THE SUNLESS CITY

FROM THE PAPERS AND DIARIES OF THE LATE
JOSIAH FLINTABBATEY FLONATIN

J.E. PRESTON MUDDOCK

"Alph, the sacred river, ran
    Through caverns measureless to man
    Down to a sunless sea."

CONTENTS

1

In one of the loneliest and most inaccessible parts of the Rocky Mountains of America is situated a strange lake or tarn.

The lake lies "silent, still and mysterious in the bosom of the everlasting mountains, like a gigantic well scooped out by the hands of genii."

There is no herbage; no animal life on its shores or in its depths. The unbroken stillness of death reigns there.

For generations learned and scientific men puzzled their heads about this mysterious sheet of water which takes all in, but apparently lets nothing out, for there is no known outlet by which the water can flow away, and owing to its peculiar situation the evaporation is very trifling, as the sun's rays seldom pierce the gloomy depths. Some stated that it was the crater of an extinct volcano, and that fissures in the mountains carried off the surplus waters, to discharge them again either in the sea or some other lake. Again, it was argued that a huge cavern was the escape valve, and a subterranean river was the solution of the problem; while another theory was that the rocks were peculiarly porous, and absorbed the water, which issued from the earth again in the form of springs many miles away.

It will thus be seen that it was the debatable ground for savants in various parts of the world. Philosophers with the whole alphabet of letters after their names advanced theories which were immediately denounced as "bosh" by other philosophers, who claimed the right to put a string of capitals after their names also. Stormy discussions, distressingly clever papers, and huge volumes of learned writing were the result of this natural problem. While the wiseacres, however, were thus squabbling about the correctness of the various theories advanced, a certain gentleman was seeking for a more practical solution of the mystery.

Josiah Flintabbatey Flonatin, Esq., or, as he was more familiarly known amongst his fellows, "Flin Flon," was a gentleman conspicuous for two things --- the smallness of his stature and the largeness of his perception. His origin was lost in the mists of antiquity, but he boasted that he was a descendant of the noble Italian family of the Flonatins, for centuries resident in the ancient city of Bologna, who were conspicuous for their learning and power during the Middle Ages. Being unfortunate enough to espouse an unpopular cause during a revolution they were stripped of their power, deprived of their wealth, and banished, many of them dying in exile and poverty. Possibly, if his pedigree had been traced, the statement might have been proved correct, but it is sufficient for the purposes of this veracious history to say that at this time Flin Flon was a grocer in a small way of business. In recording the fact I hope it will not be thought that a slight is intended upon the memory of a great man. Flin Flon could not help being a grocer. His father and grandfather before him had been in the same line --- or, as they were pleased to term it, "profession" --- and the business had been handed down from father to son through several generations. But that was in the good old times when men did not trouble themselves about the abstruse sciences or the laws of unknown quantities. And when, instead of attempting to soar into regions of speculation about the mysteries of the universe, they were content to smoke the pipe of peace in the cosy chimney corners of the country inns.

The business to which Flin had succeeded on his father's death was a snug little concern. There was a very profitable cheesemongery and bacon trade in connection with it, chiefly amongst country families, who wanted long credit but were content to pay a big price for the accommodation. And it was said that the profits on this branch of the trade were as much as eighty and ninety per cent.

Such paltry profits were scarcely worthy the consideration of a philosophic mind. At any rate one thing is tolerably clear, Josiah Flintabbatey Flonatin began to neglect his business and to frequent debating and other learned societies. Some ill natured persons said that this was owing to a "disappointment." They hinted at an engagement between Flin and a buxom widow, who proved false to her plighted troth and married a very worldly farmer, her excuse being that she thought Flin Flon was a "little cracked." This perhaps was a malicious scandal.

It may very safely be inferred, however, that the true cause of the good man's disgust for his progenitor's grocery business arose from the fact that he had a soul above sugar and spice, and cheese and bacon. No disparagement to the trade in these excellent commodities is meant by this remark. Flin Flon was born to do great deeds, to become a hero whose name should pass with honour.

"Down the ringing grooves of time."

At least this is what he told his friends. He was desirous of living in the memory of men, and being intellectual he was destined to make his way in the world, which he succeeded in doing in a very remarkable manner, as will be hereafter seen. In fact no man before or since has ever made his way in the world in such an extraordinary fashion.

Flin laboured hard for the advancement of science, and when but a young man he became a Fellow of the "Society for the Exploration of Unknown Regions," and it was with no small degree of pride that he placed after his name the imposing array of capitals, F.S.E.U.R., and was always particularly careful to write them boldly, so that the possibility of their being overlooked or mistaken was out of the question.

Flin's election to this ancient and learned body was a very distinguished honour, and was a fitting tribute to the man's great genius.

There were a few of the members who vigorously opposed his election, on the grounds that to admit a "common grocer" into their Society was to bring them into disrepute. But it is gratifying to be able to say that this opposing faction represented but a paltry minority, and the subsequent and glorious achievements of the immortal Flonatin covered his enemies with shame and confusion, so that they were glad to hide their diminished heads in obscurity.

In personal appearance Flin Flon was as singular as his name. When Nature constructed him she must have suddenly run short of materials, because she commenced a head that would have done credit to a giant in stature as well as intellect. But getting as far as the neck the old dame found apparently she had made a mistake, so finished him off hurriedly. From the neck downwards he was strangely disproportioned and very scanty.

He had pendulum-like arms; a body that might have been taken for a section of a fourteen-inch gaspipe, and legs that may not inaptly be described as corkscrews.

He was bald --- almost perfectly bald. But then all intellectual men are bald.

Another infallible sign that Flin was possessed of extraordinary brain power, was that he always wore spectacles. He was never known to be without them, although his eyes did not indicate that he was troubled with either long sight or short sight. On the contrary, judging from their keenness and brilliancy, it might be said, to use a very common metaphor, that they were quite capable of seeing through a millstone. But then clever men always do wear spectacles.

His nose was large, exceedingly large, and it was rather conspicuously red.

His face was somewhat long and thoughtful. Near the right-hand corner of the mouth was a mole, from which sprang a few silver hairs, and under the left eye was a tiny pimple.

In age Flin Flon was nearly forty when he undertook the astounding journey which has immortalised him.

He had many virtues and a few vices, and one of the latter was an inordinate love of snuff.

Whatever pride of birth Flin had, he certainly had no pride of personal appearance. But is not this another sure and certain sign of genius? Slovenliness and cleverness go together.

Tightly-fitting smalls and an old faded green coat closely buttoned up to the chin were Flin's invariable costume. And when out he wore a broadbrimmed hat, which set off his genial and intelligent face to advantage.

It happened that amongst the hundred and one things that Flin Flon interested himself in was the mystery of the strange tarn away in the Rocky Mountains, and on one occasion he had had the boldness to organise a little band of daring adventurers who started on an expedition to examine the lake by means of a boat, and report thereon. The boat was the great difficulty, for not only were there no roads, but the water could only be reached by means of a tortuous and dangerous way down the jagged ledges of rock near the waterfall. But with the enterprise and determination so characteristic of the man, Flin Flon had a small boat constructed in sections, and conveying these by rail to the nearest point, he engaged the services of a party of friendly Indians, and by their aid the boat was safely launched on the bosom of the dark waters, and thus the lake was thoroughly explored.

When the adventurous voyagers found themselves afloat, it was impossible to suppress a shudder. Far above them the sky could be seen like a little square patch of blue. A weird gloom pervaded the place, and the air was cold and damp. Not a blade of grass, not an herb of any description could be seen, and the voyagers proved that there was no life in the water, for every means were tried to catch fish, but there were no fish there, and microscopical examination revealed the fact that there was not a trace of animalcul'. Round and round the mysterious lake the boat was pulled, but no outlet for the water could be discovered. What then becomes of the surplus? was the question these savants asked one of another, but the answer was not forthcoming. Flin Flon was silent on the subject. He offered no remark, he suggested no theory. But in his great brain a thought was taking shape, that when the time came to clothe it in words was destined to startle the world. Soundings were tried for. A hundred fathoms of line were let out. Then two, three hundred, a thousand fathoms, and when two thousand fathoms were gone one and all cried, "Alas! the lake is bottomless."

The expedition having resulted in no scientific or geographical discovery, the learned "Fellows" were compelled to return, having first named the place Lake Avernus. At the first meeting, after the return of the adventures, of the "Society for the Exploration of Unknown Regions," the public flocked in hundreds, so anxious were they to have some account of the tarn which had puzzled the learned and the scientific for generations. But great was the disappointment when it became known that the combined intellect of the members of the expedition had not been able to solve the problem, and that the mystery was as much a mystery as ever.

The Society's great hall in New York, where this meeting was held, was packed from floor to ceiling with a brilliant assemblage of the most learned geographers, professors, and scientists that the world could produce, and they were not slow to express their sorrow when they learnt that the object of the expedition had not been attained.

There was one of the members who had as yet made no observations, though it was notified on the Society's programme that this gentleman would read a paper on "Lake Avernus and its probable outlet." The gentleman was Flin Flon, and his rising was eagerly looked for, as something good was always expected from him, while his wonderful intuitive perception enabled him to arrive at theoretical conclusions which were often startlingly accurate.

It was late in the evening when the Chairman, in an appropriate and neat speech, introduced Josiah Flintabbatey Flonatin, Esq., to the notice of the meeting, alluding in graceful terms to the great benefits this gentleman had already conferred upon the scientific world by his energy, determination and wonderful powers of intellect. And he (the Chairman) felt quite sure that the meeting would listen with eager interest to the paper Mr Flonatin would now have the honour of reading.

The meeting fully endorsed the Chairman's flattering remarks by a storm of applause that did not subside for some minutes.

Then the great Flin Flon arose, calm, dignified and grave. By the chair beside him reposed his large gingham umbrella, and in Josiah's hand rested a huge gold snuffbox, bearing an elaborate inscription, setting forth that the box had been presented to the present owner by "a circle of friends in acknowledgment of the great services rendered to science by Josiah Flintabbatey Flonatin, Esq., and as a token of respect for one whose wisdom and rare intellectual gifts, combined with largeness of heart and the kindest of natures, have won him troops of friends."

When the meeting had settled into silence again, and Flin Flon had refreshed himself with sundry pinches of the fragrant dust from the gold box, he straightened the wrinkles out of the green coat that was tightly buttoned round his gas-pipe like body, and with two or three swings of his pendulum arms, as if thereby he set the vocal machinery in motion, he commenced his "paper," having first placed his much-prized umbrella on the little table before him.

"Mr President, learned Fellows, and ladies and gentlemen, --- I have the distinguished honour of appearing before you to-night as a member of this ancient Society, but I must also add with regret as a representative of the expedition to Lake Avernus, whose mission has entirely failed practically."

"In dealing with the subject in hand it will be necessary for me to digress somewhat, but I respectfully claim your indulgence on this point, and hope that what I have to say will not altogether be uninteresting."

"It is a well-known fact, ladies and gentlemen, that we live upon a globe; that is, on the external crust of a huge ball. There is one thing which science has proved beyond all doubt, and that is, that this ball is not solid but hollow. Now the capacity of that hollow must almost be beyond comprehension. From time immemorial it has been supposed that the hollow is filled with seething fire and molten lava. I say supposed, because it is only a supposition. But I boldly denounce the theory of internal fire as incorrect. I say science has been at fault.

Central heat is a delusion unworthy of the consideration of great men. And now having demolished the monstrous and ancient fable with one blow, I have a theory of my own to advance that will startle you. I know it will, but I cannot help it. Nay, it is more than a theory, it is a conviction; and I say that in the centre of the earth are subterranean rivers and buried seas; more than that, ladies and gentlemen, I go so far as to say that the interior of the earth is as likely to be inhabited as the exterior."

Flin Flon paused. He took snuff excitedly. His audience, however, remained silent. The daring proposition had awed them.

"To resume."

"By the light of science it has further been revealed to us that the crust of the earth upon which we stand in no part attains a greater thickness than fifteen miles; and it is stated as a scientific truth that if we could dig down to that depth, and break through the inner surface of the crust, we should come to fire. I assert that that is a monstrously absurd theory; that we should do nothing of the kind, but that we should break in upon a new world, a new race of beings. That we should find a land of beauty and fertility; that we should find rivers, seas, mountains and valleys. The inequalities of the bottoms of our valleys will form mountains there; and our mountains will be their seas. Like unto a pudding-mould, whereon the fruit and flowers are convex on one side and concave on the other."

Flin Flon had worked himself into a state of enthusiasm and excitement, and as he gave utterance to the clever simile he caught up his favourite umbrella, and with a wild flourish brought it down again on to the table, shivering the water decanter to atoms, and just shaving by a hair's breadth the nose of the President, which was rather a large one.

This was the signal for a burst of applause from the audience, that was mingled with loud shouts of disapproval. The excitement was intense. The densely packed masses of people rose and swayed backwards and forwards. Some few persons cried out, ---

"No, no."

"Humbug."

"Absurd."

"What has this to do with Lake Avernus?"

When Flin had wiped his heated brow with a large bandanna handkerchief, and restored himself to composure by a dose of snuff, he again addressed the assembled multitude.

"In commencing my speech," he went on, "I told you I should digress, and I asked your indulgence; but I may state here that the theory I have set forth has everything to do with Lake Avernus. I say fearlessly, I say, ladies and gentlemen, that this mysterious tarn is the entrance to the inner world."

Again the cheers and discordant cries broke forth, and the audience grew more and more excited. Ladies waved their handkerchiefs frantically for it may be parenthetically stated here that Flin was a great favourite with the softer sex --- gentlemen tossed their hats up, and other gentlemen sat down upon them and crushed them into an unrecognisable mass. Such a scene had never before been witnessed in the Society's hall; but Flin preserved his composure. He stood as firm as a rock. His right hand was inserted in the breast of his green coat, and his left toyed with the gold snuff-box.

The attitude of the wonderful man must have been a study, and it is much to be deplored that no one amongst that assembly of clever men and women had sufficient presence of mind to whip out paper and pencil and sketch Flin as he then stood. The picture would have gone down to posterity as the most precious relic of a brilliant orator and distinguished savant.

When silence had once more been restored he continued his address.

"Pioneers in knowledge, like pioneers in exploration, have always to endure great hardships, but I know my fellow men too well to expect to meet with no opposition. I am, however, prepared to brave that opposition, to stand firm to my faith, and, if needs be, to lay down my life in the glorious cause of attempting to extend our knowledge of the earth we dwell upon. I repeat that the interior of the globe is inhabited. By what kind of beings I am not prepared to say. They may be monsters; they may be pigmies, or both; but that is a question

I hope to be able to answer at some future day. Ladies and gentlemen, as the Creator has adapted a race of beings to exist on the surface of the earth, I fearlessly assert that He may have adapted a race to exist in the interior. If I have startled you by the boldness of my propositions, I shall startle you still more when I say that I intend, at all hazards, to attempt, in the interests of this honourable Society and the world at large, to penetrate into the bowels of the earth."

"How, how?" arose from a hundred throats. "By descending to the bottom of Lake Avernus."

"Impossible! impossible!" cried the audience.

"Nothing is impossible to the resolute and energetic man of science. If I fail in my project I shall be but one more martyr added to the many who have been sacrificed in a noble cause."

Flin said this very proudly, and took snuff with the air of one who felt that he was destined to reveal great and startling truths to unenlightened mankind.

"I now come to the third and last part of my address," he went on, "which deals with the means I propose to adopt to find the answer to this knotty question. I intend to have a small boat constructed upon peculiar principles, the details of which it is unnecessary to enter into here. Suffice to say the boat will be built upon a principle never yet applied. It will be sufficiently large to contain myself, a few animals, and stores to last for a month. By an arrangement, which at present I intend to keep secret, I shall be enabled to create sufficient pure air to enable me to live, while a series of valves will discharge the foul air, and give me the power of rising or sinking the vessel at pleasure. If my theory of the subterranean river be correct there will be, on reaching a certain depth of the lake, a strong current setting towards it. My vessel will be carried along by this current, and before the month has elapsed I shall emerge again somewhere in mid-ocean or find myself in a new world."

"Or be food for fishes," exclaimed a voice in the centre of the hall.

"Possibly so," Flin answered. "But it will be some satisfaction to my friends to know that I sacrificed myself in the glorious cause of science; that I am but one more martyr added to the already long list of those who have unselfishly devoted themselves to the enlightenment of their fellows. I am desirous of extending our knowledge; of writing another page to the history of the world of wonders. Moreover, if there is a race of beings inhabiting the centre of our globe, they may be living in a state of spiritual darkness. And in that case I should make arrangements to send a number of missionaries in to them. They may be naked and cannibals. Then I should clothe and civilize them. In short, I deem it to be my duty to endeavour to solve the great problem as to what is in the interior of the earth; and I shall not flinch from that duty. Ladies and gentlemen, I shall devote myself to the cause, and if I perish I shall perish nobly."

He resumed his seat amidst a storm of applause. Even those who differed from him could not but admire the undaunted courage of the little man.

A vote of thanks to Flin Flon was proposed and carried unanimously, and the Chairman stated that in a few days further particulars would be announced in reference to the daring scheme proposed by that gentleman, whose experiments would be carried out under the auspices of the Society for the Exploration of Unknown Regions.

2

On the following morning all the papers published long accounts of the meeting of the Society for the Exploration of Unknown Regions, and of Flin's strange proposal. Nearly every journal had a weighty editorial article on the subject. Some denounced the scheme as impracticable and the emanation of a madman's brain; while others were strongly in favour of it, and thought the plan quite feasible.

The excitement in New York City was intense. Flin Flon's lecture was the one topic of conversation. Everything else seemed to be forgotten. The startling theory advanced by the lecturer, and the boldness of his proposition, had broken upon the city with the suddenness of a thunderbolt. It is to be doubted if even a volcano in the centre of Broadway could have caused more astonishment. Everybody exclaimed to everybody else, ---

"Is it not wonderful?"

"How strange to be sure!"

"I wonder that it has never been thought of before."

All the papers published special editions in the afternoon, containing every scrap of information bearing upon the subject. It was a rich harvest for the penny-a-liners. With the indefatigable energy so characteristic of these gentlemen, they rushed about from one end of the city to the other; a few of the most zealous even neglecting their usual forenoon "nip," though it must be confessed that the few represented a very small minority indeed, as the greater number of these "gentlemen of the Press" made the occasion one for indulging in sundry other nips, over and above the usual matutinal dram; and it is highly probable that the news which was published for the information of the public was nearly all concocted in the liquor stores.

In Wall Street, and on the Exchange, the speculators, the hangers-on, the penniless stockbrokers, the gamblers in scrip and shares, seemed to quite forget their ordinary business and go mad upon the all-absorbing topic. Several daring and needy speculators offered to form a limited liability company, to be called the "Central World Exploration Company (Limited)," with a capital of twenty million dollars; and in the event of success attending Flin's adventure, and if inhabitants were discovered, the company were to take steps to open up commerce with them immediately. This proposal, however, did not meet with any very favourable reception, as the projectors were known to belong to that clique which fatten and batten upon the public, and take advantage of every excitement to float bubble companies, by which nobody profits but the promoters, and they make big fortunes. In fact, these very men would have undertaken to have formed a company to be called "The Lunar Steam Navigation Company," its object being to run a daily service of first-class, high-pressure steamers, carrying goods and passengers at cheap rates, from the earth to the moon. Nor would they have wanted shareholders, as fools and their money are soon parted; and persons are always to be found who are ready to subscribe to the most Quixotic expeditions that were ever planned.

However, in this instance, the "Central World Exploration Company, Limited," scheme did not meet with general approbation, although a few persons expressed their willingness to subscribe. But one enthusiastic and shrewd Yankee offered to risk three thousand dollars' worth of dry goods in the proposed vessel, and to commission

Flin to dispose of them to the best advantage to the Central Earth dwellers, should he find any; while a benevolent and philanthropic old lady, who was well known for her piety and charity, undertook to supply Flin with fifty dollars' worth of suitable tracts for distribution. A celebrated firm of distillers offered him a very handsome commission if he would undertake to introduce their far-famed and noted Bourbon whisky to any people he might discover; while Professor Bolus, the universally known pill and ointment man, most generously agreed to allow the explorer fifty per cent. upon every box of pills or ointment he might dispose of. And "The Great Monopoly --- do all and buy up everything Company," intimated their willingness to appoint Mr Flonatin their chief agent in the centre of the earth, should he discover any people dwelling there.

If fact, these and similar liberal offers continued to flow in for some days, but it is almost needless to say that they were one and all firmly but respectfully declined.

During all the excitement, which continued for some weeks --- the papers taking every opportunity to keep the agitation up to boiling point --- Flin Flon was quietly superintending the construction of a curious vessel, the design of his own ingenious brain. One of the largest New York firms of engineers was carrying the work out. And so day by day, while the populace were growing more excited, and the journals teemed with letters on the subject pro and con., Flin's fish, as it was hereafter to be know, was rapidly nearing completion, and at the expiration of six weeks from the delivery of the address at the Society's meeting, the finishing touches were put to the strange vessel, and it was at last placed on view at Barnum's Museum, Mr Barnum having magnanimously consented to defray all the expenses of the construction of the vessel solely on condition that it should be exhibited in his museum for a certain time as soon as it was completed. An extra quarter dollar admission money was charged to the public during the time it was on view. But they would willingly have paid treble that amount for the privilege of seeing the wonderful vessel.

The shape of it was that of a huge pike, thirty-four and a-half feet long from the extreme end of the tail to the tip of the snout. The diameter was eight feet and a-half in the thickest part. The fish was constructed of small copper plates, beautifully joined together by countless numbers of minute rivets. In the interior was a casing of sheet-iron, and between this and the internal walls of the machine a space of a foot in width was left for the purposes that will be presently explained. In the exact centre of the fish was a crank made of highly- polished steel, which could be connected or disconnected at pleasure. And owing to an ingenious system of counterweights, the slightest manual labour would cause the crank to revolve freely. This crank communicated with a small pair of patent-float paddle wheels, so that the occupant of the machine could propel the vessel under water. The diameter of the wheels was three feet. The frames were composed of galvanised steel and the floats of mahogany, the edges being protected by brass plates.

The fish was so constructed that it would descend to any required depth head first. The centre of gravity could then be brought to the belly of the fish by moving a lever which acted upon a hydraulic pump, so that the vessel would float horizontally, and by means of the paddles could be driven along under water, at no matter what depth, the speed averaging from five to seven knots an hour.

It will be necessary to explain here that this alternation in positions from perpendicular to horizontal, and vice versa, was effected in a very ingenious manner by means of ballast, the ballast being water contained in the iron tubes that were placed between the outer skin of copper and the inner skin of sheet-iron. The water was acted upon by compressed air.

In the event of the voyager wishing to rise to the surface at any moment, he opened a valve and the compressed air would force the water out. The machine would then rise; while a suction-hose, worked by a small hand force-pump, gave the occupant the power of filling the ballast tubes again, thereby causing the fish to sink once more into the watery depths. In the head of the vessel were place two large eyes, constructed of thick plate-glass, protected by fine copper netting. Each eye was constructed to hold a small electric lamp. This lamp consisted of a piece of platinum wire, connected with a coil for producing currents of induced electricity of great intensity. The coil was of copper wire insulated by being covered with silk, and could be instantly connected with a very powerful voltaic battery. When the apparatus was in action the platinum became luminous, and produced a white and continued light that penetrated the most profound obscurity. These lamps, being very small, could also be carried by the traveller in a small leather case, which was hung around his neck, a miniature battery in this case being used.

The tail of the fish was so arranged that it could be used as a rudder, and was worked from the inside by means of a wheel placed in the head, thus enabling the traveller to keep a lookout and steer at the same time.

The internal arrangements were as near perfection as human skill and ingenuity could make them. In the tail was a small iron reservoir containing a combination of chemicals, which by a process of very slow decomposition evolved the properties of oxygen and hydrogen in such proportions as to keep up a constant supply of pure air inside the fish, while the carbonic acid gas was forced out by a complicated arrangement of pipes which communicated with the mouth of the monster, and were so constructed with trap valves that while allowing the bad air to escape they did not admit the water. It was estimated that this reservoir contained a sufficient amount of chemicals to last for two months. At the end of that time the vessel could be brought to the surface, and the reservoir refilled from a spare store. In the neck was a circular flooring, occupied by the voyager during the descent. When the fish was horizontal this formed a bulkhead, to which was attached a bunk that could be closed up or opened out at pleasure. The gills were represented by two oblong slits of strong plate glass, so that a clear lookout could be obtained. There were also two small windows in the tail.

The centre of the vessel was fitted up as a storeroom, laboratory and study. Here were compasses, a barometer, several thermometers, and a brass dial plate, in the middle of which was a delicately-poised hand. The plate was marked with a graduated scale, and the hand was connected with a strong spring. This again was enclosed in the tube, the mouth of which projected from the back of the fish. Inside of this was a balance which was depressed by the weight of water, so that the exact depth was accurately registered on the dial plate. There was also a somewhat similar plate for registering speed, and a peculiar clock for marking off the days. By closing a door at each end of the compartment it could be made perfectly water- tight, a measure rendered necessary by the possibility of an accident occurring to the head or tail. In the hinder part was a series of lockers to hold provisions sufficient to last for three months. In various parts of the inside there were also placed bottles of prepared phosphorus, which emitted a soft and pleasant light, so that the venturesome traveller was not altogether dependent upon his electric batteries. Each compartment was comfortably fitted with seats, the roof and sides being luxuriously cushioned and padded. There was also accommodation provided in the stern for a few birds and small animals.

During the time that this remarkable and ingenious vessel was on view, enormous crowds flocked to the museum to see it, and the astute Barnum netted vast sums of money; though it must be told, to his credit, that he generously placed one per cent. of the receipts at the disposal of Flin towards the expenses of the expedition.

A day or two before the time for Flin to take his departure, he and the other members of the Society for the Exploration of Unknown Regions were entertained to a grand banquet by Mr Barnum, which was given at Astor House, in the Broadway, New York. With his usual liberality the genial showman sent a free ticket to each newspaper, and there was a very strong muster of Pressmen.

All the elite of New York society were there, and a gallery was fitted up at one end of the hall expressly for the accommodation of ladies. And such a galaxy of youth and beauty had seldom been brought together under one roof. It was jocosely remarked by a certain wag that the enterprising Barnum had taken care to send tickets to those ladies only who were noted for youth and superb beauty.

Perhaps this was true, for more lovely and enchanting creatures it would be difficult to imagine. The bright eyes, the bewitching smiles of the dainty mouths, the snowy necks, the well- formed arms, and heaving busts of those fair women, caused them to be the cynosure of all the male sex; while as for the diamonds that sparkled in the hair and on the necks of the lovely creatures, they produced an effect that is indescribable, though one of the reporters spoke of it ---

"As a scene of exquisite loveliness. It seemed as if the angels had gathered all the early dewdrops from the roses in Eden, and then scattered them with a lavish hand amongst this group of earth's fairest creatures; illuminating them with luculent rays of great purity, caught up from the jasper river that rolled its course through the peaceful plains of heaven, these rays produced a hundred prismatic hues, dazzling the beholder, and helped to complete a scene that mortals could gaze upon only once in a lifetime."

This was a little too flowery, but then it was pretty and peculiarly American. The guests numbered nearly a thousand.

Of course the toast of the evening was "The Health of Mr Josiah Flintabbatey Flonatin, and success to his bold undertaking."

Flin responded very briefly. His bashful and retiring disposition would not allow him to say much about himself. But he expressed the strongest hopes of the success of the undertaking, and said that he was determined to either succeed or perish.

This brought forth a storm of applause, and the ladies, dear creatures, waved their scented cambric handkerchiefs at the speaker. And one beautiful girl of about nineteen summers was heard to murmur, ---

"Wal, I guess that licks creation, it does. I should like to hug the old man, I should, God bless him!"

In her enthusiasm she drew a magnificent little bouquet that had reposed on her fair bosom from the front of her dress, and pressing the gorgeous flowers to her lips, she leant over the front of the gallery and gracefully cast the bouquet down to Flin.

The face of the great man was suffused with blushes as he stooped and picked up the flowers, pressed them to his lips, bowed low to the charming little lady, and then placed them in his buttonhole. This act was the signal for another burst of cheering that did not subside for some minutes.

When order had once more been restored, Mr. Barnum rose to his feet to give the toast of "The Society for the Exploration of Unknown Regions."

He alluded in graceful terms to Flin Flon. He was a man of whom everyone ought to be proud, and he firmly believed that he would succeed in carrying the glorious stars and stripes into the very bowels of the earth. At anyrate, if the attempt failed, it would be another bright page added to the history of American enterprise. He felt that he could not sit down without taking the opportunity to contradict, in the strongest and most indignant terms, a scandalous report which had been published in some low English journals, that he (Mr. Barnum) had got up this affair as a money-making speculation, and that the whole thing, from beginning to end, was a swindle and a humbug. The idea was not his but Mr. Flonatin's, and though he had lent his museum for the purpose of exhibiting the wonderful vessel, the designs for which had had their birth in the giant brain of the originator of the expedition, he had done so purely in the public interest. He felt proud that Mr. Flonatin was a New York citizen, and he hoped that every gentleman of the Press then present would not fail to inform the Britishers, who were eating their hearts with envy and jealousy, because they had no Rocky Mountains and no strange tarn, that this bold scheme was originated by an American gentleman, and was worthy alike of him and American enterprise.

Mr. Barnum resumed his seat amidst a perfect hurricane of applause, even the ladies joining in the cheering, waving their fans, and clapping their hands in their excitement.

The banquet came to an end at last, as all things must; but it was with the greatest reluctance that the guests departed from that hall of beauty. In going into the streets it seemed like passing at one step from the realms of fantasy and fairy-land to the murky regions of a nether world.

3

When the morning dawned for Josiah Flintabbatey Flonatin to leave New York with his novel craft, the excitement and enthusiasm of the people rose to an extraordinary pitch.

Business was entirely suspended. The militia and the police were drawn up in double file along the whole of the route through which the expedition was to pass. The windows and roofs of all the houses were crowded with people. The streets were gaily decorated with flags, and bands of music were stationed all along the route, and played "See the Conquering Hero Comes" as Flin Flon approached.

Mr. Barnum was determined that nothing should be wanting to make the affair one of an imposing nature, and so he had at an immense expense procured a white elephant. Some snarling cynic avowed that the animal had been whitewashed for the occasion, but Mr. Barnum was not likely to have lent himself to any such imposture. On its back was placed a magnificent howdah, with curtains of cloth of gold backed by blue satin. In this howdah Flin Flon was seated, and behind him marched another elephant, carrying the strange fish vessel. Then came a long string of carriages, bearing the members of the Society for the Exploration of Unknown Regions and their friends --- that is, the friends of the members, not the regions. In many of these carriages were ladies superbly attired, for Flin was an especial favourite with the ladies, and they had taken an unflagging interest in the object of the expedition. Mr. Barnum and his company from the museum brought up the rear. The company included a giant nine feet high, two dwarfs, four Circassian ladies whose hair reached to their feet, two wild savages from the Carabboo Islands (an obscure English journal said that these savages were natives of Wicklow, in Ireland, but there is no doubt it was an unfounded and malicious statement), a two-headed woman, who, it was said, could talk in two different languages at one time. It was commonly reported that she had been married three times, but each of her husbands, poor fellows! had died raving mad. There was also a bearded lady, an armless man, who wrote and did everything with his toes, and a spotted Ethiopian, so that there was altogether a very fair collection of lusus naturæ.

One of the great railway companies had offered to convey the vessel to Lake Avernus free of cost, and when the station was reached a special train of cars was in readiness for the embarkation of the expedition.

Some considerable time was taken up in getting the expedition on board the cars, but at length it was safely accomplished.

Every member of the Society for the Exploration of Unknown Regions was to accompany Flin to the Rocky Mountains. And when all the gentlemen had taken their seats Mr. Barnum shook hands with Flin and wished him God-speed. This was the signal for at least a hundred ladies to rush forward and shake the hand of the little man, and hundreds more would have done so had they not been ungallantly kept back by the police.

When all was ready, the train, which was decorated with flags, evergreens and flowers, commenced to move slowly out of the station, amidst the din of musketry, the playing of the bands, the hurrahing of the excited crowds, who were struggling frantically to get a last look at the hero of the day. Many of the ladies sobbed piteously, and as though their dear hearts would break. Then as one enthusiastic, wild shout of God-speed rose from thousands and thousands of voices, the train steamed away and was lost to view.

After a long and fatiguing journey the base of the mountain in which Avernus was situated was reached. Here a party of Indians and mules were engaged, and not without considerable difficulty the fish vessel, the stores and instruments were landed on the shore of the lake. Preparations were at once commenced for the descent into the unknown depths of the lake of mystery. The stores were put on board and packed away in the proper quarter. Then the air-producing reservoir was got into working order, and everything being ready, the adventurous Flin Flon commenced to bid adieu to his friends.

It was a strange, wild scene, and such a one as never before nor since disturbed the solitude of the awful place.

On the unruffled bosom of the dark waters was to be seem what might have been taken for a buoy, shaped like the tail half of a fish. From the tail floated the stars and stripes, and at the back was a small open door. On the shore were several small white tents, for the party had been there some days, while the final preparations were being made, and these tents contrasted strangely with the dark rocks, at the foot of which were gathered quite a little army of bald-headed and bespectacled savants, who talked in various languages, who chipped off pieces of rock with little hammers, and then delivered learned dissertations one to another upon the geological formation of the district, and the age of the various strata. They spoke of the "tertiary formation," of the "eocene," "miocene," and "pliocene." They said that geology was a subject upon which an autoschediastical judgment could not be pronounced. That the study of the "pocilite" would teach many truths with reference to the world's formation, and that amygdaloid was a book upon the pages of which the world's age was legibly written. They also touched upon the cylantheae and the cyclobranchiata, the gasteromycetes and the byssaceae, and likewise the zechstein. With such simple and delightful words these old gentlemen made themselves understood, and thus were enabled to pass away the time pleasantly during the preparations for Flin's journey.

At length all was ready for a start, and when Flin had shaken the hands of his friends, not a few of whom were affected to tears, he stepped into a small boat and pulled a few yards out to where the fish floated. Then by means of a ladder he mounted to the doorway, and waving a farewell with his umbrella to the spectators on the shore, he descended into the body of the vessel, and having refreshed himself with a huge pinch of snuff, he closed the door and proceeded to screw it up from the inside; it fitted like the cap of a man-hole in a boiler.

It should be mentioned here that his travelling companions were six pigeons, a small goat, two fowls, six rabbits, a black cat, and a little white dog. These, with the exception of the cat and dog, were stowed in the tail.

When Flin had made the door water-tight he set his force-pump in motion, and commenced to take in his water ballast, and when the desired quantity had entered the tube the fish began to slowly sink.

It was a solemn moment was that. The onlookers began to ask themselves whether they had done right in allowing Flin to start upon such a strange journey. And that if his life were sacrificed would they not be accessory to his death? Not a few of them were really alarmed, and regretted that they had lent any serious hearing to the proposal of the expedition when first mentioned. But, in justice to them, it must be said that this feeling was very ephemeral. One of their number was risking his life in the noble cause of science, and even if he should never return they had no right to think ill of him, but should honour and respect his memory, and believe that he was actuated by the best and purest of intentions in setting out upon his adventurous journey.

The fish gradually went out of sight. First the dorsal fin was submerged, then the tail sank, until the glorious stars and stripes alone floated on the water.

It was the signal for a wild burst of cheering from the spectators, and the gloomy hollow reverberated with a thousand echoes, while far above, the eagles, startled by such an unusual noise, wheeled round and round and gazed down in bewilderment on the bald-headed intruders.

In a few minutes the flag itself was lost to view, and a large circle of air bubbles was all that was left to point out the spot where Flin's novel vessel had floated a little while before.

A small hut had been erected on the shore, and in this three men were to remain and keep watch for a fortnight. And as there was nothing more to do or nothing more to see the company turned their backs on Lake Avernus and hurried to their homes again, glad to get away from the gloomy and cheerless region.

4

For two hours after leaving the surface Flin continued to descend until the dial plate registered five hundred fathoms. As he noted this he felt a little proud as he thought that he was probably the first living human being who had ever attained such a depth. His ingenious invention was evidently a success. The reservoir was working capitally, and there was a plentiful supply of good air, and the only inconvenience that was experienced was an unusual degree of heat, the thermometer marking 82 degrees Fahrenheit, although the weather on land was extremely cold. The fish continued to descend until one thousand fathoms were marked, then bottom was touched lightly, and Flin instantly shifted the ballast and brought the fish into horizontal position. From his lookout windows he could see that he was on a shelving ledge of rock, and so connecting the crank of his paddle-wheels, he gave a few turns, and the machine glided further out and commenced to sink again. Very slowly now, owing to the horizontal position. When another hundred fathoms had been added to the depth, the fish again lodged on a ledge of rock, and instead of shelving, Flin could observe that it was quite flat and about five yards broad. Everything was satisfactory inside; the birds and animals were quietly sleeping, and the only sound to be heard was a strange, low humming noise. One peculiarity Flin noticed was, that the compasses were quite useless and magnetic attraction had ceased. As he was very tired, and the hour was late, he determined to let the vessel lodge where it was for the night, and having seen that everything was in working order, he went to bed, and was very soon enjoying a sound sleep, in spite of the novelty of his position. In all human probability he was the first mortal who, in the full enjoyment of perfect health and strength, had ever quietly reposed beneath the water at a depth of nearly two miles.

The night passed and morning came. Of course the only knowledge that Flin had that it was morning, was by looking at his chronometer watch, the hands of which indicated the hour of nine.

"Bless my life," cried Flin as he sprang out of bed, and regaled himself with a pinch of his precious snuff, "bless my life, how late it is. I declare I must have overslept myself."

Then having carefully adjusted his smalls and buttoned up his old green coat, he proceeded to attend to the creature comforts of his compagnons de voyage, and having noticed the state of the thermometer, which had risen in the night to 86 degrees, he made an entry in his diary to the effect that he had passed a very comfortable night eleven hundred fathoms below the surface of Lake Avernus. This task being completed he breakfasted right royally on a bottle of superb claret, some hard-boiled eggs, which had been prepared the day before, a few delicate slices of delicious ham, and finished off with a choice cut from a magnificent boar's head stuffed with truffles.

The next task was to get the craft off the ledge of rock, where it had securely lodged all night. Flin first of all made a careful survey of the position, as far as he was able, from his lookout windows. The electric lamps in the eyes illuminated the water for some distance, and he was enabled to see that on the left of him, and close to the vessel, rose a sheer wall of rock. And when his eyes became accustomed to the strange light he was astonished to observe that this wall was literally covered with some living things that could scarcely be called animals or fish. They had large, flat, round heads, and from each side of the head protruded an enormous eye. These eyes looked like balls of silver stuck on pins, and the creature was enabled to move them about in all directions. The bodies of these strange animals or fish were like thin pieces of pipe, about six inches in length, the tails of which were firmly attached to the rock. These things kept waving about with an undulating motion, and with a regularity that was monotonous.

"Good gracious!" cried Flin enthusiastically as he observed the extraordinary creatures, "what would I not give if I could only procure a few specimens. They are evidently an entirely new species of water animal, for I have never seen anything like them before. "

Longings, however, were vain, and so with that philosophical resignation which was part of his character he sat down and carefully entered in his diary an exact description (of which the above is a copy) of the extraordinary appearance of the living creatures; and as they partook more of the nature of reptiles than fish, he at once, with becoming modesty, classified them under the head of Reptilia Flonatin.

The entry finished, the great little man took snuff with a very self-satisfied air, and shipping the crank he set to work to impel the vessel into deep water. This was easily effected, for she rested very lightly on the rock, and being off she commenced to gradually sink again.

The peculiar humming noise which Flin had noticed on the previous evening now increased until it became like the combined buzzing of thousands of bees. It affected the drums of the ears, and produced a partial deafness. When the dial plate had registered another twenty fathoms a new and strange motion was imparted to the vessel. She went up and down like a see-saw plank, then she rolled, then described a half circle, bobbed up and down like a float, and finally commenced to spin round and round.

"Hullo!" cried Flin, as he seized his note- book and proceeded to jot down notes of the phenomenon, "this is suction. I'm going somewhere now."

Presently the humming noise increased until it became a perfect roar. The head of the fish vessel kept dipping violently, so that Flin was compelled to keep his seat. But with heroic composure he took snuff and calmly waited, pen in hand, for what might follow. He had not long to wait. The head made a plunge, until the vessel was almost perpendicular, and the little man was thrown to the floor. He gathered himself up, however, not the least disconcerted, and had just time to gain his seat when the vessel commenced to spin round violently like a newly-caught cockchafer on a pin. And all this time it was still sinking, sinking rapidly, and the roar was terrific. Any other man similarly situated would at once have given himself up for lost; but Flin did nothing of the kind. He managed to secure his precious snuff-box in the breast pocket of his coat, and then he firmly grasped with both hands the little table at which he was sitting, and which fortunately was screwed to the deck.

"Dear me!" he cried, gasping for breath, as a slight pause occurred in the rotary motion; "this is really very unpleasant, but it proves my theory correct that the lake is drained by a subterranean river and I am coming to the mouth of it."

He had scarcely given utterance to the words when again the vessel spun round, even more rapidly than before, and the noise was absolutely deafening, and rendered more distressing by the screams of the alarmed birds and animals imprisoned in the vessel with Flin.

In about twenty minutes' time the circular motion gave place to violent tossing, which, however, was less disagreeable than the other.

"Confound it!" he exclaimed. "In the interests of the honourable Society it is my privilege to represent I am prepared to encounter a great deal, but I must certainly enter a protest against being whirled round at the rate of fifty revolutions per minute."

Scarcely had the words left his mouth than the vessel commenced to rotate again, and Flin had not even time to clutch his snuff-box, which had been lying on the table, before it went flying away into a corner of the compartment. This distressed the little man sorely. The precious relic and its still more precious contents were as dear to him almost as his own life. But there was no help for it. He had to cling to the table like a leach, and his baldness in this instance was not without its advantages, for if his head had been covered with hair the probabilities are that the hair would have been whirled off.

Quite suddenly the motion changed, and swift as an arrow the vessel took a plunge down, then made a rush forward, and it became evident now that she was being carried rapidly along by a powerful current that was flowing through a tunnel.

For a time Flin was quite exhausted, and so giddy that he could see nothing. But he soon recovered, and his first thought was for his gold box. This regained, he inspected his live stock. He found them all trembling violently and suffering great agitation. The thermometer registered 90 degrees, and the barometer was flying backwards and forwards in a most mysterious manner from "set fair" to "stormy." The pressure on the dial plate indicated a depth of water of not more than six fathoms.

"Hurrah!" cried Flin, as he noted this. "I am in the centre of the channel, and not far below the surface of the water."

He went to his lookout and peered into the water, but his vessel seemed to be standing still, though he knew from the speed indicator inside that she was travelling at the rate of quite twenty knots an hour.

After four hours of this rate the speed was reduced to about ten, and the fish was perfectly steady. Nothing was to be seen but the walls of water, rendered greenish by the electrical glow from the fish's eyes. Flin occupied himself with carefully writing up his diary and examining his instruments. He felt very well satisfied, for so far success had attended his venture, and the theory he had advanced at the meeting had now become actual fact, and he was sailing beneath the surface of a subterranean river. Not a single thought troubled him as to the future. He could live in his strange abode for a month, and long before that time the end of the river must be reached; and if he should come out in the centre of the ocean he would be able to rise to the surface, and either make for the nearest shore or be picked up by some passing ship, so he reasoned. But his enthusiasm never deserted him for a moment. He longed to realize his dream and become the discoverer of an internal world. The belief was firmly rooted in his mind that all subterranean rivers must flow to the centre of the earth, and it was evident that the one in which he was now travelling had a considerable fall, as proved by the rapidity of the current. He was a least two and a half miles from the surface of Lake Avernus, and was still descending lower. At anyrate, return was impossible, and wherever this river liked to take him to he must go, even though it should be to the infernal regions themselves.

About six o'clock, no change having taken place, he sat down to dine. The dinner was quite a recherch, affair; boiled ham and delicious Indian pickles, boar's head and delicate French rolls and New Jersey butter, Catawba wine and calves'-foot jelly (specially prepared by an intimate lady friend), a morsel of Gruyere and a bottle of Moet.

Having fared thus sumptuously, Flin entered up his diary for the day, first noting that everything was going on all right. This task over he opened the escape valve for the foul air, and after that felt considerably refreshed, and, there being nothing more to do that night, he retired to rest.

He had slept about four hours when he was suddenly awakened by a violent shock, and for a moment the vessel seemed to be standing perfectly still, and there was a noise like the howling of a gale of wind through a long iron pipe. Flin sprang from his bunk. The vessel was trembling from head to tail, and the speed indicator was at "0." He realised the state of affairs in a minute. The fish had struck against a rock in mid channel. That this was the case was proved in a few minutes by the vessel swinging as the tide caught her and turned her violently round. Then with a dart and a plunge she rushed forward again, and the indicator registered twenty-two knots an hour.

Flin made a minute examination of the head of his fish, but could discover no damage beyond one of the electrical lamps in the eyes being displaced, but fortunately it was not broken.

"Confound it," he muttered, "that is a contingency I did not calculate upon, and a few such shocks would very soon bring my expedition to a premature close. It is no use meeting trouble halfway, though. I must hope for the best."

A very high rate of speed was now attained, and from a considerable depression at the head of the fish it was evident it was being carried down an inclined plane of water. Flin dressed himself hastily and took snuff thoughtfully.

"This is very awkward," he muttered, as he sat philosophically contemplating the indicator, which now marked thirty knots. "Exceedingly awkward," he continued. "We are evidently descending a rapid, and if anything should be in the way, well ---"

He had not time to finish the sentence for the fish suddenly assumed a perpendicular position, the bold explorer was sent head over heels, and found himself lying against the partition beneath a heterogeneous collection of articles which had not been secured.

He lost no time in picking himself up and hurrying to the dial plate, which marked twenty fathoms, while the indicator had stopped.

"That's a pretty considerable waterfall, I guess," he remarked, as he groped for his snuff-box.

Presently the fish commenced to rise again from the depth of water into which the momentum had carried it, and as it did so it assumed the horizontal once more. Flin seized the lever which acted upon the ballast pipe, for he was determined to rise to the surface. He pressed the handle and the fish rapidly rose, but no sooner had it reached the top than it commenced spinning again at a bewildering rate. It had been caught in the eddy. Now it dived down as the water fell upon it. Then it rose again, spun round, rolled terrifically, bumped against the rocks, darted from side to side, was one moment perpendicular, the next horizontal, and all that Flin could do was to cling tenaciously to the table and wait.

At length there was a shock, and all motion, excepting an undulating one, ceased, but the roar of the water was perfectly deafening.

Flin scrambled to his portholes and looked out. The fish was on the top of the water, and jammed in a sort of cove formed by a jutting rock. It was perfectly still there, but a few yards further away the water was perfectly white with foam, and rushing along at an incredible speed.

"It won't do to stick here," thought Flin, "and I must get out into the stream somehow."

But how? That was the question that suggested itself to him. There was but one way, and that was to open the door and push the vessel out by means of a pole which had fortunately been placed on board. But then there were two risks to be run. The first was that of foul air, and the second was the danger of the fish being carried by the eddy beneath the waterfall and swamped before the cap could be closed again.

However, to stick there was to perish miserably and ingloriously, without any chance of his papers reaching the upper world. So of the two evils he chose the lesser, and getting out his tools he proceeded to unscrew the cap, and that being done, he very cautiously opened it the smallest possible bit. The noise that greeted him was beyond all description. It was as if a thousand ponderous machines were working one against the other. At the same time a blast of icy air rushed in, and in a few minutes the thermometer fell to six below zero.

Flin closed the cap, and hurrying to his berth, wrapped himself in a blanket. This done, he

returned to the door and gradually opened it, experiencing no other effect in doing so but that of extreme cold.

The luminosity of the foaming water enabled him, when his eyes became accustomed to the gloom, to faintly discern surrounding objects, and he discovered that he was in a spacious chamber. Before leaving New York he had provided himself with a large quantity of magnesium wire, and he now hastened to procure some of this. As he lighted it a scene burst upon his view that rendered him dumb with amazement.

It was an enormous cavern with a vaulted roof, from which hung brilliantly white festoons of stalactite. Behind, at some distance, was an unbroken fall of water of a least a hundred and twenty feet, and it was over this that Flin's fish had come. Above and below were gigantic pillars of stalactite and stalagmite, and some of the rock was covered with carbonate of lime, in which were embedded myriads of crystals that sparkled and flashed in the light with an inconceivably beautiful effect.

It was truly a subterranean world. The entrances to mammoth caves could be observed on all sides. There were what appeared to be flowers, and trees, and creepers, but they were all stone. The little bay in which the fish had been caught was the entrance to a cavern, and about a foot from the side of the vessel was the floor. Having first taken the precaution to secure the vessel by means of ropes, he provided himself with a plentiful supply of magnesium wire, and some peculiar torches that had been specially prepared for him in New York. Thus equipped he stepped out of the fish, and stood dry footed in that strange cavern, nearly three miles beneath the surface of the lake.

5

As Flin stood up and contemplated the vastness of the chambers which surrounded him on all sides, he was struck with mingled feeling of awe and admiration. The strange solitudes where human being had never before entered were filled with wonders such as the upper earth could not compete with.

Before him rushed the river which might have been taken for the fabled Styx, and the gloomy caverns the abode of the grim ferryman, Charon.

To his right fell a gleaming sheet of water, and below it was a maelstrom, that made one giddy by its terrific gyrations. From the heights above Flin had tumbled into this mysterious spot, and all hope of ever returning to the upper world by the way he had come had vanished. But this thought gave the little man no uneasiness. He knew that the rushing river led somewhere, and wherever it led to he was willing to go.

He felt proud --- as who would not have done so? --- as he remembered that the invention, the child of his own brain, together with dauntless courage, had enabled him to penetrate thus far into those caverns of darkness.

The torches he had brought were about two feet long, and

composed of a preparation of resin and pitch, firmly rammed into a metal case. Each torch was timed to burn from nine to twelve hours.

Lighting one of these he fixed it in the rock against which the fish was moored, so that it might serve as a guide on his return.

The effect of the light was inconceivably grand. Myriads of brilliant stars seemed to surround Flin. Above him was what appeared to be the blue vault of heaven, studded with the jewels of night, so that Flin could scarcely believe that he was far down in the bowels of the earth, and that above him were thousands and thousands of feet of solid earth and rock.

When he had gazed long on the marvellous sight, he slung two spare torches over his shoulder, and carrying a lighted one in his hand, he started into the interior of the cavern.

For some distance the way was along a narrow passage, from the roof of which depended the most magnificent stalactites that took almost every conceivable shape. Graceful festoons of flowers, delicate lace work, beautiful banners that seemed as if a passing breath of wind would set them waving-and long, graceful creepers that twined themselves round each in the most wonderful and complicated convolutions.

Presently the way broadened into an avenue, and then a little farther on there burst on the astonished gaze of Flin a sight that caused him to stand still with amazement.

Far as the eye could reach, on all sides, stretched an apparently limitless expanse of forest. Strange trees that had no counterpart on the upper earth, and which towered up until they were lost in the darkness. Their branches were interlocked, and their trunks were covered with parasites. But there was no delicate and harmonious blending of colour as in living nature. It was all white, broken here and there with streaks of brown. And over all was the stillness of death. Not a sound but the subdued roar of the waters, not a motion but the flickering torch.

It was a world of stone. Trees, branches, creepers, undergrowth; all were stone. Petrified into hard white rock, the result of countless thousands of years.

As the adventurous voyager stood there, gazing upon all this mystery and weirdness, he pictured the time when birds sang in the branches of the now stony trees, when balmy breezes rustled their leaves into pleasant music, and thousands of bright glad insects hummed their praises among the waving grasses and the nodding flowers. Flin knew that all these things must have been in far-off ages, until some incomprehensible convulsion of nature turned this part of the world upside down, and buried for ever out of sight this glorious forest. And now, after countless ages, perhaps millions of years, he had been permitted to penetrate into that stony forest that was steeped in the silence of death.

"It is grand, majestic, awful!" Flin exclaimed at last, unable longer to control his feelings.

Then he took snuff reflectively, and waving his torch aloft, its light was reflected in a million scintillating jewels, and a scene of dazzling loveliness met his astonished gaze.

Choosing one of the many paths which ran in all directions he travelled for some distance, until the cold was intense and the atmosphere heavy, so that breathing became laborious and difficult. The traveller thereupon determined to retrace his steps, for he was hungry and a little faint. But he very soon discovered, to his amazement and alarm, that he had missed his way, and the path by which he had come he could not find.

It was a terrible predicament, but Flin was not the man to stand still when action was necessary. So he travelled on rapidly for many miles through that world of stones, trees and herbs. Now he went north, then south. Then he tried east and west, but still he could not discover the friendly beacon which marked the spot where his fish vessel was moored.

It must be confessed that at this time a feeling of despair did weigh upon him, for the pangs of hunger were keen, and nature was exhausted. To have to die thus ingloriously, and when the success of his mission had seemed so probable, was calculated to depress even the strongest minded of men. But this feeling was very temporary. Flin drew out his beloved box, and refreshed himself with two large pinches of snuff. This gave him courage, and he once more started off, selecting a path that he fancied led in the right direction. Along this he travelled for some distance, until the trees grew less dense, and at last he stood upon the edge of a plain that was treeless and shrubless. He had come wrong again, that was certain, but the plain offered new temptations to his inquiring mind, and he was determined to gain all the knowledge he could.

He again had recourse to his snuff-box for refreshment, and he raised his torch aloft and gazed around. Behind was the forest, weird and spectral in its stony death, and before was what seemed to be a vast desert, dotted here and there with hillocks. He made his way to one of these hillocks and was astounded to find that it was composed of bones. Human bones, stone encrusted. And they had evidently belonged to a gigantic race of beings.

Flin collected several of these bones, and with a pocket measure, which he had thoughtfully provided himself with, he ascertained from very careful measurement that some of the bones must have belonged to men at least twelve feet high. This was an interesting discovery, and proved the truth of Biblical history, that there were giants on the earth in old days.

Flin counted no less than fifteen of these mementoes of an era that was completely lost in the mists of antiquity.

Further on he came to a stupendous mass of skeleton that with few exceptions was quite complete. It was that of a Behemoth, whose size would have dwarfed the largest hippopotamus that ever lived in African rivers. But it was all stone. Everything in the wonderful regions was stone.

Flin fixed his torch between two pieces of stone, and drawing forth his box, he took snuff very thoughtfully. Hunger and weariness were for the time forgotten, as he stood there, the only living thing in a dead world. There was something awe- inspiring in the very thought that he was gazing upon these interesting relics of such a far-off period.

"Ah," he muttered philosophically, "I wish my worthy fellows of the honourable Society for the Exploration of Unknown Regions could be aware that I am at the present moment looking upon a specimen of the anthracotherium, that evidently lived in the pre-historic age. It is clear, too, that the human inhabitants of the earth were in keeping with the huge animals that were contemporary with them. For here the skeletons show that there were a race of giants. It is strange now," he pursued reflectively, and examining the head of the monster at his feet very closely, "it is strange now, how these pachydermata and the human skeletons came to be together in this manner. It must have been due to some very sudden convulsions of nature, in which man and beast and forest were overwhelmed in the ruins that came upon them without any warning. What wonderful discoveries might be written upon these things to be sure! Dear me, I wish I could convey some of the specimens to Barnum's Museum, and that I might have the opportunity of reading a paper on the subject before my Society. True, one could only speculate as to how this forest came to be buried and subsequently turned to stone, but these skeletons are pages in the world's history that there is no misreading excepting by those who are wilfully blind. Ah, when I proposed this journey some persons were pleased to say that I was mad, but I would infinitely rather be mad, if madness consists in learning something of the wonders by which we are surrounded, than go through life scoffing and pooh-poohing at everything I don't happen to comprehend."

After he had travelled for over a mile another surprise awaited him in the shape of a river. Yes, another river of icy cold water, flowing silently and mysteriously between two banks of stony grass and shrubs, and carrying a cold current of air with it.

"My conscience, this is marvellous," cried Flin, in an ecstasy of delight. "How I should like to trace this river to its source. I feel as if I could devote my life to exploring the hidden mysteries of the wonderful subterranean forest. But that cannot be. I have a goal to press forward to, and I must reach it or perish. These unexpected marvels, however, serve to encourage me, and give me a stimulus if that were needed."

As the glare of the torch fell upon the stream, he noticed

hundreds of queer-looking fish swimming about. They were unlike anything he had ever seen before. And one conspicuous peculiarity was that they had large white spots where the eyes would be in other fish.

"Ah, blind, totally blind," mutter Flin, as he noticed this, and stooping down he was enabled to examine the fish very minutely, as they were not at all alarmed by his presence. "Another sign of the great age of this forest," he continued, as he held his torch between his knees and made memoranda in his note book, "these fish have absolutely no eyes. Many ages of darkness must have passed to produce a family of eyeless fish; they evidently represent a species that have enjoyed the light of the sun at some period. If I mistake not, they belong to the order of megalichthys," he continued, as he rose from his stooping position. "Now, let me see, I think this river will show me the way I should go. By following down the stream I have no doubt I shall reach to place where my vessel is moored. I will put it to the test at anyrate."

He started on his journey once more, keeping close to the river, which ran almost straight. And at last he was cheered by seeing at a distance the welcome gleam of his signal torch. He hurried forward and found that the river he had followed flowed into the main one, lower down than the spot where he had started from. He found his fish vessel floating safely where he had moored her, and as soon as he got on board he began to prepare a substantial meal, for he was tired and hungry. And having fared sumptuously he wrote in his diary a full and detailed account of all the wonders he had seen.

By reference to his chronometer as soon as he returned, he found that he had been absent six hours and twenty minutes, during which time he estimated that he had travelled through the forest of stone a distance of twelve miles.

On examining his other instruments he was surprised to see that the inclination of the magnetic needle of his compass was extraordinarily great, and that for all practical purposes at present the compass was useless, as the needle was fixed. He thought possibly this was due to some magnetic attraction about the rocks in that part;

and to test this he carried the instrument some distance into the forest, but without any result. The needle pointed downwards.

"Umph, very strange, very strange indeed," he muttered reflectively, as he returned to the vessel.

He was grieved to find on inspecting his stock that the pigeons and one rabbit were dead. So he cast their bodies out into the dark stream; and being satisfied that everything else was safe and in working order he retired for the night, with the roar of those subterranean waters ringing in his ears.

On the following day, much as he would have liked to have extended the exploration of these buried forests, he felt that it would not be policy to prolong his stay in the place, and so he made preparations for his departure, having first partaken of a very substantial breakfast.

His first care was to make a thorough examination of his craft; when to his dismay he discovered a large dent in the head, the result of the collision with the submerged rock. It did not admit the water, however, and in other respects the vessel was as sound as the day he started. Having satisfied himself on this point, he got all ready for continuing his journey. But here a new difficulty presented itself, and one that he had not calculated upon.

The fish-ship had become embayed, as it were, in a small circular pool of water formed by a projecting mass of rock. Within this bay the water was unruffled, but a few yards out was the fierce maelstrom and the terrific fall of water over which the vessel had tumbled.

How was she to be got out of her present position into the stream again? That was the problem that confronted him and demanded solution. To have pushed her off before the door had been thoroughly secured would have ensured instant destruction. While even if the door was closed and the paddle-wheels were made use of from her great length, she would run the risk, if caught in the eddy while floating on the surface, of being dashed to fragments against the iron rocks. It was truly a fix from which the way out did not appear very clear.

Flin scratched his head thoughtfully, he took snuff rapidly, and he viewed things philosophically.

As the brave little man aroused from his cogitations, he indulged in another pinch of snuff, and shivering slightly muttered, ---

"This intense cold is very extraordinary, and seems to upset the theory altogether about the internal heats. The fact is, I have always been of the same opinion as Sir Humphrey Davy. That grand old philosopher did not believe in central fires, and I think I shall be able to prove that he was right. But I must get out of this mess, otherwise my great discovery will never be known to the world. But how am I to do it? that's the question!"

He sank into a brown study again and remained silent for some minutes. His giant intellect was planning how he could conquer the giants of nature, which seemed to laugh him to scorn. But they did not know the man they had to deal with. If he was small in stature he had a mighty brain, the capacity of which enabled him to find a solution to almost any problem propounded. After contemplating the gyrating waters for some time, he suddenly clapped his hand upon his hip, uttered a joyful exclamation, sniffed up a large pinch of snuff, and putting the box hurriedly in his pocket, he cried aloud, ---

"By Jove! I have it."

What it was he had must be revealed in the next chapter.

6

When Flin Flon cried, "By Jove! I have it," he meant that he had got an idea; and as subsequent events proved, it was a very brilliant one, quite worthy of the great brain from which it emanated.

It may here be briefly stated that Flin had, in common with a great many of his countrymen, visited Niagara, and knew that a person could stand beneath the Great Horse Shoe Fall without being wetted by a single drop of water, save what rose up from the river in the shape of misty spray.

The fall over which he had tumbled, and upon which he had so long fixed his eye in contemplative abstraction, which meant that he did not intend to be conquered, leapt out from the rock several yards, and came down in one unbroken sheet; and the magnificent idea due to the contemplative abstraction before mentioned was, that behind this sheet there was perfectly calm water, and in that fact lay his safety, and the only means of escape that presented themselves.

No sooner had this thought taken shape than Flin snuffed and prepared to act upon it -- not the snuff but the thought; though the question may be safely hazarded, were not many of Flin's brilliant ideas due in a measure to his inordinate love of the pungent dust?

As soon as Flin Flon had hit upon the idea-mentioned above --- he clambered along the rocks for a distance of about twenty yards, and reached a coign of vantage from which he was enabled to look behind the falling sheet, and he found, as he had anticipated, that behind the water was comparatively calm, while along the base of the rocks he had clambered over there was little or no agitation. And he realised immediately that if he could manage to keep his craft close into these rocks, and dive down beneath the waterfall, all might be well. It was a bold project, but the only one that offered any chance of escape from his predicament. Returning to his starting-point, he made a line fast to the head and another to the tail of the fish vessel, and joining them both in a loop, he put it over his shoulders and mounted the rocks again. Then with an amount of agility that would have done credit to a younger man, he commenced to scramble over the rocks and tow his craft at the same time. The tail line which he had so thoughtfully provided proving of the greatest service as it enabled him to keep the stern from floating out and so being caught by the eddy.

After a considerable amount of physical exertion and untiring energy, he dragged the fish into a little cove parallel with the fall. And having accomplished this task, he seated himself on a pinnacle of rock, some twelve feet high, with his corkscrew legs dangling at the sides. And as he panted for breath, and once more had recourse to his precious box, he exclaimed exultingly, "I believe I shall be able to manage it."

Perched up there in the weird gloom, sitting astraddle on the rock, with his crooked legs, his large head, pendulum-like arms, and gaspipe body, he must have looked a veritable gnome.

When he had recovered his exhausted strength, he prepared to descend to the vessel, which lay calmly enough in a little pool, the surface of which was unruffled. By passing the loop of the rope round a projecting piece of rock, he was enabled to accomplish the descent to the vessel with ease and safety. And having got on board, he opened a pint bottle of Moet, and drank success to his enterprise. His next care was to unhitch his rope, which he did by casting it loose from the tail, and pulling on the other end, so that it slipped over the rock and came down, and he was enabled to stow it away for future use. This done, he pushed the fish off very cautiously until he was beneath the falling mass of water. Then he lost not a minute in screwing up the door of the craft, and setting the pump to work to take in ballast.

Gradually the fish assumed a vertical position and then slowly commenced to sink, and Flin's delight was unbounded as he saw that his plan was successful.

A considerable depth was attained before Flin shifted his ballast so as to bring his vessel to the horizontal. The pressure gauge then registered three and a half fathoms or twenty- one feet. He next commenced to work the crank and impart motion to the paddle wheels, and in a few minutes the craft was within the influence of the maelstrom and commenced to spin round in a very unpleasant manner.

"Dear me, this is not at all comfortable," Flin remarked as he laboured at the crank, but owing to the gyratory motion of the fish little headway could be made. Still he did not relax his efforts, though they seemed to produce no effect, and it became evident that the vessel was rising. In a few minutes it was caught in the upper current of water, when it commenced to revolve at an alarmingly rapid rate, and Flin grew so giddy that he was compelled to give up his labour, and press his hands to his head, for it seemed almost as if the little hair he had remaining would be whirled off by the violence of the motion.

The revolutions grew more rapid. Flin could hear the thunder of the water overhead. Apart from the revolving, there was a most disagreeable see-saw motion, and this did not at all agree with Mr Flonatin, though in his boyhood days he had been particularly fond of see-saws; but then many years had elapsed since that period, and if the elasticity of his youthful energies had not left him, his stomach and head had reached an age when they were capable of entering a very decided protest against anything that was undignified. Mr Flonatin was not only painfully conscious of the fact that his position at that moment, when being whirled round like an impaled cockchafer, was so far undignified that on no conditions would he have liked his fellows of the S.E.U.R. to have seen him, but he was further aware that his head was in a very confused state, and there was a sensation in his stomach that only those who have suffered from the pangs of sea-sickness can understand; in spite of the strong effort he made to counteract the effect, he was obliged to succumb, and was soon stretched on the deck in a state of semiconsciousness.

It was a very distressing situation, to say nothing of the physical suffering he endured, and it is scarcely to be wondered at if at that moment he forgot the glorious objects of his mission, and wished himself back in his snug abode in New York, where, if he had only so much as sneezed, his faithful housekeeper would have instantly proceeded to put a copious supply of pure tallow on his nose, to have wrapped his head up in a flannel petticoat, and have administered to him a bowl of excellent gruel, in which a soupcon of nitre had been infused, and the whole rendered extremely palatable by a glass of the very best "old Jamaica."

It is impossible to say how long the iron fish continued its antics, for Flin Flon happily lost consciousness, and there is no mention made in his notes as to the length of time he remained in that condition. When he recovered, the vessel was quite steady, and he raised himself up in a sitting position and several pinches of snuff were necessary before he fully realised the unfortunate position in which he had been placed. As soon as the truth dawned upon him he jumped to his feet, and with that solicitude, which was such a prominent trait in his character, he hastened to look at his stock. He found both birds and animals living, but evidently terribly frightened, for they were crouched in the corners of their cages in a state of bewilderment. He lost no time in feeding them, and that done he drained another bumper of champagne, for nature was much exhausted and needed a stimulant. Nor was he wanting in a devout feeling of thankfulness for his preservation.

He next examined his instruments, and he found that the speed indicator marked two and a-half knots, so that he was evidently drifting with the current, and the pressure gauge noted two fathoms. He was therefore determined to rise to the surface and set the force pumps in motion to discharge the ballast, and the vessel slowly rose.

On peering through the eyes or windows in which the electric lamps burned brightly, for Flin had arranged them before recommencing his voyage, he was enabled to see that he was travelling through a vast tunnel, the top of which he could not discern. The river was very broad too, and the sides of the tunnel as they caught the light glittered in a resplendent manner as though they were set with millions of diamonds of the first water. This effect was curious and unique, and surpassed in dazzling beauty anything Flin had ever before beheld. He was desirous now of getting to some place where he might moor his craft for the night, so that he could rest with a sense of security. With this object he set the paddle wheels to work, and steered for one side of the tunnel. But he found that the wall of rock was smooth and polished by the action of the water. There was not a projecting bit of any description. It was as level as the top of a mahogany dining-table. He worked over to the opposite side, but it was exactly the same, and he could perceive that for many feet up the walls were as level as glass, so that it was evident that the river at times was very much higher than it was then.

There being no means of making the fish fast for the night the intrepid voyager resolved not to go to bed, but keep a look-out, and so he worked into the middle of the stream again, and let the vessel drift down with the current, occupying his time between gazing through the port-holes and writing up his diary --- the latter being a task that he was very particular about --- and he never failed to record the most trifling detail, even with reference to his sayings and feelings; for he knew that if ever he lived to reach the upper earth again, every scrap of paper containing information of his wonderful voyage would be precious.

He continued to watch and write for some hours, but exhausted nature was overcome at last, and his head dropped upon the table at which he was writing, and he sunk into a sound sleep.

How long he continued to sleep he did not know, but it must have been a considerable time. He was at length awakened by a sense of oppressive heat, and to his astonishment he found the thermometer marking 89 degrees Fahrenheit. He himself was bathed in perspiration, and his animals and birds were listless and evidently suffering. On looking through the ports he observed that some change had taken place, and a dull red glow seemed to pervade the tunnel, and gave it a most weird appearance.

The white points of flashing light that Flin had likened to diamonds of the first water had changed to ruby and crimson, and this, together with the reflected glow on the water, had a marvellous and magical effect.

"Whatever can be the cause of this increase of temperature?" Flin asked himself. "Why, it is positively tropical."

In a little while the walls opened out, and as the fish proceeded they continued to do so more and more, until what appeared to be a vast cathedral aisle burst upon the astonished gaze of the traveller, and he felt perfectly bewildered by the indescribable scene.

Gigantic pillars rose up on all sides and supported a fretted roof, and roof and pillars were studded with what appeared to be blazing jewels of the most dazzling colours. These again were reflected in the water until the senses became positively drunk with the wealth of beauty that everywhere greeted the astounded beholder. The opium-eater in his wildest dreamings could never have dreamed anything like this, and no vision of Oriental splendour could form a parallel to it. There was every gradation of colour --- rich ruby, pale amber, delicate green, bright scarlet, blood red, dark blue, every known hue was there, and the slightest movement of the eyes produced the most astonishing kaleidoscopic change in these prismatic glories.

But the mystery was, where did the glow come from that lit up this resplendent hall of jewels? The pillars, too, were equally wonderful in their varying shapes. Some were convoluted, others were straight Corinthian columns. Here was a delicate Grecian shaft with what seemed like leaves and flowers in ectype. There was a massive medi'val pillar with heavily moulded capitals. In fact every variety of architecture seemed to be represented --- Ionic, Doric,

Gothic, Tuscan, Composite. At any risk, and at every cost, Flin was determined to explore this region of startling wonders, and so he lost no time in unscrewing his door. As he did so a blast of hot air seemed to blow into his face, and he found a difficulty in breathing. But in a little time he got used to it, and the feeling of oppression and suffocation passed off. The river hereabout was narrow, and the floor of this vast cavern was almost flat, so that a few turns of the paddle brought the fish alongside the edge of what might have been marble pavement, it was so smooth and polished. Flin disembarked and made his vessel fast to a pillar, and then prepared to explore this new world --- that is, new to him, for countless thousands of years must have passed since the wondrous architects, Fire and Water, had commenced to construct this enchanted palace of beauty.

7

The river down which Flin had floated branched off into many streams as it ran through this hall of jewels --- for so the voyager called the place --- owing to the pillars that impeded its strange course, and as this circumstance was likely to prove very bewildering, Flin was determined not to run the risk again of being lost. He therefore procured a quantity of papers, of which he had a good supply, and tore them into small fragments, so as to strew them along the ground as he proceeded, and thus be able to retrace his steps to the spot from which he started.

This done he provided himself with a good stock of provisions, some torches, and a bottle or two of champagne. And having lighted and fixed a torch on his vessel he started off to explore the cavern. He found on examination that all the walls, the pillars, the roof, the floor, were composed of Plutonic rocks, granite, porphyry, and iron stone, and this accounted for the strange, fantastic nature of the place. As Flin speculated upon the immense time --- hundreds of thousands of years --- that it must have taken to form this hall, at such a depth below the surface of the earth, he was awed into reverent silence. Here was a page of geology that was written in characters of fire, and told in language that none could misinterpret, that the laws of Nature were immutable; that she worked slowly but surely, never altering her course, never changing her ideas, but proceeding with her ceaseless labours through millions of years, while countless thousands of generations of puny men came into the world, had their little day and then withered into the dust of the earth again, which was used by Dame Nature for her building materials.

Flin knew that the discovery of this vast cavern --- carved out of the very earliest rocks --- would for ever upset the schoolboy theories of a certain class of "tub thumpers," who shriek themselves hoarse in their assertions that this globe was suddenly blown into space like a soap bubble, and that some day it would just as suddenly collapse and be no more. That the great firmament of wondrous stars, of incomprehensible moons and glorious suns were made specially for the use of this little planet, the most insignificant and least by comparison of all. As Flin thought of this very stupid doctrine, promulgated by little-minded men, whose brain capacity is not equal to the mole which passes its life in an Egyptian night, no wonder that he grew irate, and made this characteristic entry in his diary, "Imprimis. --- All men who shut their eyes to the wonderfully simple writings of Nature are asses."

This is severe, and Flin evidently intended it to be so.

Flin could read the history of this Plutonic region with the ease with which a schoolboy with any pretensions to rudimentary knowledge could read his Greek alphabet.

Time was when these rocks were molten. So far back is that period that the mind cannot comprehend the thousands of cycles of ages that must have rolled away since. Then as they gradually cooled water came to work, but the water and the fire did not agree, though they were but agencies to carry out some great purpose. Huge volumes of gas were formed that rent, and tore, and sundered the half-cooled stone, that as it grew still harder, was shattered by the steam and gas into the fantastic pillars that Flin beheld. Then water continued its work through other thousands of years, wearing away rough angles, and polishing and smoothing down until the granite and porphyry with their embedded jewels became hydrophanous, and lo! here was a palace produced that the brain of no Eastern prince could ever have conceived.

But the mystery was, where did the light come from? It was reflected light, caught up and multiplied a thousandfold by the glittering and prismatic rocks, but where did the light have its origin? The traveller was determined to discover if possible, and he struck a course at right angles with the main branch of the river. He had brought a small pocket compass with him, but on consulting this he was amazed to find the needle flying about in a most extraordinary manner, obviously owing to some peculiar magnetic disturbance. He placed the box on the floor but the needle vibrated like an aspen leaf, one minute it pointed to the north, then flew round to the south, then west, then east, in fact it was all round the compass, and did not remain stationary at any point for many seconds together. This magnetic disturbance was very singular, and set Flin pondering, for he was anxious to discover the cause of such a strange phenomenon. He therefore returned to the vessel where he had a magnet and a quantity of steel pins. He found that the power of the magnet was quite neutralised, but that the rocks all round were highly magnetised, and that if he held some of the steel pins in his hand near the rock the pins would fly off and adhere to the nearest point of stone. All the rocks above, below, around, were possessed of this magnetic property, so that the phenomenon of the needle disturbance was explained.

Having satisfied himself in this matter, Flin noted the thermometer, which registered 79 degrees, being three degrees less than the temperature on board the fish-vessel, and he started on his journey, carrying a thermometer with him.

He steered a course as near as he could judge about S.W., but of course this was mere guess work, as he had nothing reliable upon which to base his calculation.

The cavern appeared to be limitless, though as he proceeded the pillars were closer together, some in fact being so close that he could not pass between them, but had to make a detour. He was careful as he went along to make a track with the pieces of paper, and he found that the farther he penetrated into the mysterious recesses the features of the place changed, and the temperature increased. The pillars and arches were not so well defined; the roof was lower; and the ground assumed the appearance of waves, as if the molten rock had been greatly agitated, like the surface of the ocean in a storm, and then suddenly petrified. This rendered travelling exceedingly difficult, as many of these stone waves were six and seven feet high, and the edges were jagged and sharp. But great as were these obstacles, they could not deter the enthusiastic and intrepid voyager from prosecuting his research; and though his feet were bruised and his hands lacerated, and the heat rendered breathing difficult, he still pushed ahead, and after travelling for three hours he sat down and partook of some refreshments, and after a good rest he resumed his journey, and presently came to what appeared to be a huge hill. Up this he scrambled. It was terrible work, but nothing could daunt him. The thermometer now rose to 90 degrees, and he found it necessary to take off a portion of his clothing. He reached the top of the hill, and then commenced the descent, which was very precipitous, and he found that he was far below the level of the river. The roof was so low here that Flin had to crawl on his hands and knees in many places. In fact the place might be likened to a gigantic honeycomb, and through every opening a strange, weird light streamed, which was reflected and counter reflected on millions of points of the polished rocks, until it seemed as if the whole place was hung with tiny lamps of various colours.

This sort of travelling was very exhaustive, and it took Flin nearly three hours to accomplish two and a half miles.

All this time he had been descending, and now the labyrinthian-like intricacies grew less complicated. The ground became smoother, and lost its rolling form. The roof was higher, and the pillars farther apart.

Suddenly --- so suddenly in fact that he was positively startled --- Flin found himself on the edge of a boundless chasm, and the heat was intense. But a sight burst upon his gaze that caused him to fall upon his knees in awe and wonderment, and exclaim reverently, ---

"O Incomprehensible! in the presence of such marvels I bow my head in the dust!"

He --- the daring and enthusiastic man of science --- had penetrated into the very secret heart of one of Nature's workshops.

A low muffled grumbling came up out of the gulf, and between the fissures of the rock he could see living fire flowing and seething, and from these fissures long powerful rays of light shot out, like the rays of an electric lamp.

The rocks, too, were broken and contorted into every conceivable shape. Here was what seemed to be the turret of some old castle; there an imposing and lofty house, from the windows of which lights streamed. Massive archways, ponderous gates, galleries with wonderfully carved balustrades. They were all there, until Flin almost fancied that he stood at the entrance to the infernal regions, and he would scarcely have been surprised had Pluto and his suite suddenly appeared before him.

Such a stupendous myriorama as the eyes of Flin rested upon is verily beyond the power of words to describe.

The scientific mind of the man, however, soon enabled him to comprehend the mystery. This was the bed of a living volcano, that had at some remote period extended throughout the vast cavern Flin had travelled through. There were the traces of the fire everywhere. They were marked on every inch of rock; but it was evident that the volcano was becoming extinct, since the fires were confined in such a comparatively narrow limit.

There was one thing that struck Flin as being remarkably strange, and that was the entire absence of anything like sulphurous gas. The heat was almost unbearable, the thermometer registering 112 degrees, but the atmosphere was perfectly free from any injurious fumes.

He was unable to account for this for some time, but at length observed that a strong current of air set from the direction he had travelled, and wafted the vapours over to a point on the opposite side of the gulf. Then for the first time he noticed that this point was the mouth of a huge tunnel or shaft that trended upwards. And the sides of this tunnel were aglow with a dull, red heat. It was evidently the escape valve for the internal fires when they rose in wrath. Flin made a calculation, and arrived at the conclusion that this was the base of one of the volcanoes in the Andes that had long been quiescent.

Much as Flin Flon would have like to have descended further into the gulf he felt that it would not be prudent. For enthusiast as he was, he was not --- as some scientific men are --- entirely wanting in those principles which teach that "discretion is the better part of valour." The discoveries he had already made were too valuable for him to risk his life in any foolhardy manner. He was quite willing to lay his life down if needs be for the benefit of the world in which he lived. But he did not think that any such exaction was required in the present instance. And as to descend into the heart of a living volcano would in all probability be to court instant death, he very wisely determined to retrace his steps. For there is a point at which even the most daring of men must stop, when Nature cries --- halt! And Mr Flonatin felt that he had reached that point now.

Before leaving the brink of the gulf, Flin tore a sheet of paper from his notebook and wrote upon it his name and address, the date of the month and year, and a few particulars of his voyage so far. This done, he rolled the piece of paper up and placed it in a champagne bottle, together with some United States currency, mostly five and ten cent. greenbacks, some of them being counterfeit. He corked the bottle up firmly, and placed it in a small crevasse, with the neck --- to which he tied a piece of white paper ---projecting, so that if anybody should contemplate journeying over the same route they would have no difficulty in discovering the bottle, even after this lapse of time. That is, of course, assuming that no change has taken place in the geological formation of the place.

This task completed, he snuffed freely and quaffed a bumper of wine, having first christened the place, by sprinkling a little wine over the rocks, "Pluto's Reception Hall," and casting one last lingering gaze at the mysterious gulf that he felt he should never see again, he commenced the return journey.

By aid of the pieces of paper he easily retraced his steps, but after proceeding a considerable distance he felt so exhausted that he decided upon remaining where he was for the night. By night it will be understood to mean that portion of the twenty-four hours which the traveller devoted to rest, for there was no sun or moon, or change from light to darkness, to mark the day and the night, in the region through which he was then passing.

He found that the rock was very far from a soft or comfortable bed, and repeatedly wished himself snugly ensconced in the little cabin on board the fish. But he was not a man to grumble much, for though rather sybaritic in his tastes, he was content to put up with many inconveniences for the sake of the cause to which he was devoting himself, and he knew that the preservation of his own health and strength was of the highest importance.

After tossing about for some time he fell into a troubled sleep, and he dreamed --- so he records --- that he was in the infernal regions, and that his Satanic Majesty was holding a judicial court, and he (Flin Flon) was on his trial for having entered Pluto's kingdom. The hall in which the court was held was of vast dimensions. The pavement was inlaid with the most costly and precious stones. The pillars that supported the roof were of solid gold, studded with huge brilliants. The roof itself was pure gold inlaid with turquoise, amethysts, rubies and pearls. The throne upon which his Majesty was seated was formed out of a gigantic brilliant of the first water, and his footstool was a magnificent carbuncle, while the sceptre he held in his hand was set with a cat's eye of unusual size, and every time this sceptre was moved the jewel seemed to emit sparks of fire.

All round the hall ran golden galleries that were filled with spirits in human form and all plainly labelled. There were bishops and clergymen of all denominations. There were kings and queens, statesmen, philanthropists, authors (a good many of these), tradesmen (these were more numerous than the authors), and reviewers and critics --- these were the most numerous, in fact, they represented a large majority. Each spirit wore round its neck a gold plate, on which was marked in diamonds the calling followed in life, so that Flin had no difficulty in distinguishing the kings from the critics and the critics from the tradesmen. Amongst the latter Flin states that he fancied he recognised his own tailor and butcher. But this is, no doubt, meant as raillery, for the great traveller was evidently a bit of a wag in spite of his high scientific attainments. The strangest peculiarity of all was, that each spirit was encircled in a pale blue, perfectly transparent lambent flame. The flame seemed to radiate, as it were, from the spirits themselves, whose faces wore expressions of intense suffering. The flame was all over them, though it did not shoot out from the form, but to use Flin's own words, "fitted them like a suit of clothes." And in appearance it was very like the flame given off by burning spirits of wine. His Majesty was enveloped in a flame of a deep ruby colour, that was rather pretty in its effect. If he wanted any particular person in the court to "catch his eye," he pointed his finger and a long spark, like an electric spark, darted therefrom to the spirit whose attention he wanted, It should be mentioned that all the spirits hung their heads, as if with shame, and only looked up when required by his Majesty to do so.

The spirit of one of the critics gave evidence against Flin. He said that he had observed him trespassing and making notes, no doubt with a view to publishing a book on his Majesty's dominions. The King remarked that after such evidence as that, it was useless to waste the time of the Court with going into the case any further, for the guilt of the culprit was clearly established, and for anyone to attempt to write a descriptive work of the kingdom over which he had so long reigned to the satisfaction of his subjects was a very grave offence, and must be punished in a manner altogether unparalleled. The prisoner would therefore be kept for ten million years ---"

At this point Flin suddenly awoke in a great fright. And he says that there was such an air of reality about the whole affair that for some moments he had a difficulty in persuading himself that it was only a dream.

However, a good pinch of snuff soon called him back to a proper sense of his position, and as he felt considerably refreshed, he was determined to get back to his vessel.

Following the trail of papers, he hurried on as fast as the nature of the ground would allow him, for he remembered that his pigeons and rabbits had not been fed for some time, and he feared they might die of hunger.

He reached the end of the trail and the river at last, but he could not see the fish. Then he thought that he had come to the wrong spot, but when he looked at the papers strewn on the ground he felt that he could not be mistaken. Where, then, was his vessel? Certainly not in sight. He went up the stream and then down, but nowhere was the fish to be seen. He listened with bated breath, but he could hear nothing but the weird rippling of the water. It was an awful moment. To be left there without the means of escape, to die slowly of horrid starvation, and when the success of his mission seemed so certain, was a fate that might have appalled even a stouter heart than Flin Flon's.

He rushed up and down frantically, but his search was not rewarded. And when the terrible truth broke upon him that he was indeed left there, and that his vessel had drifted away, he fell to the ground in a swoon.

8

How long Flin remained in a state of insensibility he never knew. Nor must the fact of his having swooned be taken as an evidence of either moral or physical weakness. Should anyone who peruses this veracious history be inclined to criticise Mr. Flonatin in any ill-natured or severe spirit, I would respectfully advise such person to close his eyes for a few minutes and then imagine himself in a volcanic cavern, at a depth of over three miles in the bowels of the earth, and with all means of escaping therefrom apparently gone, and thus shut off from his fellow-men; entombed alive in these halls of silence and mystery, with the prospect of a terrible death from slow starvation staring him in the face, and all his ambitious dreams and brightest hopes scattered to the winds by a sudden and unexpected mishap; if he will but realise this --- in imagination for a few moments --- his blame will be turned to pity, and he will mentally exclaim, "Poor Flin Flon! I hope he will escape."

That this hope was realised will be self-evident, as this story of marvellous adventure could not have been written if the bold explorer had not returned to the earth to bring back his papers. Again, some impatient reader may ask --- but how did Flin get back? Well, I may at once state that it is not my intention to satisfy such curiosity here. At the proper time and in the right place the almost incredible and stupendous manner in which Mr. Flonatin did succeed in returning to the upper earth will be disclosed.

Flin Flon having recovered from his swoon sat bolt upright and stared about him in a dazed sort of manner. He seemed to fancy for some moments that he had been suffering from nightmare. His vessel, which had borne him safely from the upper earth, had drifted away, and he was left without any means of escape. This was the fact he had to face, and it was well calculated to appal any man.

But Flin was not one to sit down idly and whine at his fate. Having got over the first shock, he saw that action was needed, and that no time was to be lost. If his vessel had drifted down the stream --- and it was evident that it had --- it could not have gone very far. Moreover, it had possibly got jammed between some of the pillars. But here another difficulty arose. The main river was diverted in many ways by numerous obstacles, and which of these branches to take was the puzzling question. Flin, however, selected the one he thought that the current was most rapid in, and commenced to make his way along the bank. Travelling for many hours, slowly it is true, for the floor of the cavern had got very rough and broken, and he became bewildered too at the labyrinthian-like manner in which the river wound about the pillars. He began to despair and almost gave himself up for lost. There was another fact also that gave him cause for alarm, and that was the farther he went from the volcano the less light there was to guide him. The gloom increased in a painfully rapid manner. The scintillation of the rocks died out, and the pillars assumed weird and fantastic shapes in the gathering darkness. How could he hope to find his way without a light?

He upbraided himself in the bitterest terms for having been so careless as to come away without one of the electric lamps. It was an oversight that might cost him his life. With one of these little lamps in his possession now he might have pursued his way through Cimmerian gloom. But hope died within his heart as he saw that the darkness increased. Moreover, the pangs of hunger were making themselves felt in a very disagreeable manner, and to add to his misery his snuffbox was empty. He had sniffed the dust freely during his dilemma, and without he found his vessel, where he had a good supply of Lundyfoot, he could not replenish his box.

It was a terrible predicament, despair seized upon him, and candidly confesses that at that moment his enthusiasm all left him; he wished that he was back again in New York, where he would be content to retail sugar and tea all his life, and ignore for evermore learned societies and Quixotic expeditions.

But with such a man as Flin a feeling of this kind is generally of the most ephemeric nature. The fire of energy burned within him, and he could not stand still. He must press forward, even if it was to the most fearful death; and press forward he did. Stumbling about and bruising and lacerating himself in a most unpleasant manner. Presently, finding himself on a mound of rock --- for so it really was --- he was obliged to sit down to recover his spent breath, and as he wiped his forehead, on which the perspiration stood in great beads, he bitterly lamented the emptiness of his gold box. A few pinches of snuff would have given him new strength. But regrets were useless. He had learnt a bitter lesson, and determined to profit by it, if ever he should be so fortunate as to regain his vessel.

As he so sat, bewailing his misfortune, he was suddenly startled by what seemed to be two gleaming eyes which shone out in the darkness some distance before him. Now they seemed to come nearer, then recede, then they were lost to view for a few moments, and as the astonished Flin Flon watched them, all sorts of ideas flitted through his brain.

He thought it was possible the eyes were those of some labyrinthodon, or an anopotherium or even a menopome. For although the two former were extinct in the upper world, there was no reason why they should not exist down here, and it might also prove that the menopome was not a myth after all, but that this batrachian had its home down in the fiery gulf of lava which Flin had slept behind. As he thought of this, and that possibly it was one or other of these monsters that was watching him, and would ultimately swallow him with as much ease as a crocodile would dispose of a fly, he felt very far from comfortable, and his first impulse was to beat a hasty retreat. But after a little reflection he deemed that course to be a cowardly one; moreover if this should prove to be a living specimen of one of the gigantic pachyderms which formerly inhabited the upper world, he felt that it was his duty to get nearer that he might be able to write a description of it for the benefit of his brother savants. At this thought all his enthusiasm came back, and he forgot his danger and troubles in his desire to drink at the well of knowledge. With the fiery eyes still seemingly fixed upon him, he approached slowly, but with every possible caution, making his way as best he could amongst the pillars and rugged masses of rock, but always keeping the eyes in front as a sort of guiding beacon. Presently he heard a gurgling sound, as if the huge monster was drinking deeply of the river water. And as he drew nearer still, he was enabled to distinguish very faintly the outlines of some huge reptile or fish, that was moving up and down and blinking its eyes.

"Dear me," thought Flin, "this is exceedingly interesting to be sure. I wish I could inspect the beast closer. I must try at anyrate, for this is an opportunity that may never occur again."

Crawling on all fours he proceeded cautiously and with much difficulty towards the monster, and as he drew near he found that the rocks were damp and slimy, and he was in danger several times of falling into the water. But nothing disheartened, he pressed on until he reached a jagged pinnacle of rock. Then he crouched down behind it, and peeped forth very cautiously, intending to examine the supposed monster as well as circumstances would permit. As he looked and wondered he suddenly exclaimed, ---

"Why, bless my life --- dear me, how very extraordinary --- surely I cannot be mistaken. It is --- no it isn't --- yes it is, I declare. Hurrah!"

This, it must be confessed, is somewhat incoherent, and to the intelligent reader may convey no special meaning. But it will be remembered that Flin was labouring under intense excitement, and joyful surprise almost deprived him of the power of speech.

As he cried "Hurrah!" he sprang up quickly and rushed forward impetuously, tripping as he did so over an inequality in the rock, which caused him to sprawl in a manner that was far from dignified for a member of the Society for the Exploration of Unknown Regions. He picked himself up, however. But severe abrasions on the hands, knees, face and elbows of the philosopher proved the force with which he and the ground had met. His energy was checked, but he limped forward as well as he was able towards the object that had previously startled him, and which he had taken to be some monstrous animal, but which was in reality the vessel he had all but despaired of ever beholding again.

9

It was scarcely matter for wonder that Flin Flon should give expression to his feelings of joy in a wild "Hurrah!" as he discovered, while crouching behind the rock, that the supposed monster was nothing more than his own vessel, the loss of which had caused him such intense anxiety.

It had drifted between two pillars, not wide enough apart to admit of the passage through, so that further progress was stopped. The electric lamp still burned in the eyes, and the motion of the light caused by the rocking of the vessel on the water was what had deceived Flin. The fortuitous circumstance of the vessel running between the pillars was one that caused Flin's heart to swell with gratitude. For to it he knew that he owed his life, and he almost wept tears of joy as he made the discovery. Not only was his life spared for the present, but he would be enabled to continue his explorations, by which he hoped to benefit the world in an immeasurable degree. He found that the fish was right in the centre of the stream, and some distance from where he stood. This was an unpleasant difficulty, as he was not a very good swimmer, and he had no doubt the depth of water was too great to permit him to wade out to his ark of safety. It was truly a dilemma. But with the boldness which never left him he determined to trust himself to the silent

stream, and so divesting himself of his clothing, he sat down, first of all, on the edge of the rock, and then slipped into the water and struck out energetically. The current was very strong indeed,

and Flin was carried past the pillars. He had not calculated on this, and he battled fiercely to swim against the stream. But he grew very red in the face and panted for breath, until he was in danger of sinking. Then he suddenly remembered, and was astonished that he had not thought of it before, that it would be better to turn round and get to the side, where he could scramble out and walk back again. He put this into practice, but not without considerable difficulty; and it was only after extraordinary exertion that he was enabled to effect a landing, and not then until he had fearfully lacerated his legs and body against the sharp points of rock at the side.

When he succeeded in getting out of the water, he was compelled to rest for a considerable time, for his strength was quite spent. Still he was not daunted, and having recovered he walked back, his naked feet suffering considerably. He got some distance above the spot where he had left his clothes, and then slipped into the water once more. He was more fortunate this time, and as he drifted down he was able to clutch the head of his fish, and by an almost superhuman effort to swing himself on board.

His feelings when he had accomplished this can be better imagined than described. Words would fail to convey anything like an adequate idea of his thankfulness.

His first care was to look to his animals, and it was with extreme sorrow that he found that only one rabbit and pigeon were left alive. He almost felt inclined to weep, but he knew that would do no good, and so he hastened to feed the survivors. That done, he snuffed freely; and this not only restored his drooping spirits, but brought back his strength, and he sat down to a very hearty supper, which he enjoyed immensely, consisting as it did of Staten Island preserved oysters, and very delicious they were (so Flin records), a slice of the truffle-stuffed boar's head, a portion of a pat, de foie gras, some delicate New Jersey biscuits, rendered palatable by being spread with real guava jelly. A half bottle of Catawba wine and a pint of Roederer's best brand, and a liqueur de cognac to aid digestion. After this light but elegant déjeuner Flin felt considerably refreshed, and being in *puris naturalibus* --- a state he hardly noticed while the pangs of hunger were keen; but now the cravings of the inner man being satisfied, he remembered that it was somewhat indecorous for a member of the Society for the Exploration of Unknown Regions to remain long in such a condition, even though there were no other eyes to behold.

He would at once have proceeded to have made his toilet, but the fact was he had not another suit of clothes on board. Personal adornment being about the last this he ever though of, he had omitted to supply anything like a stock of clothing. He had two or three dress shirts in his trunk, but he would not have had these if it had not been for the thoughtfulness of his housekeeper, who told him that when he found the new people he was going to discover he might have to attend receptions, and perhaps State balls. But still a dress shirt was not a suit of clothes, though it was something towards it. Taking one of the shirts from his box, he noticed the

beautiful gloss on the front, and the exquisite manner in which his housekeeper had crimped the frill, and he sighed as he thought what a pity it was to have to soil such excellent handiwork for no purpose. There was no help for it, however, so he adjusted the garment, and determined to make an effort to regain his clothes from the spot where he had left them.

To get his vessel from between the two pillars where it had got wedged was a work of time and immense difficulty, for as fast as Flin moved her a little the current drove her back again. But perseverance overcomes all things, and the savant conquered this obstacle, and his labours were rewarded at last by the fish swinging clear. He tried now to work the vessel up stream by means of the paddles, but the current was too strong; it carried him down rapidly, and he found it necessary to bestow all his attention on keeping her from being injured by coming in contact with the rocks, and so he had to abandon the paddles and take the tiller. He drifted farther and farther away, and it was with alarm and mortification that he saw that he would be unable to recover his clothes. This in itself was a great loss, for his costume of dress shirt only was scarcely one in which he could present himself before anything like civilised people with propriety, and he felt a little delicate about the matter. But this loss was nothing as compared with that of his beloved snuff- box. The clothes might be replaced, or substituted, but the box could not. He mourned as if it had been a child --- he had never had any children, so he scarcely knew what a loss of that nature would have been--but the fact of being compelled to leave his box behind cut him to the heart, and though he does not record it, it is inferred from his papers that he actually wept.

He steered the fish with admirable skill for nearly four hours, and then the pillars were fewer. The river broadened, the roof was lower, and in a little while he was once more in a tunnel and the surface of the water was quite free from obstacles. He now screwed up the door and examined his instruments. The speed dial indicated a rate of five knots an hour. The needle of the compass was very much deflected and very unsteady. The thermometer marked 75 degrees Fahrenheit, while his chronometers showed him that there was a difference in time between where he then was and New York of two hours three minutes four seconds. Having seen that his chemical apparatus was in working order, and that the electric lamps were burning properly, he prepared to sink his vessel. After having taken in sufficient ballast he descended no less than one hundred and fifty feet, or twenty-five fathoms, before he touched bottom. Here the vessel rested motionless, a circumstance that Flin was thankful for, as he felt that he could now sleep in security for some hours. And in a very short time he was locked in slumber and dreaming that he was reading a paper on his wonderful discoveries before an excited and enthusiastic audience in New York.

Flin enjoyed some hours of most refreshing sleep, and when he awoke he felt a buoyancy of spirit that was really delightful.

Having finished his toilet --- that is, combed his scant grey locks and adjusted his dress-shirt --- he examined his instruments and found that no change of importance had taken place excepting a considerable rise in the thermometer, which was accounted for by the air being so confined within the narrow limits of the fish vessel. This duty ended, and his diary written up, he made a hearty break-fast, and then proceeded to discharge the water ballast, so as to allow the vessel to rise to the surface of the stream.

As he floated along the tunnel narrowed considerably, and the strength of the current increased to six knots an hour. The walls and roof of the tunnel were stratified, but were dull and unrelieved by any of those jewel-like scintillations which had so astonished the traveller in the hall of pillars. The darkness was intense save for the light from the electric lamps.

Flin unscrewed the door so that the temperature of the vessel might be lowered, and as he did so and put his head out he quickly withdrew it again, for the air was rushing through the tunnel with the velocity of a hurricane. He was surprised to find that the fish was going through the water at a tremendous pace, acted upon by the pressure of the wind from behind.

Flin studied this phenomenon for some time, and concluded that the tunnel was a sort of air shaft, and the ultimately he would reach some open place where the atmosphere was warmer than that he was then travelling through, which was quite chilly and caused him to shiver.

His theory was that the extensive range of caverns through which he had passed had been at some time or other filled with water, after the volcanic fires had ceased their action. In fact they had been, as it were, a series of gigantic subterranean reservoirs. Then, as the water had accumulated by additions from the upper earth, it had commenced to wear a passage through the lower strata, the tunnel through which Flin was then travelling being the result of this action, and he did not doubt that the waters would presently spread out into either an open sea or another series of caverns.

The journey was continued for some hours without any change taking place. But at length the speed increased, the water became very turbulent, and the vessel tossed about a good deal. This circumstance caused Flin some uneasiness, for it was evident he was descending a rapid, and that the river was passing over a series of steps, as it were, and going farther down into the bowels of the earth. Flin deemed it prudent to screw up the door and sink the vessel to about three fathoms. This was done, and she was carried along smoothly though very rapidly. But presently she was brought up --- as sailors would say --- with a round turn. There was a tremendous shock that threw the voyager off his feet, disturbed all the instruments, and caused the fish to quiver for some moments.

"Bless my life, this is very extraordinary," mused Flin, as he picked himself up and hurried to the dial plate, which was at zero, indicating that there was no speed at all. In short the vessel had stopped. One of the electric lamps had been displaced by the force of the collision and had ceased to act. Flin lost no time in getting it in order again, and the vessel --- save for a slight wavy motion --- had become quite still he determine to rise to the surface and discover the cause of the sudden stoppage. He therefore commenced to discharge the ballast very slowly, so that the vessel might rise gradually. As it did so the undulating motion increased, and a muffled roar broke upon Flin's ears, that he could not account for. It was very far from a pleasant situation to be placed in, and he was powerless to do anything, his sphere of action being so very limited. He was subject to the mighty forces of Nature, and might be likened to a straw in the hands of a giant. How should he act? what could he do? To remain sunk in the depth of the stream was to die, and it would be better at all risks to rise to the surface and discover if possible his true position.

So he continued to discharge the ballast, and as the vessel rose the roar increased and, as he emerged from the waters, became deafening. It was as if a thousand blast furnaces were at work. The motion of the vessel was the same as it would have been had she been at anchor in a rough sea way. She would go half round, then come back again, then bob up and down, grate unpleasantly against the rocks, roll, pitch, and altogether cut such a series of capers as to both alarm and puzzle the traveller; for a while it was apparent that she was subject to the influence of some powerful current, she made no progress, but appeared to remain in the one place. He scrambled to the eyes of the fish and peered out, and as he did so such a sight met his gaze that he drew back suddenly, and clasping his hands together exclaimed, ---

"Good gracious! this is appalling and marvellous."

10

The sight that met Mr Flonatin's view as he gazed through the portholes, or eyes of his fish, was truly appalling and marvellous. As far as he could make out --- for the line of vision was necessarily circumscribed --- he was in an extensive chamber of circular form. From the surface of the water millions of blue stars were incessantly shooting up, while to roof and walls seemed to be burning with a pale blue flame.

The phenomenon was striking and wonderful. And at first Flin thought it was due to some electrical disturbance. But the needles of his compass did not indicate that any electrical waves were moving about. On the contrary, the needles were steady, which would not have been the case had the external atmosphere been overloaded with electricity. The phenomenon must therefore be sought for in some other cause --- and that cause Flin concluded was a chemical one. Consequently very great caution would have to be exercised, as the cavern might be filled with dangerous gaseous vapours, that, if inhaled, would be fatal to human life.

This was a contingency that he thought it probable --- when he set out on his journey --- that he might have to encounter. And he had therefore provided himself with a filter- respirator, the invention of an ingenious friend.

It was so constructed that it fitted closely over the mouth and nostrils, and was composed of layers of fine cotton wool between perforated plates of platinum. The external casing was of india-rubber, and was kept close to the face by means of steel springs. From this apparatus two india-rubber pipes led to the back of the neck, one on each side. They were there connected with a small tin case, that was half filled with water. On the top of this cylinder or case was a small bell-shaped funnel which admitted the air, that was drawn through the water, along the pipes, and through the cotton wool in a purified state, by the wearer at every respiration. The respirations were made by the nostrils, and the mouth was kept firmly closed. But when the breath was discharged, the mouth was opened, and the foul air was expelled through an escape valve which was opened by the force of the breath. By means of this clever invention a person was enabled to remain for a considerable time in the deadliest of atmospheres.

When Mr. Flonatin had adjusted the apparatus he got the remaining pigeon out of its wicker cage and proceeded to unscrew the door of the vessel very carefully; and having taken the precaution to tie one of the legs of the pigeon to some fine thread which he held, so the he might recover the bird again, he opened the door sufficiently to allow of the pigeon passing out. As soon as that was done Flin rushed to the porthole, having first secured the door again. He saw the pigeon fly for a few minutes in a confused sort of manner. It wheeled round and round two or three times, and suddenly fell into the water exactly as if it had been shot. It spread its wings out, beat the water, and soon was perfectly still. Flin drew it in by means of the string and found that it was dead. It had evidently been suffocated.

Much as he regretted the death of the poor bird, he felt that the experiment had been warranted, as it proved to him that he had deadly risks to contend with, and to be forewarned was to be forearmed. It would not do to remain where he was, and to understand the exact position of affairs it would be necessary to get out and make a survey. But he felt that the sooner he was clear of such a fatal region the better.

He again opened the door, and getting on the outside of the fish he closed the door behind him.

The sight was indeed startling. Small blue stars seemed to bubble up, as it were, in the water, and as soon as they reach the surface they burst into a blue flame, that shot up into the air and expired, leaving behind a flimsy haze of vapour.

Close to the vessel was a great mass of rock, that was worn into the shape of a bow by the action of the water. Into this bow the vessel had drifted, and save for the motion caused by the circling eddies, she remained stationary, though on the outside of the bow the river sped along like a millrace.

Flin was able to step on to this rock, and as it was full of indentations he managed to scramble up, though his legs and feet, which it will be remembered were without covering, suffered severely. But then enthusiasm burned strong in his breast again, and he did not feel much of the pain at that moment.

From his elevated position he observed that the cavern apparently stretched away to a limitless extent. It was like a huge chamber with a domed roof. The water was everywhere, but always flowing down with great force, and swirling with a savage roar round the rocky islets which everywhere dotted its surface.

The roof, the islets, the walls were all covered with what seemed like luminous vapour, of that kind which a common lucifer match makes if rubbed on anything in the dark. And as Flin noticed this he accounted for it by the theory that from the bottom of the lake or river streams of phosphuretted gas were continually rising, which burst into flame as soon as they reached the surface; and he hit upon the happy though paradoxical name for the place of "The Waters of Fire," for it really seemed as if the lake was emitting tongues of flame, which in truth it was. He felt that this wonder alone, to say nothing of those he had already witnessed, was well worth a journey into the bowels of the earth to see.

"But where was the outlet of this great stream?" he asked himself;

"and how was he to reach it?" He was convinced that there must be a tremendous dip in the earth here, otherwise the current would not be so rapid.

As it was impossible from the nature of the place to extend his research, he deemed it to be the wisest course to get back into his vessel and endeavour to leave the spot where he had become embayed. So he returned on board, screwed down the door, and then set the paddle to work, and, by great exertion, succeeded in getting into the fairway of the stream, and the fish moved rapidly along.

By means of a small wheel near the eyes Flin was enabled to steer and keep a lookout at the same time. The navigation was most intricate, and as the motive power of the vessel was the current itself the helm was of little use; and several times the fish grated unpleasantly and dangerously against the rocky island.

It was a most exciting time, and the brave traveller felt that he held his life by a very insecure tenure. But, thanks to the substantial manner in which the fish had been built, the collisions with the rocks were not productive of any serious consequences, and as the water swirled rapidly round the rocks the swirl itself carried the vessel clear after she had bumped.

After two or three hours of this kind of work the obstacles were fewer, and at length the fish shot into a narrow tunnel. Here the water was perfectly smooth, but so great was the difference in the levels between this and the upper lake that it was like an inclined plane, and down this the vessel rushed as straight as an arrow. Flin managed to keep her in midstream, and watched at his look-out ports with breathless anxiety, not unmixed with alarm as to what the end of this wild career might be. He thought it was quite probable that he was being borne on towards a mighty maelstrom, and if that were the case all hope of ever seeing the upper world again would be gone.

It was an appalling thought, and if something like a shudder passed through Flin's frame at that moment it certainly was no evidence of weakness, for he was as brave as most men, and had faced dangers without flinching that would have turned some men's hair grey. But here that tremendous force of Nature --- water --- was tearing along through a narrow channel, and it was plain to the most common reason that it must ultimately discharge itself with a power that was beyond human comprehension.

Would the comparatively frail craft be able to with- stand this power? Upon that everything depended.

The current which flowed from the bottom of Lake Avernus had hitherto been the only motive power upon which he had to depend. By a natural law the water was seeking its level, and it was this very law of gravitation that had induced Flin to undertake the journey. He knew that if there was a current at the bottom of the lake it must flow inwards --- that is towards the centre of the earth, or the centre of gravitation. What was there at the centre? He was far below the earth's surface; down in the very heart of the primitive rocks, so that he could not now expect to come out in one of the known oceans. Did all the great waters flow to that common centre, and there, with a fury that almost made the heart stand still with awe to think of it, form a whirlpool of such stupendous magnitude that the human brain was incapable of grasping it? These were the thoughts that agitated the great traveller.

But this feeling of dejection soon passed away, and he took courage from the thought that fortune had so far favoured him.

So rapidly and smoothly did the vessel glide along with the swift-flowing current that there was very little motion. As an evidence of the tremendous fall there was it may be mentioned that the head of the fish was lower by fifteen degrees than the tail.

To better illustrate this Mr Flonatin thought of a very happy simile. He said that if you could take the huge sheet of smooth water which flows over the Horse Shoe Fall at Niagara, and cut it into long strips about six yards broad, then tack the strips on to each other, and stretch them out with a dip of 15 3/4, a correct representation of the stream down which the fish rushed would be obtained.

No change took place for some hours, and Flin was worn out with watching. The temperature of the vessel had sunk very considerably, and the cold caused him to tremble so much, owing to the absence of clothing, that he got one of his blankets and wrapped it round him.

The speed dial marked twenty-two and a half knots an hour, and the chronometers showed that it was six o'clock, New York time. It may be asked how did Flonatin ascertain the number of days he had been out as he could not see the sun? Well, at first sight this might seem a difficult thing to do, but with that fore-thought which characterised all his movements he had provided a little instrument for measuring the days. It consisted of a dial upon which were marked the hours, and round which a hand revolved, worked by complicated mechanism. When Flin commenced to descend into Avernus he set this hand exactly at twelve, New York time. Then every hour the hand had moved until it had ticked off twenty-four. That done, a number appeared on a disc which encircled the dial. This number was ONE, indicating one day had gone.

So each day was marked, and as nine now appeared on the disc --- it showed that Flin had been out nine days --- while the hand marked the sixth hour of the tenth day afternoon, that is, six o'clock at night.

His chemicals were lasting very well, as when he had been out of the vessel he had not used the air apparatus at all. He had also abundance of provisions yet. So on that score he had no fear. His only anxiety was about his vessel. As long as that was sound he was sanguine of prosecuting his explorations to a successful issue. But should she be wrecked by any untoward circumstance his mission would be ended, and his brother savants and the world would say that he had sacrificed his life in a foolhardy cause, for he was aware how unfortunately true it was that men were apt to sneer and call a person a fool who did not succeed in what he undertook, forgetting that non-success did not always imply a want of wisdom. On the contrary, wise men sometimes fail where fools succeed. This may often be seen in the lack-brain individuals who sit in high places, and shake their heads as if they were truly Solomons.

For instance, a youth with no brains but plenty of influence at Court will get on where a youth with more of brains but no influence will be neglected and passed over. Mr Flonatin knew that this was a glaring and crying shame in his own day, and he had repeatedly raised his voice against it, for he had seen genius and merit sitting in the gutter starving for the lack of a patron; while shallowness, sycophancy and hypocrisy prevailed. If the good man could only revisit the scenes of his earthly labours he would be shocked to observe that, with all our advancement, this state of things has not improved, and that honest merit has just as much difficulty in making itself heard now as ever it had.

Flin continued at his post for some time longer, but it was with the utmost difficulty he could keep his eyes open. To use a common phrase he was "dead beat," and he would have hailed with delight any place where he could have moored the vessel, so that he might have lain down in security. As it was he felt that it would be impossible to conquer the desire to sleep much longer, and that he would have to go to bed whatever the risks might be.

Since leaving "The Waters of Fire" the tunnel had been quite dark, save for the illumination of the electric lamps. But now he observed with astonishment that the walls were opening out, the river was getting broader, and a strange, weird, ghostly sort of light was spreading through the place. This was new matter for wonder, and for a time he forgot his weariness and exhaustion, and peered eagerly through his look-out windows for the cause of the phenomenon.

The light grew rapidly stronger. The fish rushed madly on. Then suddenly Flin uttered a cry of horror as he saw right before him, but at some distance, what appeared to be a huge cauldron, from which rose immense volumes of steam, that were illuminated by an intense bright light, while an awful roar, that is indescribable, almost deafened him.

"This, then, was the end of all his devotion to the cause he had so much at heart," he thought.

Before him was a tumbling, seething, boiling cauldron of gigantic proportions; a world, as it were, of water and fire. The two elements in contact, like too mighty giants, struggling for mastery, and in their struggles shaking the firm earth to its very foundations. On to this his vessel was rushing, and he was powerless to stay her course for one moment.

He would be boiled or roasted, it scarcely mattered which. It seemed certain he would be annihilated, and whether that was effected by fire or boiling was of no consequence. It was an awful and appalling ending to his ambitious dreams. He believed that his time had come, and with a cry of anguish he sank upon the floor of the vessel and buried his face in his blanket, expecting every moment to find the temperature of the fish rising, and himself baking like a joint of meat in an oven.

11

Some time elapsed, it really seemed an age to the trembling Flin.

The roar was now awful. Presently the vessel was suddenly lifted up, then shot forward like an arrow from a bow, then rolled round and round, like a skittle ball, sending Flin and all the loose articles flying about in mad confusion. He managed to grasp the legs of the table, and hold on --- so he says --- with the tenacity of a leech. But the horrible manner in which the fish went up and down, rolled round and round and waltzed about, cannot be realised by any amount of word picturing. Flin was terribly bruised but otherwise uninjured by being knocked about, though he got a little light-headed by being whirled round and round.

This violent motion continued for a long while, and then gradually grew less, until it gave place to a gentle undulation, when, exhausted and faint, Flin Flon sank into a sound sleep, and continued so for some hours. On awakening his first thought was that he had been dreaming some horrid dreams, but, on attempting to rise, he found his limbs so stiff and swollen and lacerated that he could only regain his feet with the greatest difficulty. He was really in a pitiable condition, and he sunk back upon the cushioned seat near the table, to try and collect his scattered thoughts. As he surveyed the interior of the vessel it seemed to him to be a perfect wreck. Everything was in a state of chaotic confusion. One valuable chronometer was lying on the floor smashed to pieces, a barometer was also rendered useless, and several bottles of the prepared phosphorous, which had been used for the purpose of giving light in the interior of the vessel, were displaced, and were lying on the deck. Fortunately these bottles had been enclosed in copper netting, otherwise they might have been broken, and the consequences then would have been serious, as the phosphorus would have burst into flame. In short, everything that had not been secured was displaced, and the sight was a woeful one.

Poor Flin sat for some time surveying the mischief. One thing was clear, his stout little vessel had passed through some terrible danger, but had weathered it safely, and he himself lived. In that fact there was matter for intense gratification. As he gradually recovered from the effects of his tossing about he saw that immediate action was necessary, and that he must make a careful survey of the fish, as well as of his instruments; for after all he might be hallooing before he was out of the wood. He managed to struggle to his feet, and, feeling a little faint, he thought it was owing to the badness of the air in the interior, so he inspected the chemical apparatus, and was not a little alarmed to find that it had been displaced, and the decomposition of the chemicals that produced the properties of atmospheric air was all but stopped. Attached to this apparatus was an ozonometer, but it indicated that there was absolutely no ozone in the air. The cells containing the nitric acid from which the nitrogen was evolved were deranged, and as Flin noticed this he saw how wonderfully narrow his escape from death had been; for not only had dangers without threatened him, but dangers within also, as he must have died if the air-producing apparatus had ceased to act entirely.

But before proceeding to rectify matters, he felt that it was necessary to recuperate his strength with some stimulant, and he therefore crept to his little sleeping apartment, where he kept his stock of snuff, and the first pinch of the fragrant dust seemed to have an almost electrical effect upon him. It inspired him with new hope, new courage, new energies. And when he had drunk a pint of champagne he felt quite a different man. A cursory examination of his person proved that there were no bones broken, nor any serious injury, and he was so reinvigorated by the refreshment that he scarcely felt the pain of his bruises.

"But where am I?" he suddenly exclaimed, as he began to think it was high time he found out the position of the vessel, which, with the exception of a slight undulating motion, was as steady as a ship riding at anchor in a calm bay.

From the windows in the head a beautiful light was streaming in. One lamp had been displaced and was lying on the floor, the other was still burning, but its light was paled by the brighter light outside.

As Flin looked through the little portholes his eyes were dazzled for some moments, but when they had become used to the glare he uttered a cry of astonishment.

On one side was what appeared to be a pier or jetty, and as far as the eye could reach on the other side stretched a calm sea that seemed roseate-flushed as if with the rays of the rising sun.

He literally sprang to the door of the vessel and opened it, and as he stepped out on the back of the fish such a view met his gaze that he was speechless with wonder. What had seemed like a jetty was the end of a long ledge of rock. A sort of breakwater in fact, the top of which was perfectly flat as if formed for a promenade. Then for miles was a coast-line of the most wonderful and fantastic rocks the imagination can possibly conceive. They were pointed like pyramids, jagged like the teeth of a saw, ridged like the roof of a house, carved with minarets, rounded into domes, humped like a camel, curling like a wave, curved like the seat of a saddle, and between the rifts, and clefts, and broken masses of rocks a thousand waterfalls tumbled. Some had the appearance of mere trickling rivulets; others again were giant cataracts that thundered over the mighty cliffs.

To the right was an open sea. But the most wonderful thing was that far above the air was filled with cumulus clouds, that floated through an azure sky. The clouds were of the most beautiful tints. There were rose colour, amber, purple, magenta, crimson, yellow, silver and pure white that looked like well- washed fleece. It was a marvellous sight.

A soft balmy breeze blew over the water, scarcely ruffling its surface. The light evidently came from the clouds, the white being so intense as to dazzle the eyes. But the various rays blending together threw a fairy-like glamour over the scene.

At first Flin thought that he had come out in one of the upper oceans, near some tropical coast, though a very little reflection served to convince him of the error of this. He had reached a central sea, and as he realised this fact he fairly clapped his hands with joy. There was no sun, that was a certainty. The clouds answered the purpose of a sun, and his philosophic mind was not long in accounting for the phenomenon. The roof of this stupendous cavern was the inner crust of the earth, and to it the vapours were attracted in enormous masses, and were there highly electrified by the earth's currents of electricity, the various colours depending on the density of the vapours and the strength of the currents. That this was so Flin had little doubt, because where the clouds were loose and fleecy, the light was silvery or golden, but where they were heavy and dense they emitted a light of a darker tint. He also noticed that the rocks were striped in different colours, though the prevailing one was a white band, and he felt pretty sure that this was due to nitro magnesite. The waterfalls he accounted for by the bursting of the masses of clouds as they were caught by the splintered aiguilles.

Turning round and looking in the direction from which he believed he had come, Flin saw that the horizon was filled with what appeared to be smoke, illuminated by coloured flames, and he felt that his explorations would be far from complete unless he discovered the cause of this smoke, as well as found out the way by which he had entered this beautiful sea.

He had much to do, however, before he could continue his voyage of discovery. There was his vessel to get in order again, the chemical apparatus to set right, and various scientific observations to be made.

He found that the compasses were quite useless for all practical purposes. The needles had a tendency to point upwards. And this convinced him that the magnetic north was above, he being in the centre of the earth. The temperature of the air, out of the vessel, was 70 1/2 degrees, and that of the water was 60 degrees. He made some calculation with reference to the height of the cliffs, and computed the minimum height at 300 feet, and the maximum at 2000. He tried for soundings alongside the vessel, but his line went plump down for one hundred fathoms without finding bottom.

Having completed his work and got things ship-shape again, he set his paddle-wheels in motion, and ran clear of the ledge of rock which had given him such safe shelter.

I have hitherto omitted to mention that the vessel was provided with a most ingenious sail. It was triangular in shape, and not unlike the wing of a flying fish. It was constructed of light but very strong silk, made specially for the purpose. It was attached to a light iron mast, and shut up like a fan, so that when it was closed it lay in a groove along what represented the spine of the fish.

As soon as the traveller had got clear of the rocks, he set this sail for the first time, and as the mast worked on a pivot he was enabled to trim the sail any way that was necessary; the sheet was made of very strong silk line through which a fine thread of wire was twisted. He turned the head of the vessel towards the horizon where he saw the smoke, and set his sail to catch the air. The fish was soon bowling along at a rapid rate, so that Flin was astonished at first as there did not seem to be much wind. But he soon remembered that at great depths the layers of atmosphere were very dense, and, consequently, had immense propelling power, so that what really seemed to be nothing more than a zephyr was equal to a moderate gale of the upper world, where the air was expanded and not compressed. As he recollected this he shuddered as he thought how awful the effects of subterranean storm would be when this compressed air was in violent motion.

However, at present there seemed to be no cause for fear. All Nature was smiling. The soft electric light filled the region with a beauty and warmth that was delightful.

As he sailed along the coast the scene was grandly wild. In some parts the water fell over the cliffs in an unbroken fall of a thousand feet, and presented all the appearance of a fairy fountain, as the spray was illuminated by the various lights. Again rugged gorges, dark and grim, stretched away inland, and down these the water rushed impetuously over masses of boulders, and presented the appearance of a mountain torrent.

As Flin drew nearer to the supposed smoke he found the air filled with fine mist that fell like dew and wetted him through. But it will be remembered that he had not much in the way of clothes to wet, for his only garment was the dress shirt, and that was now very torn and soiled. Of course in that great central sea of the inner earth it did not matter, for he apparently was the only living thing. Nevertheless the little man regretted that he had not a pair of smalls to cover his lower extremities.

As the voyager drew nearer the object of his curiosity a low muffled roar broke upon his ears, and this roar increased as he proceeded, until it became terrific, and he was astonished to find that what he had taken to be smoke was columns of spray. In a few minutes he was startled to observe that he was approaching what appeared to be a waterspout of incomprehensibly huge proportions. The sea around him had now become agitated and milky white, and a tremendous current was setting against him, so that the vessel only made very slow progress. He now took the precaution to screw down the door of the fish, though he determined to remain outside, having lashed himself with a cord to the mast. He soon became aware that ahead of him was a massive barrier of rocks, towering up hundreds of feet, but which were almost obscured by the smoke-like spray and the showers of water. The din was terrific and deafening. And, as the sea got rougher, Flin altered his course and ran parallel with the barrier or reef. He continued on this track for some miles, till the end of the reef was reached, and he then hauled up and sailed between it and a line of frowning, rugged cliffs, whose tops were lost in the clouds. The sea here was very rough, and the fish was tossed about in an alarming manner. But not a muscle of Flin's face quivered. The awe-inspiring sight thrilled him, and he was determined to go on even though he perished. Soon his courage and perseverance were rewarded by a spectacle that can only be expressed by the one word --- awful. From a huge cavern in the cliffs mighty volumes of water were rushing out with a force that was appalling, and striking against the reef, were flung into the air in the form of a spout, hundreds of feet high, and fell again over an area of three or four miles in a terrible deluge.

Flin furled his sail and watched this natural phenomenon in awe-stricken silence, and he saw how much he had to be thankful for, and what an incredibly narrow escape he had had. This was the outlet of the river, down which he had travelled from Lake Avernus. It was in point of fact the mouth of a monstrous culvert that drained off the surplus waters of the mysterious tarn. He had solved the problem at last. Down here he had been carried in his fish, then sucked into the vortex of the stupendous whirlpool, thrown up by the upward rush of waters, and had fallen on the other side of the barrier, and been carried by the current to where he had found his vessel when he awoke from his sleep.

As he did not deem it safe to approach any nearer the whirlpool, lest he might again be drawn within its influence, he made sail and steered away. But he noticed that the iron barrier of rocks against which the surf beat with such appalling fury was worn perfectly smooth. There was evidence, too, in the masses of island-like boulders which were scattered about on the sea side of the reef, that it was gradually being reduced by the action of the thundering waters, and Flin had no doubt that in the course of ages this solid breakwater, formed by Nature's own hand, would succumb to the terrible force brought against it, and ultimately disappear; or, at anyrate, cease to obstruct in such a remarkable manner the great outpour from the upper earth.

He steered his fish once more out into the open sea, and taking his bearings from the barrier, he was determined to keep a course to a diametrically opposite point, which he believed to be east. He based this belief on the tendency the needles of the compasses had to point upward; and so he thought the true magnetic north of the earth was upward, and the south below him, so that the points corresponding to the north and south were not so in reality in the central world. Moreover, he did not clearly see that he had reached the level of the waters. His own opinion was that they were still flowing downwards, and that this was but an upper sea, and a lower one would yet have to be reached. If this theory was correct, the currents would naturally be setting away from the barrier, and that this was the case was partly proved by the vessel having drifted so far down the sea after it had been thrown over the barrier.

Having got well out again, Flin unscrewed the door of the vessel, and procuring a small bucket, he dipped up some of the sea water, and tested it. He found that it was intensely salt and slightly bitter.

As he was desirous of exploring the coast a little, he steered for the ledge of rock under which he had found himself when he awoke after being thrown over the barrier. Arrived here he made the vessel fast with a stout rope, and found no difficulty in getting on to the ledge, along which he walked for a considerable distance, until he reached the strand from which the ledge projected. His feet suffered very much owing to the want of boots, but he did not allow this to interfere with what he considered to be his duty.

A careful inspection proved that all the rocks were Plutonic. There were traces of fire everywhere, and this accounted for the great rifts which formed the gorges. For, as the rocks cooled, and water came in contact with them, they had shivered and splintered in every imaginable way. Now that he stood upon the shore he thought a more weird or gloomy place could not be imagined. It was like the realisation of some of Dante's pictures.

Having collected a considerable quantity of the nitromagnesite, which abounded everywhere, and chipped off some pieces of rock, in which he was surprised to find traces of gold, he was about to return to his vessel, when he was startled by a strange noise that was something between a pig's grunt and a lion's roar. He turned quickly round to behold a gigantic turtle seated on a point of rock. The animal was evidently no less astonished at him than he was at it. And he stood spellbound, for the monster surpassed in size anything that he had dreamt of in his philosophy. He had often seen in the upper world portraits of the megalosaurus and other supposed extinct gigantic animals and reptiles. But nothing approaching this living specimen now before him had ever come under his notice. He calculated that in the broadest part of its back it measured thirty-five feet, and from the tip of its nose to the end of its tail seventy-five feet. And, lest it should be thought that his spectacles had caused him to exaggerate the size of this brute, Mr Flonatin distinctly mentions in his diary that he took his spectacles off and saw the creature with his naked eyes. But not feeling disposed --- and very wisely so --- to approach nearer the monster with his naked body, and unarmed as he was, Flin hurried back to procure a gun which he had fortunately provided himself with, for he was determined not to lose the opportunity of being able to say that he had shot at an antediluvian animal, and for which he would have sacrificed five of the best years of his life, had it been possible, to have conveyed the thing alive to his friend Barnum's museum. However, he thought it was within the bounds of probability that, could he succeed in killing the beast, he might, with the instruments he had provided himself with on board, be able to cut the shell up into sections, and should he ever reach the upper world again, place them in the museum.

His gun was a heavy double-barrelled one, and he put a large charge of powder into each barrel, and then rammed home two bullets, weighing an ounce each.

He had been a keen sportsman in his day, and accounted a good shot, but he had never before had to deal with such huge game. This did not daunt him, however, and getting within range of where the turtle still sat, he lay down at full length, and resting his gun on a boulder, he took long and deliberate aim, and fired. The first bullet glanced harmlessly off the horny back of the monster, and Flin quickly fired his other barrel, with a like effect, though the creature evidently deemed it politic to remove from the neighbourhood of an animal that spat fire, and it coolly turned round and slipped into the water.

About five minutes after the last barrel had been discharged, Flin was returning to the vessel, when he suddenly stood rooted to the spot by what seemed to be a clap of thunder that fairly shook even the granite rocks. The most terrific peal that he ever heard in the upper world --- and he had heard a good many thunderstorms --- sank into insignificance when compared with this clap. It rolled all round the cliffs, then gathered up strength again, and burst overhead, then partly died away, and came up once more from across the sea, and was repeated amongst the cliffs, until poor Flin, who had crouched down on the rocks, was positively deafened by the awful roar, though he very soon guessed that it was not thunder at all, but the echo of his own gun. Those persons who have heard the multiplying echoes of Killarney, and the Swiss Alps, will be able to understand this. The sound of firing down in this central sea, not being able to escape into the limitless expanse of space, and being intensified by the compressed air, was simply stupendous. It took a full hour before the echo died away. Mr. Flonatin blamed himself very much for his want of caution, as he says a moment's consideration would have convinced him what the effect of a gun being discharged in such a place would be. Moreover, he had run the risk of disturbing the electrical clouds, and had he done so he trembled as he thought what the consequences might have been. He made up his mind not to act so precipitately in the future.

Having had ocular demonstrations that there was animal life in the regions, he began to speculate as to whether there might not be human beings. It was in quest of inhabitants that he had chiefly undertaken this journey into the centre of the world. And the conviction that he would find people was considerably strengthened by what he had already seen.

On getting on board of his vessel he decided not to set sail until he had thoroughly rested, for he was very weary and his limbs ached.

His day marker indicated that he had been out eighteen days, and the chronometers marked 4:30 p.m., New York time. As he had two of these instruments remaining --- he had had three when he left, but one had been ruined when the fish was thrown over the barrier --- he decided to alter the time of one, so that he might have a night and day. That is a time for labour and a time for rest, because there was no atmospheric change to mark one part of the twenty-four hours from another. He therefore set the chronometer to ten o'clock, and considered that to be his bed- time, and he would rest till eight o'clock when that would be the commencement of a new day for him.

Before retiring to rest he thought he would christen the sea, he therefore opened a pint bottle of champagne, and sprinkling the wine on the rocks and in the water, he said, with great solemnity, ---

"I, Josiah Flintabbatey Flonatin, F.S.E.U.R., hereby, in the name of the President of the United States and the great American Republic, and on behalf of the Society for the Exploration of Unknown Regions, take possession of this portion of our globe, and call the place the Sea of Echoes, by which name it shall ever be known."

Having performed this ceremony he had his supper, screwed up the door, and went to bed.

12

Poor Flin Flon raised himself when he awoke from the recumbent position with extreme difficulty, and it cost him much pain to do so.

His whole body was so sore and his joints so stiff, owing to the tossing about he had had on his entrance to the Sea of Echoes, that he could scarcely move. Moreover, he had caught a violent cold in the head --- due no doubt to the loss of his clothes -- so that he did not by any means feel in very good spirits. But had the appliances been at hand he would have put his feet in mustard and water, and have well greased his nose with tallow, and then, wrapping his head in a flannel petticoat, have gone to bed again. But in the absence of any of these excellent, yet grandmotherly, remedies he did the next best thing, and that was to pull his woollen nightcap well down over his ears, and enveloping himself in a blanket, he managed to lower himself to the floor. That done, he produced a small spirit lamp from amongst his stores, together with a bottle of prime "Old Jamaica," and drawing some water from a cask which he had brought in case of emergency, he proceeded to brew a stiff glass of most excellent punch (he was famed for brewing punch), flavoured with just a soupcon of lemon juice. And having quaffed this with very great relish, he wisely went back to bed again.

The "Old Jamaica" had a very soothing and soporific effect, and Mr. Flonatin sunk into a healthful and pleasant slumber, from which he did not awake for four or five hours. By that time he felt so very much better that he got up and dressed himself; well, that is, he exchanged his night shirt for his "dress" shirt, and his toilet being thus completed, he partook of a capital breakfast. That over, he unscrewed the door of the vessel and looked out.

There was no observable change excepting a slight darkening in the electrical clouds. The tints had deepened, and the silver clouds had become a sort of dirty brown. Though Flin certainly noticed this, he did not attach any serious import to it, but on returning to the cabin he was rather surprised to find that the compass cards were spinning round in a very extraordinary manner, stopping suddenly, then going on again. And, happening to glance in his looking-glass, Flin was still further astonished to observe that his own silvery fringe of hair was standing out erect, each particular hair being stiff and straight.

"By Jove!" he cried, "these phenomena indicate some powerful electrical disturbance in the atmosphere."

He raised his hand to his head, and then noticed for the first time that a pale blue light was playing about the tips of his fingers.

Now to an unscientific mind these things would have appeared very startling, but Mr. Flonatin thoroughly understood the cause and the laws which governed them. The whole atmosphere was surcharged with electricity, and a storm was about to burst.

What took place is given in the great man's own words: ---

"The beautiful colours of the clouds gradually died, and with them the light, so that for the space of an hour a darkness that was horrible was over all things. It was truly an Egyptian night. But presently a silvery electrical radiance gleamed from the sea, and though this only partially dispelled the gloom, the effect was marvellous and beautiful. Inside the vessel every piece of exposed metal was illuminated with a blue flame, my own hair and extremities were also luminous, and when I wrote with the pencil it seemed to mark the paper like a lucifer match. In fact everything was actually immersed in the electrical fluid. Suddenly the clouds discharged one awful, blinding sheet of flame, that extended from horizon to horizon. And this was immediately followed by a burst of thunder that made me think the firm earth had been shattered into a million fragments. No known words could possibly convey anything like an adequate notion of that fearful peal. The vessel trembled as if she had received a violent blow. The surface of the water was agitated as if tons of small shot had been sprinkled over it from a gigantic sieve. Then the echoes of the peal were scarcely less terrible than the grand crash itself. These echoes came and faded with startling suddenness. They seemed to bound from peak to peak, and from crag to crag. To be one minute down in the gorges, the next amongst the pinnacles of rock, and then again afar off on the opposite side of the sea. The effect of these echoes was the most marvellous thing I ever experienced, and I feel that my pen is quite powerless to convey anything like a proper notion of the awfulness of the storm which raged for upwards of two hours. It seemed sometimes as if the whole region were literally bathed in fire. An electric spark would shoot up from the water, and in mid- air would be met by another spark from the clouds, and as the two came in collision they separated into thousands of little balls that darted about with astonishing rapidity. Then every now and then some prominent rock appeared to be suddenly illuminated, as if it had been saturated with spirits of wine and set on fire. This phenomenon would last for a minute of so, when there would be a tremendous explosion, and from the illuminated rock millions of sparks would shoot into the air, and all would be dark again. This was the most appalling sight that could possibly be imagined. Another extraordinary appearance was that a transparent cloud of fire --- or what seemed to be fire --- appeared as if by magic overhead. The colour of this cloud was sometimes red, at others mauve or blue. It would float along very quickly, while it seemed to come in collision with something, when it would burst with an awful roar, and a flash that was horrifying. Gradually the storm ceased, and a deathlike silence took the place of the roar and crashing that for two hours had fairly shook the solid rocks. This silence seemed to be due to some change in the atmosphere, which had caused it to lose its acoustic properties. Because up to this time the roar of the waterfalls had been almost deafening; but now not a sound, however faint, could be heard, and not a gleam of light could be seen. The silence was absolute. The darkness was palpable. I confess that I trembled with awe. I felt humbled into the very dust in the presence of such awful evidence of Nature's wonderful power. Here the pent-up electric forces had been disturbed, and the storm that followed made the most terrible of storms of the upper earth pale into insignificance by comparison. I have wondered whether I was not responsible in a measure for this storm which broke over the Sea of Echoes, as I have reason to think that the report of my gun when I fired at the turtle disturbed the electric currents, and caused the clouds to discharge their streams of the subtle fluid on to the earth below. This theory, however, may be incorrect, though I have faith in it myself."

"The noiseless silence --- and in using this somewhat tautological phrase I do so that a better idea may be gathered. Because even in the most solemn hours of night in the upper world some sounds may be detected, however faint, but here it was a region of death. The air was perfectly stagnant, and the sound waves had ceased to flow. There was not a motion in the water, not a motion in the vessel --- I say that the noiseless silence and the perfect darkness lasted for some time. I waited in dread suspense, for I did not know what might happen next. I thought that there might be one grand final crash, in which I and my puny vessel would be annihilated. But fortunately all danger had passed. Very gradually the darkness seemed to melt away, and a sort of phosphorescent glow spread over the surface of the water. The air was set in motion again. Sound awoke, and the roar of the waterfalls grew more and more distinct. The clouds became luminous, and the colours were even more beautiful than before. The storm had passed. I lived, and gazed upon the wondrous scene, over which an unseen yet warm and beautiful sun seemed to be shining, endowing the whole place with fairy-like glory. A strong breeze sprang up, and the sea was broken into short, chopping waves."

Mr. Flonatin was now determined to continue his journey, and after a very sumptuous meal, of which he stood very sadly in need, he set the interior of the fish in order, and opening the door he stepped outside on to the little platform over the tail, which formed the deck. He found that the temperature of the atmosphere had lowered very considerably since the storm, and the cold was not at all pleasant to him in the absence of proper clothing. This set him thinking upon his condition, and the necessity of devising some means of obtaining a suit of clothes, for he thought if he should come upon inhabitants his appearance was scarcely compatible with the laws of good society; and as a representative of a most enlightened nation, he was desirous of upholding that dignity and modesty which had ever been distinguishing traits in America's sons. After some reflection he hit upon a brilliant idea. He had ample stores of cotton and sewing materials, and like most bachelors he knew how to put on a button, and more than that he could sew, hem, fell, make tucks, put in gussets, back stitch, run, and do many other peculiarities of the expert needlewoman's art, and this too without breaking his needle every two minutes or pricking his fingers or putting the thread through his skin instead of the cloth upon which he was at work. In short he was an expert in the use of needle and thread, and I very much doubt if he could not --- had he been so disposed --- have made a lady's fancy ball costume or even a "duck of a bonnet." Well, his idea was that he should make some clothes. He had a spare red blanket, that would do capitally for a coat, while two or three excellent pairs of trousers might be constructed out of the sheets. Then came the question of shoes, and although he had never had any experience in the shoemaker's trade his ingenious brain was not at a loss. He had some leather on board amongst his stores, and out of this he could construct sandals. Having made up his mind on the subject, he thought it was better to carry the idea into effect at once, and so he moved his vessel over to the ledge of rocks and there moored her, and was very soon deeply absorbed in his tailoring operations. He cut the blanket into the shape of a coat, put in some sleeves, sewed on leather buttons, and the thing was done. He next tried his hand upon the lower garments, and succeeded capitally. It is true they were a little baggy and of Dutch pattern, but then they were comfortable, and Flin always studied comfort more than personal appearance. It is also true that the tout ensemble of his costume was a little bizarre, but he did not mind that, as it answered his requirements for the time being.

Having dressed himself in this "home-made" suit and fastened some leather sandals on his feet, he cast off the moorings, fixed a small American flag at the mast head, and hoisting the sail got under way, and was soon speeding along at the rate of fourteen knots an hour, for the morning air acted with great force upon the sail and the vessel was light.

For some distance Flin kept along the coast. There was no change at all in the general features of the place. The same gorges, the same roaring waterfalls, the same rocks, and the same sterility. A few trees or shrubs or even grass would have given the region the appearance of a veritable paradise, but after the storm Flin had witnessed he had no difficulty in accounting for the utter absence of vegetable life. The very hardiest of plants or trees must have been withered by the electric fluid which permeated every crevice, and even the solid rocks and depths of the sea. He pondered upon this, and his theory was --- arguing from the fact that the rocks were Plutonic --- that at some distant period of the world's history, so distant that he seemed to think it quite possible that millions of years had intervened between the then and now, this place had been one huge cavern of liquid fire. He expresses himself a very strong adherent to the belief that the whole world in remote ages was a burning globe. That gradually the extreme crust cooled, and the fires were confined to the centre, but, chafing at their imprisonment, they had struggled to burst their bonds, rending and shattering the crust in all directions, throwing up mountains, and carving out valleys. Then the waters descended and filled up the valleys, forming oceans. And these waters helped to still further cool the burning earth, and prepared the way for coming life. That the germs of all vegetable, if not animal, life (though he speaks very cautiously on the latter point) were washed down from the upper regions of space by the falling waters, --- that these germs, under the influence of heat, developed rapidly, and attained enormous growths, so that the whole of the external globe was one stupendous forest. But the fires which for ages had been accumulating their mighty powers rose again in rebellion, and, bursting their bonds, once more produced chaos. But this time the fire forces had to fight the water forces, and the latter succeeded in driving back the fires to the centre. Then the stupendous masses of vegetation sank down, and were destined in the course of time to form the coal measures, and the overwhelming waters left their traces even on the tops of the highest mountains. This was succeeded by ages of rest, during which the world was becoming clothed again with vegetation. And while continents were being upheaved by the action of the imprisoned gases, the great waters were washing other continents away, forming islands, and carving out great rivers. That gradually the fires had been driven farther and farther into the centre, and were now dying out altogether, and that only isolated patches of fire --- so to speak, such as that in "Pluto's Reception Hall" --- existed, and even these in time would become extinct. This was Flin Flon's theory, and the further he travelled through the bowels of the earth, the more convinced he became that he was right.

As he sailed along he took soundings repeatedly, but in no instance was he able to get the bottom, though sometimes he had five hundred fathoms of line out. But lowering the sail occasionally, and bringing the vessel to, he ascertained that a very strong current was flowing obliquely from the land, and he determined to follow the set of this current, for he felt sure it was his most reliable guide. By steering this course he soon ran out of sight of land, and continued so for some hours. Then other land loomed up ahead, and in time he made out a bold coast-line, but on approaching nearer he found it did not differ from that he had left behind. He ran in under some overhanging rocks, where he was enabled to moor for the night and get some rest. The next day he set sail at ten o'clock. He found that the current was now setting along this coast at a tremendous rate, and what with this and the sail the speed of the vessel was almost incredible. In six hours' time he found himself approaching a gigantic headland, and at right angles to this was another range of mountainous rocks. There was evidently an opening between the range and the headland, and as the water seemed very broken thereabouts, and the current was setting with the swiftness of a mill-race, Mr. Flonatin deemed it prudent to lower his sail, and, taking sufficient ballast on board, partly submerged the fish. This was accomplished, and the opening reached. The place was appallingly weird. On either side the burnt, black rocks rose up like perpendicular walls, not more than twenty-four yards apart. Far above their tops were lost in the electric clouds, which sent down a stream of red light, the effect of which can scarcely be described. But it seemed as if the rocks were dripping with blood, and that the vessel itself was moving through a sea of blood. Between these walls the tide rushed furiously, and the fish was borne on at a tremendous pace, the voyager feeling that new wonders were about to burst upon him.

Presently he found that he was approaching the base of what appeared a huge mountain, and as he drew near he saw a most tremendous opening, into which the river rushed. This opening was like the entrance to some of the mammoth caves of worship that are found in many parts of India and China. It was, in fact, a kind of colossal doorway, almost square in shape. He felt that this was the portal to another region. What that region might be he could form no possible conception. But go on he must. He could not turn back, for the tide was carrying him down at the rate of twenty-five knots an hour. There was one thing he saw very clearly, and that was that this was the outlet for the surplus waters of the sea that he had left behind. He got his electric lamps in order, and, having seen everything snug in the vessel, he waited in anxious suspense for the next revelation. In a few minutes the fish rushed into the tunnel, where all was profound darkness save for the gleam from the lamps.

13

The fish continued its course through the tunnel at a very rapid rate, borne along by a current that evidently flowed down a considerable incline. Mr. Flonatin estimated that the fall was about 1500 feet, and this proved that the sea he was leaving drained into a lower sea or lake. The vessel travelled through the tunnel for nearly twelve hours, and the time seemed even longer to the adventurous voyager, who could not retire to rest until he had come to a place where he might moor his craft. The walls of the tunnel were almost perfectly smooth, though the roof was broken and worn into fantastic shapes. Sometimes it was low down, at others high up. In some places long, jagged pieces of rock protruded in a very unpleasant manner, and rendered extreme vigilance on the part of the navigator of the highest importance, otherwise a collision with one of these obstacles might have proved disastrous, and have brought the scientific journey to a premature close. This subterranean passage or tunnel was very remarkable, and Mr. Flonatin's opinion was that it had originally been a volcanic fissure. That the water had gradually percolated through, and, having once got an entrance, carved out a way for itself.

After long and weary watching Flin was agreeably surprised to observe that the intense gloom of the place was yielding to a soft and pleasant light, and in a little time the vessel shot out of the tunnel into an open river, and then a wonderful sight burst upon the view of the astonished beholder. Looking behind he noticed that the exit of the tunnel was considerably less than the entrance. Long, reddish-looking grass covered the rocks, and as this was the first vegetation he had seen since leaving the upper world he was no less surprised than grateful. A sloping bank on each side of the river was covered with the richest verdure that mortal eyes had ever seen. The most beautiful tree ferns waved gracefully in a gentle breeze. Tall palms shot up straight, and round their trunks twined creepers that were loaded with flowers, the colours of which were of the most brilliant hues. Far overhead floated soft and delicately- tinted electric clouds, and not only did they send down great heat, but their light was intense.

Flitting about amongst the grass and ferns were millions of tiny insects of a species new to Flin. But it almost seemed as if the gems from some jeweller's shop had taken wings and were flying through the air. Strange birds, too, whose plumage rivalled the rainbow tints, flew from tree to tree. And now and again Flin noticed the bright eyes and head of some curious animal protruding from among the luxuriant foliage. Strange fruits and flowers were everywhere. No adequate notion can be conveyed of the wealth of colour which everywhere greeted the eye. But all things seemed to be in perfect harmony. There was not a line that wanted softening or a colour that was misplaced. It was a veritable Paradise, and Flin Flon's joy was boundless as he realised that his daring was at length rewarded, and he had actually reached an inner world. His goal was gained; or, at anyrate, he had so far succeeded in proving that his theory of a central world was correct. And he was then looking upon tropical beauties before which those of the upper earth must pale. As he gazed and gazed, feeling absolutely intoxicated with the wealth of glory that surrounded him, he asked himself if there could be such a wondrous land as this without inhabitants. He almost trembled with excitement when he thought of it. Was he destined to see a race of beings different from those with whom he was allied? He felt strangely agitated. And perhaps he was moved too by a little conscious pride. When he had first broached the subject of this journey into the interior of the world, men had laughed at him and called him mad, and a fool, and a blind enthusiast. But he had meekly borne all that, as a pioneer in knowledge should, for it is one of the inherent principles of human nature that men should scoff at what they do not comprehend. But now, as Mr. Flonatin saw that he had successfully solved the great problem that had puzzled the learned in all ages, he certainly felt a little proud, and he just as certainly did not entertain any great bitterness against his fellows of the upper world. Mr. Flonatin was a fair and honest man, and he felt it would be better to live even in solitude in that world he had succeeded in reaching, than return to one where

"Man's inhumanity to man made countless thousands mourn."

But he did not continue long in this frame of mind, for it was impossible for him to be selfish. He recognised the duty he owed to society, and that he had no right to withhold any information that would tend to let in light upon the ignorance of his fellows. If it were possible to return after his labours of exploration were completed, he would do so, and lay a faithful record of the wonders he had learnt before the world. And he trusted that it would at least be a lesson to sceptics and doubters, who would not see with other men's eyes, or hear with other men's ears. Further, he hoped that when he had made his discoveries known, those who had been so ready to throw stones at him might feel humbled, and act with greater mercy in the future.

Mr Flonatin continued his journey until the river broadened out into a sort of lagoon, and here in a beautiful little bay overhung with luxuriant foliage he determined to moor his vessel and recruit his strength with rest and sleep. A few turns of the paddle quickly ran the fish inshore, and leaping out he made it fast to a tree.

The beauty of this spot could scarcely have been excelled. The water was perfectly pellucid. The palms and ferns on the shore grew in clusters, and peculiar flowers covered the ground with a carpet that was a perfect bronze, that being the prevailing colour. The air, notwithstanding that it was very hot, was balmy and heavy with a thousand perfumes. Lulled by the grateful fragrance, and the cheery songs of the birds, Flin Flon sank into a sound sleep, from which he did not awake for many hours. He was then surprised to find that the glare had given place to a sort of beautiful twilight. The songs of the birds were hushed, and a myriad voices of chirping insects had taken their place. Fire-flies were everywhere. They flew over the water until it seemed studded with reflected stars. They were in the trees, and on the grass, and amongst the flowers. The sight was wonderful. The clouds had lost their coloured light, but seemed to give off a soft, silverlike radiance. Flin was puzzled about this. It was evident some change had taken place, and it set him wondering, until he at last concluded that night had settled upon this central world, and he accounted for the change in this way.

The light of these inner regions was entirely due to electricity passing through vapour --- or, in other words, clouds. These electrical currents were affected by the changes of the upper earth, and were stronger when the sun shone above, and consequently gave off more light. But when the sun's influence had been withdrawn from the upper world, the currents of the central world were less strong, and these changes marked the day and the night. This will be better understood when it is remembered that the electric forces permeated the whole globe, and those laws which govern the outer part of the world must affect the inner part. Mr. Flonatin subsequently proved this beyond dispute by observing that the tides of the internal seas regularly ebbed and flowed. The darkness --- though this is merely a conventional mode of speaking, for the whole country seemed bathed in moonlight --- lasted some hours, then gradually the clouds became more brilliant, the silver radiance gave place to gold and chrome, and a light as from a tropical sun broke forth, and the air grew sultry. This effect was no less beautiful then it was startling --- startling, because it was so totally unexpected. Flin wondered how it was he had not observed the same thing in the "Sea of Echoes," and his theory was that the space being less there and the power of the electric currents greater, they were not affected in the same degree as here, where it was open country. Moreover, when he came to remember it, some slight change had taken place there, though he believed now that he had slept through what was really the night, and so had been unable to mark any very decided alteration in the light thrown off by the clouds. Having breakfasted he cast off his moorings and continued his journey. As he proceeded the river grew broader and the country became more wooded with a stunted growth of trees, until he sailed through miles and miles of dense jungle that was a mass of gold and bronze. He saw silvery streams meandering through meadows of delicate emerald grass. As he proceeded a bend in the river brought him to an open plain of many miles in extent. This plain was scattered all over with disrupted rocks, but they glittered like burnished gold. Trees there were a few, but flowers or herbage there were none. The whole place, in fact, seemed nothing but yellow metal.

Flin steered his vessel into a little cove and sprang ashore, which was not soft ground, but hard, solid metal. He stooped down to examine what it was, and fairly gasped for breath as he discovered that it was gold --- pure gold --- polished and worn smooth by the action of water. He jumped up excitedly, and ran to the nearest boulder, which weighed many tons. It was solid gold. The whole plain was gold. Gold was everywhere. Flin almost staggered with astonishment as he beheld the countless millions of tons which lay around of that precious metal which was said to be "the root of all evil" in the world he had left. If the whole wealth of the upper earth had been collected together it would scarcely have been equivalent to one of the boulders upon which at that moment Flin rested his hand; and yet here there were millions of these boulders. In his wildest imaginings he had never dreamt of such a thing as this. He had often thought that down in the bowels of the earth there were immense masses of gold; because mining operations had proved that the richest gold-bearing strata are deep down. But that there were solid fields of the precious metal scores of miles in extent had never once occurred to him. As he surveyed this stupendous tract, and assuming that the gold was only two inches in depth --- though he proved by the crevasses and fissures that it was many feet thick --- he made a rough calculation that there was sufficient gold there to pave the streets and roads of every large city and every town and village in the United States, as well as to enable all the citizens to build their houses with it, and even use it for all those purposes that iron was then used for.

Mr. Flonatin was no hypocrite, and so he confesses that as he gazed upon these fields of wealth he sighed with regret, and wished that he could have found means to have reached the upper earth there and then from the spot where he stood. As it was --- and knowing how useless such wishes were --- he stooped down and filled his pockets with pieces of the yellow dross. And then he ran down to his vessel and procured a pillow- case and filled that. And the more he procured the more he desired to have, and he clutched frantically at the glittering lumps, and carried them on board, and stowed them in every available spot. He spent hours in doing this, until he found that the vessel was sinking so deep in the water as to be unsafe. But he says that this did not trouble him. And at that moment --- he records this with heartfelt sorrow --- he forgot everybody --- everything --- even his glorious mission, in his mad wish to possess himself of the wealth which was so lavishly scattered about. The gold had suddenly become his god. He literally fell down and worshipped it. He lifted up great lumps, and staggered so under their weight that he was obliged to put them down again. And then he almost wept because he could not convey them away. He stood in a world of gold --- master of all --- and yet not a single grain of it was of the slightest use to him then. On the contrary, it had a positively evil effect. It corrupted his soul, it almost turned his brain. His genial, pleasant face was distorted with a horrid, selfish expression. And he writes that he firmly believes that if at that moment there had been only one other human being there who had attempted to have taken a single ounce of the metal he would have dashed out his brains without one feeling of remorse or pity. Mr. Flonatin is of opinion that he was not responsible for his acts at this period of his journey. He thinks that he was literally mad, though it was the only time that ever he was so in his life; and it subsequently cost him many pangs of keen sorrow.

When he had crammed his pockets full of gold, and filled the available space in his vessel with it, he cast off the moorings and left the place with intense regret. Looking back every now and then his heart ached at being obliged to leave this wonderful region, and he was frequently tempted to turn again. But he conquered this feeling as he remembered that he had brought hundreds of thousands of pounds' worth of the stuff with him.

His pockets were bursting with it; he had filled his pillow-cases, the lockers, the shelves, his own boxes, he had piled it up on the floor, on the seats, everywhere in fact. And he watched it hour after hour, and was fearful lest he might lose even a grain. Almost every sound startled him. He thought somebody was coming to steal his hoards, for he forgot at that time that he was down in the bowels of the earth.

He neglected to take his meals, and even to snuff. His own life --- his safety --- the objects of his journey --- everything gave place to the one and all-absorbing thought of his suddenly-acquired wealth. At last exhausted nature asserted itself, and, unmindful of where his vessel was drifting to, he sank down upon the floor and fell into a profound sleep.

14

Of course Flin Flon woke after having had sufficient sleep, and he rubbed his eyes, sat bolt upright, looked round in bewilderment, and then cried --- "Where the deuce am I?"

He found himself in a vast hall which seemed to be built entirely of pure gold, excepting the roof, which was composed of some highly-polished timber, supported by massive pillars of gold. The floor was formed of large squares of massive glass of different colours; or, at anyrate, what at first seemed like glass; though Flin afterwards discovered that these squares were slabs of garnet, rubies, emeralds, amethysts, diamonds, and various other stones that he had hitherto been in the habit of looking upon as "precious."

But it was not the gold walls and pillars and floor of jewels that astonished him just then. He was surrounded by a crowd of persons, who were at once the most extraordinary beings he had ever seen, and it was not to be wondered at that he thought he was dreaming.

They were small people with large heads and small bodies, and, what was still more astounding, they had tails. Their features were very prominent, and they had narrow foreheads and long hair that hung down to their necks. In general appearance they were not unlike what the gnomes are supposed to be. Seated on a sort of throne was a person who was evidently the King. He had a long tail, and on his head was a crown of tin.

Flin found that he himself was the object of much interest on the part of the King and his Court, for he had little doubt that he was in one of the Royal palaces of the Central Earth Dwellers. As this idea occurred to him he rose to his feet and bowed low, for Flin was the very acme of politeness.

"I trust your Majesty will pardon my seeming rudeness for having sat so long in your presence," he observed, "but I am a stranger and a foreigner, and am quite ignorant as to how I came to be in your Majesty's presence."

At this the people burst into a loud laugh. The King laughed louder than the rest. Then they shook their heads as a sign that they did not comprehend him, and they conversed among themselves in a language that was quite unintelligible to Flin.

Presently a grave-looking person stepped forward at the bidding of the King. From his manner Mr. Flonatin took him to be one of the Court physicians. He approached Flin and examined him very minutely, especially his head and his back, and then, bowing with his back towards the King, he addressed his Majesty as follows, though Flin states that it would be impossible to convey any idea of the correct way to pronounce this curious language; but he gives the following phonetically: ---

"Tisrucco ot em ruoy ytsejam taht siht tsum eb emos suorobrab egavas morf emos trap fo eht htrae hcihw ruoy ytsejam swonk ton fo. Eht ecnesba fo a liat dluow dael em ot refni taht siht dehcterw erutaerc tsum tneserper a ecar yltsav roirefni ot eht denethgilne stcejbus fo ruoy s'ytsejam mlaer. Eno dluow tsomla kniht taht eh saw eno fo eht yradnegel stirips ohw era desoppus ot llewd no eht edistuo fo eht htrae."

Now Flin was a very fair linguist; indeed, it is to be doubted if even Mezzofanti himself could have surpassed him, and he had thoroughly mastered five-and-thirty languages, besides having a smattering of Hebrew, Greek, Sanskrit, and low Dutch, but for the life of him he could not understand the language spoken in the Court of his

Majesty King Gubmuh, for he subsequently discovered that this was the name of the august person in whose presence he had the distinguished honour of standing. Mr. Flonatin was really puzzled, and he thought that he should like very much to write a learned paper, to be read before his Society, "upon the origin and peculiarities of the language used by the Central Earth Dwellers," but he consoled himself by remembering that this pleasure was, in all probability, reserved for him in the future. But, as he stood there, and --- as he honestly confesses --- stared through his spectacles somewhat rudely at the King, he puzzled himself in trying to comprehend the language he had heard, though it bore no resemblance to the Sclavonic or the Celtic, nor could he discover traces in it of any of the Latin or Gothic families. He therefore concluded that it was pure, and not derived or compounded from any of the languages spoken in the upper world. As he thought this his eyes beamed with intelligence and his face flushed with noble enthusiasm as he pictured himself reading a "paper" on this original language to the Society and its members.

But, while Flin was thus mentally engaged, the King, and his physician, and his courtiers were in deep and earnest conversation, the subject of which was the distinguished traveller himself, as was evidenced by the frequent looks they directed to him and the manner in which they pointed at him.

Now Flin could not help feeling slightly annoyed at being thus pointed at, and he thought it was not strictly in accordance with the etiquette of his own country. But in the charitableness of his heart he was not at all disposed to quarrel with these people, for he considered --- judging from the apparent barbaric splendour around him --- that they were in all probability heathens and uncivilised, and as such deserving of his pity. He half regretted, too, that he had not accepted the offer of the fifty dollars' worth of tracts, so magnanimously made by the Christian old lady of New York. A free distribution among these people of those beautifully simple legends which are told so sweetly (albeit ungrammatically at times), and in which the goody-goody people are invariably transported to the realms of bliss, there to play on silver trumpets, and drink ambrosial nectar during the whole of their eternal lives; while the naughty persons are most justly condemned to be roasted in the lakes of brimstone, could not fail to have a very beneficial effect, even though these poor and unenlightened barbarians did not entirely comprehend the legends aforesaid, though that was a point of no material importance, as very few people do understand them. But then Flin knew that, even if the tracts were never read --- and it was very seldom they were excepting by the devils (i.e., printers' devils) and the correctors for Press --- they possessed a Christianising influence --- at least so he had been told by several old ladies, who were distinguished for their exemplary piety no less than as champions for woman's rights --- ; and this influence (a sort of pure moral aroma) always had a very marked effect upon those who were subjected to it. This has often been beautifully illustrated in the cases of the noble savages who, by the timely gift of a tract, have reluctantly consented to give up the sybaritic pleasures of dining upon plump missionaries, and confine themselves to the more ascetic regimen of their own juiceless grandmothers. But to resume.

After the King and his Court had conferred together for some time, and had talked very rapidly and gesticulated rather frantically, as is the wont of foreigners, a messenger hastily left the hall. Flin did not feel at all comfortable. He considered that his reception by the King was not at all compatible with Court etiquette, and that, being there in the position of an ambassador --- as it were --- from the great American Republic, he ought to have been treated with more condescension and courtesy.

He attempted to remonstrate with the King --- of course in a very polite manner --- and he addressed him in Spanish, Italian, French, German and Low Dutch but every time he spoke the whole Court was convulsed with laughter; and the King so far forgot his exalted rank that he fairly shook again until his tin crown slipped down over his eyes, and one of the gentlemen-in-waiting was obliged to set it straight.

Mr. Flonatin's face flushed with indignation at being thus made a laughing-stock, and he expressed himself rather warmly in the choicest American vernacular, but it was only the signal for another burst of laughter on the part of the Court.

At this moment the messenger returned, and he was accompanied by an old man, who had a remarkably long tail, and long white hair that hung down his back. He was also attired in a white robe of some peculiar material, which was quite new to Flin. Mr. Flonatin also observed that this person was followed by an immense crowd of people --- quite a multitude, in fact --- and they were all dressed in the same sort of material, but their dresses were different in pattern. Another peculiarity that struck the savant was that many of these persons had only one sleeve to their dresses, the other arm being left bare, and just below the elbow they wore a narrow band of tin.

These persons elbowed each other, and pressed forward to stare at Flin in a manner that was not at all pleasant. And they "jabbered" so loudly, and, in fact behaved in such an unceremonious manner that one of the Court officials by order of the King addressed them as follows in a stern voice: ---

"Nemeltneg siht ylmeesnu ruomalc si yllaer elbanodrapnu ni sih S'ytsejam ecneserp. Dna tonnac eb desucxe neve no eht sdnuorg taht siht dehcterw egavas seticxe ruoy ytisoiruc. Uoy lliw erofereht eb doog hguone ot llaf kcab dna evreserp luftcepser redro."

This reproof had its effect, as the crowd kept at a distance, though they still craned their necks to catch a glimpse of the distinguished foreigner who had arrived at the Court in such an extraordinary manner.

The person with the long beard and tail approached to the foot of the throne, and bowed very low three times. Then he and the King conversed together for a considerable time, and during this conversation the long-tailed gentleman repeatedly pointed with his finger upwards, as if he was anxious to direct his Majesty's attention to some peculiarity about the ceiling. But the King never once cast his eyes aloft. His face was very grave, and he listened thoughtfully to whatever it was the gentleman with the beard was talking about.

Mr. Flonatin was very much exhausted; moreover, his feelings were wounded, as he considered that he had not been treated at all in a proper manner; and he was determined, even though it might be opposed to the dignity of the Court, to refresh himself with a good pinch of snuff. He thrust his hand down into the pocket of his blanket coat to feel for his paper of snuff, and in withdrawing it he pulled out a lot of the gold he had collected, and it was scattered on the floor.

At the sight of this the person with the long tail sprang forward, and picking up some of the pieces, he held them in his hand before the King's face, and pointed upwards ever so many times, gesticulating so wildly that poor Flin began to think that he had fallen among a lot of lunatics, more especially when the other members of the Court uttered a chorus of groans.

In spite of this, however, he unscrewed the paper and took a pinch of snuff, and no sooner had he done so than again the white bearded person sprang forward, and snatching the paper from Flin's hand, he showed it to the King, and gesticulated even more frantically than before.

From the King downwards everybody seemed to be getting most excited, and Flin was by no means comfortable. He concluded, notwithstanding, that there was an outward show of civilisation, that these people were unchristianised savages, or, what was even worse, that they were raving lunatics. At that moment he was sorry that it had been reserved for him to discover them. He would rather have been pursuing his peaceful though lonely journey through the hitherto uncivilised bowels of the earth than have come upon a people whose chief characteristics seemed to be an utter absence of breeding or manners. He was also exercised in his mind as to how he came to be in the palace. When was he brought there, for it was clearly evident that he had been brought there. And what had become of the fish vessel? he asked himself, not without some anxiety, for if that had been destroyed how could he hope to leave the place. But really just then he considered that all hope of leaving had for ever gone, as he believed that the savage King and his myrmidons were plotting how best to cook him.

He continued thus in a state of dreadful suspense for some time, during which the King and the long-tailed gentleman continued to talk excitedly, and the subdued hum of hundreds of other voices reached the unfortunate Flin's ears. He stood there the cynosure of all the Court, and yet was unable to make himself understood, or to understand.

Presently the King seemed to give some command to the man in the robe, who raised his arms aloft, flourished his tail, and coughed. At this there was a dead silence. Then he approached Flin, and drew a circle round him with a small crystal stick which he took from his girdle. He next uttered some strange and (to Flin) unintelligible jargon, and everybody excepting the King fell down on his knees, and bowed his head.

"Bless my life, this is altogether a strange and undignified proceeding," muttered Flin. "This fellow is a priest, I dare be bound; in fact, were I a betting man I should be much inclined to bet my bottom dollar on it. He is evidently going through some heathenish rite before offering me up as a living sacrifice. This is altogether an unpleasant position for a member of the S.E.U.R. to be placed in, nor can I hope that my country can avenge my death, for how could troops penetrate into such a region as this. At anyrate I will set these cowardly people an example, and show them how a brave man can die."

Mr. Flonatin compressed his lips, folded his arms, stood firmly on his feet, and waited for the dread moment. But the man with the long tail had no such sinister intentions as Flin imagined. He raised his hands over the bald head of the savant and pronounced some more jargon. Then he made several rapid mesmeric passes, and Mr Flonatin began to feel the "influence." For if there was anything he was susceptible to, next to the bewitching voice of a charming woman, it was mesmerism. In a few minutes he was perfectly passive, and his will subdued. Then the mesmeriser led him to a small stool, and motioned him to be seated. In that state he was enabled to understand the language spoken by these strange people, and the bearded man addressed him in a solemn voice as follows.

15

"Wretched and despised being," the man commenced, "know that I who address you am the great high priest and magician of this happy and peaceful realm of Esnesnon, over which his most gracious Majesty King Gubmuh has reigned for two hundred years. My name is Ytidrusba, and I am commanded by the King to inquire why you have left the infernal regions to penetrate into this land of civilisation and beauty. I give you the power of free thought, so that you may answer me."

"Really, Mr -----. I beg your pardon, sir, what did you say your name was?"

"Ytidrusba," replied the priest.

"Mr. Ytidrusba," continued Flin, "I must really correct a very grave error into which you have fallen. I assure you, sir, that I do not come from the infernal regions. My name is Josiah Flintabbety Flonatin, I am an American subject, and have the honour to represent a very learned body known as the Society for the Exploration of Unknown Regions. I may further inform you that the enlightened and highly civilised people of the world I have left have generally been in the habit, from time immemorial, of fixing the locality of the regions you speak of as being situated somewhere down here. I undertook to make a journey into the centre of the earth purely on scientific grounds, and to prove the truth or falsehood of that theory. And I can only say that if this is Hades, and if the gentleman with the tin crown is a certain person whose name I need not mention, that you are altogether a very strange lot of people, and very much wanting in politeness to a foreigner."

Ytidrusba's brow darkened with a frown, and he seemed to be very angry indeed, though it was evident he was trying to preserve an even temper.

"You are a presumptuous and daring man," answered Ytidrusba.

Flin bowed.

"Thank you, sir," he said; "while not owning to presumption, I think I may fairly lay claim to being daring."

"Listen to me," continued the priest. "You must understand that the nation over which King Gubmuh reigns is the most civilised in the whole world." (Mr Flonatin records that at this point he felt very much inclined to laugh outright, but not wishing that these semi-savages should consider him wanting in politeness as the representative of a great nation, he constrained himself with considerable difficulty). "The barbarous, blood-thirsty people from whom you have come have ever been looked upon with horror by us. It is given to me and my brother magicians to know something of the awful regions in which you dwell. We are aware that scattered all over the outside crust of this beautiful earth are millions of wretched beings like yourself. They are, in fact, the spirits of those who have lived in the inner world, and who for misdeeds done here are doomed for a purgatorial period to take upon themselves the forms of men and women and pass a life of most awful suffering on the crust, and which is, in fact, a kind of probationary Hades, as proved by our sages and philosophers from time immemorial. But the most dreadful degradation of all to which you are subject is to live in a tailless state. There could be no surer sign of utter barbarism and degenerated nature than that, as you will observe that this enlightened people is distinguished by a most graceful caudal appendage. The longer the tail the higher is the rank of the person. The lower orders are not allowed to wear long tails, and so they are clipped in childhood. The greatest mark of distinction among the subjects of King Gubmuh is the ancient order of the Blue Ribbon of the Tail. But this order is only conferred upon those who have rendered signal service to the State, and whose lives have been blameless."

"Really, sir, you astonish me very much," Flin observed. "I could scarcely have believed, had it not come from such undeniable authority as yourself, that any such order existed among human beings."

"You will permit me to correct you, Mr. Flonatin," answered the priest, "we are not human, but prehuman beings. The human state is that awful darkness in which you dwell --- it is, in fact, a state of degeneration, and we grieve deeply for those who are doomed to pass into it."

"Dear me, dear me," Flin remarked thoughtfully, and wishing to propitiate this very self- opinionated gentleman, "this is odd, very odd indeed. You are possibly, sir, not aware that situated on the crust of the earth is a very small, and somewhat insignificant, insular spot which we call England."

"I beg to remark that I am quite aware of this fact," answered Ytidrusba.

"Upon my word this is startling," cried Flin.

"Why, your knowledge seems to be infinite."

"No, sir, you are mistaken," the priest observed sadly, "our knowledge is extremely limited. We, as priests, have the gift of being able to know, by a sort of spiritual intuition, what takes place on the exterior of the world, but this gift is not given to the lower orders, nor even to the kings. I may tell you that our high calling does not always command that respect that it should, and our teachings have been attacked by some of the most learned men of this country. I regret that we have unbelievers and hard-headed sceptics amongst us who have dared to impeach our noble order of propagating unsound doctrines. Even his Majesty King Gubmuh is not free from this infidel scepticism --- if I may so term it. He, in common with thousands of his subjects, has doubted the possibility of there being an outer and purgatorial world. In our great public library there are hundreds and hundreds of massive tomes, written by the ablest men who ever lived, and who have endeavoured, by logical reasoning, to prove that living beings could not exist on the crust of the earth. We call these writers materialists, in opposition to those who believe to the contrary, and who are known as spiritualists."

"Then I take it, sir, that you are a spiritualist?" said Flin.

"Unquestionably so."

"Bless my life, this is very strange. But I was about to observe before you interrupted me that in the little spot known as England is an author of some eminence, who has written a very great deal upon what he is pleased to call the 'origin of species.' And he has brought upon himself no small ridicule by asserting that the people who inhabit the exterior of the earth formerly had tails."

"Oh, miraculous!" exclaimed Ytidrusba joyfully; "this is indeed confirmation strong in support of our doctrine."

He hurriedly moved to the throne, and in rapid language told the King what he had heard, but the monarch only shook his head, and a smile of incredulity sat upon his royal lips.

"It is very shocking," the priest observed, as he crossed again to where Flin sat, "it is very shocking indeed that even the sight of a tail-less and degenerated being cannot convince his Majesty that the existence of races in another state is anything more than a fable. This gentleman to whom you refer to as dwelling in England must be a man of incomprehensible wisdom, and I confess that my knowledge does not enable me to tell why he should be doomed to pass a term in such an unenlightened place and among such awful savages. I have no doubt that you will be surprised to hear that we have several eminent authors among us who have written learned treatises also upon the origin or our species. They have sought to prove that we have descended from races who lived in the far-off past, and who spoke no language, wore no clothes, but were covered with long hair and lived like beasts in the jungles. I am happy to say, however, that these gentlemen have only had contempt and ridicule for their pains. That we, enlightened, skilled and highly civilised as we are, should have descended from animals of the monkey tribe is a monstrously absurd theory. But that the writer you speak of should be enabled to tell that you who are human are degenerated from us who are pre-human, shows how deep must be his learning; and that he should have to preach to unbelievers is truly lamentable. Here we have evidence of all he has written. We are as a nation immeasurably superior to the people which you represent, and you see that we have tails. And that your people are without tails is --- as I have before observed --- one of the most dreadful marks of degradation. But when some of our writers try to prove by shallow argument that we have sprung from monkeys, it is really heartrending. We must draw the line somewhere, you know, and we draw it at tails, sir."

Mr Flonatin smiled inwardly at the self-satisfied air with which the priest said this, and he thought that he might have been taken as a fair representative of certain pig-headed people who lived in the upper world, and who believed only in themselves and ridiculed everybody else who differed from them. But at the same time he was also grieved to think that this principle of inherent selfishness was so very widespread. He had indulged in a hope that when he left the upper regions to descend into the lower he would leave all such human weaknesses behind him. But here he was actually among a race who were pleased to style themselves pre-human, and to assert that to pass from the pre-human to the human state was to be utterly degraded and to fall. Possibly, thought Flin, could the apes of the jungles have spoken they would have said that to pass from the monkeyfied to the pre-human state, and to have the gift of speech, was to fall into the very deepest depths of humiliation and bondage.

"The knowledge you possess of the upper earth, Mr. Ytidrusba, is, to say the least, very remarkable," observed Flin, "and I take it that this knowledge springs from some inherent principle; in fact, a sort of second or spiritual sight."

"Precisely," the priest answered. "I must really compliment you upon your astuteness, which shows an amount of intelligence that is very extraordinary for a human being. I may inform you that we priests are true spiritual media and clairvoyants, and that this power is confined entirely to the priests, who are a distinct race in this central world. Amongst your people there are professing spiritualists, but they are all shallow impostors and arrant knaves, and their dupes are imbeciles and fools."

Flin coughed. Although not a spiritualist so called himself he did not like to hear that belief which had become almost a second creed in his country spoken of in such an irreverent manner. However, he thought it was better not to interrupt, and so the priest proceeded.

"The vile trade carried on by your people who call themselves spiritualists is a disgrace, if anything can be a disgrace to human beings; and since they trade upon the credulity of the ignorant and vulgar, they should be suppressed with a strong hand."

"Really, Mr Ytidrusba, you are using very strong language," Flin remarked, unable longer to restrain himself.

"No stronger than is justifiable, sir. Impostors should be dealt with boldly. And I really feel that nothing I could say about the lying humbugs of the upper world who call themselves spiritualists would be too strong. They are a set of miserable, deceiving rascals, and ought to be burned with brimstone."

"I am afraid you are very severe."

"I am, and rightly so. For here we are too enlightened and too highly civilised to play the humbug. We worship truth, and anyone detected uttering that which is not true for the sake of gain is instantly put to death."

"Then I venture to infer from your remarks, sir, that sectarianism is not known among you?"

"Certainly not, sir. We have one universal creed known as Esnes Nommoc. It is alike the religion of the King and the humblest subject in his Majesty's realm, and those who differ from it are killed."

"Then I presume executions are not uncommon in this kingdom of Esnesnon?"

"I regret that they are not," answered the priest.

"If it be true, then," Flin remarked, "that the wicked pre-human people who die here take upon themselves the human state, and dwell outside of the earth, it may account for differences in opinion on religious matters being so rife amongst us."

"Exactly!" exclaimed the priest delightedly.

"You are a very clever person. Sectarianism is one of the tortures to which the human race is doomed. Another certain sign of the degradation to which you are made to suffer, as tailless beings, is your awful, savage gluttony for that commonest of all metals --- gold."

"My dear sir, you labour under a wrong impression as to the metal in question being 'common.' I assure you that we look upon it as being very precious."

The priest laughed contemptuously.

"Poor fellow," he observed sympathisingly, "how very apparent your human nature is. I repeat that this gold is the commonest of all metals. Here we have whole plains of it, hundreds of miles in extent. We quarry it out, and build our palaces and houses with it. But you fight, and tear, and mangle each other to pieces for a mere handful of the rubbish. It is, in fact, the god of the infernal regions. You bow down and worship it, and it binds you in the most terrible and cruel slavery."

"I must admit that there is some truth in what you say," observed Flin; "but may I take the liberty to inquire if you have no equivalent for gold?"

"We have a metal that is very rare --- we call it tin, and it is brought from mines that are situated in a far off and lonely region."

"Indeed, and who are the people who work these mines?"

"They are people who have been guilty of breaking the laws, and so they are doomed to work as slaves for periods ranging from twenty to a hundred years."

"Then what is the average duration of life here?"

"Three hundred years; though we have had extreme cases of old age, where persons have reached four hundred years. These are, however rare."

Mr Flonatin was thoughtful for some time. These people were on the priest's own showing full of those weaknesses so characteristic of the human family above. Like a good many other persons whom Flin could have named, this very self-satisfied gentleman was very desirous of plucking the mote out of his brother's eye, but could not see the beam in his own.

"As I am very desirous," he observed, "of learning more of your interesting country, and of the habits and customs of its highly-cultivated and enlightened people, so that I may be enabled to show my own unfortunate fellow-beings the error of their ways, I respectfully crave permission to sojourn here for some time."

"I will solicit his Majesty to grant your request," answered the priest; "but I think it right to inform you that it is our rule to send all foreigners who may intrude upon our kingdom to work in the mines. At a long distance from here is situated another race ruled over by King Thgirenivid. He is a very low and uncivilised person, and scarcely superior to your own wretched people. For centuries our two nations have been enemies, and some terrible wars have been the result. But King Thgirenivid has always been the oppressor. This barbarian is bound by none of those rules which we as enlightened and peaceful people recognise. Whenever any of his subjects are caught within our dominions we instantly put them to death."

"May I venture to remark, sir, that I consider that rather a harsh measure," said Mr Flonatin.

"Oh, nonsense," cried the priest, "nothing can be harsh that is justified, and we are beyond all question of doubt justified in putting these miserable savages to death, because their object is to try and corrupt our morals, and poison the minds of King Gubmuh's most loyal subjects. They are jealous of our happy and flourishing condition, and take every opportunity to harass us. We have occasionally sent missionaries to them, but they have never returned. And though we have not been able to glean any accurate information, we have reason to believe that our unfortunate emissaries have either been made slaves of or put to death."

"Ah, very shocking indeed, very shocking," observed Flin, a little ironically.

"However," continued the priest, without seeming to notice the interruption, "as you do not come from King Thgirenivid's people, you may possibly be allowed to remain here for a little time, so that the curiosity of our scholars and scientific men may be satisfied, for you are sure to be the subject of much discussion; and there will be those among us who will doubt the evidence of their own eyes, and refuse to believe that you have descended from the infernal regions to visit our happy realm. I shall therefore strongly recommend King Gubmuh to let you remain, as you will not only afford amusement for the lower classes, but be excellent pabulum for the savants of our learned societies, and we shall no doubt have many clever works written about you."

Flin felt a little annoyed at this. He by no means relished the idea of being exhibited in the same way as in his own country any rare and curious animal might have been shown and written about. "Afford amusement for the lower classes indeed" --- the mere suggestion of such a thing was a base indignity to one of the most distinguished men of his time. A fellow of the important Society for the Exploration of Unknown Regions, and enjoying the personal acquaintance of all the great men of the United States, from Mr. Barnum down to the President, for him to be treated in every way as his own countrymen would have treated a heathen Chinese or a naked savage from Equatorial Africa, was simply monstrous, and he felt that he must enter a protest.

"You will pardon me, Mr. Ytidrusba," he said calmly, although he was burning with indignation, "you will pardon me, sir, but I find it necessary to inform you that in the United States, of which it is my proud privilege to be a native, I have the honour to be looked upon as a man of considerable scientific knowledge. In fact, sir, I hold a very high and important position, and as a public man am respected and looked up to as a leader in the paths of knowledge. You will therefore, I trust, sir, understand that it is not at all agreeable to my feelings as a man of superior intelligence and great intellectual culture to be treated as if I were some strange fish or animal, and to be paraded for the amusement of your lower orders, and as a debatable subject for your philosophers."

The priest smiled rather contemptuously, and he patted the bald head of Mr. Flonatin in a soothing sort of way.

"Poor fellow, poor fellow," he remarked, "the exalted notion you entertain of yourself is very shocking to my civilised ears, and it points to a defect in your brain, for which some of our great physicians may be able to prescribe a remedy. Coming as you do from a degenerated and tailless race, your attempt to lay claim to anything like civilisation or superior knowledge is simply absurd. You are but a poor representative of fallen greatness, and possibly having, in common with your people, some instinctive knowledge of the state you occupied when with us, you ape our manners, our customs, and lay claim to some of our wisdom. But it is a sorry attempt, a sorry attempt. You are all impostors. No doubt if some of the huge animals which we capture in the jungles and exhibit for the amusement of the people could speak, they would enter such another protest as you have done, and have the audacity to talk about the high positions they held amongst their fellows, and how infinitely superior they were to every other animal, and so on. But you, my poor fellow, are very small in stature, and your intellect corresponds, so I will pardon your presumption."

Mr. Flonatin was really boiling over with rage. To be spoken about in such a disdainful and contemptuous manner by a person who seemed to him to be only one remove from a monkey, was almost more than human patience could stand. By a great effort he managed to control his wrath, for he knew that he was in the power of the enemy. But he made a resolution that if ever he escaped he would have revenge by letting his world know what wretched barbarians the people who inhabited the interior of the earth were.

The priest moved over to the King, and with him had a long conversation, during which his Majesty frequently burst into fits of uncontrollable laughter, and Flin felt that he was the cause of it, because the priest was holding him up to ridicule. At length the man came back and said, ---

"I have obtained his Majesty's permission for you to remain, as he has no desire to stand in the way of his subjects acquiring knowledge, and he considers that you will be an excellent study for them for some time. Before releasing you from the mesmeric state I may give you the key to our ancient language. You read from left to right, but we read from right to left, so that with this hint, and if you are diligent, you will soon be able to make yourself understood by our people."

16

When Mr. Flonatin recovered from the mesmeric state in which the old priest had placed him, he felt very confused and bewildered, and by no means well. In fact he experienced that depression which follows on an unchecked indulgence in after- dinner wine. Not that he was in the habit of going to excess in the gratification of his appetite. But he knew those who did, and he had studied them with considerable advantage, so that, had he felt disposed, he might have written an elaborate treatise on the evil effects of alcoholic drinks.

He found that he was quite alone in the hall. The King and his suite had gone.

"Dear me, this is very extraordinary," he muttered, as he rose from the seat on which he had been sitting, and feeling cramped, stretched himself and yawned, "very extraordinary," he repeated. "Why, I must have been dreaming, for that old rascal of a priest would never have dared to have insulted me in such a manner. To think of my being exhibited and shown about for the gratification of their monkey- like people is preposterous. I, who occupy such an eminent position in my own country, to be treated altogether as if I were some new species of animal, is almost unbearable. Oh, I must have been dreaming; of course I have; there can be no doubt about it."

He strolled round the hall, which was of vast dimensions. He found that all the walls and the pillars were of pure gold. And this in a measure seemed to be corroborative evidence that he had really talked with the priest, for unless the gold was very plentiful indeed it could not have been used in such a lavish way. But that it was plentiful Flin himself had witnessed when he went ashore in "The Valley of Gold." He stooped down and examined the floor, and found that it was formed of huge slabs of highly-polished gems, the colours being blended in beautiful and perfect harmony.

While he was admiring the exquisite workmanship of this part of the building, he noticed the old priest coming down the centre of the hall, and he hurried forward to greet him.

"Ah, good-morning, Mr. ---- let me see, Mr. ----, I really beg your pardon, but for the moment I forget your name --- bless my life, how very stupid of me --- "

The priest smiled and shook his head, as a sign that he did not understand.

"Umph, I forgot that the old savage could not understand the language of a civilised being," Flin muttered, and feeling at a loss how to act, for no more awkward position can be imagined than that of two persons speaking different languages and not understanding each other standing face to face and having no means to render themselves intelligible.

The priest motioned Flin to follow him, and then led the way into an ante-room, and pointed to a seat. Flin sat down, and the priest made a few passes, and the traveller began to comprehend him again.

"Kindly permit me to once more inquire your name; it is such a very difficult one that I cannot remember it," said Flin.

"My name, sir, is Ytidrusba, and I am High Priest and Magician-in-Ordinary to his Majesty King Gubmuh."

"Thank you, sir" and Flin bowed respectfully; "and now will you be good enough to inform me, Mr. Ytidrusba, whether I am at the present time wide awake or under the influence of some spell you have exercised over me?"

"You are under the influence of mesmerism, for it is only while in this state that you can comprehend me."

"Most singular," Flin observed; "but I should like to know how long I am to continue like this?"

"Until you have learnt our language. A few hours' study will enable you to do that if you remember what I told you, that you must read from right to left. On that shelf there you will find some books. I must leave you now, but in a little time will return and see what progress you have made."

When Flin was alone he crossed to the shelf and took down some of the books indicated, and by following the old man's suggestion he found it was by no means a difficult language to master, and in a couple of hours he was able to read quite well.

A short time afterwards Ytidrusba returned and said, ---

"I think I may release you now," and he passed his hands over Flin's head, so that he awoke. "You have slept very soundly," the old man observed.

Flin still felt confused, though he understood the priest very well now.

"I was not aware that I had been to sleep," he answered as he rubbed his eyes, and felt strongly inclined to pinch himself, for he was not quite sure yet whether he was not comfortably tucked up in his own bed in New York and dreaming a dream.

Ytidrusba laughed loudly, and seemed greatly amused at Flin Flon's confusion.

"Indeed, you have slept very long and soundly," he replied. "I threw you into a trance, but the influence passed off some twelve hours ago, and since then you have been asleep and snoring loudly."

"Then am I to really understand that I am amongst a new race of people; that I am not out of my mind and the victim of some strange delusion?"

"As regards being amongst a new race of people, you err there. We are a very ancient race indeed. Our scholars say that this city of

Esnesnon is built on the site of a city that flourished two million years ago."

"Impossible!" exclaimed the astonished listener.

"Nothing is impossible, sir, and for you to use such a term serves but to show how pitiably ignorant you are. With reference to the other part of your question, that is not difficult to answer. We do not look for mind in such a sorry specimen of a degraded race as you. You possess no mind, and therefore could not go out of it. And as for your sense, it scarcely enables you to grasp the commonest of truths."

"Really, Mr. Ytidrusba," cried Flin, "such language as this is unpardonable, and if you continue to insult me in this manner I shall demand such satisfaction, sir, as a gentlemen has a right to expect. I would remind you that I am a man of science and learning, and that my countrymen are the most learned and civilised in the whole world. Therefore, your treatment is very far from what it ought to be. I hope, sir, you will withdraw your insulting remarks and make a suitable apology."

Ytidrusba's face darkened a little, and his tail moved angrily. It was very evident that he was annoyed. He made an effort to control his temper, however, and succeeded, and replied calmly, ---

"You are a most contemptible little animal, and for one so insignificant to assume such airs and graces is very absurd. Your statement that your countrymen are the most learned and civilised in the whole world is another certain sign of your imbecility. We are perfect, and consequently the highest in the scale. You are imperfect and degenerated, consequently are the lowest. Under these circumstances, and taking into consideration the position I occupy in his Majesty's service, I can afford to treat your ignorance with the contempt it merits. Your threats, however, are another thing, and I would politely hint that we have a public officer to whose care we shall have to submit you if you continue to be so saucy. His duty is to publicly flog anyone who is guilty of insulting a member of his Majesty's Court, or those holding high office. As such an insignificant, distorted little animal as yourself would look a very conspicuous object, if placed in a state of nudity upon the scaffold, and flogged before many thousands of our subjects by the public flagellator, I hope you will endeavour to behave in a proper manner for the future, and learn to appreciate the kindness of great King Gubmuh in having given you permission to remain for a time in his beautiful kingdom."

Mr Flonatin felt literally crushed by the insulting language of Ytidrusba. It is no confession of weakness to say that he almost wept. To be spoken of as "a most contemptible little animal," and "an insignificant, distorted little atom," was bad enough in all conscience. But a philosophical mind like that of the distinguished member of the S.E.U.R. might have borne this, attributing it to the ravings of "an illiterate and lamentably ignorant person." But when he was told that he would be publicly flogged it almost broke his heart.

When his temper had cooled a little he made reply and said, ---

"Your threats I treat with contempt, and I am truly sorry for your ignorance. But long experience in life has taught me that humble resignation to trials and persecutions is the duty of the true philosopher. I undertook this journey purely in the interests of science, and whatever suffering I may be exposed to I shall endeavour to endure it as a man should. Moreover, I am content to believe that there is a power which neither you nor I can control, but which will throw around me an aegis of protection in consideration of the manner in which I have devoted myself to the great cause of searching for truth. I shall therefore, sir, submit to you in all things. But as a foreigner and a stranger I claim protection and respect. And I would most respectfully hint, that should I be subjected to an outrage, full and ample apology will be exacted by my country. Indeed I do not hesitate to say, so great is American enterprise, that the Government would not hesitate to fit out an expedition, and despatch it by submarine vessels to this country, to avenge any insult offered to me, even at the point of the bayonet. The American people, sir, stick at nothing. I repeat with pride, they are a great people, a mighty people, and I am their representative."

Ytidrusba laughed immoderately until he grew dangerously red in the face, and he was obliged to press his long hairy hands on his fat sides.

"Well, upon my word," he cried, when he had recovered his breath, "you are a miserable, self-inflated little humbug. But there, I'll forgive you. Our philosophers and scientific men will revel over you, and as for the common people, why, you will afford them amusement for a long time to come. But there, my little fellow" --- he added with withering sarcasm and with mock gravity --- "you mustn't get so terribly savage, or else we shall have to confine you in a cage. Why, do you know, sir, we have a celebrated showman in this city, whose name is Gullthemall, and he keeps a large museum of curiosities in the principal part of the town. He would positively give his tail away if he could only get hold of you to make an exhibition of you. But there, don't let us quarrel. I should be sorry to resort to extreme measures to keep you in order, because I am rather interested in you. In a little while the very elite of our scientific world will arrive at the palace to see you. In the meantime you can make yourself comfortable. And here is the Esnesnon Gazette for you to read. You will see what it says about your arrival."

"The Esnesnon Gazette!" cried Flin; "why, you do astound me. Pray, sir, may I inquire how long you have known the art of printing?"

"How long --- ; well, now let me see," mused Ytidrusba, tapping his forehead thoughtfully. "I suppose it will be quite ten thousand years since Old Caxton first brought printing into use."

"Caxton, sir, Caxton! Why, it is said in the upper world that printing was invented there by one Caxton."

"Ah, very likely, very likely. It would be the same old man. After he died here he no doubt passed into the human state. In fact, I think there can be no question that whatever little knowledge your wretched people may possess they owe to those who have existed before in a pre-human state; and, passing from this to the upper world, they have carried some of their intuitive genius with them. I have an idea that you yourself formerly existed here. We had a cantankerous, insignificant little fellow who was very fond of poking his nose into other people's business. He was attached to the Court as one of the 'gentlemen of the back stairs,' and was always talking about penetrating here and going there, and was never at a loss for a theory for everything. But he tumbled down the back stairs one day after dining and broke his neck, and it is very possible that he lives again in you."

Mr. Flonatin did not condescend to notice this last insult. It was true he had heard of people in the upper world who firmly believed in a pre-existence. But that he himself should have existed before in the person of a contemptuous "gentlemen of the back stairs" was preposterous and absolutely unworthy of contradiction.

"There is one thing I should like to mention, Mr Ytidrusba," he said, "and that is, in my country we eat and drink, and at the present moment I am suffering from a vacuum that is far from pleasant."

"My dear sir, you must really pardon me," the priest exclaimed with genuine concern. "Our conversation has been so interesting that I had quite forgotten to ask you to take refreshment. The oversight shall be remedied directly."

Ytidrusba left the room, and in a little while a servant entered bearing a bright tin tray, on which was spread a variety of food. There were fruits and fish, both of a variety that was strange to Flin. There was also a stew, and a dish of very small birds that were swimming in sauce. Flin attacked these birds first, and he found them very delicious, and as he proceeded to try the stew he muttered, ---

"Well, these barbarians know how to cook if they don't know anything else."

There was a sort of tankard made of tin on the tray, and this was filled with some tempting-looking wine. It was a pale amber in colour, and there was a delicate bead floating on top. Mr Flonatin tasted this wine, which was veritable ambrosial nectar. It was delicious, and he drank deep. Having finished a very agreeable meal, he told the servant --- who had watched him with curiosity and astonishment --- to take the things away. This man had a very short tail, but the hair of his head was long, and his eyes were extremely small. He did not speak, though as he removed the things there was a contemptuous grin on his face.

Flin felt very much more comfortable after the d,jeuner, and having undone the top button of his home-made trousers, he threw himself on to a very elegant couch and proceeded to read the paper. The first article that his eye fell upon was one with the following heading: ---

"WONDERFUL CAPTURE OF A HUMAN BEING --- SUPPOSED TO HAVE DESCENDED FROM THE INFERNAL REGIONS --- HIS RECEPTION BY THE KING --- HIS EXTRA-ORDINARY APPEARANCE AND DRESS DESCRIBED --- EXCITE-MENT AT COURT --- ALL THE SCIENTIFIC MEN AND PHILOSOPHERS SUMMONED TO EXAMINE THIS STRANGE BEING --- THE KING'S PRINCIPAL ARTIST IS ORDERED TO DRAW THE CREATURE'S PORTRAIT, WHICH WILL BE HUNG IN THE GREAT CHAMBER OF KNOWLEDGE --- ALL THE LATEST INFORMATION UP TO THE HOUR OF GOING TO PRESS.

"As some of the Kings's fishermen were pursuing their occupation on the River Greenwater two days ago they were suddenly startled by the appearance of what seemed at first sight to be a large fish of an unknown species. As the creature floated along the men determined to capture it, if possible. They advanced along the bank very cautiously until they were abreast of the fish, and then discharged two large spears at it. But the weapons simply glanced off, and fell into the water, while the strange thing proceeded on its way as if wholly unconscious of the attack. Again the men discharged two shafts, striking it this time on the head, but with no other effect than before. Exasperated at this they jumped into their boat, and getting some ropes, made running nooses, and so captured the fish. But their astonishment may be better imagined than described when they found that the fish was nothing more than a vessel constructed of some peculiar metal. There was a small doorway in the tail, and entering through here they found themselves in a very comfortable apartment. But their eyes almost started from their heads, and the blood curdled in their veins, on beholding a strange being lying there fast asleep. From his extraordinary appearance, and owing to the entire absence of a tail, the men naturally concluded that it was some infernal creature, and fearing evil, their first impulse was to fly. But one, having more courage than his fellows, suggested that they should secure this wonderful creature and convey it to the King's palace. On looking round they were surprised to find that great piles of gold from the gold quarry were lying on the floor. And from this they concluded that the creature must have been ashore in the King's quarry, though what could have been his object in bringing so much of the rubbish away did not seem very clear, unless it was to ballast his strange vessel. The men proceeded to bind the intruder very securely with ropes, though they state that they trembled very much during this operation, for the thing roared through its nose and made a great noise. When they had finished their task they got into their own boat and took the other in tow, and made for the King's dock-yard. Here the astounding news soon spread, and reaching the ears of his Majesty, he ordered that the stranger should be brought into his presence immediately. The excitement was now intense. The people about the place literally tumbled over each other in their eagerness to catch a glimpse of this wonderful arrival. The intelligence spread like wildfire, and even reached the great business mart in the city, where for a time it caused quite a suspension of business, and the place was deserted. Thousands of persons flocked towards the Palace, so that it was necessary to have some public flagellators and a body of spear-throwers to keep order. In the meantime we despatched two of our most trustworthy reporters to the right glorious and supremely honourable Taerg Ytidrusba, High Priest and Magician-in- Ordinary to his Majesty. This gentleman, with that courtesy and kindness which have won for him the respect and goodwill of every person in the realm, received our representatives and promised them every information. They learnt that the strange creature had been brought up from the docks, and was at that moment in the presence of his Majesty. When the King heard that two gentlemen from the Esnesnon Gazette were in the Palace, he most graciously ordered them to be brought before him, and he was then kind enough to address them, and say that they were to be particularly accurate in any information they might send to their paper. Our readers can therefore depend upon our report, and as no representatives of our contemporaries were admitted to the Palace, the Gazette is the only paper in which facts can appear. Our reporters having gained admittance to

THE AUDIENCE HALL,

they found his Majesty seated on the throne, surrounded by the nobles of the Court. In the centre

was the strange creature that had made its appearance in such a mysterious manner. In form he is somewhat like a pre-human being, but is perfectly tailless, and his head is white and highly polished, and quite destitute of hair, with the exception of a little fringe round the back part of the skull. Anything like symmetry or beauty in the creature is entirely wanting. His arms are long and ungraceful, and his legs are twisted. He is small in stature, and wears over his eyes peculiar pieces of glass, which are bound in small frames that are apparently made of common gold. It would seem as if this yellow stuff had some peculiar fascination for the unfortunate barbarian, as all his pockets were filled with it. And when some of it fell out on the floor, even the King could not refrain from laughing. Scarcely less strange than his personal appearance was

THE CREATURE'S DRESS.

This was composed of a peculiar and unknown fabric, and hung in great folds round his meagre body. On his feet he wore pieces of wood, which were tied on. His ludicrous appearance caused everyone to laugh, but as this seemed to annoy the poor creature his Majesty gave orders that silence was to be observed. The man --- for so we Suppose we must call him for the want of another name --- was quite ignorant of anything that was said to him, and shook his head in a dull, stupid kind of way when even a question was put to him. Seeing that there was no hope of making him comprehend, the Right Glorious and Supremely Hon. Taerg Ytidrusba asked his Majesty's permission to be allowed to exercise his magic art, and, this permission being most graciously accorded, Mr. Ytidrusba proceeded to mesmerise the little stranger, and was then enabled to ascertain beyond all dispute that he had really come from

THE INFERNAL REGIONS,

or Upper World. This discovery was startling, no less than interesting, as it enabled this great magician to verify his teachings that the infernal regions are situated on the outside of the earth, and that they are peopled by a degenerated race of beings who have once lived in a pre-human state. At present we are not allowed to make public the subject of the conversation that took place between the savage and Mr. Ytidrusba, but we shall not be guilty of any breach of confidence when we say that the great magician learned some most astounding information that will enable him to put to the blush all those persons who have hitherto had the daring to doubt the correctness of his theories. We are very glad to hear that this is so, for it is high time that the carping doubters and miserable sceptics, who have so long been a disgrace to our city, should be for ever silenced."

"At a subsequent interview Mr. Ytidrusba had with the stranger he learnt that the name he was known by in the regions from whence he has come was the very heathenish one of Flonatin. The King has been graciously pleased to grant Mr. Flonatin permission to remain in Esnesnon for some little time."

LATEST PARTICULARS.

"The excitement caused by the stranger's arrival has greatly increased. The people in the city seem verily to have gone out their wits. We hear that the enterprising Gullthemall has been making efforts to secure Flonatin, with a view to exhibiting him in the museum. But the King is not likely to countenance this. There is to be a grand conference at the Palace of all the savants in the city to-day. The King's portrait- painter has been ordered to paint a full-length portrait of the strange being. The celebrated Doctor Yrekcauq has also received instructions to make a minute examination of Flonatin and note the differences there are between him and civilised beings.

At the moment of going to press we hear that an extraordinary meeting of the Society for Explaining Away Everything will he held in a few days, at which an elaborate paper by the celebrated Professor Loofmot will be read. This paper will deal with the much-vexed question as to whether the external crust of the earth is inhabited or not, and the existence of tailless beings. The opportune arrival of Flonatin among us has satisfactorily settled the latter point, and the hard-headed materialists, who have so long made capital out of theory that it was impossible for tailless creatures to exist, will now have to take to some other subject."

Mr Flonatin read this article with considerable annoyance, though occasionally he could scarcely repress a smile. It did seem so preposterous that he, an enlightened and scientific man, should be written about and talked of for all the world as a naked savage from the centre of Africa would be if he were suddenly set down in the middle of the Broadway, New York.

"I shall have to study these people," he muttered, as he cleaned his spectacles with the corner of his blanket coat; "they are interesting, though apparently little better than barbarians. But surely, ignorant and superstitious as they evidently are, they cannot seriously believe that the so-called Infernal Regions are situated on the crust of the earth, or that I have had a pre-existence. I think that this is about the most empty-headed theory it has ever been my lot to hear propounded."

At this moment a servant entered, and though scarcely able to keep from laughing as he looked at Mr. Flonatin, he wagged his tail and said, as gravely as he could, ---

"The right glorious and supremely honourable Taerg Ytidrusba, High Priest, and Magician-in-Ordinary to his most gracious Majesty King Gubmuh, commands you to attend him in his private chamber."

"The right glorious and supremely honourable," and "high priest and magician," so tickled Flin Flon's fancy that he felt as if he must burst out laughing, and in fact had to stuff his handkerchief into his mouth to keep from doing so, for he did not want the servant to think he was rude. So motioning the fellow to lead the way he followed him.

17

The apartment to which the servant led Flin Flon was a large one, and very handsome in appearance. The walls were composed of polished gold, upon which designs in colours were drawn. There were long windows filled in with extremely fine mica, and at the sides of the windows were elaborate curtains of some peculiar substance, which on examination Flin found to be asbestos. These curtains were ornamented with tiny tin stars. The room was filled with a number of persons, who all turned round and stared very hard as Flin entered. He had no doubt whatever that they represented the elite of Esnesnon, as mentioned in the Gazette, and that this was the conference, and he was to be the subject of discussion.

It was not a very pleasant thought, but as it was useless to offer any protest, he was determined to submit with the best grace imaginable.

He noticed that many of these savants wore a large blue ribbon on the tail, this being the order of the Blue Ribbon of the Tail mentioned by Ytidrusba. All their clothing was made of asbestos, which was dyed in various colours and had rather a pleasing effect. Some of their faces were extremely ugly, at least so Flin thought, for they were pinched up and wrinkled, and Flin further thought that, if he had a few of these strange creatures in New York, he might have put them in a cage and exhibited them for talking apes, that is if they would have talked then. Each person had a round plate of glass, about the size of the top of a tea-cup, hung round his neck by a small chain. This plate was set in a frame of tin, and the use of it was for closer examination. In fact, instead of wearing spectacles, as civilised and intelligent people do, these "barbarians" (this in Mr. Flonatin's word) encumbered themselves with a great magnifying glass, though subsequently Mr Flin learnt that they were not glasses at all, but very thin diamonds peculiarly cut, so as to have great magnifying power.

When the distinguished traveller entered the room there was a great buzzing of voices. It seemed as if everyone was speaking at the same time. Mr. Ytidrusba came forward, and taking him by the hand led him to a small table upon which was a chair, and he requested Flin to take his seat thereon. And when he had done so the savants crowded round and examined him through their diamonds. His clothes in particular seemed to excite their curiosity, as they felt the blanket, and pulled his trousers about, and altogether acted in a manner that was very far from pleasant. The hubbub increased. Each one seemed as if he was trying to talk his fellow down, while the scientific jargon they used was beyond the comprehension of even the gigantic mind of Mr, Flonatin. He had endeavoured to give a very free translation of some of this, but he states that he much fears he has not done justice to the subject. When the inspection was over the savants retired to their seats round the room, while one person remained at the table, and while he twiddled his diamond magnifier about in his fingers he proceeded to deliver a lecture to his fellows on Flin. This person was the celebrated Dr. Yrekcauq, that is, celebrated of course in Esnesnon, and after two or three preliminary coughs, and sundry flourishes of the tail, he commenced his address, the following being a free translation:---

"Most learned brethren, during a very great number of years it has been my distinguished privilege to be a member of your honourable body, and I have ever endeavoured during that time to do all in my power for the advancement of science and general knowledge; and I trust I shall not be accused of sounding my own trumpet if I say that I feel conscious that this great and enlightened city owes something to my years of study and thought."

There was tremendous applause and great wagging of tails as this was said. When order had been restored, the learned Doctor proceeded, ---

"Your applause," he said, is a most gratifying assurance that I have done my duty, and I can assure you, learned brethren, that my heart swells with pardonable pride at the proof you have given me that I have merited your esteem and approval."

"You are a humbug," thought Flin, though he did not express this thought.

"There have been times, however," the Doctor continued, "when the opinions I have ventured to express as the result of long and anxious study have not always met with approval, but on the contrary have subjected me to the ridicule and insults of the rabble of this country, who are represented by a corrupt press. Perhaps no opinion I have ever advanced had incurred more opposition than that of there being inhabitants on the outside of the earth. I am sorry to say that this opposition has not always come from the lower classes, but persons who by position and learning ought to have known better have been pleased to contradict my theories --- theories that were only arrived at after profound research and anxious thought. I have ever stoutly maintained the possibility of the existence of being differently constituted from ourselves, and greatly inferior in mental and physical organisation. For I think, nay I am sure, that we are the very highest and most intelligent of created beings. (Loud applause.) It is, therefore, very gratifying, no less than it is startling and wonderful, that a specimen of a lower race has been permitted to penetrate the almost boundless thicknesses which separate us from the outside of the globe, and which, but for its enormous thickness, would be liable from many causes to crack and rend asunder. And if such a catastrophe were to take place, the dreadful gases and winds which surround the outer world would rush in and annihilate us. It is well known that the opinion I have entertained with reference to a new race has been shared by Mr. Ytidrusba. Though that gentleman has differed from me, inasmuch as he maintains that the outside of the world is peopled by beings who have once lived here, and who, having died here, have for their sins been transported in another form to what he is pleased to term the 'purgatorial regions.' I am bound to confess that I do not agree with this idea. Though I know that this confession will lay upon me open to the accusation of being a hard-headed materialist if not an infidel. I allow myself, however, to be guided by common sense, and I stoutly maintain, in spite of all opposition, that the outside of the globe is peopled by an original though greatly inferior race. (There was some applause and much disapproval expressed at this assertion, but the Doctor was calm and dignified.) I fear, however, that I am somewhat wandering from my subject. I have to deal at the present moment with this being, I am afraid I can scarcely call him a man." (Here the Doctor laid his hand upon the polished head of Flin, who was absolutely writhing with indignation). To be told that he was not worthy to be called a man by such a pompous, monkeyfied-looking rascal as this Doctor was almost more than human nature could endure, and the distinguished traveller and philosopher felt strongly tempted to knock the impudent fellow down. "Discretion is the better part of Valour" was a motto, however, that Flin had ever been guided by, and he was determined not to depart from it now. Insults were to be expected from persons whose ignorance was only excelled by their conceit. So he swallowed his choler, and remained silent, but he pushed the Doctor's hand away in a manner that plainly said, "You are a fool." At this the assembly broke out into a roar of laughter, and Flin's face flushed scarlet, but still he did not speak. The Doctor resumed his address.)

"The arrival of this tailless individual in our city is no less wonderful than it is astounding. From the account which he has given he has travelled down from regions where, if the people are not mad, they are at least savages. His arrival forever sets at rest a much-vexed question as to whether the crust of the earth was inhabited or not. It will be fresh in your recollection that when some years ago I issued from the Press a work entitled The Crust of the

Earth, and the Possibility of its being Inhabited, I raised a storm of abuse from all sorts of people. But when I went further, and said that a race of tailless beings was as likely as not to exist, the whole nation was furious, and the Press and the people vied with each other in heaping abuse and satire upon my head. I am thankful, however, to think that I have lived that down and that my countrymen are becoming more enlightened. They begin to see now that the horizon of their science is very limited, and that beyond that horizon there may be wonders which even in their profoundest philosophy they never dreamt of. It is a proud triumph for us, brethren. It is a greater gain for the scientific world. And I forget myself in the grand thought that a mighty truth has suddenly been brought home to us, and that the knowledge of our world is extended. (Applause.) And yet I venture to add, with all becoming modesty, that the doctrine I have preached for so many years with such pertinacity has at last been verified by what is little short of a miracle. It is as though a spirit had been sent from the land of the dead to open men's eyes and say 'Behold, ye unbelievers, and doubt no more.'"

The doctor paused, but there was a solemn silence. His eloquence seemed to have awed his listeners.

When the Doctor found that his brilliancy had not aroused the enthusiasm of his audience as he had expected it would have done, something very like a sneer of contempt sat upon his intelligent face, and no doubt he thought that those around were pigmies compared to his own giant intellect, and that to pass the slight unnoticed was the most dignified course to pursue. He felt hurt though, nevertheless.

"Time will not permit me to do more now," he continued, "than to glance hurriedly at the possible origin of the race represented by this being. A degenerated race, I think, you will all admit, my learned brothers. (Loud applause.) The opinion long entertained by my esteemed friend, Mr. Ytidrusba, that the spirits of our dead dwell on the crust of the earth, is one that I have never been able to reconcile myself to. And yet, in justice to Mr. Ytidrusba, I am compelled to say that the opinion of such a high authority is worthy of the most respectful consideration. But if I differ from him I do so in that broad spirit which should characterise all searches after truth. I know that the great magician is sincere in his own belief, and I venture humbly to say that I am equally sincere in mine. We are certain now that the outer world is inhabited. We know from the specimen before us the sort of people who dwell there. And the question for our consideration is how did these people come there, and what was their origin? a question by no means so difficult to answer as at first sight it would appear to be. We have long had traditions that our world here was inhabited long before our written records state. I assert now that these traditions are based upon truth. People did live in ages that are lost in the mists of antiquity. They were indolent, luxurious, worldly and thoughtless, and as a punishment for their errors some violent eruption of the world took place; in short, it was turned inside out, and what few beings remained after the commotion was over found themselves the solitary dwellers on a strange earth. The physical changes that had swept over all things had also changed them. They were tailless, and they knew that from then to the end of time the sign of their fallen state should be the absence of that which so distinguished us --- the tail. This, my learned brethren, is a rational, a feasible, no less than a morally certain theory. And no amount of discussion can ever alter what appears to me to be an incontrovertible fact."

"But how do you account, Doctor" --- asked a little old man, whose tail waggled with evident delight, as if its owner knew that he was putting a poser, "how do you account for there being tailed races in existence still?"

"It is difficult to account for it, sir, very difficult," answered the Doctor, as a frown contracted his brow. For the truth was the learned Doctor, like a good many more savants, was particularly fond of theories, but did not like to be questioned too closely as to facts. "I propose, however," he continued, "to read a paper on the subject at no distant date. I will conclude my address, brethren, by humbly suggesting to his most gracious and mighty Majesty, King Gubmuh, that this tailless wonder be exhibited to the common people at a small charge, by which means the national exchequer may be replenished."

There was considerable applause at this, the courtiers and the hangers-on at the Palace being particularly audible, for the fact was they had not received their salaries for a very long time owing to the impoverished condition of the King's purse, so that it was scarcely matter for wonder that the suggestion was met with an outburst of applause.

18

When Doctor Yrekcauq had finished his lecture, the company prepared to depart, and Flin was allowed to descend from the table. He was by no means sorry for this, as he was cramped and stiff. When the company had all gone, a servant informed Flin that Ytidrusba wished to see him, and, following the man, he led him to the magician's apartment.

"Well what do you think of Doctor Yrekcauq?" asked Ytidrusba, as Flin entered.

"What do I think of him? Why, very little. I think he is an old --- "Flin was about to use a word that would have been decidedly wrong, but he checked himself in time. "Well, that is, I mean to say," he continued, "that the old gentleman is lacking in courtesy. In fact, he does not know the simplest law of etiquette."

The magician smiled, and wagged his tail. Flin had thus early discovered --- for it must be remembered that he was a close observer --- that this wagging of the tail indicated delight on the part of the owner.

"Pray be seated, pray be seated," said Ytidrusba, pointing to a seat. "Your expressions, perhaps, are a little strong for such a united and peaceful community, but it is just possible they are not altogether undeserved. You see Dr Yrekcauq has made enemies --- ahem, that is, I mean to say --- I pray you will not misunderstand me --- that he had not been quite as agreeable as he might have been."

"Ah, just so," answered Flin, not a little amused at Ytidrusba's confusion, for our traveller saw in a moment that the artful old fellow thoroughly hated the Doctor, but he was afraid to say so. "Ah, just so," Flin repeated; "but to be candid, Mr. --- pardon me, your name is such a funny one that I have really forgotten it again."

"Ytidrusba."

"Ah, thank you. Well, now, Mr. Ytidrusba, I may as well speak my mind, as I hate beating about the bush, and not to put too fine a point on it I believe the Doctor to be a perfect humbug."

"Dear me, how very strange," answered the magician "that is rather strong language for our happy city, where everything is as clear as daylight. But I fear you will feel a draught" --- here Ytidrusba crossed the room and closed the door, and returning to his seat resumed the conversation. "Anything like jealousy, personal abuse, or ill-feeling are not tolerated here amongst the upper classes, but in the best of society there is sure to be some black member, and I will admit to you that I too consider the Doctor to be a humbug."

"Do you indeed?"

"Yes, a consummate humbug. I have a decided objection to back-biting, and though I am aware that jealousy exists to an alarming extent in the awful regions from whence you have come, I can assure you with pride that we are free from anything of the kind here. But though I hate and detest jealousy I love the truth. We are very truthful here, very truthful indeed. Now, in your regions, they are all false."

"I must really correct you there, sir. You labour under a very wrong impression."

"Pray do not interrupt me, Mr. Flip Flap --- "

"I beg your pardon, Flin Flon is my name."

"Ah, Flin Flon. Well, sir, I repeat that falsehood is one of the punishments of the infernal regions, but we know nothing of the kind here. Truth, truth is our guiding principle. But, as I before observed, black members will creep into the most carefully guarded communities, and I have reason to believe that the Doctor is such a person as you have mentioned."

"Pray speak out," Flin remarked, for he saw that the cunning old man had something on his mind that he was anxious to ease himself of. "Well, the fact is," answered the other, "I do not altogether like the Doctor."

"Oh, oh," thought Flin, "some rivalry, I suppose."

"I do not consider that he is a proper person to hold the position he now occupies."

"May I ask what position that is?"

"Yes. He is Physician-in-General and Professor of Philosophy to his Majesty. But in my opinion he is a sham. His knowledge is exceedingly shallow. But what he is deficient in in this respect he makes up for in cool assurance and consummate impudence. I have spent the best years of my life at the Court in trying to teach my theory of spiritualism, which is truth. But I have always been counteracted and opposed by the Doctor, who preaches his abominable doctrine of materialism. He has influenced the King greatly against me, and though Yrekcauq speaks of me as his dear and valued friend, I firmly believe nothing would give him so much pleasure as to see my remains committed to the cinerary urn."

"Bless me, how very odd!" observed Flin thoughtfully, as he remembered that he himself had had to counteract much jealousy and rivalry in his own country. He could not forget the time when, as a humble grocer, he had first turned his attention to science, he had been opposed on all sides by shallow-brained people. And though he did not altogether hold with Ytidrusba's principles, he certainly sympathised with him, as he had taken quite a dislike to the Doctor.

"You must understand," Ytidrusba continued, "that Dr Yrekcauq is a person who has no thought for anyone else. He is thoroughly selfish. And by unscrupulous dealing he has managed to gain considerable influence over the King. As a result I have suffered. I had at one time nearly succeeded in converting his Majesty, but Yrekcauq, by very much cunning diplomacy, undid the good I had done, and I am grieved to have to say that his Majesty still remains in a state of darkness."

"Ah, very shocking indeed, very shocking," said Flin, with the air of one who thoroughly felt what he was saying. "I am inclined to think you are a much injured man, Mr. Ytidrusba."

"I must give you credit for keenness of perception," answered the magician, "though you are, unfortunately, a dweller in the infernal regions. I should say you represent a very high order of intelligence."

Flin bowed.

"Entertaining this view, I shall be happy to do what I can for you."

Flin smiled inwardly, though at the same time he felt annoyed with the old fellow's patronising manner.

"You are exceedingly kind," he observed, as he bowed low, "and your extreme condescension merits my eternal gratitude. I may be permitted to say that I think that the dwellers in this favoured city of Esnesnon, where all is peace and love, and where backbiting and jealousy are unknown, ought to be very proud of you."

"Thank you, thank you for your good opinion," cried Ytidrusba, a little excitedly. "You are a most excellent person, and very discerning. I regret, however, to have to say that I am not appreciated here. The fact is I am before my time. The people are not yet ripe for the great truths I preach. They are matter of fact, exceedingly so, and the school I represent is not appreciated. I have often said that even a dweller in the infernal-regions coming amongst them would not be able to convince them, and the truth of this is proved now. They do not seem disposed to believe that you were once an inhabitant of this world, and that on your death you passed to the other region."

"Ahem, coughed Flin, "that may or may not be so. I must in the interest of truth say that I cannot altogether bring myself to believe the doctrine; but no matter, my poor abilities, such as they are, are at your service, and if I can aid you, pray command me."

"Thank you very much," answered the other. "I could not have conceived that the upper world could have produced a man of such wisdom as yourself. You would scarcely discredit a tailed race of beings. You can be of service to me, and I accept you offer. I should like you to become a follower of mine. I can assure you you have much to gain by doing so. The King is weak-minded, and you and I together may be able to convince him, and by our united efforts counteract the intrigues and false doctrines of Doctor Yrekcauq. You have nothing to gain from him, nothing whatever. He will in fact, make your existence here miserable. As you are aware, he is desirous of exhibiting you as a show, but we must oppose that."

"I thoroughly appreciate that idea," exclaimed Flin, who had already conceived a positive aversion for the Doctor from the fact of his having made such a proposition. On the other hand, he did not, by any means, think much of Ytidrusba. "What do you propose?" he asked after a pause.

"Be guided by me in all things."

"You will find me an obedient follower."

"That is good. I shall endeavour now to obtain you an interview with the King, and you must strongly protest against the proposed exhibition. You must use every endeavour to gain his Majesty's permission to move freely about the city, and you will have to convince the people that you descended from the infernal regions specially to warn them against their wickedness in opposing the truths I have so long preached. You will get many converts, and our party will be so strengthened that we shall be able to annihilate the Doctor and his clique."

"Ah, capital idea," observed Flin, but he did not at all approve of it in his own heart. To represent himself as inferior to these wretched beings was by no means pleasant, but there was no help for it. He had many interests to serve beside his own, and he felt it was a duty he owed to the honourable society of which he was a member, as well as to the glorious Stars and Stripes, to learn all that it was possible to learn about these strange beings. Moreover, he thought it was just possible that by able diplomacy he would be able to induce King Gubmuh to recognise the American flag, and in time Esnesnon might even become a dependency of the United States Government. That was a noble end to strive for, and he felt that to reach such a goal he was justified in resorting to any legitimate means, and "legitimate means" under the circumstances was capable of a very wide interpretation.

"By the way, it has struck me that, with a view to strengthening our hands, a little harmless artifice may be resorted to," said Ytidrusba. "You are young, and of prepossessing appearance (Flin blushed and bowed). The King has a daughter, a lovely creature, charming in manner, and with a heart brimming over with affection. But she has been kept very secluded, owing to a tendency to wildness, and her father will not permit her to move in society at present. She is very anxious to see you, and I have no doubt that by perseverance you will be able to make a very favourable impression upon her. She may even pay you considerable attention, and possibly indulge in a little flirtation."

"Really, Mr Ytidrusba," interrupted Flin, "I think I must decline to lend myself to any such scheme. I am too old to trifle with the feelings of any fair creature, and --- "

Ytidrusba burst into a loud laugh, and Flin felt considerably annoyed, for he did not like to be ridiculed. It made him absolutely angry.

"Pardon my seeming rudeness," said the magician. "You are such a comical little chap that one cannot help laughing. Why, you are only a baby yet compared with our people. And if you had a little more hair on your head you would not be at all a bad-looking young fellow. Why, the lovely Princess Yobmot, who is a little given to flirting, I am sorry to say, will be quite delighted with the novelty of making love to you for a time."

"Really, sir, I am very much shocked to hear you speak in such a manner. For you to say that a young lady and a Princess is 'given to flirting,' and that she will make love to me, sounds very strange, and is scarcely compatible with my notions of etiquette and propriety."

Ytidrusba laughed loudly again. When he had recovered himself he said, "I must really beg your pardon. I had quite forgotten that in your miserable country the gentlemen make love to the ladies. Here in our civilised region it is quite different. The order is reversed. The ladies make love to the males; and I assure you they are terribly wild flirts. No young male with any pretension to looks is safe from the designs of the girls. Our young males are very carefully guarded by their mammas, but I am sorry to say that they are led astray in spite of the watchfulness and care of their parents. We are governed here, sir, by women."

"Governed by women!" exclaimed Flin.

"Yes; we have a grand parliament composed entirely of ladies. The King can do nothing without the sanction of this parliament. The fact is, the women rule us with an iron hand. We groan under their despotic sway. We have no voice. At least, we may talk ourselves hoarse, but they will not hear us. Our girls have far too much liberty. I have long tried to get an Act passed making it an offence against the State for them to flirt."

"Dear me! how very strange to be sure!" mused Flin. "I cannot say that I should altogether like this mode of petticoat government. In my country there are loud complaints heard from individuals who are strongly ruled at home by their better halves. But that is a private matter, and the remedy for that or rather the prevention, is for men not to get married at all. But if it came to a question of having old women in our council chamber, I very much fear I should be false to my allegiance and forsake the dear old Stars and Stripes."

"No doubt, no doubt," Ytidrusba answered, "but here the wisdom of our women is considered infinitely greater than that of the males. Though, to make a confidant of you, our men would rise in rebellion tomorrow if they could only get a resolute leader. The artful ladies, however, exert such a bewitching influence over the male population that I fear it is hopeless to look for anything like a universal rising. But to the point. I will introduce you to the Princess, and you must endeavour to make yourself agreeable. She has influence with her father, who really dotes upon her; and she also has a voice in the parliament. If she takes a fancy to you she will be able to aid us very materially. You see she is young and childish yet, and youth must have its frolic. In other respects you will find her a very nice young lady, but an awful tease."

"I shall be delighted to make her acquaintance," answered Flin;

"but I beg to assure you that I have long since passed that period when flirtation is enjoyable. Though if the beautiful Princess Yobmot can influence our cause, I shall use every endeavour to render myself agreeable."

"I am glad to hear you say so," said Ytidrusba. "A little finessing under the circumstances is allowable. But come now with me, and I will see if I can procure you an interview with the Princess."

19

Ytidrusba led Flin down several corridors, and across a courtyard, and into another wing of the building. Here he left him, but returned soon afterwards, and announced that the Princess was willing to see Flin, who, following his guide, was ushered into a very magnificent apartment. Seated on a sort of raised dais was the "lovely princess" Yobmot, who rose as Flin entered, and stepping from the dais held out her hand, which Flin took, and pressing his lips to it he bowed low. But the feeling with which he kissed the hand of the maiden almost amounted to disgust. His own was small compared to it. Hers was a coarse and hairy hand. From the representations of Ytidrusba he had expected to see a young lady who might have justly laid claim to some beauty. But though Flin, with the gallantry and courtesy characteristic of him, does not say all he thought of the Princess, it is very clear that he was by no means very greatly impressed. In age she must have been close on sixty, though, as he had learnt, this was simply childhood in Esnesnon. But used as he was in his own country to look upon a person who had reached that age as being in the sere and yellow leaf, he could scarcely reconcile himself to the fact that this blushing damsel was as yet but as a maiden in her teens.

The lady's face was by no means conspicuous for its beauty. Flin only makes a passing and delicate allusion to it, but from that we gather that the nose was a very prominent feature, and slightly retrouss,. The eyes were small and somewhat sunken, and the forehead was low. The mouth was boldly cut, and lips unpleasantly thick, and when they were opened they revealed a set of irregular and somewhat discoloured teeth. Whether this lady had a long or a short tail Flin was not able to judge, as she wore a long, loose-fitting, but very elegant robe, made of asbestos and trimmed with feathers. Her hair, which was long, was twisted into a massive plait and hung down her back.

Having introduced Flin, Ytidrusba withdrew --- the artful old fellow --- and left Mr. Flonatin alone with the Princess. He says that he felt exceedingly uneasy, as with a gracious smile he offered his hand to her, with a view to leading her to a seat. But he was abashed by the look of astonishment which came into her face, and she exclaimed, ---

"How very badly you have been brought up to be sure." Then she immediately checked herself, and added quickly: "There, there, I will excuse you, you are a stranger in our city. You have never been used, I suppose, to civilised society before, and so you may be pardoned."

"Permit me to lead you to a seat," the lady said, and Flin allowed himself to be led like a lamb to the fold.

The Princess seated herself beside him, and staring at him, especially at his bald head, in, as Flin thought, rather a rude manner, she remarked, ---

"You are very young to be travelling alone. How is it your papa did not come with you, or send a competent guardian to take care of you? I am afraid that this is a very bad place for an unprotected young male who has any pretension to beauty. The ladies here are terrible creatures."

The Princess smiled, though Flin says that her smile was a "horse laugh." It is only charitable to believe that he made this assertion while smarting under some fancied wrong, for his well-known gallantry would scarcely have permitted him to be rude to one of the fair sex.

"Really, madam," answered Flin, "you need some information as to the customs of my country, where I should be considered quite capable of protecting myself. In fact, I may inform you that there the ladies are generally guarded and looked after, and that it would be considered the height of rudeness for a lady with any pretensions to good breeding to make the slightest advance to a gentlemen."

"Dear me, can it be possible that you are such barbarians!" cried the Princess in astonishment, as she played with a large feather fan. "The gentlemen make advances to the ladies?" she asked with a look of incredulity; and then breaking out into a little laugh she added, "No, it really cannot be possible. You are given to joking, you naughty little fellow, and you are trying to deceive poor me."

She closed the fan and tapped him playfully on the head with it -- - a familiarity which Flin by no means liked, but then, poor man, what was he to do, and how was he to resent it? The only thing was to submit calmly. Still, for the credit of his sex, he felt it to be a bounden duty to endeavour to improve this young lady, so he replied, ---

"My dear madam, I cannot for a moment doubt that the attention you are pleased to honour me with is well meant, but you must really make some allowance for my bashfulness as well as for the novelty of the position in which I am placed."

"You are really most charming," remarked the Princess admiringly, and caressing Flin's hand --- an indignity he put an end to by quickly withdrawing his hand from hers. "Come, now," she said in a soothing tone. "I didn't mean any harm, I assure you. You are really so fascinating as to be irresistible."

"Madam," cried Flin, "this is unpardonable in a young person of your sex."

"Why, what an irritable little fellow you are, to be sure," answered the Princess, with a merry laugh, and passing her arm round Flin's waist. He pushed her away --- as he says --- somewhat roughly, but she only laughed the more and struggled to retain her hold. Flin's face burned with indignation, and his lips quivered with suppressed rage, but he was so astonished that he could not find words to give utterance to the feelings that were surging within him. "You are very cruel to repulse me thus," she murmured. "You have awakened in my heart a feeling of admiration that I cannot conceal. Deign to give me one little smile in return." Again her arm went round his waist, and again he wriggled away, and felt strongly inclined to rise up and leave the room. .What a hard-hearted little male you are, to be sure. Why do you repulse me so? But there, you are only tantalising me; are you not now?" and again she tried to draw him towards her, but he frustrated her design, and in a voice that quivered with indignation, he exclaimed, ---

"Your Highness, I am really surprised at you; nay more, I may go so far as to say that I am shocked. I would remark that, even if I had been in the heyday of my youth, anything like fastness on the part of a lady would have raised in me a feeling of disgust. But when I remember that I am a grave and sober man of science, I can scarcely find words sufficiently strong to express my aversion for such unpardonable behaviour on the part of a lady occupying the high position that you do."

The Princess burst into a fit of most immoderate laughter. Flin's manner had amused her so much that she felt it impossible to control herself. But when she was able to speak she said, while her eyes were filled with tears through excessive laughing, ---

"Do, my dear, forgive me for laughing at you. I really cannot help it. You are such a funny little fellow, and you simplicity is charming, upon my word. I cannot tell you how much I admire it. Do you know there is nothing I detest more than a forward young male. And you are so retiring and bashful that you are simply delightful. Why, there are some of our young males in Esnesnon that, if I were to make love to them, they would very soon allow me to caress them. But I don't like such easy conquest. The greatest pleasure you know is in the pursuit of pleasure. Now, I dare be bound that in the course of about an hour I would undertake to kiss the very highest-born young male in our land, in the same way that I am now going to sip the nectar of those beautiful lips of yours."

She made a motion as if about to kiss him, but Flin put up his hands and drew quickly back, so that her design was frustrated.

"You are too cruel, really," she said, "and ought not to treat me so. Why, do you know --- but there, of course you don't --- and so I will tell you that his Majesty has kept me confined to the palace for I don't know how long, and it is quite a change to enjoy the company of such a charming creature as yourself."

"It is a pity, your Highness, that his Majesty does not place you under the care of a strict governess, who would teach you propriety."

"Oh, you curious little creature," exclaimed the Princess. "It may surprise you to know I have just finished my education, and having been annoyed with teachers so long, it is only right I should have a little liberty now. But the King will not let me enjoy freedom. He says I am very wild and a little fast. Now, isn't that a wicked libel, don't you consider. Do I look as though I could lead a young male astray?"

"You ask me a question, madam, and I am bound to answer it. I think that your conduct is most reprehensible, and highly improper. Why, if a young lady were to conduct herself in my country in such a manner she would be shunned by every respectable person."

"Oh, but look what an uncivilised and wretched country yours is. Why, Mr. Ytidrusba tells me that the people who dwell there are the very lowest of beings."

"You will pardon me for contradicting that statement, madam, it is a gross untruth. I am proud to say that under the glorious stars and stripes the perfection of civilisation is reached. There the ladies are made love to by the gentlemen."

"Can it be possible?" exclaimed the Princess in wonderment. "Oh, what a horrid fashion. I shouldn't like to live there then."

"I do not suppose you would, madam," Flin replied. "I think, your Highness," he continued, "that after the frivolities I may venture to claim your serious attention to a little matter concerning myself, and in which I am desirous of soliciting your aid."

"Pray, my dear, command me," she answered. "I will fly to the ends of Esnesnon if you but command me."

"You are exceedingly kind," he said, "but I am not desirous of putting you to any such personal inconvenience."

"No inconvenience, love, if it would serve you," and again she tried to draw him towards her, but he held her at arm's length.

"Your Highness, will you try and be a little more reserved? This familiarity is shocking in the extreme."

"What a delightful creature you are, to be sure," she laughingly exclaimed. "Your childlike innocence is charming. But now tell me how I can serve you. Has any woman in Esnesnon dared to insult you. If so, one of my maids shall call her out and have revenge."

"Considering that I have not left the palace since I came to it, I have not suffered in the manner you suggest. But if I may believe that your Highness is a fair representative of the female population of this city, I can well imagine that even a venerable gentleman like myself would scarcely be safe in the streets."

Again the Princess roared with laughter. And when she had recovered sufficient breath to speak, she cried out, ---

"Do not be so absurdly funny, there's a darling. You really make my eyes water and my sides ache. Why, you are such an interesting little creature that all the maidens in our fair city will be fighting about you. But let us to business. What is this great favour you require?"

"Well, you are aware, madam, that I am looked upon here as a curiosity."

"Yes, indeed, a very great curiosity."

"There has been a meeting of what I suppose I must call the savants of this place. And one Dr Yrekcauq suggests that I should be made a public exhibition of."

"Oh, what a horrid fellow?" exclaimed the Princess.

"That is just what I think, your Highness. The thought of being shown as if I were a wild animal is very shocking indeed to me, and I venture to pray that your Highness will use your influence with his Majesty --- your father --- in my behalf, and entreat him not to sanction the proposal of Dr Yrekcauq."

"That will I do with pleasure, sweet creature. I will worry the

King's life out until he grants my request. I do not like that doctor at all. I believe him to be a bit of a humbug."

"Just my belief, madam."

"Ah, you see how well our ideas coincide. There is a mutual sympathy between us, and yet you treat me so unkindly. Now, is there anything else I can do?"

"I think not, at present. But I shall not fail to avail myself of your powerful influence should I need it."

"Command me at any time, I beseech you. I am going though to claim payment in advance for the service I shall render."

"I fear, madam, I have nothing to repay you with."

"Oh, you innocent little creature," she exclaimed, and with sudden movement she threw her arms round his waist, and drawing him quickly towards her, she kissed him.

At that moment, and before she could release him, or he disengage himself, the door opened, and the King and Ytidrusba stood upon the threshold.

20

A very severe frown darkened the King's brow as he observed his daughter caressing Flin, and it was very evident he was angered so as to be unable to speak his thoughts. The Princess was by no means confused, though her face reddened a little. She released Flin, and moving quickly towards her father she said with sweet simplicity, ---

"I am so glad, sire, you have come. This young male has been telling me his woes, and aroused my sympathy deeply, as I am sure yours will be when you have heard his trouble."

"Peace, child," cried the King. "I thought that you were gaining some wisdom, but, alas? I fear that you are just as giddy as ever."

"Ah, your Majesty, you judge me harshly," moaned the charming Princess, with a pretty pout. "I did but sympathise with the poor young barbarian. You know that my heart was never proof against a tale of woe."

"A tail, you jade," cried the enraged King, mistaking his daughter's meaning, "why do you mock me? the wretch is tailless, and therefore too inferior to perform even the most menial office for the daughter of a King. And yet I find you flirting with him in every way as if he were one of us. It is shocking, absolutely shocking and unpardonable."

"Dear King," sighed the artful Princess, as she gently wound her arms round his Majesty's neck. "Do not be angry with your little pet. She did but sport innocently with this funny being. He is such a novelty, you know, and so young too."

A smile spread over the old King's face, and he looked down proudly on the face of his daughter, whose head had drooped gracefully on his breast. "You are a naughty little child, Yobmot, to anger your father so."

"I will not do so any more, your Majesty."

"False promises, child, false promises, I fear. You have made them so often, only to break them again, that I am compelled to doubt."

"Believe me this time, your Majesty, for I am sincere."

"Well, well, it shall be as you desire. Ytidrusba informs me that you have a request to prefer, and I am here to hear it."

"Was ever girl blessed with such a dear parent?" remarked the Princess, as she playfully patted the King's cheek. "You are the very embodiment of wisdom and generosity."

"Cease your flattery, daughter, and let me know your wishes."

"I wish to plead for this miserable being, whose very wretchedness and misery should excite our pity. Dr. Yrekcauq would exhibit him as we have the alligators and other strange beasts shown for the gratification of the common people. However amusing such a show might be --- for no one can doubt that he is a most extraordinary and comical wretch --- I venture to think that it would be detrimental to the dignity of an enlightened and mighty people to make an exhibition of a creature who in some measure can claim kindredship with us."

The King was thoughtful. He bit his finger nails, and his daughter still fondled him, for she was a very artful young lady.

"Our exchequer is low, Ytidrusba, is it not?" he asked sadly.

"It is, your Majesty."

"That being so, we can replenish it well by showing this novel being in an iron cage, as some strange beast who bears an extraordinary resemblance to a pre-human being."

"Your Majesty will surely spare me such an indignity," chimed in Flin, who felt that he could no longer remain silent. "I am an American subject, and in the name of my Government I protest very strongly indeed. In the United States we are in the habit of treating aliens with the greatest amount of consideration and respect. I trust, therefore, that you will have some respect for my feelings. And in the event of your nation and mine ever being able to communicate with each other, you would find that any respect shown to me would be amply repaid."

The King burst into a loud and contemptuous laugh, in which Ytidrusba joined.

"I must give you credit for one thing at least," his Majesty observed, when he had recovered himself, "you have an astonishing amount of assurance, if not impudence. If you are a fair specimen of your countrymen --- and I take it that you are --- that land of yours must be a pretty warm place to live in. Are you aware, sir, that I am the mightiest monarch in all the world?"

"Are you indeed?" said Flin, ironically, "I was not aware of that interesting fact."

"Then know it now, and henceforth respect me. I have no doubt that the beings among whom you dwell have a very exalted notion of themselves. But possibly so have the smallest insects that crawl through our land. But you must remember that you are for ever stamped with the awful brand of degeneration, and that you belong to a fallen race. Save that you speak, you are no better than the wild animals in our woods. This may not be your fault, but conscious of your own littleness, you should not be guilty of presumption."

Flin was terribly annoyed at the old King's remarks, but he bowed gracefully and said with withering sarcasm, ---

"Your Majesty is undoubtedly a highly civilised and most polished gentleman, and the nation you honour by ruling over it must be a happy and mighty nation, indeed, with such a wise King to govern it.

But, while in justice I admit this, I trust you will permit me to say that amongst the nations which dwell on the crust of the earth America stands preeminently the highest and most glorious. I guess it's a mighty tall nation and wants some licking. It can give points to every other nation on the crust of the earth, but of course it is not equal to your own kingdom."

The King smiled, for he liked flattery. It was a lucky speech of Flin's, and completely won the old monarch, whose vanity had been touched.

The Princess also was not slow to perceive the effect Flin's words had had upon her father; for she possessed all the keenness of a woman's penetration, and was a practised hand in the use of those cunning little artifices which are the weapons of the softer sex, and which are used with terrible effect on poor, weak men.

The charming Princess, seeing that His Majesty was moved by Flin Flon's appeal, determined to follow up .the advantage thus gained --- what a sly little puss she was, was she not? --- and so, caressing her parent very lovingly, she simpered, ---

"What a dear, dear delightful pa you are to be sure. Was ever girl so blessed as I? Heigho! I fear, pa dear, I am not so deserving of you affection as I ought to be, but then, you know, I am going to be ever so good in future."

"Humph!" murmured the King, and though his hairy face beamed with a pleasant smile, he looked suspiciously at his daughter as if he didn't quite believe all she said. But he patted her head, and observed, "Yobmot, you are an artful little dear. I know you want to wheedle your old father out of something. Come now, is it not so?"

"I declare this is too bad," cried the Princess, as she stamped her foot, and with an air of injured innocence drew back and pouted her lips. "It is really too bad," she repeated, pulling out a very large amber handkerchief and pressing it to her eyes. (Alas! woman's nature seems to be much alike in all worlds. We have no authentic accounts from the moon, but if there be female dwellers there, and it is very probable that there are, they no doubt are just as experienced in the value of tears as a most effective weapon against man's heart as their sublunary sisters. At any rate Princess Yobmot --- sly little minx --- knew their use too well.) Her loving and gentle sire drew the fair head to his broad chest, and toying with her locks, he said ---

"There, there, my pet, spoil not those pretty eyes with weeping."

But the naughty little thing only sobbed the more. So that the King caressed her still more tenderly, and whispered, "There, there, my darling, dry your tears. I did not mean to hurt your feelings so. Tell me what I can do for you. I promise that I will grant any reasonable request. I will really."

"Oh, you dear, kind, cruel, naughty, delightful old pa," suddenly exclaimed the Princess, at the same time smoothing her back hair, which had been ruffled by the King's arm, and having arranged her tresses, she kissed her father, and added, "You are so awfully nice." (The observant reader will note that the paradoxical style of expression, which is at once so pretty and so absurd, is by no means peculiar to the young ladies of the upper world, but seems to be general.) "I have only one little tiny favour to ask, and, after having wounded my feelings so terribly, you must grant it."

"And pray what is it, pet?"

"For the honour and credit of our great nation, you must let this miserable, tailless barbarian have his liberty, and be free to move amongst our people and improve himself by studying our customs."

The King sighed. He was unable to resist his daughter's persuasive powers. Alas! he was by no means the first King who had fallen through lovely woman.

"I fear, my dear," he remarked, "that if I comply with your request it will not be very much to our credit --- which we shall have to pledge --- as our exchequer is so exhausted. But it shall be as you desire. Our royal promise is given."

"Oh, you are kind," cried his daughter, casting a sly glance at Flin and Ytidrusba. The latter gentleman was particularly delighted, as he saw what a triumph he had gained over his adversary, Doctor Yrekcauq. "I intend to be ever such a good little girl now, pa," she added, as she once more kissed him.

The old King was visibly affected. This might have been caused by the great display of his daughter's affection; but it was very possibly owing to the thought that he would have to devise some other plan to refill his empty coffers. It was a great sacrifice to give up the scheme of exhibiting Flin, but there was no help for it, as he was disarmed of all resolutions when his daughter wept.

"I confess that I have yielded to my daughter's request very reluctantly," observed the King, turning to Flin. "I have no doubt at all that if one of my subjects was to stray into your country he would be instantly seized, places in a cage, and exhibited to gaping ignoramuses." (Flin thought this was exceedingly probable, for a being with a tail would be a curiosity indeed in the upper world.) "However," pursued his Majesty, "the customs of savage nations do not, I am pleased to say, affect us. We are desirous to set an example by which we hope other nations will profit. You will, therefore, consider yourself at perfect liberty to go where you like in Esnesnon, and if you are an observer you cannot fail to benefit by what you see, and I trust that, if you should return to the Upper World, you will do all in your power to reform your fellows, and instruct them in the arts and politeness of a highly civilised people, such as, I am proud to say, we are."

Flin bowed low. But he could scarcely repress a smile as he compared the great American nation with Esnesnon. It seemed to him so ludicrously absurd for an old savage only one degree removed from an animal of the woods, like King Gubmuh, to talk of "politeness" and "arts," and to imagine for a single moment that the American people had anything to learn in this respect. He was determined, however, not to seem wanting in that delicate courtesy which as an American subject he knew so well how to exercise. And so dropping on his knee, he pressed his lips to the hairy hand of the monarch, and said: "I beg that your Majesty will accept the expressions of my most perfect gratitude and esteem for the unlooked-for favour which you have been pleased to extend to me. And I beg to further assure your Majesty that should I be so fortunate as to return safe and well to my beloved country, I shall never cease to uphold your Majesty as a generous and kindly monarch. And though I cannot admit that my nation is altogether what you believe it to be, I do go so far as to say that your Majesty's example might very fairly be copied by other crowned heads. One thing I may safely state, and that is, that the representations I shall make of your Majesty's goodness and generosity will win for you the entire good-will of the mighty people who live under the glorious stars and stripes."

"Tut, tut," cried the King, "this is mere bunkum."

Flin was astounded that King Gubmuh should be acquainted with a noun that was so singularly expressive and peculiarly American. And it must be confessed that he was annoyed at being accused of talking "bunkum." But he considered it would have been an act of weakness to let his Majesty see that he had noticed the insult, and so he merely bowed again and said, ---

"Permit me to observe that you Majesty's generosity is only excelled by your exceeding great wisdom." Whereat the King smiled, and motioning to Ytidrusba, withdrew.

As soon as the door was closed, the Princess Yobmot burst into a loud laugh, and capering round the room like a young colt just let loose, she cried, ---

"Oh, you delightful little humbug! Why, I declare, the governor almost believed that you meant what you said. I saw the old buffer's eyes twinkling as though they were going to water."

Mr. Flonatin was terribly shocked at the levity of this young creature. To hear her speak of her father as the "governor," and "old buffer," was painful, and he replied, ---

"Really, your Highness, I would remind you that I am a sedate and grave man of science, and such giddiness as you display troubles me. I am not given to speaking what I do not feel, and you may believe me when I say ---"

The Princess here interrupted him with a perfect roar of laughter, and exclaimed, ---

"Oh, do give over, you funny little creature, or I shall faint. We shall have some jolly fun together if you are a good little fellow and only do what I tell you, and between us we shall be able to gammon the governor into anything."

She threw her arms round Mr Flonatin's waist, and set off him in a waltz round the room, spinning round and round like a top, until the poor fellow was bewildered and giddy, and sank down on a seat perfectly exhausted, while the lively girl fanned him with her amber handkerchief and laughed immoderately.

21

The excitement in the city of Esnesnon caused by Flin Flon's strange arrival promised to be something more than a nine days' wonder, and public opinion was very much divided as to who he was, and where he had come from. In fact two "parties" were quickly formed --- the one led by the celebrated Doctor Yrekcauq and the other by the great spiritualist and magician, Ytidrusba. It may be as well to mention here that the word "magician" was not used in the city of Esnesnon in the same sense as it is used by upper world people. It was in point of fact a title of great honour, and indicated learning and attainments of a very high order. Mr Ytidrusba was, as has been shown, well acquainted with the science of mesmerism, and he was also a "professor of spiritualism." This was a degree peculiar also to the central world. For although there are spiritualists in the upper world, they are simply practisers, and not professors. And after the power displayed by the learned Ytidrusba, I am afraid it will have to be admitted that the spiritualists of the upper world are very shallow impostors indeed. One thing was very remarkable. Mr Ytidrusba did not resort to the childish nonsense of making the chairs and tables dance, and knocking flower-pots about in order to convince his world that spirits did exist. But he professed to have an intimate knowledge of the occult sciences, and he preached a doctrine that certain of the dead of Esnesnon took their departure to the outer regions of the globe; that there they assumed another form, and went through a probationary term previous to voyaging to a new world. Of course such a doctrine as this will sound very ridiculous to civilised ears. But it is a trifle more rational than that preached by the canting hypocrites of this favoured region, who impiously assert that they are enabled to hold communion with the disembodied spirits of another sphere. I am bound to confess my inability to account for the very remarkable knowledge possessed by Ytidrusba, nor would I for a single moment believe that Mr Flonatin was guilty of anything like "bunkum" in making the statements that he has done. His upright conduct and noble disposition must for ever place him above the breath of slander or calumny. He was the very embodiment of truth, and the good man's bones would surely rattle in his grave if any reader should for a single moment doubt the truth of anything he has written. Anyway I feel it is but justice to his memory to say that if any trifling inaccuracies or exaggerations have inadvertently crept into this history, they must be laid to my charge as the historian. Though I have no fear but what will bear favourable comparison with the generality of histories. In fact, I venture to think there are fewer misstatements than might have been expected in a work of such magnitude, and dealing as it does with a new world and a new race of people. But as I fear I shall be accused of egotism, I will say nothing more about the merits of the work, for I hold that if there is anything that is objectionable it is surely the blowing of one's own trumpet. In fact, since the noble and high-souled race of critics came into being, there is no longer any necessity for one to praise oneself, as these gentle creatures do it for you, and in such a delicate and polite manner as to leave nothing to be desired. These gentlemen critics are above suspicion, and as for the ladies, why, they are simply perfect. Any work possessing a scintilla of ability is sure to receive the most gracious consideration at the hands of these good people. In fact, they delight in giving praise, and their lives are one long round of enjoyment and pleasure, as must ever be the case with those who live, not for themselves, but for the benefit of others less favoured than themselves. But spotless and chaste as is the race of critics, they do not escape the breath of calumny. Unprincipled and shameless persons have at times hinted at bribery and corruption in connection with criticism. They have even gone so far as to say that critics are jealous, cross- gained, envious, splenetic, captious, spiteful, snarling, stony- hearted, shallow-brained, one-sided, mercenary, champagne-drinking, supper-eating, favour-hunting, office-seeking, falsehood-telling people. But it is a remarkable fact that these libellers have invariably come to some bad end, or met with violent deaths, which speak plainly of that providence which protects the good and punishes the guilty.

But to once more take up the thread and return to that city of moral gloom, Esnesnon. There the State was torn with the feuds of contending parties. And the peace and goodwill so conspicuous in the upper regions were not enjoyed there. There were contentions, bickerings, backbitings, jealousy, hatred, malice, uncharitableness; and, in short, so much evil that it would almost justify the belief indulged in by the pious people of the upper world that the centre world was verily the infernal regions.

The Press of Esnesnon was also very corrupt. The Gazette was the State organ, and its toadyism was fulsome. All official notices appeared in it, and it was practically the voice of the King and the Government, of which more will be said by-and- by. The opposition paper was the Anti-Humbug News. This was, in fact, the people's journal, and professed to be the only vehicle of public opinion. It prided itself upon its incorruptibility, and "gassed" a good deal about its "pure tone and outspoken honesty." There is reason to believe, however, that this was only "bosh," and that it really existed by trading on the credulity of an ignorant people, and by misdirecting public opinion. As to whether the latter charge is correct, my readers will be able to draw their own inferences from the following extract, which has reference to Flin Flon's arrival. It will be remembered that the Gazette was the only paper which was allowed to have a representative at Court, and consequently the only journal able to supply its readers with accurate Court information. There can be little doubt that the News smarted from this exclusiveness, and was exceedingly bitter against its rival. But the relative value of the opinion of the respective papers will be best judged when the following is contrasted with the notice taken from the Gazette. This is what the Anti-Humbug News said: ---

"A few days ago we briefly announced the arrival in this city of a strange being, supposed to have come from some savage region, as yet undiscovered by our geographers. We refrain from giving any detailed account of the creature until we had been able to learn something more about him by a personal interview. With this object we immediately despatched one of the oldest members of our staff to interview the stranger. But we regret to announce that our representative was resolutely and insolently refused admission into the palace. We were not altogether unprepared for this, knowing as we do the amount of cliqueism and favouritism which unfortunately prevail at his Majesty's Court. Our policy has always been to speak out boldly, without fear and without favour; as our readers are aware, this has brought us into bad odour in certain quarters. But in the interests of this great people, and the country generally, we do not hesitate now to inform the King that it is his duty as monarch of a mighty realm to study the interests of his subjects, and to recognise no party. Unhappily --- and we say this with all due respect --- his Majesty allows a few interested office-seekers to stand between him and his people. For a long time the government of the country has virtually been in the hands of Mr. Ytidrusba and Doctor Yrekcauq, and as it is notorious that a bitter feud exists between these two learned beings, we fearlessly assert that they should no longer be allowed to make the Court and the Senate the arena for their personal quarrels. That both gentlemen are endowed with extraordinary ability must be freely admitted, but their high attainments are sullied by a smallness of spirit that would discredit barbarians. The arrival of the strange being is the signal for a renewal of the jealousy which has so long been a disgrace to his Majesty's palace, and both Mr Ytidrusba and Doctor Yrekcauq forget what they owe to the public in their desire to air their own opinions. We would, however, respectfully inform these gentlemen that we, as the organ of public opinion, object to have mud thrown in our eyes. We claim to have a voice in all matters affecting the public weal, and anything like chicanery or humbug we shall oppose with all the energy at our command. We believe that the public are being humbugged with reference to this stranger, whose chief claim to singularity seems to be the absence of a caudal appendage. We understand that there was a meeting yesterday at the Palace of all the learned men and savants of our city, but that they arrived at no definite conclusion, though both Mr Ytidrusba and Doctor Yrekcauq had their pet theories well paraded, as is usually the case when anything strange occurs. Without entering into the merits of the disputes of these scientists we feel called upon to denounce the statement that the stranger has come from the exterior of the earth, as one totally unworthy of a great mind, and equally unworthy of a moment's consideration by intelligent people. Our philosophers and scientific men have proved beyond a doubt that the exterior of this earth is perfectly smooth, and shrouded in eternal night. The idea, therefore, of anything having life being able to dwell upon a smooth ball, and in total darkness, is so ludicrously absurd that it is an insult to ask a person, even of the most ordinary intelligence, to believe it. But science has proved even more than this. It has established the fact that the exterior of the earth is surrounded with gases of such a deadly nature that nothing --- neither animal nor vegetable life --- could possibly exist there for a moment. It is, in short, a region of gloom, silence and death. To say, therefore, that a person similar in being to ourselves could possibly have made his way from there to here is a monstrously-absurd falsehood. This may be strong language, but the time has come when only plain speaking can avail. We have so long groaned under the despotism of cliques, who, from self-interested motives, have not hesitated to cram ridiculous notions down the public throat, that we are determined now to combat this. We feel it to be a duty, and we shall not flinch from doing that duty. Do not let our meaning be misunderstood. We write in the broad spirit of brotherly love and charity. But DUTY is our watchword. In the meantime, we caution the public not to be gulled by the nonsensical idea that this tailless wretch has come to us from the mysterious and unknown regions of solitude and darkness which surround our world. The commonest of logic will disprove this. He was found floating in his strange vessel on the Green River. Now the source of that river has never been discovered, notwithstanding the many attempts that have been made to trace it. It will be remembered that many years ago a powerful electrical vessel was fitted out to ascend the river, and after travelling for a considerable distance she came to the mouth of a huge tunnel, from which the water poured in such force as to render it impossible for the vessel to proceed further. There is no doubt that the new arrival came down this tunnel, and it is equally certain that, dwelling in another part of our world, and connected by the Green River, is an extraordinary race, of which this person is a representative. He had probably been boating when by some mischance he was carried away by the currents, and so found himself, much to his astonishment, amongst civilised people. But to suppose that he could have dropped down from regions that are, for aught we know, thousands of miles above us, is at once childish and ridiculous. If what we have stated is not true, then all we can say is that a cruel hoax is being perpetrated, for reasons that we confess we are unable to define. We shall jealously watch the movements of the Government with reference to the matter and shall not hesitate to expose anything like humbug."

Thus did the Anti-Humbug News pour out its vials of wrath, begotten by disappointment. As Flin Flon read the article he could scarcely refrain from smiling.

"Alas!" he mused, "there is little difference between those races with tails and those without. And if we could only get the monkeys to tell us what they thought of both human and prehuman beings, we should be very much astonished as well as shocked. "

The reader will probably acquiesce in this. And in the next chapter some very peculiar information will be given that will have special interest for the ladies.

22

It will be remembered that the roguish little Princess Yobmot had succeeded in wheedling her father into allowing Flin Flon to have his liberty. And this concession was no less welcome to Flin than to the lady herself. Mr Flonatin was by no means pleased with the exuberance of animal spirits displayed by the Princess, but under the circumstances he felt it was to his interest to put up with some inconveniences, and therefore he was determined to be silent, as she might prove a valuable ally.

On the day following Flin's interview with King Gubmuh, he was unexpectedly, and, as it proved, clandestinely visited by the Princess, who, suddenly bursting into the room, exclaimed, --- .

"Oh, I am so delighted to see you, you jolly little male! But do you know, my dad has prohibited me from coming, though that does not trouble me. Love laughs at locksmiths, you know, dear, doesn't it? "

Mr. Flonatin blushed. He could not help doing so, for he was particularly bashful and retiring in the presence of ladies.

"Really, you Highness," he stammered, "your attentions are no doubt well meant, but I must again remind you that I have long passed the hey-day of youth, and that love-making was an art in which I fear I never even reached mediocrity, as testified by the fact that in my old age I am still a bachelor and childless."

The Princess fairly roared with laughter as Flin spoke. She was evidently greatly amused, though he, poor man, had not the slightest intention of joking. His bachelorhood was a tender subject upon which he seldom touched. Nor shall I presume to deal with such a delicate and sacred matter, though I am selfish enough to feel some slight degree of gladness that the immortal traveller never was trapped into the net of Hymen. For had he settled down into a humdrum Benedict, and become the proud father of a large family, his roving propensities would not have been gratified, and, as a consequence, I should not have had the pleasure of writing this history. But to return to the Princess, who, when she had recovered, exclaimed, ---

"Oh, you funny little quack-quack, you talk in such a comical manner that I really cannot refrain from laughing."

Then she pressed his cheeks with her by no means delicate hands, I am sorry to say, and kissed him two or three times --- an act of gracious condescension which he by no means relished. And he showed his reluctance to be treated so familiarly by forcibly drawing back and frowning his severest frown, which only caused the Princess to break out again and cry, enthusiastically, ---

"You darling, you will drive me mad with laughter if you persist in being so funny. Do try and be sedate, there's a dear."

For her to be any madder than she was Flin thought would be morally impossible. In fact, his own private opinion, it may be freely confessed, was that everybody in Esnesnon was very decidedly mad, an opinion in which I by no means share. In fact, I do not hesitate to say that Mr. Flonatin was a little too severe, and since we do not know exactly the precise opinion entertained by the prehuman people for the human race, beyond that they believe us to be very degenerated, a belief in which I fully coincide, it is as well to be a little lenient and sparing of abuse, remembering that those who live in glass structures should not fling stones.

"Really, my dear madam," Flin remarked, "I must respectfully beg that you will be a little less volatile. I am so unused to such behaviour that it quite confuses me."

"What a splendid actor you are, to be sure," she answered, with a look of mock gravity. "Why, you would almost make one believe that you were in earnest. But do, for goodness sake, try and be a little serious yourself, there's a dear. It is not good for one to laugh so."

"I really protest, your Highness --- " Flin continued; but the Princess interrupted him by putting her hand playfully over his mouth, and saying, ---

"There, there, you funny little thing, don't joke any more now, or else I will get ever so angry with you."

Mr. Flonatin sighed. He felt that he was thoroughly mastered by this young lady, and that to attempt to convince her would be a perfectly hopeless task. He was not the first man who has had to confess himself beaten by a strong-minded woman. In fact, there is reason to fear that at the present day man is becoming decidedly the weaker vessel, and that henceforth his station will be in the kitchen, where he can exercise his ingenuity in making pastry and washing up the plates. But if woman has thoroughly made up her mind to drive us there, I call upon all men to rally round and make a bold stand against this revolutionary measure. Let us show the dear creatures that we know how to resent this last indignity. We will die, die bravely, piling up our dead bodies at the kitchen doors rather than submit.

"Now, look here," continued Princess Yobmot, addressing Flin. "I tell you what I am going to do. There is a meeting to-day of 'The Society for the Protection of Males.' I was one of the founders of this society, and it is supported by some of our best ladies. There is often some jolly fun there, and so I intend to take you. But, mind, on one condition only."

"And what is that, you Highness?" asked Flin, not a little pleased at the opportunity which offered itself to him to see some of the inner life of the New Worlders. The Princess sidled up to him, and looking into his face very roguishly, and patting him on the head, she said, ---

"Why, you artful little creature, as though you did not know. Well, it is that you do not allow any of the ladies there to make love to you; or I shall be so awfully jealous."

"Really, you Highness, I cannot believe that you wish me to accept this seriously. Surely the members of a Society whose business is of such a serious nature will not be guilty of such a dereliction of duty as that you name."

"You silly little thing," answered the Princess, "you don't know what my countrywomen are yet. It is very doubtful if they are capable of really serious business. And they are such flirts. I am afraid they sadly deceive their husbands, poor, confiding creatures! Oh, do you know, if I had a husband I should be so good to him. And I should always take him out whenever I went, and I shouldn't belong to any club, but always be home early at night, and never look slyly at any other young male. In fact, I should be a perfect model of a wife."

"I fear, your Highness, that you promise far too much," Flin observed. "I have heard men in my own country make similar promises, but I know they have seldom been kept. And the husband has cared more for his club than his wife after marriage."

"His club!" the Princess almost shrieked, throwing up her hands in horror. "His club," she repeated. "You don't mean to tell me that the husband has a club?"

"What I state is perfectly true, madam."

"And the husband goes away and leaves his wife at home?"

"Such I am sorry to say is too often the case."

"Oh, the brutes!" the Princess cried; "but tell me, why do the wives allow it?"

"Simply because they cannot help themselves. You must understand that in most civilis --- I beg your pardon, that is, I mean to say --- in the upper world regions man is invariably the ruler and the woman is ever the weaker sex."

"Oh, horror, I shall faint!" exclaimed the Princess. "Can it be possible that such a state of things can exist, even amongst barbarians? How I wish I could visit your country. I would very soon alter all that." Then she moved closer to him, and winding her arm round his waist, she broke out into an incredulous smile, and said, "You naughty, gay, little deceiver. Fie on you! You have been trifling with my feelings, and you know that what you have stated is false."

Flin by no means liked to have his veracity impugned, and gently disengaging himself from his too ardent admirer's grasp, he remarked, ---

"Your Highness is slightly discourteous to doubt my word --- "

But before he could finish his sentence she kissed him rather boisterously, and said, ---

"Now don't get cross, you little tease, for you know that what you say isn't true. The idea of trying to make me believe such a thing, you naughty little fellow. Now, now" --- as Flin was about to speak --- "it is no use saying anything else because I won't hear you. Why, if I thought that even in such a terrible place as that from which you have come my sex were so degraded I would drown myself, I declare I would. It is horrible to think of it even as a joke. So please not to be so funny any more, or I won't speak to you for a whole day."

Flin saw that it would be perfectly useless to attempt to convince this dreadful young lady. And he breathed a silent prayer of thankfulness that in his country her counterpart was nowhere to be found, and "the lords of creation" still held sway.

Alas! in the purity of his nature, and his childlike simplicity, he believed this to be the case. But things have altered since then, and if the good Flonatin's spirit could revisit earthly scenes he would weep to see how the Esnesnon fashions are becoming general throughout the upper world.

"Come, we must not waste any more time," the Princess remarked, "or the Society's meeting will be over." As she spoke she struck a polished stone disc with a sort of hammer, and a strange, low, musical note resulted. This stone was the equivalent for our bell. A servant appeared. "Order my chariot immediately," she said imperiously. The slave bowed and retired. Returning in a few minutes he announced that "the chariot was ready." Then, all smiles, the Princess turned to Mr Flonatin and said, "Come, dear, let us go." She caught up an elegant asbestos shawl which was lying over the sofa, and throwing it over Flin's head so as to conceal his face, she offered him her arm, and gazing on him with a look of admiration led him out of the room.

23

The chariot, which waited at the door ready to receive the Princess, was circular in shape, not unlike the half of an egg-shell. This shell was fitted into a framework that bore a strong resemblance to an egg-cup. The cup rested on a wooden platform that might very well be likened to a table without legs. In the front and back part of the table were two wheels, and at the sides were two more like the driving-wheels of a locomotive. The motive power of this strange vehicle was electricity, which was generated in a battery fitted beneath the body of the carriage. By means of powerful currents of electricity a crank was turned which set the wheels in motion, and, the concern being circular, would run backwards or forwards. A servant stood on the platform to control the battery and steer the carriage.

Mr. Flonatin examined this machine with considerable curiosity and surprise, for he had no idea as to the kind of conveyances these strange people might use, and the application of electricity in such an ingenious way excited his admiration.

As he had not yet forgotten his upper world customs, he was about to hand the Princess in; but she looked at him with astonishment and said, ---

"I trust I am too much of a lady to enter a carriage before a male. You should remember that women in this country always give way to the weaker sex."

Flin could scarcely help smiling at the girl's arrogance, but he made no reply and allowed her to assist him in. When he was seated she sprang lightly after him, and the coachman drew some elegant curtains, which were suspended from a light framework round the vehicle, thereby secluding the occupants from the gaze of the vulgar.

"May I inquire, madam," said Flin, when they were seated, "if all your vehicles are built upon this principle?"

"Nearly all. We have some which are used out of the town which are propelled by means of compressed air acting upon an enclosed sail. But they travel so rapidly that we do not allow them to come into the streets. They are used chiefly to carry passengers and goods to distant parts."

"Then I presume you have no horses."

"Horses! horses! Whatever kind of things are they?"

Mr. Flonatin pitied her for her ignorance, but he did not like to be rude, and so he explained that horses were four- legged animals, and were extremely useful in the upper world.

"I never heard of such beings," the Princess replied. "The only animal we use as a draught animal, and then only for heavy loads, is the anoplotherium."

"Bless my life, is it possible?" cried Flin in amazement. "Why, we have always looked upon the anoplotherium as an extinct animal. Occasionally his fossil remains have been found in our country, but a living specimen would arouse the interest and enthusiasm of the whole scientific world."

"Why, what a funny place your country must be to be sure," the Princess observed with, as Flin thought, just a touch of irony in her tone; though, as it is scarcely possible that a Princess of the royal house of Gubmuh could have been guilty of anything like rudeness to a gentleman, he may have been mistaken in so thinking.

"As you are so favoured with regard to the Anoplotherium," Flin remarked, "it is possible you have also the menopome here."

The Princess smiled.

"Why, of course we have," she replied; "whatever do you think we should do without it? He is a most useful beast, I can assure you."

"Ah, possibly, possibly," said Flin, feeling a little incredulous, for the great salamander had ever been looked upon by him as a mythological reptile, but now he was actually in a place where it was utilised. "And may I inquire, madam, for what purpose these strange beasts are used?"

"Yes. In our great gold foundries, where there is much heavy work, the menopome is taught to carry massive beams and girders into the furnaces. The gold is placed on the backs of a couple of the beast, which, when loaded, crawl into the furnaces, and then wait until the metal gets sufficiently hot for whatever process it has to go through, when they bring it out again."

"Wonderful, wonderful," cried Flin enthusiastically, and finding it very hard to bring himself to believe that such a thing was possible. He almost felt inclined to clap his hands with joy as he made notes of these wonders. "By the way, my dear Princess," he said suddenly, and in his enthusiasm quite forgetting himself, "can you inform me what has been done with my vessel by which I arrived here?"

Instead of answering him directly her arm stole around his waist, and she drew him to her.

"Ah! speak to me again like that," she murmured; "to be called dear by you is so very nice."

"Really, madam, you have mistaken me," he stammered indignantly, and trying to disengage himself; but she held him firmly.

"Do not be so cruel," she whispered; "you have awakened within my breast a feeling of

devotion for you, and I shall hope yet to win your love, my pet. Nay, do not push me away. I am

sincere, let me not plead in vain, or I shall sigh myself away. Give me one word of hope and I will kneel at your feet and plead for a loving smile. Command me to travel the earth through and I will do it if you but wish it. I would even go to that awful region from which you say you have come."

"I --- I --- madam --- let me entreat you to be a little more decorous," Flin stammered, for he was utterly bewildered and ashamed. To be made love to by a female in such a manner was quite a novel experience, and though it might be the custom of the country which he was then in, he felt it was a custom he could not reconcile himself to, though he had no doubt that when one had become thoroughly used to it, it would be by no means unpleasant. "You should really make some allowance for my inexperience," he continued.

"Ah! sweet creature," she chimed in, "how ingenuous and innocent you are."

"I thought," he went on, "that such nonsensical language was confined to my own country, and even there only used by love-sick boys, whose proper place is at school, where they should be birched regularly and fed upon water gruel until they had learnt reason."

The Princess was by no means daunted. She exhibited much of that characteristic perseverance which is so marked in male lovers in our own country; and instead of feeling offended, she smiled sweetly, and snatching a kiss, which act caused Flin's face to become scarlet, even to the very roots of his few remaining grey hairs, she murmured, ---

"Sweet male, you are cruel, very cruel, but I shall still hope." She squeezed his hand, and would have kissed him again, but he repulsed her. And at this moment, much to his relief, the chariot stopped. The Princess jumped out, and then gave her hand to Flin. They were at the entrance to a magnificent building, the front of which was composed of polished gold, which apparently was the universal building material in Esnesnon. Princess Yobmot gave her arm to her companion, and then conducted him up a flight of very noble stairs, which were made from what seemed to be massive slabs of ruby glass.

"You were asking me, darling, about your funny little vessel,' she remarked."I should tell you that it is being exhibited in Doctor Yrekcauq's museum, and thousands of people flock to see it every day."

What heathens, Flin thought, but he did not say so. At the top of the landing a servant was waiting. He wore a huge wig, which hung right down his back, and Flin could scarcely keep from laughing, for the fellow looked such a guy, what with his short tail and long wig. He bowed almost to the ground as the Princess approached, and stared in stupid astonishment at Flin, so that he remarked, ---

"How very rude the fellow is to be sure."

"He has never seen such a handsome barbarian as you before, dear," she answered, and then motioned the servant to lead the way. This he did, until he stood before a large door, which he flung open, and in a stentorian voice announced, ---

"The Princess Yobmot, and the strange savage from the infernal regions."

Flonatin looked daggers at the fellow, and felt that it would have been a relief to his feelings if he could have kicked him downstairs. But the Princess only smiled, and led her blushing companion into a large apartment.

As the distinguished arrivals entered there was such a buzzing of voices as to be almost deafening, and Flin Flon was positively confused. It seemed like Babel, and as if hundreds of persons were trying to talk each other deaf. Ranged round a very long table were about seventy Esnesnon dames, and so the cause of the hubbub will be readily understood; and it will be further comprehended that amongst such a large gathering of ladies who had assembled together for the transaction of public business that there was a pretty considerable amount of jealousy and backbiting. As the Princess entered, all the ladies bowed and rose from their seats, and one lady,

whose summers and winters together would have made up a respectable sum of years, so large, in fact, that ill-natured people, especially expectant heirs, might have said of her that it was high time she got herself comfortably cremated. But, judging from her lusty lungs and apparent vigour, she had no intention of taking her departure for the upper world for some time, which was rather fortunate for the upper world, though there is strong reason to believe that she has since come to dwell amongst us, that is, assuming Mr. Ytidrusba's theory to be correct. This dear creature's name was Sregdorpittemmocaig, rather a sweet thing in names when pronounced quickly. Well, Mrs. (please take the name as written) rose and said, ---

"I vote Her Royal Highness takes the chair."

Which being duly seconded, and unanimously carried, the Princess took the chair accordingly, and having done so she proceeded to address the meeting as follows: ---

"I really had no intention, my learned sisters, to preside at your meeting to-day, but since you have done me the honour of voting me to the important office I cannot very well refuse. As you will perceive, I have taken the liberty of bringing a stranger and one of the softer sex here" (at this there was much laughter and a few groans. Flin still kept his face closely muffled in the shawl in accordance with the commands of the Princess, and many of the ladies had made desperate efforts to get a peep at the intruder, but without avail, for the disguise was effectual). "I know that this is not allowable according to our rules," the chairwoman proceeded, "but a point may very well be stretched in this case when I tell you that our visitor is no less distinguished a person that the poor barbarian who has arrived from goodness knows where." At this announcement there was intense excitement among the "learned sisters," and the buzzing recommenced, as everyone asked everyone else a dozen questions all at once, and in a manner that only a lady knows how to do. When order had been once more restored the Princess proceeded, "I thought that your interest would be aroused as soon as you were informed who the person was, and I venture to express a hope, ladies, that his presence will not be allowed to interfere with the transaction of our business. And for fear your attention may be too much distracted I think it will be better for the creature to keep his features concealed." "No, no, no" was the unanimous cry, "pray let us have a look at him." "Well, ladies, if you are so anxious to see him you shall, but I trust it will not cause you to neglect duty." Mr. Flonatin felt by no means comfortable. To have to stand the gaze of seventy pairs of feminine eyes, even though the eyes belonged to people who had tails, was a trial that the stoutest-hearted man would have shrunk from. It certainly taxed all his powers. But he was no coward and he made up his mind to face even this dreadful ordeal with that fortitude and endurance which were among his chief characteristics, and so at a signal from the Princess he threw off the disguising shawl, and like the Roman slave of old before the senators, he stood revealed in all his blushing beauty, and with a sweet smile on his genial countenance he bowed politely to the assembly. Then there broke out a buzzing which resembled nothing so much as numerous swarms of bees who were disputing possession of the bough of some tree.

But every now and then Flin was enabled to catch such sentences as, ---

"Isn't he good-looking?"

"Oh, what a duck!"

"What a charming little fellow, to be sure!"

"What a fine nose he has got!"

"And what a lovely mouth!"

"And such a noble head!"

"And only to think that such a dear fellow should be a savage. How very shocking, to be sure! "

These expressions of admiration did not escape the ears of the Princess, as was evident by the severe frown which contracted her brow. She thumped on the table with her rod of office rather vigorously; this rod of office looked to Flin like silver, but as a matter of fact it was platinum, a metal in common use throughout Esnesnon. But though the Princess thumped and thumped again with her rod, it was some time before she could restore order, for, alas! the tongues of seventy ladies having once got into full swing cannot be stopped suddenly as if they were steam engines. It requires a great deal of manoeuvring and tact to bring them to "dead slow" and then to "stop." But by dint of much hammering and repeated shouting her Highness at length succeeded in getting silence.

"Really, ladies," she observed, in a tone of anger, "this is unpardonable. I declare one would think you had never seen a male before. And miserable barbarian though this one is, you ought not to forget yourselves in such manner."

At this reproof many of the ladies turned up their noses in a rather indignant way, though they did not let the Princess see them, and many more whispered one to the other, ---

"The idea!"

"Did ever you know of such a thing?"

"The forward hussy, to speak to us like that!"

"I should like to pull her hair for her, so I should!"

"The brazen minx!"

"For a child like her to talk in such a manner is unpardonable."

But of course these expressions also were not allowed to reach the chairwoman's ears.

Again the Princess thumped upon the table with her rod, and the tongues ceased, though very reluctantly, for, like a large bell that has once been set swinging, there was a clang and a ding every now and then, although silence seemed to be restored.

At length, when the dear creatures had quite ceased, Mrs Sregdorpittemmocaig rose. (In dealing with this lady in future I shall take the liberty of leaving her name a blank, as it is a very terrible one to write, and I know I shall get into trouble with the printers.) This lady rose stern and grave, as became one of her age, and said, ---

"Your Royal Highness and ladies, as one of the oldest members of this board, I may be permitted to make a few remarks."

"What presumption, to be sure," whispered a rather good-looking young lady to her neighbour.

"Yes, indeed, the stupid old thing. Why doesn't she stop at home and look after her husband and children?" was the reply whispered back.

But, all unconscious of these loving remarks, the ancient dame proceeded, ---

"What I have to say will be very brief. I cannot but think that our beloved Princess was actuated by the best of motives in bringing this curious being here. But to be candid --- and those who know me know that I cannot be anything else ---; ("Oh, the wicked story-teller!" whispered another lady) --- I must say I think it was rather bad taste. We have much business to get through, but I am afraid that certain of the younger members of the board will neglect the business to stare at that idiotic-looking savage."

"Personal, personal," cried several voices.

"Why, the old wretch is jealous," whispered several more.

"I have no intention of being personal," Mrs ---- went on. "My friends know that personalities are about the last things I indulge in."

"Oh, oh!" from various quarters.

"These interruptions are unseemly, ladies, and I appeal to the chair lady to protect me from insult. Certain persons like to think themselves of importance when they are in reality nonentities."

"Names, names," cried several of the members.

"I refuse to mention names."

"Shame! shame! apologise."

"Really, ladies, I must interfere," said the Princess, thumping the table. "Such conduct is far from polite."

"I believe, your Highness, that she refers to me," cried a young lady, as she sprang to her feet. "And if she dares to make such a remark again I will scratch her face."

"I will box your ears for you, you minx," retorted Mrs ------.

"I should like to see you do it," cried the other one in a towering rage.

"You shall soon see me and feel me too, you young chit," sneered the amiable Mrs ------.

To what extent the quarrel might have gone there is no telling, had not her Highness rose and in a loud voice cried, ---

"I command silence. Otherwise I will leave the room. Such behaviour is really disgraceful." But in spite of this threat the two ladies continued to look daggers at each other, and it was some minutes before the young one could stop her tongue, for she was determined to have the "last word," even "if she died for it." But order at last being restored, Mrs ---- proceeded, ---

"I did not think, your Highness and ladies, that ever I should have lived to suffer such unmerited insult as has been thrust upon me this day. My length of service, unremitting attention to the interests of the board, and indefatigable zeal --- "

"Don't blow your own trumpet," from a voice at the end of the table.

"That person, I won't say lady, who has dared to interrupt me ought to know that self-praise is a thing I never indulge in. I am too upright in my conduct, too honest in my motives --- "

"Order, order, to business, sit down," were the cries which arose from all sides; but the charming Mrs ---- was by no means the woman to be talked out of her rights. She scowled at her fellow-members, and looked an incalculable number of daggers at the young maiden who had threatened to scratch her face.

A scene of indescribable confusion followed. All the seventy tongues commenced to jangle again, the ladies sprang to their feet, arms were waved menacingly in the air. Mutual recriminations, jeers, sneers, and tears, were frequently indulged in, and as Mr. Flonatin surveyed the scene in alarm he raised his eyes aloft, and breathed a fervent prayer that Providence would spare dear America from such a scourge as women's societies.

24

I will not be so ungallant as to say that the fair members of the Society for the Protection of Men indulged in anything like a row, but I will say that for a time a wordy war waged, and if it is possible, by any stretch of imagination, for my peacefully-inclined readers to realise what would be the result of seventy feminine tongues suddenly let loose to talk against time, they will not be surprised to learn that Mr. Flonatin, old and experienced traveller though he was, turned pale and faint, and as he saw the seventy pairs of flashing eyes that were darting fire, and the seventy pairs of arms that were sawing the air, and the seventy pairs of lips moving with lightning-like rapidity, and seventy noses turned up in withering scorn, and seventy breasts heaving with the volcanic wrath which agitated their fair owners, I say as he saw these things he trembled, and wished himself safely back again with his old housekeeper in his snug dwelling at New York. The Princess Yobmot, noticing how agitated and alarmed he was, moved from her seat, and taking his hand led him to a couch and whispered, ---

"Don't be alarmed, dear. Although they make a terrible noise they are quite harmless." Then going back to her chair again she hammered the table in such a manner that the tongues began to move less vigorously, and when partial silence had been restored she exclaimed, in a stentorian voice, and in a manner that left no room for doubt that she was in earnest, "Ladies, ladies, ladies," repeating the word three times, and raising her voice each time, "this is absolutely disgraceful, and if you do not preserve order I will dissolve the meeting. I command you to be silent. Remember I am your King's daughter."

And there was silence, save for an intermittent outburst, that gradually grew fainter and fainter, like the mutterings of a dying thunderstorm. And at last the dear creatures commenced to smile, and the smiling was contagious, until the whole seventy faces were as bright as the radiant beams of the rising sun of the upper world. It was a glorious sight to behold.

Then the Princess, all smiles too, once more addressed the meeting.

"I am very much obliged to you, ladies, and now we will proceed to business."

Two of the young members here caused some slight interruption by having a dispute about some fashions which had appeared in the Esnesnon Fashion Guide, but the disturbance was quickly quelled, and harmony and good feeling prevailed --- that is, apparently, for what the true feelings of those seventy dear hearts were there are no means of knowing. A woman's heart is a profound and awful mystery. Even Mr. Flonatin is silent on the subject.

"The first business I have on the paper, ladies," said the Princess, "is the case of an unfortunate male who has been deserted by his wife. He is a mere youth, being but fifty years of age. He has two infants, aged seventeen and twenty respectively. They are both girls, and he applies to us to protect him and these babes from his wife, who may probably return and squander the property, and turn the father and children out. This seems to me to be a very deserving case, and I think we may safely pass a resolution to apply to the Court for the necessary protection order. It is very evident that this wife is a very worthless and bad woman, and the poor husband should be protected from her violence."

Some slight discussion here arose, but it was very short, and the resolution was put to the meeting and carried unanimously.

"The next case, ladies, is that of a youth aged forty, who was inveigled away from the legal guardianship of his parents by a young woman. She kept him a prisoner in a house in a low part of the town for some time, but he was subsequently turned out and sent home."

"What evidence is there, your Highness," asked a lady, "that this boy was taken away against his will?"

"According to the paper here there is the evidence of his parents, as well as his own statement. He says that he was not party. "

"Then I think it is a matter for our consideration," observed another lady. "I am sorry to say that cases of abduction of young men and boys is sadly on the increase, and should be dealt with a firm hand. It is really a disgrace to a civilised country like this that such things should be possible."

"I quite agree with your remarks," said the Princess; "I have been shocked of late to see the number of cases in the papers of young men who have been led away. It is terrible, indeed, and the severest punishment should be meted to any woman who is guilty of such a crime. It is high time that there was reform."

"Why doesn't she set an example?" simpered a blushing damsel to another blushing damsel on her left. "She is worse than anybody else in Esnesnon."

Fortunately this remark did not reach the Princess's ears, or it might have fared badly with the fair libeller.

"The next case," pursued the chairwoman, "is a very sad one indeed. It is that of a young male with several children, and for years he has laboured to support his family, while the wife has remained at home in idleness. The other day he came home, and his wife asked him for some currency, which he refused to give her, where-upon she commenced to beat him, knocking him down, breaking one of his arms, injuring an eye, and his tail, and otherwise maltreating him, and rendering him incapable of pursuing his occupation. He applies to us to enable him to get a separation from the woman, so that he may live in peace and follow his calling for the benefit of his children without interruption. It does occur to me, ladies, that this is a most pitiable case. This poor young male has been struggling for years to support his dissolute wife and his children respectably. But his efforts have been useless, and he has repeatedly been most severely beaten and maltreated. I hope you will be able to pass a resolution to meet the young man's wishes."

"What is his occupation, your Highness?" asked a member.

"He is a public chariot-driver; very hardworking and steady. But his earnings are barely sufficient even to supply necessaries."

Here Mrs ---- rose up suddenly. Her face wore an unusual look of sternness.

"I must oppose this application," she said.

A roar of laughter greeted the announcement, but, unmindful of the interruption, the lady proceeded , ---

"I repeat that I oppose the application, on the grounds that a male who drives a public conveyance cannot be a respectable person." ("Oh, oh!" and cries of "Shame!")

"Somebody cries 'Oh!' and 'Shame!' but I may be permitted to say that I have made a study of the whole race of chariot-drivers, and have had as much experience of them as anyone in Esnesnon." (Loud laughter.)

"You may laugh as much as you like, ladies, but I assert fearlessly that my experience has been bitter. You are aware that scarcely a week passes but what I have to summon one or other of these wretched people, male of female, for overcharging me."

"Why don't you keep a chariot of your own?" from a voice at the end of the table.

Mrs ----looked in the direction from whence it came, and had she recognised the owner of the voice at that moment it might have gone hard with the owner.

"I will not notice that insulting question further than by saying that the reason I don't keep my own chariot is entirely my own business. I choose to patronise the public vehicles in the public interest; and the single handed war which I have so long waged against these chariot-driving sharks ought to have earned for me the public esteem and support, instead of ridicule and contempt. My disinterested exertions --- "

"Humbug," from a lady.

"Who says that I am a humbug?" roared Mrs ---- but no answer was forthcoming, and so she continued: "I repeat that my disinterested exertions --- "

"Twaddle," from a little woman at the extreme end of the room, opposite the speaker.

The veins in Mrs ----'s forehead were dangerously distended, and her countenance was a pea green. So great was her wrath that she could not find words, or rather the words rushed to her lips in such numbers that her tongue could not move fast enough; but presently she managed to stammer, ---

"Who dares to accuse me of talking twaddle? Let the wretch stand up and repeat it, and I promise her such a boxing of the ears as she has never before experienced. Who is the culprit? I call upon her to stand out, and if not I brand her as a coward and a --- "

"Order!" cried the chairwoman, just in time to stop Mrs ---- from saying something very naughty.

"You may well cry order," remarked Mrs ---- sarcastically, "but why don't you keep the other members in order? I am always being insulted. I am one of the most amiable and peacefully-disposed members at the board --- (loud and derisive laughter) --- but I have to put up with more insults than anyone else. It is too bad, that it is. Who is the wretch who said I talked twaddle? Why does she not speak?"

But the culprit showed no signs of declaring herself, and so Mrs sneered, ---

"She may well keep silent, the miserable minx. It would be better if she were to stay at home and keep the dwelling clean, instead of coming here to interrupt a lady."

"Mrs ----, I call you to order," cried the Princess, rising suddenly and banging the table with her rod. "You shall not indulge in such personalities in my presence. It is really disgraceful, and this board is getting quite a reputation for squabbling. You will please to confine your remarks to the business before the meeting; and any personal quarrel you may have with any member you must settle elsewhere."

"This is too bad, that it is, I declare," exclaimed Mrs ---- bursting into tears. At least she drew forth a large handkerchief which was made from asbestos and buried her face in it, and between hysterical sobs she managed to stammer, "I am a most ill-used and persecuted woman, that I am. Everybody is against me, and yet I never quarrel with anyone, and always carefully avoid saying anything that is calculated to give offence. It is shameful, so it is, and it is seriously affecting my health. I can't stand it. I will resign, that's what I'll do."

("Hear, hear," from all parts.)

In an instant Mrs had dried her tears, and was looking round defiantly at her tormentors.

"No doubt," she said, "many of you would be delighted if I were to do that, but I won't. You shall not have the satisfaction of saying you drove me from the board."

"Mrs ---- ," roared the Princess, "I will dissolve the meeting if you do not confine yourself to business."

"Very well," answered the lady, "but permit me to say, your Highness, that you might show me a little more consideration, even though the young members of the board know no better. But to return to the subject, though I may mention that if anyone else is vulgar enough to interrupt I shall treat them with profound contempt. With reference to the case of this chariot-driver ---- though I may first parenthetically remark that if I am insulted again I shall consult my woman-of- law ---- I say that this male is not deserving of our support. I would just pause for a moment to remark that I shall write to the editor of the Gazette and complain of the treatment I met with here. A male who drives a public vehicle cannot be other than a worthless vagabond. Just one caution to those ladies who treat me with such marked disrespect. I shall in future provide myself with a whip, and shall not hesitate to use it. But to return to this chariot-driver. I cannot support his application. He is unworthy of any consideration. I confess that I don't like chariot-drivers, they are as objectionable to me as vermin. I like to prosecute them, torment them. I should like indeed to improve them off the face of our beautiful world, which they only serve to befoul. I therefore oppose this application."

"Upon what grounds?" asked the Princess.

"On the grounds of his being a chariot- driver."

"Have you no other reason?"

"None whatever."

"You don't know the male personally?"

"No."

"Nor anything against his personal character?"

"No. But he is a chariot-driver, and that is sufficient."

"There I differ from you. It is not sufficient for us to merely consider what his occupation is. The fact of his being a male, and subject to ill treatment at the hands of his wife, ought to arouse our tenderest sympathies, and I hope, ladies, those sympathies will not be withheld. It is ever woman's duty to protect her weaker brother, and personal animosity ought not to be allowed to stand in the way of our doing our duty."

"I beg to correct your Highness," growled Mrs ---- . "I have no personal animosity --- "

"We will proceed to vote, ladies," said the Princess, with supreme contempt for the speaker. "I regret that I have no person ---; "

"Vote, vote."

"You shall hear me. I have no --- "

"Vote, vote"

"Sit down."

"I sha'n't sit down. I have --- "

"Silence, order!"

"I won't be silent, I won't keep order," shrieked the irascible lady. "I --- "

But the rest of her sentence was drowned by the roar of voices which hailed the declaration that the vote had been carried with only one dissentient. The chairwoman now announced that the business was concluded, and so the meeting broke up, and then once more the seventy tongues were set in violent motion. And as the ladies put on their shawls and wished each other good- bye there was as much kissing and shaking of hands as if all these dear creatures were angels inhabiting a peaceful Eden. And Mrs ---- was profuse in her compliments to this lady for the elegant cut of her robe, and to that one for the simple yet refined manner in which she dressed her hair. And the good- natured soul kissed and shook hands just as though she was in earnest, and then she invited several of her dear friends to a quiet little Scantonguedal drinking party. Scantonguedal is a favourite beverage with the fair sex in the inner world. It is made from a peculiar grain that grows there, and its effect is to exhilarate and induce a freedom of expression which enables the dear creatures to speak about their friends without any sense of responsibility or restraint. On that account the ladies are much given to indulgence in it.

25

When Dr. Yrekcauq heard that his plans had been defeated by a stroke of diplomacy on the part of his rival Ytidrusba, he was naturally very much annoyed, for he could not bear defeat of any kind. While such a defeat as this was certainly a crushing one.

The intelligent and discerning reader --- and it is pleasant to think that there are none but intelligent and discerning readers --- will long ere this have discovered that King Gubmuh was a weak, if not an impotent monarch, and that the responsibility of governing such a vast state of Esnesnon devolved in reality upon the great men Ytidrusba and Yrekcauq; and though they might have differences, they arose pure and simply from the earnestness with which each gentleman tried to do his duty. Both saw that the King was a mere puppet, and in endeavouring to guide him the right way it must not be thought that they had any self-interested motives. Oh, dear, no! Such a supposition would be the very height of absurdity. They were statesmen, you see.

Doctor Yrekcauq knew that the national exchequer was in a state bordering on bankruptcy, and the arrival of such a curiosity as Flin offered an unusual opportunity to raise revenue. Of course Yrekcauq might have been actuated by some personal feeling, as he and Ytidrusba had long struggled for supremacy, and any advantage gained by one was zealously resented by the other. The fact is, the two great men belonged to exactly opposite schools, and the theories of Ytidrusba were contemptuously snubbed by Yrekcauq, and vice versa, though both, under the guise of that savoirfaire, as we should say, which should ever distinguish leading men, endeavoured to hide the hatred they bore each other, and which rankled in their breasts. Be that as it may, Yrekcauq was unquestionably very bitter. It was said that he had been one of the most servile of courtiers, and a sort of lickspittle at Court. But of this, of course, there is no accurate information. The statement herein made is based entirely upon mere hearsay, and so much be received with caution. However, when he saw that his opponent had gained such an ascendancy over him, he placed his resignation in the hands of his Majesty's secretary, and immediately two "parties" were formed. The one, which may be called the Yrekcauqites, supported by the Anti-Humbug News; and the other, the Ytidrusbaites, represented by the Gazette. Amongst the former, one of the staunchest, and certainly the loudest, opponents of the Government was Mrs Sregdorpittemmocaig. This prettily-named lady had conceived the most intense dislike for Flin Flon, and it is possible she was the only lady who had ever done this. Why she should have shown so much enmity it is difficult to tell, though it was hinted that she was jealous of the Princess, and would like to have appropriated Flin herself. But not being able to do this, and being peculiarly splenetic, she allied herself to the opposite faction, and poured out her vials of wrath, which were peculiarly vitriolic. She flooded the News with articles from her pen; and while, ostensibly, she attacked the distinguished traveller, it did not need half an eye to see that she had a grievance, and she took this opportunity to air it. As a specimen of this strong-minded lady's style the following article from her pen, which appeared in the Esnesnon News, will not be without interest. It will be observed that the virulence could scarcely be surpassed even by certain American papers, and the only wonder is that the News should have opened its columns to the contributions of a lady whose mind was so visibly inflamed. This is the article, which is in the form of a letter and was addressed to the editor: ---

"It has generally been supposed that our government of Esnesnon would bear favourable comparison for wisdom and impartiality with any government either in this or any other world, if there are any other worlds. We have hitherto boasted that we were the most civilised, most learned, most enlightened, and most refined people in existence, but, alas! this has been a pleasant dream from which we have been rudely awakened, and I fear that it must to our shame be admitted that, after all, we have not reached the point of perfection upon which we have prided ourselves, and that we are simply living in a state of moral darkness. Had the nation been told a little while ago that the unexpected arrival amongst us of a deformed, inexpressibly ugly and tailless savage, who in appearance would not bear comparison with some of our loathsome animals, would have caused such a change at Court, and even amongst the people the assertion would have been looked upon as monstrously ridiculous, but we are suddenly shaken from our torpor to find that the very base of our Governmental fabric is rotten, and the Court itself full of corruption. This is a sad confession, but its truth is too glaring to be glossed over. The King has proved himself to be no longer fit to reign over a great and free people, and in the name of that people I call upon him to abdicate. Not the least of the causes why he should do this, apart from his recognition of this horrid barbarian, is his constant refusal to recognise my petitions for a reform in our public chariot laws." (This was the lady's favourite hobby, and she never lost an opportunity of riding it.) "This is a subject, as the public are well aware, to which I have devoted some of the best years of my life --- a life, in fact, that has disinterestedly been devoted to the public welfare. Petition after petition have I sent up to his Majesty, and from a careful calculation I estimate that for these petitions I have used one and a-half tons of paper, two tons of ink, and have spent twenty years in writing them. Surely such perseverance as this might have met with better recognition at his Majesty's hands. But I have reason to think that my papers have ever been kept back by the miserable, cringing, dust-eating toadies who swarm around the throne, and are ready at any moment to sacrifice their dignity, their manliness, their dearest friends even, for the sake of a royal smile. Such filthy servility makes one shudder for the safety of the high-souled honour which has hitherto distinguished our males. Our chariot laws are a disgrace; and though 'reform' has ever been my watchword and battle-cry, reform has never come, and we poor citizens are still left to groan under the barbarous yoke of these spawns of venomous reptiles --- the chariot-drivers. Citizens! I ask when is this to end? When are these vile poison-breathing vipers, the drivers, to be swept from the face of our fair earth? I call upon you to arise and annihilate them. Royalty has turned a deaf ear to our prayers. It is useless to any longer look for help from that quarter. We must help ourselves. We must rise strong and determined, and show those in office that we, the enlightened, the brave, the noble, the highly civilised citizens of this fair land are not to be treated as if we were born slaves. Reform ---;Reform --- Reform --- is my cry. Brave women throughout the length and breadth of the land rally round my standard, the standard of freedom. Let us demand our rights from the King, who is simply the puppet of miserable cringing males. We should have a woman on the throne, women at the Court. Let Parliament take the matter up vigorously. Let them call upon his Majesty to abdicate in favour of his daughter, and then indeed will our day of glory have arrived. Then shall we see the loathsome race of drivers exterminated, as we should exterminate any other foul and obnoxious insects. We shall no longer be charged double fares. We shall no longer have to stand at our doors and wrangle with the vermin for the sake of a paltry sum, which we now dispute on the highest of principles --- the principle of right, of truth, of justice. Not for myself do I battle. My disinterestedness and retiring disposition are too well known. But in the name of our weak brethren I cry aloud for freedom. Gentlemales should be able to travel in comfort and security without being liable to be taken advantage of when unprotected by a lady. These execrable and foul toads, the chariot-drivers, should no longer have it in their power to overcharge us; they should no longer be able to insult every helpless male who is forced from necessity to avail himself of the public vehicles. They should no longer be allowed to sneer at and insult us when we offer them their bare fare. They should no longer be allowed to refuse to carry me whenever they happen to recognise me. If I have prosecuted them it has been in the public interest. I have fought tirelessly and unflinchingly in the good cause, and I venture to think that I have earned well of my country. Arise, brave countrywomen; arise and strike for freedom. Bring down the iron-shod heel of Liberty on the back of the Hydra-of-Imposition and crush it. Grind it into the earth. Annihilate the odious, filthy monstrosities, public chariot-drivers, and then indeed will peace and goodwill be amongst us. We demand free chariots. Their drivers should be supported by the State. The time shall come when there shall no longer be a charge for being conveyed through the public streets. Let us hasten that blessed time. We groan and sweat under the tyranny of the drivers. They are a bane and a curse in the land. Is our bread dear? it is owing to the drivers. Is our fuel outrageous in price? it is owing to the drivers. Is meal beyond the reach of the poor? it is owing to the drivers. Is our army degenerated? it is owing to the drivers. Are our courts corrupt? it is owing to the drivers. Is our national exchequer empty? it is owing to the drivers. In short, these demons of darkness are the root of all evil. They have made us slaves. They are pestilential blots upon the face of our fair land. Banish them to the infernal regions above, where only are they fit to dwell. From this hour let us never rest until we have got our rights. Let our voices be heard in the busy day as well as in the silent night. Let us shriek from the house tops, from the street corners, from the public platforms, from the courts of justice, or rather injustice, and let us never cease shrieking." (God help the peaceful citizens, thought Flin, as he read these lines. If this dreadful woman was to carry out her threat and never cease shrieking, it would be a blessing if doomsday were to arrive. He knew certain ladies in America who were somewhat given to shrieking, and who wanted to reform everything and everybody and build a new world, but then they did not shriek ceaselessly. Sometimes their tongues got tired and they stopped. But in Esnesnon, where woman ruled, her tongue seemed to be even more pliable than her upper-world sisters, and that was saying a great deal. To be subjected to the ceaseless shrieking of strong-minded women was so unutterably horrible that the seven plagues of Egypt must have been rather nice by comparison). "Send me to Parliament," continued the nobly constituted and gentle, dove-like Mrs ---- , "send me to Parliament. Make me the champion of your rights. I will battle in your behalf for freedom. No longer shall you groan under the curse of chariot-drivers; you shall have everything for nothing, and be able to do as you like. Agitate! agitate! agitate! This must be our rallying cry until we have swept away those barriers which separate us from that long-looked- for and happy time when woman shall reign supreme in the land, and the whole race of miserable, helpless males shall be taught to know their place, and not aspire as they do now to offices that they are totally incompetent to fill. Once more I say, send me to Parliament, and than I promise such things shall be done that males shall tremble and women shall rejoice. The Court shall be entirely reconstructed. It shall no longer be sullied by the helpless imbecility of such men as Ytidrusba, whose vanities are sufficient to fill our lunatic asylums with patients. A woman on the throne, women in Parliament, women only at Court, women only in the council chamber, and then, then indeed will the long- foretold time of eternal and universal peace have dawned upon our fair land. Help me to bring about this desired end, and I promise that until our rights have been obtained my tongue shall never cease to be heard day or night.

"SREGDORPITTEMMOCAIG."

As Flin read this he sighed, and thought that a universal prayer-meeting should be called in Esnesnon to offer up prayers that the unfortunate citizens might be saved from the awful threat of this dreadful lady. For her tongue to be kept going day and night would be an infliction that would surpass all the diabolical tortures that were ever invented for the inhabitants of Hades.

But Flin's alarm on behalf of the Esnesnons was unnecessary. They were pretty well used to the gentle creature, and simply smiled as she shrieked herself hoarse, for experience had taught them that she was all bark and no bite. She had long been the bane of the unfortunate chariot-drivers' lives; she had persecuted them with relentless hatred until it had come to be a saying that the sight of one of the detested race made the amiable lady rabid.

On the other hand, if she hated the drivers, they returned the compliment, and they had banded themselves together to protect their interests from the repeated attacks of the lady. So that there was a constant war being waged in Esnesnon between Mrs ---- and the drivers. To a foreigner this state of affairs seemed incredible. It was hard to believe that in a country which boasted of its pre-human civilisation such a thing should be tolerated. Mr. Flonatin felt sure that even in darkened England, to say nothing of his own beloved and enlightened country, such a person as Mrs ---- would soon be popped into a straight jacket, and allowed to howl herself hoarse in the padded room of a lunatic asylum. But then Esnesnon was not America nor England. It was a peculiar country, to say the least of it, and they were curious people too who dwelt there. Prehuman they might truly be said to be since --- according to Mr Flonatin's notions --- they had not reached that stage of civilisation which even the most unenlightened of upper world people enjoyed. In fact, he could not help thinking that it was a veritable land of lunatics. And when his own countryman had fixed the locality of the infernal regions in the centre of the earth they had not gone very wide of the mark.

The violent letter of Mrs ---- which appeared in the News caused some little excitement amongst the faction which she led. And it called forth an equally abusive article in the Gazette, in which it was asked: ---

"How long is the peace of the land to be disturbed by the horrible howling of this mad-brained creature? When are the peaceful subjects to be protected from the seditious ravings of this hag? When are the unfortunate and long-oppressed drivers to be relieved of this terrible virago who has pressed upon them like a horrid incubus? When is this desperate and unprincipled woman's tongue to be bridled? The time has arrived when something must be done. Man has groaned too long under the iron sway of feminine rule, rendered the more galling and the more unendurable by this person's ceaseless shriekings, which have been heard for the last hundred years. It is time that man should now assert his independence. He must arise and make his voice heard from the four corners of our land. And the first step gained towards this sighed-for freedom will be the downfall of Mrs ---- . The King must be protected from her insults. And so far from the citizens sending her to Parliament they should send her to an asylum. Every woman in Parliament should, for the honour and glory of her beautiful country, feel that it was a sacred duty she owed to pass a bill making it an unlawful offence to talk as this person has talked. And until this is done our boasted freedom will be but a mockery, for women have made us slaves. Under their merciless sway we have been compelled to grovel in the dust. We have been humiliated before our children, and our hearts could scarcely be called our own. This state of things must no longer be allowed to continue. The end must be hastened, for it is our firm belief that man was never intended to be a woman's slave. Parliament should be constituted of an equal number of males and women. And only when this is done will many of the evils now complained of be remedied."

The paper war was carried on day after day for a considerable time, but like all such wars there was a great deal of noise and not much harm. The poor old King did sometimes tremble in his sandals a little as he heard the uproar, and there were moments when he felt tempted to abdicate, so that his daughter might ascend the throne and he himself be relieved of the cares of State. But he had a few faithful advisers around him who counselled him to hold out bravely and never show the white feather. Amongst these counsellors Ytidrusba was the loudest and most persevering. He positively hated Mrs. ---- and perhaps no one more than himself had groaned so deeply under feminine rule. His wife was particularly strong-minded, and half inclined to enlist under the rebel standard of Sregdorpittemmocaig. She kept her husband in a state of feverish suspense, and almost a state of poverty, for though she had a large income of her own she barely allowed him sufficient for his personal necessities. Though his office at Court was worth but little, and that little, owing to the state of the nation exchequer, had not been paid for a long time, this was shocking condition of things, and Flin could not help but think that the system of government was rotten to the foundation; and furthermore, he was daring enough to think that this was entirely due to the freedom which women there enjoyed. But though he thought this he had sufficient discretion to keep it to himself, as he was in a land where the power of woman was absolute, and he trembled to think what the consequences might be if he had ventured to open his lips in support of suffering man.

He could not refrain, however, from sympathising deeply with Mr. Ytidrusba, for whom he entertained considerable liking. He pitied him from his heart, and felt inclined to make an attempt to get more consideration shown to him by his wife, for Ytidrusba had made a confidant of him. Not without much misgiving and some inward trembling did the old magician hear the proposal; but Flin's argument, that he as a foreigner would in all probability be able to make an impression on Mrs. Ytidrusba, was considered a good one, and Mr. Ytidrusba told Flin that if he liked to take all the responsibility on his own shoulders he might venture to talk with the lady, but under no circumstances, and as he valued his life, was he to tell Mrs. Ytidrusba that her husband knew anything of the matter. This was agreed to, and it was arranged that Flin should lose no time in seeing Mrs Ytidrusba, and the result of that interview will be duly chronicled in the next chapter.

26

In undertaking to see Mrs. Ytidrusba and endeavour to work upon her feelings, so that the husband's position might be ameliorated, Mr. Flonatin was actuated by the broadest of philanthropic motives, and the fears of Mr. Ytidrusba that such an interview could scarcely fail to lead to unpleasantness Flin laughed at. He had always been used to see woman in her proper station, and the idea of her ruling and keeping man in a state that was only one degree removed from serfdom was so contrary to all his ideas that he could not realise it, and thought that such a condition could only be due to the want of some proper manly feeling on the part of the male sex in Esnesnon. Under these circumstances he believed he was perfectly justified, in the interest of his sex, to try and emancipate Esnesnon from feminine rule, and that by beginning with Mrs Ytidrusba the thin edge of the wedge would be got in. Nor did he, on consideration, anticipate much difficulty. He had hitherto flattered himself that he possessed considerable influence over ladies. This was certainly the case in his own country, where the dear creatures worshipped him, but like most travellers he was inclined to judge every other nation by his own standard. He went into a strange country. He saw new customs, new ideas, new systems, new beliefs, and because they were new and strange to him, he at once made the common error of imagining that they must be ridiculous because they were unlike those he had been used to.

In saying this much I hope it will not be thought that I am supporting Esnesnon against Mr. Flonatin. Far from that. But I am strongly desirous of being impartial, and I know that the error into which our traveller fell is such a common one with all persons who go out of their own country, that I feel that something ought to be done to correct it. If anyone were to travel to the moon, and discover that the inhabitants of the planet walked upon their heads instead of their feet, he would not be justified in returning here and reporting that the lunar orb was peopled by lunatics, as the peculiar custom would no doubt be suited to the peculiar country.

It will be readily understood that unused, poor fellow, as he was to female rule, Mr. Flonatin could not help looking with contempt upon the male population. He had not been ground under the iron of wifely rule, and therefore it would have been difficult to have imagined anyone less qualified for the task he had set himself. But though Ytidrusba cautioned him of the risk he ran, he only laughed, and seemed to treat it as a good joke, for he imagined petticoat government to be the very height of absurdity.

Unfortunately for him at this time the Princess Yobmot was away, as she had gone to a far distant part of the country on some political business in connection with her father's Court. And before going she had given Ytidrusba strict injunctions to take every care of Flin, or, as she playfully called him, her little sweetheart. The magician was therefore very reluctant to give his consent to Flin's scheme, but the latter ultimately overcame the old man's scruples, and it was arranged that Flin should see what he could do with Mrs. Ytidrusba. This lady was a power in the land. Her influence at Court was immense, and in the Parliament her voice was, perhaps, one of the loudest and strongest. This is to be taken in a moral sense, for, physically, her voice was rather weak and decidedly squeaky.

The day fixed for the interview came at last, and Mr. Flonatin was ushered into the great lady's presence, who received him with frigid dignity, not altogether unmingled with contempt. She was a woman of very commanding presence, towering far above Flin in height; and if she ever had possessed anything like beauty, it had long ago faded out, and left nothing but a sour, crabbed look. As the distinguished traveller entered the room he bowed very low indeed. The lady returned his bow by a very stiff movement, and then, raising a large diamond magnifier to her eye, she examined her visitor curiously, and it was evident that she only refrained from bursting into a loud laugh with the greatest difficulty. Mr Flonatin was, of course, very much annoyed, and he states that he cannot imagine what she could possibly have found either to laugh at or stare at, and he could only pardon her rudeness on the ground that she was an utter barbarian.

The lady was the first to speak.

"Well, my funny little fellow," she remarked, with a good deal of sarcasm, "and what is your pleasure?".

Flin's face went very red. He thought that this marked disrespect would have disgraced even the most vulgar and the lowest-bred female in his own country. Moreover, he could not imagine why she addressed him as a "funny little fellow." He had never in his life had the slightest pretensions to funniness. Comicality was out of his line. He was a thoughtful, grave, scientific man. This was evidenced by the total disregard he had for anything like dandyism. In fact, he had been in the habit of looking upon that man who paid much attention to dress as decidedly effeminate; and, therefore, he was considerably exercised in his mind to know in what way he was "funny." Possibly Mrs Ytidrusba would speedily have given a reason for so addressing him, had she been requested to do so. For we cannot always see ourselves as we are seen by others. However, Flin managed to keep down his choler, but he was strengthened in his purpose to use every endeavour to awaken the male sex of Esnesnon to a sense of their utter degradation and to incite them to revolt against the feminine rule. As a stranger in the new world, this was, to say the least, a very dangerous resolve; and it is more than probable that had he been better acquainted with the fearful risks he would run, he would have shrank from the danger. But it was this very ignorance that made him bold. The heart does not fear the danger it knows naught of. And this was Mr Flonatin's case. Moreover, he was desirous of serving his friend Ytidrusba, and this desire gave him courage. He bowed to the lady once more, and was about to offer her a seat, when she put out her hand, and, taking his, led him to a couch.

"And so you are the singular being who has come from some horrible and nameless region," she observed, as she applied a handkerchief highly scented with some powerful and peculiar scent to her nose, which was exceedingly large. "Well, I must say you are a perfect natural curiosity."

"I may be permitted to set you right on one point, madam," Flin replied. "The region I have come from is neither nameless nor horrid. I have the honour to hail from America, and I am thoroughly American in blood, in sympathies, in ideas, in --- "

"Why, bless me, how curiously you talk, to be sure," interrupted the lady. "You are very bold and forward, too, for a male, who ought to be retiring and bashful."

"There I beg to differ from you, my dear madam."

"Tut, tut," cried the lady. "Why, I declare this is positively shocking."

"If you will graciously listen to me for a few minutes, madam, I think we shall be able to understand each other better," remarked Flin firmly, and in a tone that, had the lady had any perception, ought to have convinced her that Mr. Flonatin was by no means an ordinary man. But, unfortunately, the lady had no perception. In fact, it is doubtful if any of the Esnesnonites were gifted in this way. Their intellects, such as they were, would seem to have been much clouded, and only such things as directly affected their own interests struck them with any force.

Mrs Ytidrusba was evidently much astonished. To be talked to in such a manner by a male was something so extraordinary for Esnesnon that she opened her eyes in a manner that plainly indicated her profound amazement. She raised her diamond glass to her eye, and stared at Flin as though she was microscopically examining some wonderful and singular insect. Perhaps she did think so.

"Un-der-stand each other," she said, when she was tired of staring, and drawling the world out.

"That is what I said, madam," Flin answered, by no means abashed, though greatly annoyed, for his pride was wounded. "I beg to explain that in my beloved country the men rule and not the ladies."

"Oh, gracious!" exclaimed Mrs Ytidrusba, sniffing at her scent as though the very idea was horribly repugnant. "What a barbarous country, to be sure."

"So far from being a barbarous country, I assure you it is the most enlightened on the face of the earth. The only cares which a lady has are the cares of her own household, and even there she is subject to her husband's sway."

"Oh, what poor, miserable, degraded creatures they must be," said Mrs Ytidrusba.

"On the contrary, madam, the American ladies are noted for their liveliness, their general happy dispositions, and their entire freedom from anything like servility."

"You extraordinary being, do talk sense," exclaimed Mrs Ytidrusba, petulantly. "How is it possible for women to be anything but the vilest and most grovelling of slaves if they have to acknowledge the rule of men?"

"That is a rule that will better apply the other way. Man is by nature endowed in a manner which peculiarly qualifies him to be woman's protector her breadwinner, her ruler. His intellect is greater, his powers of endurance are greater. Woman in the senate, at the Bar, or in the professions, is out of place. And when once a woman quits her sphere she ceases to be a woman and becomes objectionable. In my country we surround woman with a halo of romance. She is the recipient of our loves, the keeper of our hearts, the guardian of our children, the ornament of our homes. We place her on a pedestal, as it were, and worship her beauty, respect her feelings, treat her with tenderness, but I guess, madam, we keep her in her proper place in the States, you bet we do."

"Oh, you humbug, you miserable barbarian," exclaimed Mrs Ytidrusba, passionately. "How dare you sit there and tell me such monstrous fictions, and expect me to believe them? If there be even a grain of truth in what you say I cannot conceive any beings more utterly degraded than are your wretched women. They must be lost to every sense of dignity, of nobleness, of freedom."

"That is a point I cannot concede you, madam," Flin remarked, determined not to lose one inch of ground. "All that you say with respect to our women may be applied with tenfold force to your men. May I venture to cite your husband as an example? He is gifted, intellectual, studious and farseeing, but he would be an infinitely better man if he was not subject to petticoat government."

Mrs Ytidrusba almost shrieked with horror, but Flin, nothing abashed, continued, ---

"I say that if your husband occupied his proper sphere his mind would expand more as the responsibilities of his position increased. The greatest incentive for a man to labour, to aspire, to struggle for fame, and to fight for glory is the knowledge that on him woman depends. But reverse the order, and man becomes a mere machine, while the height that he might attain, if in his true station, can never be attained by her who assumes man's responsibilities, because nature has not fitted woman for the office." He paused to wipe his face, for he had grown a little warm with his enthusiasm, and it gave the pent- up fires of wrath which smouldered in the lady's breast an opportunity to burst forth.

"Well may it be said that you come from the regions of darkness," she cried, "for you have the daring that we ascribe to the fiends. But while I do not believe that you have come from any such place, I denounce you as an unmitigated humbug. A presumptuous, inflated, yet miserably insignificant fellow, who ought to be whipped through our streets until you have learnt to know your true position."

"Madam, this is strong language," Flin commenced, but the lady stamped her foot and cried passionately, ---

"Hold your tongue, sir, when I speak to you. We do not allow our males here to contradict us, nor would any male in all Esnesnon have had the audacity to talk to a lady as you have talked to me."

"Poor creatures," Flin muttered.

"Woman is infinitely superior to the other sex. She has beauty of form and beauty of mind. She is shrewd, far- seeing, cautious, quick-witted, has powers of discernment which man has not, and therefore is she adapted to rule. It is her mission to rule, and before I would see our privileges surrendered I would head an army of women to sweep the males off our earth."

"Shocking, shocking," Flin murmured.

"I tell you,' the lady continued, "that the woman who would consent to have man as a ruler is a wretched, degraded, lost creature, and deserving of a reptile's death."

Flin could restrain himself no longer. To be talked to in such a way by a female was almost more than flesh and blood could stand. Small though he was in stature, he had a mighty brain, and a big heart that swelled with love for all women, when women were women, and not men. So indignant did he feel that he allowed his valour to overcome his discretion, and rising excitedly he cried, ---

"Madam, the time has come for me to speak out boldly for the honour and credit of my sex. I will endeavour to emancipate your men from their slavery. I will teach them their true position. I will show them that it is their duty to burst their bonds, and I will set them an example how to rule. All my energies, all my strength of mind and body shall be devoted to the good cause of freeing your unfortunate men from their social degradation."

"Ah, traitor, traitor!" screamed Mrs Ytidrusba, in a towering passion, "this is treason, and your life will be forfeited." She crossed the room hurriedly, and beat upon a gong of gold twice. A servant appeared in answer to the summons. "A guard," she cried. The man bowed and withdrew. "We shall," she continued, "see whether you can come to our peaceful realm with you revolutionary ideas and endeavour to carry them our with impunity." The door opened, and a body of Amazons, armed with long pikes, marched in. "Secure this wretched being, and march him to the citadel," she said imperiously.

In an instant Flin was arrested. He offered no opposition, but said, as firmly as he was able, ---

"Madam, this outrage on an American subject will be avenged."

The excited lady waved her hand haughtily, and cried, "Away with him!" and Flin Flon was led away as a captive.

27

The unexpected ending to his interview with Mrs. Ytidrusba considerably astonished Mr .Flonatin, though he had little time for reflection, as he was hurried down the stairs by the female guard, who placed him in a closed-up conveyance; and after being rapidly whirled through the streets, the vehicle stopped. He was told to alight. Then led up some broad steps, enclosed between high walls, and finally he was thrust into a dismal, dank and dark sort of dungeon.

Then, when he had recovered his breath, and his excitement had cooled a little, he muttered, ---

"Well, I little thought I was going to place my head into such a scorpion's nest. What a frightful Tartar that Mrs. Ytidrusba is, to be sure. I don't wonder at her unfortunate husband suffering. But the fact is, this is altogether a strange world, and I feel a difficulty sometimes in realising the fact that I am really awake. It is very horrible to contemplate what the power of a woman is when once she has succeeded in gaining the upper hand. Unfortunately for America there are but a few strong-minded ladies; they have never reached above a certain height, where, if they are left alone, they soon fall back again into oblivion. But here man is a nonentity --- a poor, simple, patient, long-suffering fool, domineered over by woman, crushed and ground out of all manly recognition. Alas, it is very sad!"

As soon as Flin's arrest became known, which it very speedily did, the excitement through Esnesnon was intense. For the power and influence of Mrs. Ytidrusba were well known, and it was also as well known that she was very jealous of any male who attempted to gain a position, and that Flin being a degenerated male, she was likely to be all the more incensed against him. Speculation was rife as to what the end would be. For anyone to attempt to revolt against the established rule was a most serious offence, and when proved against the person was generally punished with death, the victim having little bits cut out of him every day until he died.

The arrest also caused the newspaper war to rage fiercer than ever. The Gazette said that Flin, being a foreigner and under the protection of the King, ought not to be placed in prison. But the good-natured Mrs ---- in the News went perfectly frantic with delight. She yelled --- if the word be admissible, and really it is not inapropos to the lady's style --- I say she yelled with glee, and in a very strong article indeed on the subject she so mixed Flin up with the drivers, and the drivers with personal abuse of the King, that it was rather difficult for the calm and deliberate reader to tell exactly what she meant. But then it was not of much consequence. A bull, it is said, can never control its temper when it sees a red shawl, and this very excellent lady's nerves were just as sensitive to the sight of a driver. How this aversion had arisen, or why it had arisen, was hard to say. But it is pretty clear that, viewing it from our upper world point of view, she suffered from a monomania, and ought, poor thing, to have had her head shaved, and then been put in a large room, and on the principle of giving persons who suffer from dipsomania alcohol until it literally oozes out of them and they begin to loathe it, portraits of chariot-drivers might have been hung round the room on every inch of the wall. Even the ceiling and floor should have been covered with them, until the unhappy lady had become reconciled to the unfortunate race, and so a cure effected.

But in Esnesnon, where according to our ideas every body

seemed mad, nothing of this kind was attempted, and the poor creature was allowed to rave and put her ravings in print unchecked. Of course in our own country such a state of matters would never be tolerated for a single moment. We have no lunatics excepting those who are confined within the walls of an asylum.

When Flin's arrest came to be known to the King his Majesty was exceedingly annoyed, but he was afraid to say much, for he was well aware of the influence Mrs Ytidrusba possessed. He had a positive dislike for her, but he, poor fellow, in common with all his sex, groaned under this petticoat rule. It is a lamentable fact that he was nothing more than a puppet, and only held his kingship by virtue of hereditary right --- a right that had been established in very distant ages. But the women had tried to abolish this right and make a law by which only a woman could be on the throne. In this they had not succeeded. But they made the King's life such a wretched one that his crown was truly a crown of thorns, and many a time he wished that he occupied the position of one of his poorest subjects. His court, his retinue, his ministers, his advisers, his guards, the keeper of the Privy Purse, were all women. The horror of such a position as this cannot be realised excepting by those who have been similarly placed. The privy purse was very strictly kept indeed, and the miserable King's pittance was doled out to him at the petticoated keeper's pleasure. And if at any time he ventured to enter a protest against the smallness of the sums he was allowed for his own private use, the keeper would appeal to the ministers, and the ministers would inform his Majesty that they considered him to be very extravagant, and that it was not safe to trust a male with money.

Now such a state of affairs as this would really be positively ludicrous were it not so sad. But our laughter must give place to pity, lest such a dire infliction should some day visit our own beloved country. It is true the King has been very vacillating and weak-minded. But alas! poor fellow, how could he help that? The ceaseless din of the female tongue would have turned a far stronger brain than his.

He, however, sympathised with Flin, and he sent one of his most trusted male courtiers to the prisoner with a message that he would do all he could to support him. Flin was grateful for this, for he felt that he had got into an awkward scrape, and the ending of the affair might be of such a nature as to prevent him carrying out his plans, and would in fact bring his interesting journey to a premature close.

Flin languished in gaol for some time. Nobody knew exactly what he was charged with, as there was much secrecy and mystery about the whole affair. But it was very well known that he was the victim of Mrs. Ytidrusba's jealousy and strong- mindedness. This lady's position of wife to a person holding such high office as Ytidrusba gave her immense power. In fact, the truth is that the husband found the brains, and his wife enjoyed all the influence, honour and emoluments of his labours. For in this woman-governed kingdom man was looked upon as a sort of useful animal, if a tight hand was kept over him, and he was made to know his place. And a very tight hand indeed was kept over him, so that the Esnesnon males had long sunk into a state of apathetic effeminacy, though at times their souls rose in rebellion against the tyranny exercised by the fair creatures. Some few bold spirits had even tried, by means of secret societies, to overthrow the ruling power and make man the master. But the system of Government espionage was so perfect that the conspirators were invariably detected while their plots were in embryo, and after a hurried trial they suffered a violent death, being strapped to the backs of menopomes, which were driven into thrice-heated furnaces.

The delay in Flin's case was caused by the red-tapeism of the officials. For alas! red-tapeism, even in Esnesnon, was a bugbear under which the unhappy citizens groaned. It was necessary for Mrs Ytidrusba to impeach the prisoner, and then for that impeachment to be thoroughly examined by the Government, for it must be remembered that this was looked upon as high treason. And the Government, with a false show of impartiality and justice, affected to be very scrupulous, and to give a prisoner who was charged with an offence for which his life was liable to be forfeited every opportunity to defend himself. But it was very much to be feared that this was all humbug, and that the true cause of delay in such cases arose from the difficulty which was experienced by the ladies in coming to anything like a unanimous agreement.

Some ill-natured and dyspeptic bachelor once said that after women had kissed each other a dozen times they always fell out. I should be very sorry to endorse such an obviously unfair verdict as this. Though, under cover of all reserve, I will remark that in my own country, whenever I see two ladies after five minutes' acquaintance kiss each other, and then address each other as "dear," I tremble for the consequences. I know what such signs presage. This being so here, some idea can be formed of the state of affairs in Esnesnon, where in Parliament there were ten hundred female members. During a debate, and when the benches were full, the Tower of Babel and the confusion of tongues must have been rather pleasant as compared with the Esnesnon Parliament.

And of course, amongst such a large number of ladies, there was necessarily considerable diversity of opinion. Each lady considered her own opinion to be infinitely superior to her neighbour's, and the consequences of such a state of affairs may be better imagined than described.

The Parliament was constituted on precisely the same principles as our own, with the exception that a general election took place every three years instead of seven, though at times there was an election much oftener than this. For the Government, though indulging in personalities, often forgot their public duties, and consequently fell into a state of inextricable confusion, and the result was that an appeal to the country had to be made. These appeals were frequent, and the excitement an election caused passeth all understanding. Every woman in Esnesnon considered herself highly qualified, both by nature and art, to sit in Parliament, and as there was universal suffrage, some idea may be formed of the unpleasantness of election time. The poor men were neglected. The unfortunate husband had to wash and dress the babies, cook the dinner, and perform other degrading and menial housework, while the wife went down to spout nonsense at the hustings; and that woman who did not get elected made rather a hot time of it for her husband until she, sweet creature, had cooled down from her excitement.

In the House of Parliament there were, as I have before stated, one thousand members. Think of that, reader! Ponder upon it, and thank goodness that our own country is saved from such an awful visitation. One thousand ladies all trying to speak at once. One thousand pairs of arms excitedly sawing the air. One thousand pairs of eyes flashing like burning coals, and one thousand tongues moving with the rapidity of lightning. It must indeed have been appalling. The gallery reporters, who reported the debates, were all women. One of the papers had tried the experiment of employing two or three males for a short time, as they were so much cheaper than women; but they all went mad, and died miserable deaths.

There was no House of Lords corresponding to our own, but there was an Upper House and Final Court of Appeal. This was composed of three hundred old ladies, who held the highest position in society, and the right to sit in the House was hereditary. There was not much business done in the House. It was a dreamy kind of place, for whereas their sisters in the lower chamber talked against time, these pleasant old dames chatted quietly, and dozed frequently with their handkerchiefs over their faces.

I have before mentioned that the King was a mere automaton. He could do nothing without the sanction of his Parliament.

He was allowed forty thousand chequers per annum by the nation. A chequer was made of tin, and was equivalent to our sovereign. Tin was an exceedingly valuable metal in Esnesnon, and gold was as common as tin is here. In fact, it seemed as if when the various forces of nature had contrived to dispose the minerals throughout the strata of the earth, they had concentrated the gold in the very centre, for here solid layers of metal ten and twelve feet thick were common. In fact, so common was gold that it was generally used for building purposes, as it was so much cheaper than stone. Precious stones were also common. The abounded everywhere, and as they made good and pretty pavements, they were generally used for this purpose in the houses of the better classes, while diamonds were so lavishly scattered about by nature that they were cut thin and used for window glass even in the poorest houses.

With these few necessary particulars I may return to Mr. Flonatin, who languished day by day in his prison in a state of misery and suspense, and though he addressed frequent petitions to the King, they did not ameliorate his condition, for reasons already explained. The King was powerless. Mrs. Ytidrusba was powerful and spiteful, and Parliament was long-winded.

The King's magician, however (Ytidrusba), did all he could for the prisoner unknown to Mrs. Ytidrusba. The governor of the prison was a young and rather good-looking woman, and she sympathised with Flin, if she did not fall slightly in love with him; as a result she allowed him many liberties not allowed to ordinary prisoners, and but for this his case would have been very much worse than it was.

At length, after some very stormy discussions, and many nights spent in debate, Parliament decided that Flin's offence was very serious indeed, and that he should be indicted on three separate counts, and tried by the State.

The first of these counts was "undignified and insulting language to one of the highest ladies in the land, to wit the most mighty and gracious lady, wife of Ytidrusba, the King's Magician and High Priest." The second was treasonable and seditious language, and the third an attempt to interfere with the peace of the realm. All these, being grave and serious offences, were punishable with death should the accused be found guilty.

Of course to the sober and sensible reader this will seem very absurd, and certainly incredible that people calling themselves civilised should have raised such a storm about nothing. But then it must be remembered that the rulers were women. The State lawyers were women, and they saw that a splendid picking was to be got out of this affair, and so they kept the pot boiling, and strongly advised his Majesty's ministers to prosecute. The Gazette, which was the organ of the King, and partly supported by him out of his own privy purse, and edited by a male, opposed this resolution on the part of the Government very strongly. But the News, which was entirely conducted by women, including the dreadful Mrs ---- , advocated the sternest measures, and tried to howl the Gazette out of the field, The result was that there was such a rumpus as had scarcely ever been known before, and at one time the two parties got so violent as to threaten a disturbance and the Amazons were called out.

During all the time that Parliament was wrangling, and the lawyers were squabbling about Flin's case, and the indictment was being framed, the Princess Yobmot was absent in a distant part of the realm, and so the unfortunate traveller was left without his most powerful friend. For being a woman she could of course do more than could Ytidrusba or the King. The old magician's wife was not slow to perceive that her husband's sympathy was with the accused, and this served to make her more bitter. It is a painful fact that she disliked her husband very much. And with a true woman's spirit she opposed him because "she chose to do so."

When Ytidrusba heard that the day for the trial had been fixed, he was determined to lose no time in letting the Princess know of the true state of affairs, and so he dispatched a trustworthy messenger to her Highness. She was exceedingly angry when she heard of it, for I think it must be confessed that her Highness was a bit of a Tartar, and liked to have her own way. And as she had made Flin a sort of prot,g,, it annoyed her to think that anyone should have dared to have taken such a liberty during her absence. Moreover, between her and Mrs. Ytidrusba there was a deadly feud. This of course was greatly in Flin's favour, and he could scarcely fail to profit by it.

As soon as the Princess heard the news she immediately hurried back, and arrived in Esnesnon the day before that appointed for the trial, and she lost no time in obtaining an interview with Flonatin. She found him very dejected. A man in such a position could scarcely help being cast down. He was in such a singular world, where the customs were so totally different to those in his own country, that he looked upon it almost as a forlorn conclusion that his life would be forfeited. Not that he had any craven fear on this score. Far from that. When his

right time came he was not the man to shrink with cowardice

from the inevitable. But he did not feel this to be the right time. He had risked much and dared much to accomplish the journey. And now when the goal had been won, when the dearest wish of his heart had been realised, and his favourite theory about the interior of the world being peopled had been proved true, all his labour and devotion and sacrifices were to be rendered useless through the will of a stupid woman. This is what galled him, and as he thought the records of his journey would never reach the hands of the Society for the Exploration of Unknown Regions, he almost wept.

The Princess's visit was therefore as welcome as unexpected. And as she entered the apartment in which he was confined he rose, and taking her Highness's hand, kissed it. But she, with less conventionalism and more warmth, kissed him. He was a little abashed, and would rather have dispensed with such unpleasant honours, but not wishing to offend her, he did not say anything.

"Well, my dear little fellow," was her first exclamation, as she led him to a seat, "whatever made you get yourself into such a scrape as this?"

Flin briefly told her, and for a time the Princess seemed a little grave.

"You have been very indiscreet, very indiscreet," she observed, with more gravity than ever he had seen her assume. And he began to fear that even she considered his offence so terribly serious as to place him beyond the pale of her assistance or sympathy.

28

In this thought, however, Flin was greatly mistaken. The Princess was not of that mind. Not that she as a woman looked favourably upon his offence. On the contrary, she really felt that his crime was one which merited the severest punishment, viewed politically. For she, in common with the rest of her sex, and young as she was, was too fond of commanding to brook anything like an innovation from a male. The only male authority she had hitherto recognised had been that of her father, and only then because he was her father. But the fact is that, though an Esnesnonite, she was a woman, and that is saying much. It seems that woman's nature is very much alike all over the world. As a consequence of this, she felt a good deal of warmth for Flin. I don't know whether I should be justified in saying love at this time; but she certainly looked upon him with much favour, and in the corner of her heart perhaps there was real affection, that time would develop; and again, Mrs. Ytidrusba was her enemy. This lady, for some reason that only a woman could explain, had taken a great dislike to the Princess (women do take dislikes to each other in such an unaccountable manner). She said that she was wild, and a great flirt, and ought to be curbed; and had repeatedly spoken to the King; but one of the laws of Esnesnon was, that up to a certain age, when the mother was dead, the father had absolute control over his daughters.

The Princess therefore --- as what young girl would not --- felt extremely irritated by the meddlesome interference, and had once gone so far as to tell Mrs. Ytidrusba to mind her own business.

This had led to open rupture; and from that moment the ladies became sworn enemies. The Princess therefore felt that in indicting Flin Mrs. Ytidrusba had been actuated by personal animosity against her Royal enemy, and so far had succeeded in playing a trump card.

"But I will thwart her," thought her Royal Highness; and then turning to Flonatin she said, "It is most unfortunate that you have got into such a pitiable mess, and I shall have the greatest possible difficulty getting you out of it. The very best counsel in Esnesnon shall be engaged, and though I think it will be a hard fight, we may succeed in defeating the plans of our enemies."

"This most gracious condescension on the part of your Highness," answered Flin, "begets in me a gratitude that I cannot find words to express. But I will take this opportunity to say that, should I survive to return to my native country, all America shall know how well you have served one of her sons."

"And is that all?" sighed the Princess, taking his hand and looking him full in his face.

"That all!" repeated Flin in astonishment, and not understanding her. "What else can I do for your Highness?"

"Much," she answered; "but this is not the time to speak of it. The future shall reveal to you what I desire. In the meantime your defence must be prepared, for the ablest State lawyers will prosecute you, and as they are nearly all very old women, I fear I can look for little mercy from them. But keep your heart up, and it is very likely we shall come off triumphant."

"I hope so, I hope so," was Flin's answer. The Princess squeezed his hand and kissed him, and in a few minutes he was left to his own reflections again.

Flin's trial commenced on the following morning, and there was intense excitement in consequence. The circumstances of the case were so romantic and peculiar. A person from an unknown world had come down to Esnesnon, and then, in return for the hospitality shown him, he had endeavoured to raise a revolt. The thing was altogether unparalleled, so the people said, and people here will admit that it was.

Through the instrumentality of the Princess, some most able counsel for the defence had been engaged. One of these was a young woman named Hturtehteraps. She had already greatly distinguished herself in her profession, and the success of many of the causes celŠbres of Esnesnon was entirely due to her eloquence and skill.

The Court where the trial was held was an immense place. It was built in the form of an amphitheatre, and was surmounted with a doomed roof that was elaborately carved and set with ornamental, or as we call them, precious stones of immense size.

The floor of the theatre was occupied by the professional ladies and the reporters for the public papers, while the judges sat beneath a magnificent canopy on one side of the circle. There was no jury as in our own country. But Esnesnon was composed of twenty-seven provinces, and each province had a judge. In great trials every province sent its judge. And all the judges were ladies noted for uprightness of conduct no less than their great ability.

Flin Flon occupied a position on a raised seat placed on the floor of the theatre, and as he surveyed the scene, its vastness and magnificence, as well as the novel arrangements, stuck him with amazement, more especially when he contrasted it with the cramped-up, miserable places used as courts of law in his own country. There the prevailing characteristics were foetid atmosphere, murkiness, foul odours, bad acoustic properties and general inconvenience. But here, in this circular and lofty building, not only were an immense number of the public accommodated with seats, but every word that was uttered could be distinctly heard. The air was pure and refreshing. The judges were comfortably disposed, and the lawyers and pleaders were provided with every accommodation and convenience for transacting their business.

From the floor up to the very dome the building was packed with an eager and excited throng, and the women were far in excess of the men, for large numbers of the latter had been ordered by their wives to remain at home and look after the children. The buzzing of the female voices was like the whirl of a thousand spinning looms, and almost deafening. But when the judges had taken their seats, and the Court was ordered to be silent, there was silence instantly. Then the indictment was read over. It was a most voluminous document; but I will not weary the reader by printing it. It set forth that the crime with which the accused stood charged was one punishable with death, and Flin was asked if he pleaded guilty or not.

By the advice of his lawyer he simply said, "Not guilty," and then the trial proceeded.

It was evident from the first that the struggle would be a severe one, for there was an amount of animus infused into the opening address that was astonishing; and it was hinted that Mrs. Ytidrusba, having heard that Princess Yobmot was interesting herself in the case, grew very excited, and made use of language not at all polite, and she had stated without reserve, that not a stone should be left unturned that could possibly help her to gain a triumph.

The prosecution was infected with the lady's spirit, and seemed equally determined to secure a conviction. The leading counsel for the Crown spoke in a most contemptuous manner of Flin, and said that his guilt was too clear to admit of any doubt as to what the issue would be, but when considered it was paying him an undeserved honour to try him at all. "A person who was so inexpressibly insignificant as he was ought to have been dealt with summarily, for nothing could be possibly clearer than that he was a miserable, wretched barbarian and adventurer, whose sole object in intruding upon that peaceful city was to stir up revolution and anarchy. Such a thing could not be tolerated. This human wretch had had the daring to tamper with one of the highest ladies in the land. Not only had he tried to corrupt her, but he had spoken in the most scurrilous tones of the grand old institution of woman rule, a rule that had made Esnesnon the happy, peaceful, wealthy city it was --- a rule that could not be surpassed for gentleness, suavity and mercy --- a rule that had left nothing undone --- that was just and equitable alike to rich and poor. There had been a few restless spirits who had expressed dissatisfaction with this grand old institution, and they had endeavoured to inflame the minds of others, but in this they had ignominiously failed. Esnesnonites were too peaceful, too law-abiding, too fond of those who governed them, too happy, and too well cared for, to listen to seditious language. (Flin would have liked to have heard what the people themselves had to say about this.) Woman had ever been powerful in the land, and when she ceased to be powerful the end of Esnesnon would have come. (At this there was considerable applause, which was with difficulty suppressed.) In her rule she had left nothing to be desired. Her ears were ever open to the cry of pity, her heart to the wail of distressed males. It was true there had been males who, possessed of a boldness that was awful to contemplate, had attempted to gain some power and supplant woman, but the end of all such persons had been so indescribably terrible as to serve as a salutary warning to others who would attempt to follow in their footsteps; and if ever the day should come when males gained power in the land, it would be a sorry day indeed for Esnesnon. The crime of this miserable, degenerated being, who, it had been suggested, had come from the infernal regions --- and for her part she was very strongly inclined to believe it --- was of the blackest description; and one that, in the interest of justice and the general peace, should shut him out from all mercy. He was deserving of none; he should have none shown to him. It was hard for her to have to speak in that way even of one so low in the human scale as he obviously was. But the enormity of the offence caused her to close her eyes to sympathy, and open them only to a stern sense of duty. And it was that very sense of duty which made her, even against her will, speak in the way she had done. When she had been instructed to take up the case she had examined into it very carefully to see if she could discover any palliation. But she regretted to say she had looked in vain. She regretted it the more because the offender was a stranger; and had it been possible to have found any excuse she would have liked to have done so on that account. But there was none to be found. The fearful nature of the crime must have sent a thrill of horror through the breast of every peacefully-disposed person in the realm. He would have remorselessly aroused the Demon of Revolt, and have let it loose to prey upon the vitals of a ruler- fearing and woman-respecting community. He would have thrown the whole social machinery of the country out of gear. He would have raised a whirl-wind of desolation, and cast the electric bolt of dissatisfaction at the great throbbing heart of a happy people. (These similes were very fine.) But he had been foiled. The great lady whose loyalty he had attempted to assail was staunch and true. Her honour was impregnable. Painful though it was for her to have to do so, she did not shrink from her duty and ordering the instant arrest of the dastard who had thus attempted to tamper with the State. This lady's truth is unimpeachable. Therefore, my ladies, you cannot fail to convict the miserable being of the crime for which he stands charged--the crime of treason. For what sane woman can doubt for a single moment that he has been guilty of treason? and that having been so, that he is deserving of death. In conclusion, my ladies, I would venture to remark that the eyes of the world are upon you, and that the action you take in this matter will be watched with the most jealous interest by every woman in the realm."

As this lady resumed her seat the female portion of the audience applauded rapturously, but a few hisses were mingled with the applause, and it was very evident that they came from male throats. At this the learned counsel sprang to her feet again, and with a great deal of bitterness in her tone said she hoped the chief judge would order every male to leave the Court if such a disgraceful uproar should occur again.

There was an uneasy movement amongst the males as this was said, for they knew from the stern look on the judge's face that she would not hesitate to do as desired. This judge was very old, and had never been married. She had been heard to say that she hated males, and if she could do as she liked she would exterminate them.

It will be seen from this little incident how terrible was the lot of the males of Esnesnon, and how they must have groaned and sweated under the tyrannical rule of the females.

Flin's blood boiled as he saw to what a terrible depth of serfdom his unfortunate sex were reduced in this so-called "happy city," and his great and good heart panted to strike a blow for freedom. Much as he loved woman, he felt that he could not brook her rule as she ruled there, and sooner than submit to it he would gladly die.

29

When the excitement in the Court consequent on the speech for the counsel for the prosecution had subsided, people whispered one to another that it would go hard with the accused. And this inference almost seemed justified by the very grave faces of the judges. Some of these ancient ladies looked at the prisoner in a very severe manner through their diamond glasses, and then they shook their wise heads, and consulted their written notes in a manner that seemed to imply that they considered Mr Flonatin's offence was one that ought to be visited by the direst punishment. And yet to a very close observer, and to a physiognomist, it might have been seen that under the stern and stoical expression which the faces of these judges wore there was a feeling of pity, as though in their hearts these dignified administrators of the law were saying,

"Ah, poor young male, how very nice he is to be sure, and what a pity it is for such a dear creature to be placed in so unenviable a situation."

Of course it will be thoroughly understood that I do not say for certain that the judges really thought this. But then woman's heart is such a profound mystery that one may almost say anything he likes about it without being very far wrong. For my own part, if I were on trial for my life, and I had the option of selecting my own judge and jury, I should certainly choose ladies, and in doing so I should be cheered by the inward conviction that whatever the weight of evidence might be against me, I should be able by those cunning little artifices so well known to upper world men to touch the sympathetic chords of the dear creatures' hearts.

However, as subsequent events proved, Mr Flonatin did not stand in need of any such artifice to obtain his acquittal. The brilliant eloquence of his charming counsel, and his own sweet naivet,, were quite sufficient to move even the law-encrusted hearts of these Esnesnon judges. But then of course it is not every man who is blessed with "sweet naivet,," and in the absence of it he would have to resort to the means I have suggested. I am afraid, however, that I have in these remarks anticipated the verdict. Though every reader of this history will long ago have come to the conclusion that no lady or any number of ladies could have possibly condemned such a distinguished man as Flin Flon. But to proceed.

When the excitement had quite subsided, and silence and order had been restored, the young and able counsel for the defence, Hturtehteraps, arose. There was a look of quiet dignity and self-assurance on her face. She bowed to the judges, and then turning to Flin and the Princess Yobmot, who was near him, she smiled to them and bowed also.

"My most noble judges," she commenced, "it is my very proud privilege this day to have the honour of defending a prisoner who is a native of another world, and who in ours stands charged with a crime of such unparalleled atrocity that as every honest woman contemplates it she must shudder. I will here divide these preliminary remarks under two heads. Firstly, as to the prisoner being a native of another world. That is, I am bound to confess, a somewhat bold statement, but it is perfectly evident that he does not belong to our own fair earth; his degenerated appearance is sufficient to convince us of that, though as to where his world is situated it is not for us to inquire here. It is sufficient to know that he is an unenlightened foreigner, and I say, my most noble judges, that that fact alone, I repeat it most emphatically, that that fact alone ought to be sufficient to ensure his acquittal. We are a great, a civilised, a refined, a merciful, a charitable, an oppression-hating people. And being all these it is a paramount duty we owe to ourselves to set other worlds an example. Better that we should be destroyed, better that we should be annihilated, better I say that we should sink for ever into oblivion, than that it should be said in other worlds that we as the most cultivated of people were wanting in the commonest principles of charity or of mercy. It is not for us to consider where this human male has come from, though it be, as has been suggested he is, from the infernal regions."

"It is sufficient to know that he is a stranger amongst us, and as such demands our consideration and pity. Shall we, as women, withhold these from a male, even though he be a fallen one? Weak, helpless and friendless, he appeals to our better natures, and shall we, as the protecting sex, turn a deaf ear to the cry of the forlorn? I answer, no. I cry aloud, no, no. For, if we did, our names would go down to posterity with execration, and other worlds would ring with shouts of horror at our barbarity; while generations yet unborn would weep tears of blood as they heard of the blot that rested on the escutcheon of the fair city of Esnesnon. This is a fearful thing to contemplate; it would be a thousand times more horrible if it were to become reality. But whether it shall, or shall not, is a matter which is entirely in your hands, my most noble judges. The balances trembles. A touch one way will plunge our city for all time into a depth of ignominy, disgrace and darkness at which I shudder, while a touch the other way will elevate us to the proud position of being the nation of nations, and will stamp us at once as the most humane and merciful people ever yet, or that ever will be, created. It is for you to give it this touch. It is for you to raise us to this glorious pinnacle. Where, to use a simile, I may say we shall be as a statue representing dignity and love, teaching young worlds the first principles of prehuman justice. If I have allowed my feelings to lead me into somewhat poetical language, it is because my soul thrills with sentiments that struggle to find utterance by my own weak voice, but which, alas! I can only too feebly express. But I am sure, by noble judges, you will catch something of the spirit which animates me. The chord which vibrates in my own heart will find a responsive echo in your own. And the voice of the inward monitor will cry aloud, 'Acquit him, acquit him.'"

The learned counsel paused; there was immense applause; it was very evident that her splendid eloquence and flowers of rhetoric were telling upon her listeners.

When the applause had subsided she resumed her speech.

"I have hitherto contented myself" she went on "with appealing to those feelings which should burn in the breast of every woman, as she beholds a weak male in the unfortunate position that this one is placed in. For is it not ever woman's nature, in this beautiful land at least, to rush to the rescue of the weaker sex when danger threatens him, and to thrill with pity at the sight of a male in distress. But now I must deal with the second head of my address, and must appeal at once to your sense of justice. And I say it boldly, defiantly, and without fear of contradiction, that the charge brought against my client in a monstrous one, and entirely without an atom of foundation."

At this statement there were some murmurs of disapproval, but the learned counsel turned to the quarter from whence they proceeded for she knew that there the opposing faction was congregated and as her eyes flashed fire, she said, with the most withering scorn ,

"The truth hits hard, and some persons groan under it. I am glad, however, that I have sent a shaft home, and the contempt of Court shown by those persons who are evidently smarting under my fire cannot fail to strengthen my hands." (At this there was considerable applause, and the learned lady smiled and bowed gracefully.) "I repeat," she went on, turning to the judges, "I repeat that there is not a particle of truth in the charge brought against my client. Could anything be more preposterous than to suppose that he, a poor, simple, ignorant, half-witted waif, from a region that lies beyond the ken of prehuman beings, could possibly be guilty of attempting to overthrow this Government? Even assuming that there was truth in it, the attempt to upset an institution of woman- rule, built upon such a solid foundation as is ours, would too surely betray symptoms of a dreadful insanity that would cause every right-feeling woman throughout the length and breadth of this happy land to weep scalding tears of the tenderest sympathy. And instead of clamouring for the life of the unfortunate male, she would with tender hands nurse him in his affliction, and with soft lips and kisses of pure love soothe him in the paroxysms of his madness. But the prisoner is neither insane nor guilty. I say that the charge is a monstrous, diabolical, and wicked conspiracy against an innocent life. I am aware that the lady who impeached him is high in power, and the influence she possesses in certain quarters is too well known for me to dwell upon here. But I venture to say that these very facts should cause you to view the accusation with all the legal acumen that it is possible to bring to bear upon the case."

Here the counsel for the prosecution arose and objected to her learned friend's remarks this was said with a most scornful sneer. The imputations she sought to throw upon the prisoner's accuser were un-ladylike, and incompatible with the dignity of the Bar.

At this Hturtehteraps struck the table with her open hand in a manner that told how terrible was the volcano of wrath which raged in her fair bosom, and at the very top of her voice she screeched,

"That she would not stand there to be insulted in such an unwarranted manner, nor would she yield the palm to anyone for the respect which she entertained for the dignity of the Court. Before she proceeded any further she must demand an apology from her learned friend the counsel for the prosecution "

Here the opposing counsel struck the table violently in return, and shrieked that no apology should ever cross her lips, when a scene ensured that to our tastes was very shocking indeed. The two "learned ladies" glowered at each other form their respective ends of the table, and in voices that could only be likened to the screech of a hurricane through a pine forest, they hurled epithets at each other that I will not repeat. But I do venture to assert that if the long table had not separated the fair disputants it would have been necessary to have called in the sweeper to have swept up the loose hair.

The battle raged fiercely savagely for some minutes. The chief judge entreated, commanded, then stormed and raved; and her sister judges also raised their voices, until there was such an unearthly clamour of female tongues that it is a perfect miracle that poor Flin Flon did not go raving mad. Dreadful as this must seem to civilised people, it was nothing for Esnesnon. The people there were used to such scenes, and ever will be while women rule.

After repeated threats by the judge to commit the wordy combatants for contempt of Court, order was at length restored, and panting and exhausted, though still eager for the fray, the two gallant ladies wiped their heated faces and ground their teeth at each other. But when Hturtehteraps had cooled a little she broke out into genial smiles again, and bowing to the judges, who bowed in return, she observed pleasantly,

"I am very sorry, my most noble judges, that the order of the Court should have been interrupted by this pretty passage-of-arms. But a little pleasant banter serves to clear our heavy legal atmosphere and enables us to breathe more freely."

I think my readers will unanimously be of my opinion, that if this was only "pleasant banter" a row in Esnesnon amongst the ladies would have been rather serious, and unpleasant for human and civilised beings. But as the judges smiled, and the two learned counsel smiled lovingly at each other, and the audience laughed, it is to be presumed that it was only "pleasant banter," and that the Esnesnonites relished such scenes with as much zest as Spaniards do a bull- fight. But alas! it is fearful to contemplate the tremendous amount of hypocrisy there must have been there to be sure.

The legal atmosphere having been cleared, the counsel for the defence continued her speech.

"As I was saying before my learned friend the counsel for the prosecution interrupted me, this unfortunate male, the prisoner at the bar, cannot be guilty of the charge brought against him, and should therefore be acquitted. His accuser is a lady. It is not for me to enter into the motives which led her to place my client in his unfortunate position. Her reasons are best known to herself, but I say that it would have been better for her, and better for this mighty nation, had she shown more consideration for an alien, even assuming that he had been guilty." (Here the opposing counsel jumped up again and protested strongly against her "learned friend's remarks," and another rumpus seemed imminent, but the presiding judge threatened in a tone of awful severity to quit the Court if order was not kept. At this the two ladies looked daggers at each other, and turned up their pretty noses, and resorted to other feminine means of expressing the bitterness and jealousy which rankled in each heart.)

"In conclusion, I would remark," said Hturtehteraps, "that the unsupported charge of Mrs Ytidrusba cannot be sustained if we would wish to preserve unsullied the character for justice which this great nation has ever borne. Therefore, I ask for his acquittal in the name of truth, of justice, of mercy. Let it be said by future generations of women yet unborn, that here the foreigner found refuge and protection from the machinations of those who would have encompassed him, and who desired his fall, from the basest and most wretched of motives."

The learned counsel, after this brilliant peroration, resumed her seat amidst a storm of applause, and as she wiped her heated brow there was a look of conscious satisfaction on her face, and a roguish twinkle in her eye, which seemed to say, "I think that has done it, or I am not a woman." And that it had done it was pretty soon self-evident. The trial was speedily concluded after this, and the presiding judge's summing up was a masterpiece of analytical rhetoric. She cautioned her learned sisters against being led away by false sympathy on the one hand or prejudice on the other. The prisoner was a foreigner and a male, she said, and therefore, even if the weight of evidence was considered to be against him, some palliative circumstance might be found. The offence with which he was charged was a very grave one. In fact nothing more diabolical could possibly be imagined than for a male to try and upset the rule of woman. It was an offence, indeed, that, if proved against the person, no punishment that could be devised by the ingenuity of woman would be adequate to meet. But its very awfulness called for the most impartial and deliberate consideration. For the name of a male who should be proved guilty of such an offence in Esnesnon would for ever be execrated, while his children and children's children would be branded with the brand of infamy. It was therefore imperatively necessary that every scrap of evidence should be carefully weighed, and the motives of the accuser analysed. And if there was a doubt at all in the minds of the judges, even though that doubt should be infinitesimally small, the prisoner should have the benefit of that doubt.

The trial after this came at once to an end, the unanimous verdict of the judges being "Not Guilty" a verdict that was evidently a popular one, for the Court rang with applause, that was taken up by the multitude outside until it had spread throughout the town, and the whole population, especially the males, seemed to go mad with excitement.

30

As soon as the trial was over, the judges, the counsel for the defence, Princess Yobmot, and several other ladies crowded round Flin Flon, to congratulate him on his acquittal, and there was quite a disturbance amongst the fair creatures as they struggled to get near Flin and offer him their arm; though these little designs were frustrated by the Princess, who drew his arm through her own and led him into an ante-room, where a little bit of a banquet had been prepared, and into this room all the other ladies and the old judges crowded. Amongst the latter it was very evident that the flame of jealousy was burning fiercely, although they had reached an age when wisdom ought to have come with their grey hairs. But it would almost seem as if the old females were far greater flirts than the young ones. It is equally certain, too, that Flin savage though they called him was a bone of contention amongst them. In fact, there is reason to believe that a very large number of the Esnesnon ladies felt in their own hearts that the country would by no means suffer if man was allowed an innings at ruling. The supreme power which women had there was by no means beneficial to the country. The King, owing to womanly despotism, was a poor, weak, half imbecile puppet; while the Parliament itself might truly be said to be the common wrangling ground, and on a night of a grand debate there was such an uproar amongst these female M. P .'s that the place was more like Pandemonium.

Mr. Flonatin, gifted as he was with a wonderful amount of natural shrewdness, was not slow to perceive this. He saw, in fact, that the country groaned under petticoat sway. That its sources of wealth were undeveloped from the same cause, and that man was a long-suffering, much-imposed-upon and uncomplaining creature, whose fallen condition was pitiable to see.

Much as he would have liked to have done so, Mr. Flonatin felt that he was powerless to alter the condition of his suffering brethren in Esnesnon. Long persecution and tyranny had taken all the spirit out of them, and he, as a stranger, could not hope to arouse them to any sense of their utter degradation, so that they might rise and throw off the yoke. In fact, to have done this, a gigantic conspiracy would have been necessary, and Flin had already seen the danger that would have to be incurred by anyone who attempted to interfere with the present mode of government. He therefore deemed it advisable to do as the Esnesnonites did, and conform with the best grace he could to the female oppression.

The Princess Yobmot took the chair at the luncheon which had been provided, and in a neat speech she expressed her satisfaction at the result of the trial. She considered that Flin Flon had been the victim of a paltry and unwomanly jealousy, and, for the credit and honour of that great country, a gigantic public meeting should be held to express disapproval at the way in which the unfortunate foreigner had been treated.

This suggestion found favour with the company. For many of the ladies present were anxiously looking forward to the time when the Princess would come to the throne, so that they might drop into snug little sinecures. And it may be that this was the secret of Flin's acquittal, for if the Princess had not been on his side he would in all probability have been unmercifully executed.

Of course there was a great deal of speechmaking at this little banquet, and each lady spoke of the other as "her dear and valued friend," and the "you butter me and I'll butter you" business was carried on until it became fulsome, and amongst the upper world people it would not have been tolerated. But then Esnesnon is not the upper world; and the Esnesnon weaknesses have not yet pervaded our own society, thank goodness. When the luncheon was over there was again a good deal of struggling for the privilege of escorting Flin. In fact, many of these dreadful old ladies burned with a strong desire to flirt a bit with the "uncultivated foreigner." But the Princess was determined to frustrate all such designs, and unmistakably expressed her disapproval of the unladylike conduct, and while the dear creatures were smarting from the reproof she hurried Flin out, and handed him into her private chariot. Then, when they were once more alone, she took his hand and said,

"My dear, I am so glad you have escaped. If anything had happened to you I think I should have died."

"Really, your Highness," he answered, "the kind interest, you take in my welfare overwhelms me, and makes me feel that I shall never be able to repay you."

"Say not so, dear," she murmured. "What is there I would not do for you if I could but win one gracious smile?" (Flin thought that this was a little bit of bosh, but he did not say so.)

"Since you came here," she continued, "I have not felt the same being. You have awakened a feeling in my heart that is entirely new and strange. You have taught me to love you "

"Really, your Highness," Flin exclaimed, colouring very deeply indeed, "this is shocking to my aged ears. Besides, your Highness forgets the barrier that exists between us. I, alas! belong to a degenerated race far below your own." (He felt that this was profound humbug, but he considered that under the circumstances he was justified in using any amount of humbug.) "I was unworthy of you, and your affections would be misplaced."

"Nay, say not so," she sighed. "Love recognises no barrier it can break down or build up, it can raise or level. You have taken me captive. I feel that you are my only light, and without you all will be dark and drear. Blight not my hopes. Turn me not away in despair.

My heart is yours. None other can hold a corner in it. Your voice is my music, your touch can thrill me, your gaze charms me I live for you only."

Mr. Flonatin felt dreadfully disgusted with the Princess, for he knew that this was frightful hypocrisy, and he had no doubt that she had used the same language to dozens of young males in Esnesnon. Even assuming that she was sincere he reasoned with himself he did not see his way clear to reciprocate her passion, as there was such a wide difference between them morally and physically; but when he came to dwell upon the subject he began to think that the thing might not be so impracticable as at first sight it seemed. The Princess would one day come to the throne, and Flin thought that if he could succeed in winning her, or rather in allowing himself to be won by her, he might be the means of liberating hundreds of thousands of wretched males from a terrible bondage, and of restoring woman to her proper sphere. This might have been considered a wild, mad scheme, but he asked himself if, after what he had already accomplished, he could not accomplish this, and whether he would not, on the broadest principles of humanity, be justified in taking the steps. He had no selfish motives in the matter. But the liberation of a people, whether they chose to call themselves prehuman, or even superhuman, was such a grand thing to struggle for, that he felt as if he could dare all the powers in nature if he could but accomplish his purpose. But still it was a step requiring much consideration. He was troubled, for he had no desire to commit himself on the one hand, or to lose an opportunity of setting free a longsuffering and sorely-oppressed race of men. But then he had only been acquitted from a charge of conspiracy, and now he was contemplating a move that if it failed the consequences would be terrible, but life or self-interests were nothing when the welfare of a nation was a stake. It was true that there was not much in the Princess to admire, bachelor though he was, and consequently the sacrifice on his part would have to be great. She saw that he was troubled, and so she said, as she pressed his hand,

"You are uneasy in your mind, dear. Confide in me. Tell me your woes that I may solace them. Let me be your trusted friend."

"Ah, your Highness," replied Flin, "that is the word. Your friendship is what I require."

"And is that all?" she murmured.

"What more can I expect?" he returned, a little confused.

"You may expect all that a woman can give to a male love and protection."

"Really, your Highness," he stammered, "you place me in a very awkward position, and one that is no less novel than awkward. You will remember that I told you that in my country the gentlemen made love to the ladies "

"Ah, but then they are so uncivilised there," she interrupted.

"That I admit," he continued, with a roguish twinkle in his eye. "That I admit, but then you must make allowance for my inexperience in the new way, and not forget that the customs of your country must strike a stranger as being very singular."

"But then you come from darkness to light as it were," she replied, "from ignorance to knowledge, from utter barbarism to refined civilisation." "Humph, just so."

"And so you should adapt yourself at once to the situation," she continued, without noticing his interruption, "more especially when it is to please one who loves you." She bent down and would have kissed him, but he drew back. He found it very difficult indeed to reconcile himself to her caresses.

"Why are you so shy?" she asked.

"I fear I am not worthy of your love," he replied, drooping his head, and finding great difficulty in refraining from bursting into a loud laugh, for the whole situation was so ludicrous. But still he felt that the game was worth playing out. Much as he respected woman he could not help thinking that in Esnesnon she was out of her place, and to put it in his own and facetious language, "she wanted taking down a peg or two," and he was determined to take her down and put man in his right sphere. And every right-thinking woman who reads this will say that he was perfectly justified. But some who are not right-thinking will be of a different opinion. This is very sad, and I can only hope that all the poor creatures who are of this mind will soon be brought to a sense of their terrible condition.

"It is I who am not worthy of yours," the Princess answered with well-assumed artlessness; but the wicked minx knew well enough that she was simply talking nonsense. She was like a child with a new toy. Flin was a stranger and a novelty, and therefore she like him for a time. But she meant no more in what she said than does a young gentleman in the upper world when he vows that his lady-love's eyes are "stars," and her hair "woven sunbeams," and her teeth "pearls," and "her neck like the swan" all of which language is slightly idiotic. But then, to sentimental young spoons it sounds nice.

Flin sighed. He did so because he thought the Princess was terribly wicked. She sighed in return. Not that she meant anything by it, but the naught girl knew that sighs were the true language of love, and, misinterpreting Flin's sigh, she thought she would answer him.

"I am afraid, your Highness," he said, "that you are very precipitate in this matter. You seem to forget that between you and me there is a very wide gulf that will be most difficult to bridge. I am a stranger, belonging to a race totally different from your own, and whose customs are the very antithesis of the Esnesnonites. You are a Princess of the royal blood, and I am but a plebeian."

"I forget nothing," she answered. "I only know that you have won my love, and I ask you to give me yours in return. I will be true to you. Your lightest wish will be respected, and we shall be so very, very happy, dear. Say that you will be mine."

Flin's breast was filled with mingled feelings of pity and contempt. He believed that in a measure the Princess was really sincere in her protestations, and so he pitied her. But he found it a most difficult task to conceal his disgust, though he was convinced that the present was a case in which a little dissembling was perfectly justifiable. He had succeeded in getting into Esnesnon, but how to get out was another question. And as the chances of his being able to leave seemed very remote, he thought he might do as Esnesnon did. Looking straight at the Princes, he said,

"My dear madam. If you consider that I am worthy of the notice you are pleased to take of me, it is not for me to offer any opposition to your wishes. And so by necessity I conform to the custom of this strange city, and, reconciling myself to the reversed order of things, I have the honour to say that I am yours."

She kissed him. She was very fond of doing that, but he didn't like it at all, and would have much preferred to have had a good pinch of snuff. She seemed overwhelmed with joy, and exclaimed,

"You have made me so happy, and I shall take ever such care of you, and shall insist upon the Governor placing you in some good position. Of course, when I am queen I shall be able to do more for you, but till then, dear, you must be contented."

"Quite contented," Flin answered a little ironically. "I venture to presume that the person to whom you are pleased to refer to as the 'Governor' is his Majesty, you esteemed father. And if so, I need scarcely say that any position it might be his royal pleasure to confer upon me will be faithfully filled as far as my humble abilities will permit me. In fact, I have reason to believe that his Majesty might find me of considerable service."

"Well, I will see what can be done," replied the Princess, "but you see, dear, without a male happens to be exceedingly clever, he is really of no use here, excepting as woman's companion, and so very, very few males are clever. It is obvious that in the great and incomprehensible scheme of nature they were simply intended to be woman's plaything. He is not at all fitted to fill the important offices now occupied by woman." (Flin coughed here to prevent himself from laughing at the absurdity of the idea, but the Princess did not notice the interruption, and continued). "Of course you will understand that I do not wish to depreciate you. I don't think you will do discredit to your sex. But then you see, darling, you are only a male." The last words were said with a great deal of ill-concealed contempt. And if a spur had really been needed to Flin's intentions this would have supplied it. For there could be no doubt that the Princess, when she spoke thus, but echoed the sentiments of every woman in Esnesnon. And had she wished to have completed the sentence she might have added and although you are an ornament when young, you are certainly not useful Mr. Flonatin felt the full force of the stinging remark, and it galled him. I may even go so far as to say that it embittered him against the Princess, so that he made a mental resolution that all his energies, all his talents, as well as the rest of his life, should be devoted to the attempt to emancipate the longsuffering males of Esnesnon, and to teach women that her true station in the order of things is that of a dependant. Whether he succeeded in accomplishing his noble aims will be revealed as the history proceeds.

31

When the result of the trial became known there were those who, feeling disappointed and dissatisfied, cried out that there had been a miscarriage of justice. And none were louder in this outcry then Mrs Sregdorpittemmocaig and Mrs Ytidrusba. In fact, the latter lady went so far as to hint that her husband had been guilty of tampering with the judges, and this hint seemed to promise rather a warm time of it for the unfortunate gentleman. Even ladies knowing Mrs Ytidrusba's peculiar temperament were not slow to express sympathy with the poor husband. As for Mrs. she seemed to go raving mad if she had not always been so. She shrieked louder than ever. And, of course, her favourite. grievance of the drivers was mixed up with her abuse of Flin, of the judges, of the King, of the country in general, and, in short, of everything that did not please her. And as it was very evident little or nothing did please her, her complaints were rather numerous.

Allied to this violent lady was Dr. Yrekcauq. This gentleman's bitterness so far got the better of his discretion and courtesy as to lead him to write a pamphlet anonymously, in which he heaped the vilest abuse on the head of the Court magician, Ytidrusba, saying that his knowledge was of the shallowest kind, and, in fact, that he was a "quack," a "humbug," and an "impostor."

Of course, the two leading papers entered the lists and kept the ball rolling, and so the row promised to be long and violent. In fact, so serious did it become, and public feeling was so strong in the matter, that it was considered necessary by the Government that the military should be called out. The result was something like twenty thousand Amazons were quartered in the city. They were an awfully wild lot, and in spite of the strict military discipline which was enforced, it was utterly impossible to stop them using their tongues, so that the peace of the town was broken up and the place became a Babel. Many attempts had been made from time to time to prevent these female soldiers from talking, but everything had hitherto signally failed. And it was left for a very waggish, but, alas! too daring male to suggest what seemed to be the most effectual remedy. This he did in an anonymous letter to the Government organ, in which he advocated the passing of an Act making it compulsory on every woman presenting herself for military service to have her tongue cut, as he considered that a woman had no business to talk, excepting on very rare occasions.

Although this suggestion was made with the best of motives, the end of the author was horrible in the extreme. In spite of his anonymity he was traced; it is supposed he was betrayed by some female relative. One night when he had just risen to prepare some food for his youngest baby, four masked women entered the room, and in a stern and terrible voice commanded the wretched fellow to follow them. The unhappy male appealed to his wife for protection, but she turned a deaf ear to his entreaties. Then, seeing that all hope had gone, he kissed his children, said farewell to his miserable wife, and pressing his lips firmly together, showed his tormentors how a brave male should die. He was taken away, but his fate was never actually known, although it was stated as a fact that he was led by his captors to a large cavern some distance out of the city and there talked to death by two hundred women. This, however, seems so diabolical in its fiendish atrocity that it is charitable to suppose, for the honour and credit of the female sex, that the statement was really a libel, and that some more merciful end was accorded him.

It would really be a difficult thing here to convey anything like an adequate notion of the misery caused by the disorganised state of society in Esnesnon. Owing to Flin's trial all the women seemed to go mad, and of course poor, unfortunate man suffered in consequence. The matter came before Parliament, and the result was one of the stormiest discussions on record. Many of the members suggested that, with a view of restoring things to their normal condition again, Flin should be banished or kept a close prisoner in some stronghold. But this was vigorously opposed by the Princess's party, who were largely in the majority. But it gave rise to no end of bitterness and bad feeling.

Time, however as in every other country served to heal the wounds, and after the proverbial nine days Flin ceased to be a wonder, and he was enabled to go about without attracting any great amount of attention. He availed himself of this opportunity to make himself better acquainted with the Esnesnonites and their customs, which were curious enough in all conscience.

But the thing that will strike us as being most singular was the manner in which the clothes were cleaned. Cold mutton and washing-days are institutions with us; but in Esnesnon such things were unknown. In fields situated outside of the town were large furnaces, and into these all the dirty clothes were cast, and after being subjected to the flames for fifteen minutes, they were drawn out and sent home to the owners perfectly cleansed. Burial was also unknown, but in its place inurning was in vogue. The dead body was placed in a platinum oven, and then calcined by means of currents of electricity. The ashes were afterwards collected and placed in a diamond vase. The vase was then hermetically sealed, and stood on a gold pedestal in places outside of the town appointed for the purpose. The cemeteries, if they may so be called, were amongst the prettiest sights of Esnesnon. The rows of crystal vases on the pure polished gold shafts, which stood amongst the most brilliantly-coloured flowers and graceful trees, produced an effect that was exquisite.

The most precious metal in Esnesnon was tin, and from this all the valuable coins were made, as well as articles of personal adornment. In the botanical world there were many plants that were said in the upper world to be extinct. And amongst these was asterophyllite. In the fauna, apart form the menopome, already mentioned, there were the anoplotherium and the augustherium. The latter were kept by the people as watch-dogs. The labyrinthodon was also found in the seas. After seeing one of these gigantic reptiles floating in the water one day, Mr Flonatin states that he no longer felt any doubt as to the truthfulness of the stories about the "great sea serpents" current in the upper world. He expresses a strong conviction that this reptile was not extinct as naturalists led us to suppose, but still inhabited some of the upper world oceans.

It was seldom that the Esnesnonsites went to war with other countries, for they had reached such perfection in the science of artillery and explosives that military manoeuvring was not necessary as there were no personal encounters between armies. They had a gun which threw a shell sixty miles. And this shell on exploding would almost destroy a town. It was loaded with a mineral found in the earth which was soaked for a number of days in a powerful acid, and then acquired most extraordinary explosive properties. Its power was beyond anything that the imagination could picture. A few grains when confined were sufficient to shatter a large building. They also had another gun which would discharge thousands of small round shot every time it was fired. And it could be loaded and fired at the rate of forty times a minute, by simply pressing a button that set a powerful current of electricity free, the gun being self-feeding, while a third gun was constructed to hurl showers of small poisoned arrows. This was a most fearful weapon, as the arrows were so small and fired with such terrific force that one would pass through the bodies of several persons, and if their points only happened to touch the skin death was certain.

All these weapons were the inventions of women, and all the soldiers were women. The

standing army was very small, just sufficient to keep order in Esnesnon. But in the event of war there would be a general conscription, when every woman under a hundred would be liable for military service.

War, however, was always a very remote contingency. Woman exercised all her ingenuity in inventing these diabolical engines of death, but it must be confessed that she didn't like the smell of powder. There was a story extant during Mr Flonatin's sojourn amongst them, that some hundreds of years previous to his arrival there had been a battle between the Esnesnonites and a neighbouring country. When the contending armies were brought face to face they forgot all about their weapons, flew at each other like enraged tigers, and pulled each other's hair out in handfuls. Since then there had been no battle, and the military engineers had devoted all their time to inventions. The enormous sums that were annually spent in carrying out these inventions were one of the reasons of the national exchequer being so empty. Poor old King Gubmuh knew this. But he was powerless to do anything to stay the dreadful waste. If he complained to his ministers they told him that he was not in a position to judge, and that it was quite useless to have a Parliament if the King was to interfere whenever he like. In fact, on one occasion, when the burden of his position weighed upon him more heavily than usual, he ventured to enter a very strong protest against the tyrannical manner in which he himself was governed, and in reply some of the most influential ladies at Court politely hinted that if he did not keep quiet they would find it necessary, in the interest of that great people, to call upon him to resign on the plea of imbecility and allow his daughter to ascend the throne. In fact, Flin was not slow to observe that there was a general desire amongst the female population for the King to abdicate in favour of his daughter. But as this would strengthen woman's power considerably, Mr Flonatin determined to prevent it if possible. He saw that the unhappy monarch's life was a burden to him, and that he sighed for freedom. Ytidrusba, too, grew daily thinner, for since the trial his wife led him a most dreadful life. He did not complain much, but it needed no very great shrewdness to perceive that he suffered terribly. Flin's good heart bled for him. He saw that woman in her rule was merciless. Her hand was iron, and her heart was steel. And though in her proper sphere she might be an angel, it was certain that out of it she was a devil. Mr Flonatin was a peace-loving man. He had ever had a wholesome horror of war, but he felt not that he was justified in taking every possible means to bring about a revolution and raise man to his original and proper station as a lord of creation. But the risks to be run were great. He knew that. He knew also that he had a desperate one-handed game to play, and that if he lost death and dishonour would be certain. Moreover, a well-organised and very extensive conspiracy would be necessary. And it was a question whether long years of oppression and degradation had not entirely crushed the spirit out of the males and turned them into mere machines.

Flin pondered deeply on these points. And one less bold than he might well have been pardoned had he shrunk from such a Herculean task. Much as he longed to return to the upper world and lay his grand discoveries before the Society to which he belonged, he felt that he ought to play the part of a liberator. And yet, as discretion was the better part of valour, he also considered in necessary that he should devote some time to endeavouring to discover if a return to the upper earth was practicable. It was clear that he could never go back the way he had come. But his great brain was fertile in speculation, and he believed that a way back did exist. Some distance from Esnesnon was a mountain, the top of which was always obscured by the electrical clouds. Only two or three persons had ever reached the top of this mountain, and they returned horrified, saying that it opened into a huge cavern that went up and up, and they felt sure that it was the entrance into the infernal regions. Flin had read an account of these several journeys in a book published in Esnesnon, and his curiosity was at once aroused. The travellers had all been women, and he felt sure that what woman could do he could accomplish without much difficulty, notwithstanding the boasted superiority of the Esnesnon women. Strong in this belief, he applied to Parliament for permission to start upon a journey of discovery and to explore the strange cavern. Such a request coming from a male naturally caused a great deal of surprise amongst the members.

Some of them exclaimed that the audacity of the fellow was unpardonable. Others said that he was a conceited little puppy. But others again ventured to hint that it wouldn't be a bad plan to let him go. This, of course, led to a row that raged hotly for many nights. But Flin was artful, and in a second petition which he addressed to the House he took good care to excite that most sensitive part of woman's mental organisation--her curiosity. He tickled the members' fancy with a vivid picture of the wonders that might lie concealed in those upper strata, and that if they would but give him permission to go he was willing to risk his life for their sakes and the sake of science. This argument, of course, told. For the truth of the matter is, every woman in Esnesnon was burning with curiosity, though they were all lacking in courage, and those who had gone up had funked when they had reached the portals of the strange cavern, and had hurried back as fast as they could. Thus the members allowed their curiosity to overcome their discretion, and after a very great deal of talk they gave the necessary sanction for an expedition, and also acceded to another request Flin made, that he should be accompanied to the top of the mountain by males only. But there can be little doubt that in making this concession the members that the expedition would not return, but be lost, and therefore a few old males wouldn't be missed. A sum of money was also voted to defray the expenses.

Flin's joy was great when he found that his application had been successful, and the two schemes now engrossed his attention. With reference to that of the liberties of his fellows, he was determined to take the King and Ytidrusba into his confidence. But his idea about returning to the upper world would be kept to himself.

32

It will of course be perfectly understood that the two grand schemes which now occupied Flin Flon's attention were the result of the most humane and disinterested motives.

To take every means possible to return to the upper world was a duty he owed to science and his friends, while to attempt the liberation of the oppressed, un-sexed, and long- suffering men of Esnesnon was a duty demanded in the name of humanity.

The difficulties that lay in the way of accomplishing this task were too apparent to be overlooked. Woman in Esnesnon was lynx-eyed --- I am not sure if she is not so in every country --- therefore the difficulties were increased manifold on account of this vigilance, and the most perfect organisation of any secret society would be required which had the liberation of males for its grand object.

But still Flin was not sufficiently egotistical to think that he himself could accomplish this. He saw that the chances of success were remote, and if he failed death would be certain if he were captured. It was to avoid the latter unpleasant consequences that made him desire to find out if there was a practical way to the upper world.

The story of the huge cavern in the higher regions did not appear to him by any means as a "mere traveller's story." It was true that the discoverers had only been women, and little could be expected from them. But still, while making every allowance for exaggeration on the part of those over ambitious ladies, he considered there was a wide margin left for truth, and that being so he was strong in the belief that the cavern reported to exist was really the entrance to a gallery that had its outlet somewhere in the upper world. In short, it was more than possible that it was the shaft or chimney of an extinct volcano that had existed near Esnesnon. If this theory was correct the daring adventurer believed it to be quite possible to travel upward through the bowels of the earth until he emerged once more on the crust. But he was determined to put the feasibility of the plan to a practical test, and should he find that it could be done it would offer him the means of escape in the event of the conspiracy failing.

Having got the sanction of Parliament, as well as a grant for the expedition of discovery, he lost no time in preparing his plans. Male volunteers were advertised for, and the applications were to be sent in to a Government officer especially appointed to select the candidates. It may be mentioned, as an evidence of the alacrity with which the wretched males jumped at any chance that offered a little freedom from woman's oppression, that in one week no fewer than 9,067,850 applications had reached the office. Nothing could have given more convincing proof of the awful condition of the male population than this. Even the Government themselves were astounded, and they began to hint that they had made a mistake in acceding to Flin's request. But still their curiosity would not permit them to countermand it, and so they selected a dozen of the oldest and most useless males, and when these poor fellows received the news that their applications had been successful they almost wept with joy, while the rejected ones verily wept with grief.

The members having thus been selected, nothing remained but to equip the expedition, and this was speedily done. A number of electric lamps and various scientific instruments were provided, together with a very large quantity of provisions. Flin was particular on the latter point, as he wished to have a reserve store up in the mountain in case he found it necessary to make a precipitate flight from Esnesnon.

The Princess Yobmot was by no means pleased with the idea of the expedition. She had no scientific ambition what woman has? and poohpoohed the thing as ridiculous, and not calculated to be advantageous to the country in any shape or form, while the money voted for the expenses would be a useless waste. But the true facts of the matter were she did not like parting with Flin. She thought that he was going to risk his life unnecessarily. At a private interview she kissed him so frequently and warmly that he felt very far from comfortable, and she told him,

"That when he had gone her life's light would be gone. That his voice had been music to her, his presence a joy unspeakable. But not that he was going to leave her, she would be lonely and miserable; and like a menopome that had lost its mate she would pine till he returned."

To all this Mr Flonatin mentally ejaculated "bosh"; and he wondered how any woman, laying claim to be considered perfectly sane, could have given utterance to it. But then he forgot that there was not a woman in Esnesnon but was insane.

Every preparation for the journey being completed, he set off at the head of the expedition early one morning. As he and his little band of old males filed across a plain that led from the city, the Princess appeared on a lofty tower of the castle, and waved a large asbestos handkerchief as long as she could discern them.

When the plain was crossed they came to the shores of an extensive sea. Here a vessel was waiting to take them on board. It was rather a large ship, and was driven by means of electricity. The captain and crew were all females.

After a voyage of four days the little party were landed at a point known as Cape Desolation. This place might have been reached by an overland journey, but it was very difficult, and would have taken up very much more time than the sea voyage.

The name of Cape Desolation was by no means misapplied, for a more awful or desolate region could not possibly be imagined. An immense hollow lay at the feet of the explorers. The sides of the hollow were riven and seared and burnt. It was, in fact, the basin of an extinct volcano. The whole region was composed of black lavatic rock. There was not a tree, an herb, or even a blade of grass, to cheer the eye. It seemed, indeed a valley of death, for birds there were none, animals there were none. Nothing moved, nothing grew.

As Flin viewed this place he knew he was looking on a crater, or rather on the bed of a volcano, and that the crater must be above. Here in far distant ages, as the forming fires had sunk lower and lower, this place must have been a glowing furnace, and it was more than possible the sea over which they had sailed had been connected with it. Some convulsions of nature since then had materially altering the features of the place, shattering the mountains and throwing up the headland and capes and peninsulas, until the waters rushed in into the main bed, extinguishing the lingering fires, and forming a sea. But there were still traces in the overhanging masses of mountain that the lower land and upper had been, if not quite untied, nearly so. And these subterranean fires, consequently, had their outlet on the crust of the earth.

It was necessary to journey along the edge of the basin for some time. But there was always the same blank desolation. When they had proceeded a considerable distance the clouds, which had hitherto been of a beautiful roseate colour, gradually darkened, though here and there there was a streak of blood-red light, and the effect of this was horrible beyond all imagination. The fantastic masses of black rock which were everywhere piled up the great hollow, which seemed to go down to an unfathomable depth the mighty mountains, which arose on all sides and the black streaked clouds, made up a picture that for diabolic weirdness could not have been surpassed. It was horrifying, and had a strange and depressing effect on the beholder. In fact, had Flin Flon remained there long he must have gone raving mad. But if there were another word to signify something ten thousand times worse than "awful" I should have to use it to convey any idea of what followed. The change in the colour of the clouds was observed by the males, who quickly told Flin that an electrical storm was gathering up. Those persons who have travelled in tropical countries, and experienced something of the terrific thunderstorms which occasionally break there, may be able to form the very faintest conception of what an electrical storm is like in the interior of the earth. But those who have never had such experience must of necessity fail to realise, however faintly, the incomprehensibly horrible scene of which Flin was fated to be a spectator.

The travellers took shelter in a cavernous opening in the side of a mountain. And here they waited in breathless silence. The hair upon each person's head stood erect, and gave off long sparks. And his fingers seemed to be fingers of fire, while the face of each male was to all appearances transparent, and as if a light was burning inside of the head. But Mr Flonatin says that so far from any ill effects being felt, the contrary was the case. One was exhilarated to an extraordinary degree. A weight seemed to be removed, there was a feeling almost as if one could fly. A delicious sense of mental dreaminess in which all that was objectionable was eliminated and only the beautiful retained. A strong desire every now and then to break out into rapturous song, and to clap the hands in an exuberance of joy. And then this was alternated by a gradual fading away of all surrounding objects, and a person seemed to be sinking into a most refreshing sleep. But no particular sensation lasted many minutes at a time. A constant change was going on, for it must be remembered that the travellers were steeped in an electric bath.

Presently there was a tremendous explosion for it was more like this than a peal of thunder and from every projecting point of rock, from out of the crevices, from the bottom of the hollow, and from the clouds themselves, which were now inky black, there burst forth millions of minute pale blue stars. The effect was inconceivably grand and awful. Then the stars moved about with astonishing rapidity, and explosion upon explosion followed until the earth literally rocked. The stars in time gave place to huge balls of fire that darted about like fire fiends, and with a startling, cracking noise. The roar was deafening, and the balls spun round until the spectators grew giddy, and a sickening sense of fear seized the heart as the explosions increased in intensity, and their long jagged forks of flame shot down and shattered the projecting rocks with a horrisonous crash. This effect gave place in turn to a new one. From the earth to the clouds there rose up long, spiral columns of electric fire that cracked and hissed, and sent out balls that flew round at a tremendous rate, and as they came in contact with each other exploded with a deafening roar. But the most singular and unique effect was that when all the rocks and the mountains seemed suddenly to become transparent and to be glowing with living fire inside. This scene was most extraordinary and appalling.

But the light gradually faded, and then rain commenced to fall in a perfect deluge. This, however, did not last long, and nature resumed her normal condition again while the clouds shed a soft crimson and purple light, and the storm had passed.

None of the travellers were injured, and as Mr Flonatin stepped from his shelter, his heart was filled with a silent thankfulness for his preservation. Though he felt glad at having had an opportunity of seeing the effects of this extraordinary storm, he would not have gone through the same experience again, could he have avoided it, for untold wealth.

The way now lay along the edge of a precipice, and then a plateau was reached, and from here a mountain rose, and its head was lost in the clouds.

The daring travellers commenced to ascent. It was a toilsome journey, for the road was broken and precipitous. And as Flin went up he felt convinced that it was nothing more than a continuation of the side of the basin or hollow, though some earthquake or convulsions had altered the features of the scenery.

Up they toiled for many hours, until they reached the clouds, and then they seemed to pass through illuminated mist. In time this stratum of vapour was left below, and then far, far above other layers of clouds could be observed, though they were different in colour to the lower ones, being bluish and purple. Acting on the information that had been given him, Flin now led the way along a sort of ravine that was very narrow, and the sides were almost perpendicular.

There was still the same awful desolation, The black, burnt rocks, the utter absence of all life. It was a dead world. After travelling along this ravine for about six hours their destination was reached, and the travellers stood at the mouth of a mammoth cavern, the entrance to which was broken into fantastic shapes. It was a strange place, and as Flin examined it he was more than ever convinced that it had been the outlet for fire, and that the ravine was but a continuation of it, though the roof had been shaken down and the configuration of the mountain altered entirely by earthquakes. To explore this cavern was now the object of the expedition, and Mr Flonatin lost no time in making preparations to start on the following morning after they had rested. He also formed a provision depot at the entrance, and being fully equipped with every necessary, and ample stores, as each male carried on his back about sixty days' rations, the exploring party started. It was arranged that only six and Flin should go forward. The other six were to remain at the entrance, and if the first party did not return by a certain time the second was to set off to try and ascertain their fate. At first the way was through a dismal, gloomy chamber of immense dimensions that the light from the electric lamps failed to penetrate. But after a time the path trended up. Up, and up, and up. Through eternal galleries that were broken and intersected by other galleries, though Flin was cautious enough to keep to what he considered to be the main one. In time it was almost like going upstairs, for the floor was broken, and the lava as it had flowed seemed to have cooled by successive stages.

Day after day the travellers pursued their dreary way that is dreary in one sense but Flin Flon was interested to a pitch of enthusiasm, while his companions were tasting the precious sweets of liberty, though it was only the liberty of eternal, subterranean galleries, but the poor fellows were free to act for once in their lives like men. The chains of bondage were for a time broken, and woman's terrible and enslaving influence no longer made them tremble. Her presence was not felt here. Not that she was without ambition, for could she have done so, she would have held dominant sway over every corner of the earth, but she had come here, and bold and daring though she was when she had only weak, unfortunate man to contend with, she faltered when she reached the entrance to that terrible and unknown region, and as she contemplated the dark galleries running for miles and miles into dim, mysterious solitude, she faltered, got scared, and then turned back.

Flin continued his march for many days successfully, always going up, though sometimes

they came to galleries that went down into unknown depths, but he was anxious to prove if his theory about this being an outlet was correct, and so he kept to the path that ascended until he was many thousand feet above the entrance to the cavern. The air now commenced to get bad, and this caused his hopes to fall a little, as it seemed to place an insurmountable obstacle in the way; but remembering the arrangement that had been made for supplying his fish vessel with pure air, he believed it perfectly practicable to invent a sort of headgear to contain the necessary chemical, and so enable the wearer to exist even in the foulest of atmospheres. As the journey could not now be continued, the party decided to return, and, without mentioning his thought to his fellow-travellers, Flin was satisfied that the upper world could be reached through the bowels of this volcanic mountain, for such he believed it to be. He had done all that he came to do then, and the next time that he returned it would be to reach his own beloved country again or perish.

The downward journey was quickly made, and when the entrance to the cave was reached, the travellers found their companions anxiously awaiting their return. The remaining provisions, of which they had brought a large quantity, were carefully stored away, and the party returned to Esnesnon without any special adventure.

33

The expedition, so far as Flin Flon was concerned, having been successful, returned to make its report. I say so far as Flin was concerned, because in other respects it was not a success. That is, nothing was discovered beyond what was already known. Great dissatisfaction was expressed in the city, and loud outcries were made against the Government for having voted the money. Of course, Yrekcauq and Mrs. went out of their minds as usual, and the poor old King was abused most unmercifully. As for Flin, the enemies of the Government made it rather uncomfortable for him; for a time they condemned him in language very far from polite, and suggested the advisability of turning him out of the kingdom. Otherwise the peace of the realm would be disturbed, and very serious consequences might ensue.

All these things, however, did not in the least disturb the equanimity of Flin. He laughed in his sleeve, and he winked slyly when nobody was looking at him, as much as to say,

"You have your day now; mine will come." Certainly he was very well satisfied with the result of his journey. And he congratulated himself on the fact that he had found the door which opened into his own world, and that all that was required were endurance, patience and resolution. It is well known that he possessed these qualities in an eminent degree. And if he could succeed in obtaining pure air and carrying a supply of provisions, and given that his theory was correct, there seemed little doubt but what the journey might be accomplished. At anyrate, he lost no time in maturing his plans, though to do this he was obliged to make a confidant of Ytidrusba. Although the old man did not offer any opposition, there is no doubt judging from his manner that he thought Flin was not quite in his right senses. However, Flin did not care about that in the least, more especially as Ytidrusba undertook to get the necessary head-dress secretly made. For this purpose he enlisted the services of one of the best male artisans in the country, who undertook to construct the dress from a plan which Flin supplies, and which may here be described.

In appearance it was not unlike the dress worn by divers. The head or crown terminated in a bellshaped trumpet, though which the external air entered and was oxygenated and ozonised by layers of chemicals compounds in cotton wool, and was drawn into the mouth by means of a tube. The impure air was discharged through the nostrils by means of a valve which fitted close, and which acted automatically by the force of the breath, but did not allow any of the external air to enter. There was also an india-rubber suit to be worn on the body, and this was fitted with various receptacles for provisions. This latter was a difficulty which at first seemed almost insurmountable, because it would be impossible for one person to carry anything like bulk or weight, and unless a sufficient store of food and water could be secured death from starvation would be certain.

This obstacle would have daunted many men, but it did not do so with Flin. His fertile brain was seldom at a loss to find a way out of a difficulty. Much as he liked good living, and Sybarite though he was, he could, when the interests of science demanded it, live upon as little as any man. And the problem to be solved was, how to get the greatest possible amount of nutriment into the smallest possible space. The solution was comparatively easy to Flin. He felt quite sure that if there was no actual water to be found in the bowels of the mountain, there would be sufficient moisture to afford fluid for a whole army if properly extracted. This was all the more feasible from the fact that the mountain seemed to be composed principally of pumice. The thing to be done was to extract this moisture, and then render it fit for drinking, and the following ingenious method was hit upon.

A square platinum box was made. About four inches from the bottom was a finely-perforated plate. Over this was a compact layer of sponge. Then another plate. And on the top of that a layer of salt. These layers of salt and sponge were continued within two inches of the top of the box. The moisture that would thus be absorbed by the salt and sponge would percolate to the bottom. Then it could be drawn off by means of a tap, and next distilled in a small apparatus, with heat generated by electricity. It will thus be seen that wherever there was moisture in the air or earth a supply of pure drinking water could be ensured.

For food the principle of the concentration of nutriment was resorted to. Mr Flonatin had observed that the poor people lived chiefly upon an amber gum of a sweetish taste, which exuded from certain trees in the forests. Those who ate it fattened and strengthened on it in a remarkable degree, and on analysis Flin found it contained all the nourishment necessary for the support of life. He, therefore, had a large number of wafer-like biscuits made of the gum and a little flour mixed. This flour was procured from the seeds of a peculiar shrub that grew in great profusion everywhere. The seeds were dried in ovens heated by electricity, and was afterwards ground in stone mills, the motive power of the mills being electricity. He proved, by practical experience, that these biscuits satisfied the cravings of nature, and kept up the vitality to a high standard. As he could carry a large quantity of the biscuits, one or two being sufficient for a meal, he had no fear of starving. For light he had two electric lamps, one fixed in front of the head-dress, and the other at the waist. A small electric battery was also constructed to be carried on the back, and which could be used for generating heat. When all the arrangements were completed, and the apparatus ready, Flin secretly left the city one night and took his way to the mountain. By making the detour mentioned he was enabled to avoid the sea. He reached his destination in safety, and stored his things away, ready for use whenever he should require them.

As he had not mentioned a word to anyone of his intention to go, his disappearance from the palace caused intense excitement. The Princess was affected so much that a serious illness was threatened. Then it suddenly occurred to her that some of her rivals had stolen him. This almost drove her mad with jealousy, and she persuaded her father to issue a proclamation offering a large reward for his recovery, and threatening the penalty of death on anyone who should detain him after the publication of the notice. Still he was not forthcoming, and then the Princess grew desponding again, and it was evident beyond all possibility of doubt that she entertained a feeling for him which in this world would certainly be called love.

But after many days, and when everybody about the palace was beginning to despair, Flin

turned up; and learning of the anxiety he had caused, he resorted to the pleasant fiction of saying that he had been lost.

The Princess was overjoyed at his return, and of course she quite believed him. Lovers always do believe each other. And if an upper world lady was told by her inamorato that she was a blush rose, or a sweet angel, or a beautiful star, or a vision of brightness, she would no more think of disbelieving it than she would think of not criticising her neighbour's new bonnet, and notwithstanding that she would know in her heart that it was all bosh and absurd flattery. Because a blush rose is not painted with rouge, and a sweet angel does not wear a toque at least it never has been reported that the angels do and the brightness of a beautiful star is not sullied by retiring to rest when it ought to be rising, nor does a vision of brightness wear false teeth or dress-improvers.

As before stated, the Princess was overjoyed when Flin returned, and she hugged the little man until he grew very red in the face, not by reason that he blushed, but because she squeezed him so hard.

To enter any protest against her behaviour would have been perfectly useless, and so he sighed and endured. And here I have a little secret to impart of the most interesting nature. It is not only interesting, but decidedly curious, and is intended more particularly for the ladies. Ladies of course like secrets. Not that they ever keep them when they get them; but then that fact only serves to prove how unselfish a woman is. For although she is so fond of a thing that she is often "dying to have it," the moment she gets it she passes it on to her "dear friend."

It will be understood, however, that this extreme generosity is only shown in the case of secrets; because a lady would not be so free with her bonnets and dresses. But of course, these are very different things from secrets. When a lady has a secret, she acts the same as she would if she had a fever. She tries to get rid of it as soon as possible; and if she cannot get rid of it, she is very ill. It will be remembered that Chaucer's Wife of Bath was once in possession of a secret, and was so bad that she cried ,

"When I am in danger of bursting, I will go and whisper among the reeds."

And the poor thing went, and no doubt felt considerably better. But women must have been very scarce in those days.

I knew a lady once who was told a very important secret by a gentleman on condition that she would promise very faithfully to keep it to herself. In a moment of weakness, and "dying with curiosity," she made this promise. Alas! that she a woman should have done so. But even women sometimes do foolish things. In her case it proved fatal. The gentleman went abroad, and the lady nursed the secret in her breast. But day by day it became more burdensome. It was an incubus that tortured. The colour faded from her cheeks, the brightness from her eye. Her step grew daily slower, and her friends saw with alarm that she was suffering from some strange malady. They pressed her to tell them the cause of her sufferings, so that they might suggest some remedy. But she only shook her head and sighed sadly. It was terrible and heartrending to see one so young and beautiful fade away without being able to stretch forth a helping hand to save her. Her friends sent her abroad. She went to Italy, France, Spain. She mixed in the gayest circles, she wandered amongst the most beautiful of nature's scenes. All that money and tender solicitation could do was done. But the great shadow was upon her, and from out that shadow nothing could lift her. Weary and broken she returned to her native land, for her life had lost its charms. Things that had hitherto given her pleasure now palled. She shut herself off from her acquaintances, and at last took to her bed. The cleverest physicians that wealth could procure were called in. But after they had felt her pulse, and looked at her tongue, they shook their heads sadly, pocketed their fees, and went off to other patients and more fees, and the disconsolate friends were left as wise as ever, for these doctors were not able to diagnose the malady. Some hinted at heart disease, others at consumption, diseased liver, religious mania, disappointed love, approaching insanity, cancer in the stomach, and in fact nearly every disease that flesh is heir to, for these grave, professional men had reputations to keep up, and therefore it was necessary to say something, and they said it and went their way with a sense of having done their duty.

But the end came at last. It was a wild and stormy night at the end of October. All the trees were bare, for the cold hand of winter was making itself felt. The dead leaves, swept by the gusts of autumnal winds which moaned over the land, rustled weirdly, and spoke of the departed joys of summer. No stars shone in the leaden-hued sky, though occasionally the glary moon peered from a jagged rent in the storm-clouds as they drove fiercely before the blasts.

The unhappy lady lay stretched upon her bed, surrounded with weeping friends. The shaded lights threw a melancholy gloom over the sad scene, and as the human soul struggled to break its bonds, the stillness of the room was broken by the stifled weeping of the watchers.

As the neighbouring church clock solemnly chimed out the hour of midnight, the dying woman took the hand of one of her dearest friends, and drawing her down she whispered into her ear,

"Nellie, darling, I will tell you a secret if you will promise me that you won't repeat it."

"I promise, dear," Nellie answered.

"Well, last year Mr Jones an old friend of mine, you know told me that his wife had presented him with twins. He was so ashamed of this that he made me solemnly promise that I would never mention it to anyone. I made the promise, and it has killed me."

She ceased speaking, gasped for breath, and with a low moan breathed her last.

As the weeping Nellie bent over the form of her dead friend she kissed the drawn lips, and made a mental vow that she would never keep a secret. And in a hour from that time everybody knew that Mrs Jones was the mother of twins.

The case, which is well authenticated, was very sad, and should be warning to all who read it. I at once suggested to her friends that this line should be inscribed upon the tombstone

Sacred to the memory of ..., who departed this life while yet in the bloom of youth and beauty, a victim to an attempt to keep a secret.

It would be a lasting monument of the folly of a woman attempting to do that which nature never intended she should do.

34

In the course of this history I have endeavoured to show that in a quiet, unostentatious way Mr Flonatin was enabled to influence those with whom he came in contact in a very remarkable manner. It is ever so with a true man of genius. People are all, unconsciously as it were, drawn towards him. They feel his power by intuition, and look up to him for guidance. This was so in Flin's case in a very marked degree. But perhaps the most astounding fact was the way in which he captivated the Princess Yobmot, a young lady whose flighty, volatile nature would have justified anyone in saying that she could not possibly have fixed her ideas upon any particular thing.

But though she was, as the Esnesnonites were pleased to term themselves, a prehuman being, she was, after all, singularly human according to our way of thinking. This applies in more ways than one. For like a good many young ladies, whether they be princesses or plebeians, she had some sort of undefined idea that she was pre-eminently superior to everyone else, and that, consequently, she ought to be looked up to, bowed down to, and otherwise recognised as a being of transcendent worth. But love is a mighty leveller; and however absurd it may seem to associate love with such a person as the Princess Yob mot, the truth must be told, she learned to love Flin, and silently but eloquently to acknowledge his superiority. Of course Mr Flonatin was an old man, whose life had been unselfishly devoted to the cause of science; but in Esnesnon, where people lived to be upwards of three hundred years old, his sixty odd years were but as childhood to them, and any argument he used to make them understand that as a human being the limit of his existence was very much narrower than theirs was ineffective. For there again they proved themselves to be prototypes of certain people in the upper world, who are chiefly remarkable for their small intellects and their self-importance, and who will see nothing beyond their own noses. Believing, as the Esnesnonites did, that Flin had really come from a locality where in their own stupid ignorance they placed the infernal regions, they looked upon him as immeasurably inferior to themselves. But, as I have before observed, his unobtrusive manner and his genius, which made themselves too apparent to be overlooked, won upon their feelings in a large measure; and while the men envied him, and secretly sighed that they had not been cast in the same mould, the women admired him, much after the fashion that they are given to admiring the opposite sex in our own civilised part of the globe. But mere admiration would not express the state of the Princess Yobmot's feelings. From imperiousness and superciliousness she descended to humility and submissiveness. Flin saw this not without some alarm. His contempt for her changed to pity. He tried to check her growing admiration; for however much he might have been inclined to have become a naturalised Esnesnonite, could he have served the cause of science by so doing, he felt that he would rather have died than have had to acknowledge the superiority of female over male rule.

He saw with pain the misery woman by her overweening ambition had caused in the inner world. She had rushed into places where even angels would have had considerable reluctance to have gone. She had mounted herself on a pinnacle, and imagined that, towering as she did above the heads of her fellows, she was immensely superior to man. But she forgot that the very height upon which she was perched caused her to appear to those who looked up to her as a mere and insignificant pigmy. She was, in point of fact, lost. A star of the first magnitude in her own sphere, she paled to a mere rushlight when she appeared out of that sphere. While man himself was reduced to a condition of almost insupportable wretchedness; and, unable to rise and rent the bonds that bound him, he groaned deeply as the iron of woman's tyrannical rule entered his soul.

Flin saw all these things as a philosopher should see them, and his great heart thrilled with unutterable pity. And the strongest desire of his noble soul was to break the fetters that kept man in the dust, so that he might spring to his feet again, and with a loud and joyful voice cry "Victory," while woman, acknowledging her error and her cruelty, should return to her primitive station of dependence, and be, as far as earthly beings can be, man's guardian angel.

It was a proud aspiration, and worthy the great brain from which it emanated. But, alas! he who would sweep away customs that have been rooting through long centuries, or would elevate a people out of whom all spirit and energy have been crushed, undertakes a task compared to which the labour of Hercules in the Augean stables was but as child's play.

Mr Flonatin saw the growing love of the Princess, and, as he was powerless to check it, he felt that he was justified in endeavouring to turn it to account. Moreover, another grand idea took shape in his mighty brain. It was none other than this: if it should prove possible for him to return to the upper world, it was equally possible for the Princess to accompany him, and could that be done, she would profit by what she saw of civilised nations. And when she was stored with information and new ideas he might accompany her back to her own world, where she would rule wisely and well. This, however, was too daring a scheme to be proposed suddenly, but he was determined to try and turn the Princess to his way of thinking with reference to her countrymen.

He had already taken Ytidrusba and the King into his confidence, and they were both overjoyed at the prospect however slight it might be of liberty. But while fully approving of the scheme and consenting to aid as far as they might do with safety, they refused to take any active part in organising the conspiracy. And so he had to work single-handed, and against obstacles that would have daunted a less bold spirit. But "perseverance and endurance" was his motto, and he did not flinch. Slowly but surely he worked. One by one winning men to his side until the conspiracy began to assume considerable proportions. Secretly and silently they progressed. Now undermining this institution, now that, and always moving towards a grand coup d'etat, which Flin convinced was imperatively necessary if the Government was to be overthrown.

Ytidrusba and the King watched the progress things were making with ill-concealed delight. It was for them, as for all males, the first glimmerings of a blessed liberty. Hope was rising. Its beams were warming the hearts of long-suffering man. A new era was dawning. But the daring of the person who had thus appeared as their champion and liberator awed them. They stood breathless as it were, waiting for the supreme moment when the clarion note of freedom should sound throughout the long-oppressed land, and yet trembling in themselves lest all the plans should miscarry, and in the fancied moment of triumph the plot should be disclosed, when woman, waking suddenly to a sense of the danger in which she stood, would, in her blind, mad, passionate revengeful fury, exterminate man from the earth, and then as a consequence she would die, and Esnesnon would be a buried city of the dead. But so far things had worked well. In all parts of the country societies had been formed, and the business was transacted with such silence and secrecy that no one unconnected with the movement had the slightest suspicion males of course knew how to be silent and secret.

The plan for the overthrow of woman's power was elaborate but effective, could it be carried out. At a given moment every public institution was to be seized and occupied by males. The Houses of Parliament were to be taken possession of and held resolutely, while the most strenuous efforts were being made to secure the services of a few unprincipled women whose sole desire was self-interest. These women were to be employed to tamper with the Amazons, and by promise of large rewards, and sinecure positions, induce them to remain neutral. Though the primary end for which Flin struggled was to teach man the extent of his own power, physically and mentally, and that lesson thoroughly learnt he had no fear of the rest, as he knew that if once man discovered it was his place, according to the scheme of creation, to rule, woman's reign would be at an end.

During the many weeks that were spent in maturing his plans, both for the revolution and for his own escape should he be unsuccessful, Flin was cautious enough not to offend the Princess, whose infatuation for him grew stronger every day. His power over her also gradually increased, for he insensibly led her to recognise his superiority as a ruler. He paid her those delicate attentions which he would have done to a lady in his own country, and as something new and strange she like it. He made her feel some of the exquisite pleasure there was to be enjoyed by a woman who, looking up to man as her guide and protector, ruled him with love, and could, when she sat enthroned in his heart her true position enforce obedience to her slightest wish.

He watched the progress he made in this respect with infinite pleasure, and he, the baldheaded man of science, and seared and world-worn, actually had to confess to himself that he was getting more than deeply interested in this strange woman; he was absolutely learning to regard her with something of the feelings a man regards his first love.

Visionary though the scheme might appear to certain people who never look below the surface of anything, he felt that if he could succeed in converting her that the conquest would be such a grand one that it was worth any sacrifice to accomplish it.

At length, when he considered that the right moment had arrived, he ventured to suggest to the Princess that Esnesnon would be better under the rule of man. At first she heard this in profound astonishment, and then allowing her ambition to overcome even her love for a time, she became exceedingly angry, and threatened him with the direst consequences if he dared to make any such seditious suggestions again; but this opposition only served to strengthen his determination to conquer, if there were within the region of possibility, and he said tenderly in reply to her threats,

"You should not grow angry with me. Custom has unsexed you, but some woman's feeling is still left in your heart. Let that feeling tell you that nature intended man to take the highest scale in creation, and while not inferior to him, woman is essentially a dependent on him, no less than his help- mate. Come down to your proper sphere and you will know the truest happiness. Let me show you how much man is willing to do for woman, providing she keeps her level. You, as the highest lady in this land, make your voice heard. Tell your sex they are usurpers, but the hour has come when they must go back to their true place and allow down-trodden man to come to the front. Do this, and in time your name will ring with honour, and in faroff ages your memory will be revered as one who had the moral strength to rise up and acknowledge her error."

As he ceased speaking the Princess stared at him in utter bewilderment. And then she could only exclaim,

"Are you mad, or am I dreaming?"

"Neither one nor the other. I am speaking the soundest logic. And though it may startle you at first, a little reflection should serve to show you I am right."

"You are audacious," she answered. "Nay, more, you are a conspirator, a traitor, a villain, and shall die."

Her eyes were full of fire, and her voice was stern and determined, but Flin did not flinch. There were mighty interests at stake. One false move on his part, the slightest show of faint-heartedness, and the game would be lost. But he was not the man to tremble or lose presence of mind. It was his habit to grow firmer the more danger increased. He had dared the power of nature in her most secret recesses, and he could not think of quailing before an angry woman. And so he pointedly remarked,

"If it is your Highness's pleasure that I should die, by all means gratify that pleasure. And I shall be able to show you, and your wretched countrypeople, how I can defy you, and how a brave man should die. But I would remind your Highness that you have won upon my feelings. You have touched the strings of my heart and taught me the magic of love."

"Of love," she answered, her whole manner changing.

"Yes," he answered, and feeling a secret joy at the advantage he was evidently gaining. "I have learnt to love you. And whether a woman be an Esnesnonite or any other nationality in the world, I do not believe it is in her nature to slay in cold blood the man who loves her. But do with me as you think proper. A word from you and your myrmidons would no doubt gladly lay me dead at your feet. But will you be able to survive my loss? If so, give the command and let the end come."

She drew nearer to him. She seemed to be labouring under some kind of mesmeric influence. She was literally speechless with astonishment.

You make me feel as if I were undergoing some strange metamorphosis," she said at last. "You are binding me with silken threads that are as strong as iron chains, and though I see you are doing this I am powerless to stay you. What is the cause of my helplessness?"

"Love," he whispered.

"It must be so," she cried. "I feel a new and exquisite sense of pleasure, that if I try to resist will be fatal to me. You have enchanted me, thrown a spell around me, and now you would lead me and my nation to destruction, and yet I cannot raise my voice to sound an alarm. This must not be. You must go away. Seek for some means to return to your own world. Go, I beseech you."

"Never," he cried passionately, seizing her hand, "never, without you go with me."

"I go with you?"

"Yes. I have reason to think I have found a way back. But that way shall never be travelled unless you accompany me. Why should you not go? Why should you not come with me? I will lead you to new scenes. Show you wonders such as you have never before beheld. And, moreover, you shall behold woman as woman should be."

"These are fearful words you are pouring into my ears," she

answered. "They are, as it were, a moral poison, that is changing my whole nature."

"Then is the poison wholesome if that is so," he cried enthusiastically, growing bolder as he saw that his plan was successful. "I am trying to draw you from darkness into light--to emancipate your nation from slavery and misery."

"It is a daring scheme," she murmured.

"Love makes man daring. Do not throwaway what I offer. To hesitate is to be lost. Grasp at the golden opportunity. Accept the liberty and the joy I offer you."

"I am yours," she whispered faintly.

It was a grand moment for Flin. He smiled inwardly as he saw that he had gained one great triumph. And he believed, conscientiously, that all the means he had taken to secure it were justified by the results.

"If you are mine," he answered, "then must you acknowledge my sway."

"That will I do," she replied; "your will is stronger than my own, and you have conquered."

"That is good, and now, through you, I must conquer this nation."

Then, as briefly as the importance of the subject would permit, he cautiously laid his plans before the Princess meeting all her objections by the most logical arguments, and overcoming all her scruples by a confession of his love, until at last, metaphorically speaking, he had bound her captive and she was lying prostrate at his feet.

With such a powerful ally as the Princess he was now very hopeful that his plans would succeed. The conspirators were overjoyed when they heard the new, and they promised to place Flin upon the throne if they were successful. The Princess used her influence too to get some of her party to join the conspiracy, consenting to fly with Flin in the event of a fiasco; and he had another dress made for her so that every contingency might be guarded against.

The King and Ytidrusba watched the progress of events with breathless agitation, for they knew that they must either gain power or sink to eternal ruin, according to the turn matters took.

At length all things were ripe for the blow to be struck, and an hour was fixed for the coup d'etat. But, secretly as the conspirators had worked, they had a traitor in the camp, and though this means the Government were made aware of the mine upon which they stood. Then a counterplot was arranged, and the result must be told in the next chapter.

35

Flin Flon's revolutionary movement progressed satisfactorily, or apparently so. Revolutions as a rule cannot be too strongly condemned. But if it be true that the end justifies the means, then it may be safely asserted that the end aimed at by Mr. Flonatin was such a desirable one that any means would have been justifiable that would have ensured success. It will be remembered that even the King was allied to the would-be liberator, for no one could have had stronger motives than he for the overthrow of his Government. But as an evidence of the immense influence Flin possessed, and the way in which he was enabled to sway the female mind where circumstances were favourable, it may be stated that the Princess Yobmot fell into his views, and fully acquiesced in all he desired. Of course it will be said that this young lady was in love with the great traveller, and therefore it was no wonder that she should try to please him, as anybody would do as much for the object of her choice. But I would firmly though respectfully contradict all persons who incline to this popular error, and beg to say that they know little of the female mind, which is exceedingly like a weather-cock. A lady likes to rule, and particularly rule her lover. In fact I have no hesitation in saying that a woman is a perfect tyrant to the man who is enthralled with her charms. No cannibalistic savage could possibly be a greater despot than she who is aware that the light of her eyes has bewitched some unfortunate man, and the music of her voice has charmed him into slavish obedience. Then may it be said speaking figuratively, of course that she places her foot upon his neck, and as she pierces his heart through and through she exultingly cries,

"Behold my conquest! As the power of woman was strong in the land even in the days of Eve, so is it now. Time has not weakened it, and here at my feet is a slave chained and bound, whom I, a woman frail and weak, have captured, and brought him from the enemy's country to lie prone at my feet and worship me, and he shall do my lightest bidding. I will make him fetch and carry even as I would my spaniel. He shall acknowledge my imperious will, and obey my commands. Even his thoughts shall not be his own, for I shall be his mistress, his queen, his absolute ruler, and if I tell him to look to the left he shall do it, and if I command him to turn to the right that shall he do also."

Of course this is the idea of every woman who enthralls a man's heart. But then she forgets that man submits only to make her submissive. And when he has conquered he teaches her how well the slave can rule the ruler. But remembering the awfully stubborn nature of a lady's will, Flin's conquest was the more remarkable, especially in Esnesnon, where woman's power was absolute, though it must be confessed that the Princess was very badly in love with him, and in such a desperate case the patient was very liable to do desperate things. At the same time in justice to her it must be said that he did not make a conquest of her without some difficulty.

She felt his power. She felt that she was being drawn nearer and nearer to bondage, and she struggled hard to free herself. But she was simply helpless. She could not shut him out from her sight. She could not obliterate him from her memory.

She firmly protested, she objected, she grew desperate. It was all useless, however. She struggled in vain to break the chain. He conquered. It was a glorious triumph and well entitles him to be immortalised in heroic verse to the end of time.

Of course the value of the Princess's influence could hardly be over-rated. Flin knew this, and he felt exceedingly proud of his conquest. In fact he looked upon success as a foregone conclusion. But he over-calculated his strength.

The conspirators met nightly. Both the King and Ytidrusba watched the progress of events with palpitating hearts. They panted for liberty, now at last liberty seemed to be coming, and the end of woman's rule was drawing near.

But "the well-laid schemes of mice and men gang aft agley." Notwithstanding the vigilance of the conspirators there were other persons in Esnesnon who were equally vigilant. The movements of the Princess and Flin had not escaped notice, and suspicion had been aroused. Mrs Sregdorpittemmocaig and Dr Yrekcauq were hawkeyed, and they smelt danger. They saw that there was something in the wind, and they set themselves to work to find out what that something was. Strong in the belief in her own influence the Princess had extensively tampered with the army, and regiment after regiment had promised to give her their support when the right moment came. But, unfortunately for the success of the plans, there were traitors in the camp; and Mrs soon learnt that an extensive scheme had been almost matured for the overthrow of the Government, and that the rule of woman was threatened.

This discovery seemed to drive the gentle lady madder than ever, and rushing down to the Parliament House, like an escaped lunatic, she dropped a bombshell, so to speak, into that grave and solemn assembly. That is, she shrieked out the news she had learnt to the astonished members, who, startled so suddenly from their fancied security, became as mad as she, and a scene was enacted in that Council Chamber that is perhaps without a parallel in the world's history. The daring and horrible audacity of the scheme alarmed them in a manner that nothing else could have done. To have their power threatened, to tremble on the verge of a revolution that would in all probability place woman in a position inferior to man in the social scale, was so horrible to contemplate that for a time the fair creatures were dumb with amazement, and almost paralysed with fear. But this feeling soon passed, and was succeeded by one that can only be described as dangerous lunacy. Every member jumped to her feet at the same moment and tried to speak, until the Babel of tongues was beyond the power of human comprehension to understand. Then the dear creatures set to work abusing each other, and for a long time the business of the House was interrupted by frantic gesticulations and a deafening noise. But at last some of the members came to their senses, as they realised the great danger which threatened them, and by dint of perseverance they managed to prevail upon their sister members to give them a hearing. The best means for nipping the rebellion in the bud were discussed. But while there was by no means a unanimous feeling as to the course that should be pursued, it was pretty generally acceded that it was imperatively necessary for the safety of the State that Flin should be immediately arrested, and all the troops be called out and their loyalty tested. This having been decided upon, the meeting broke up, and a messenger was despatched to the Governor of the city that she was immediately to arrest Flin Flon. But he and the Princess had already got information that they were suspected, and so, while the members were quarrelling amongst themselves in the House of Parliament, Flin was enabled to withdraw to the Palace accompanied by a considerable number of troops, who had been prevailed upon by the Princess to forsake their allegiance.

When it was revealed that not only the King and Ytidrusba were on the side of the enemy, but that the success of the plot so far was entirely due to the Princess, the rage amongst the female population was fearful, and they vowed to have the most deadly vengeance on the Princess should she be taken alive.

Mrs. went about the city inflaming the minds of the populace and inciting them to action. She called upon them to arrest Flin, the King, and Ytidrusba, and instantly execute them, while the Princess was to be slain by slow torture. But all this was easier said than done. The conspirators had made good their position, and showed no inclination to come out and be slaughtered.

The excitement in the city was immense, and words would fail to convey any adequate idea of the manner in which the leading female members conducted themselves. Stormy meetings took place, and resolutions were passed one moment only to be abandoned the next. In this critical hour no one could be found sufficiently collected and with a clear head to take the management of affairs. Each lady considered her own proposition infinitely superior to her neighbour's, and terrible confusion was the result. But after hours of talk it was at last decided that the conspirators should be called upon to surrender, and failing to respond to the call, the palace was to be besieged and battered down.

The loyal troops were drawn up in fighting order. Volunteers were enrolled, and even males were pressed into the service as servants and bearers.

The demand to surrender was made, but treated with scorn, and so the battle commenced.

The most terrible electric explosives were used, battering rams were brought into requisition, and

both besieged and besiegers fought with a fury that was begotten by the desperate nature of the cause. The war was continued for weeks. Sorties were occasionally made from the palace, and furious hand-to-hand encounters took place, the female soldiers tearing each other's hair and eyes out like so many furies. The fighting on the part of the males was only a sham, for they fully sympathised with the conspirators, and in their hearts hoped that they would be successful.

The Government, with a cruelty that was execrable, had large numbers of males executed as warnings to others, some of them being frizzled to death by means of electricity. In fact, the amiable Mrs. went so far as to suggest that all the males, excepting the very young ones, should be killed off. But this diabolical proposal was not carried out, though be it said to this lady's eternal disgrace, nearly all the public chariot- drivers were massacred at her instigation.

During this terrible state of affairs the poor old King seemed to sink more and more into a state of hopeless imbecility. His spirit was crushed and his dreams dissipated. He was conscious of having always been a puppet; woman's power had been strong upon him, but there had been times when he had dared to hope that he would be able to free himself and breathe the air of liberty, when he would be relieved of the despotic sway of petticoat rule.

Day by day the King continued to waste away, and at last died. This was a heavy blow to the little band of devoted adherents, and no one felt it more seriously than Ytidrusba, who was greatly attached to his Royal master. The old priest never held up his head again, and a week after had joined the King in some other world.

Flin had nothing more to fight for now. The Princess, whose love for him had been steadfast all through the siege, counselled him to fly. Still he hesitated, although he saw that he could not hold out much longer, for the besiegers were bringing up fresh troops, and new instruments of warfare, which discharged, by means of compressed air, terrible bombs filled with deadly gas, and a corrosive acid that caused awful torture. Further resistance was quite useless, and as the Princess consented to accompany him, he determined, in the interest of the noble Society he represented, to seek safety in flight, and favoured by the cover of darkness, and a lull in the siege operations, he and his faithful Princess quitted the palace and hurried towards the mountain, where Flin believed he had discovered the entrance to a passage which led to the Upper World.

36

The fugitives were enabled to continue their flight unmolested. The Princess was no longer the gay, sprightly, volatile girl of a few weeks previous. The terrible events that had so quickly crowded upon her had had a very marked effect, and had enfeebled her health to an alarming extent. But Flin was still sanguine that her devotion for him, aided by her perseverance, would enable her to triumph over all difficulties and accompany him to the upper world, if it were possible to make his way there. This was now the one goal to which he pressed. Devoted as he was to science, he felt that to be able to present the Princess to the American people was such a grand idea that it was worth making any sacrifices to accomplish. Moreover, she would be the best answer to any questions that might be put, and would effectually silence all doubts. After considerable difficulty the fugitives succeeded in reaching the mouth of the cavern.

Flin found his stores and apparatus exactly as he had left them. The Princess was much exhausted, and so he decided to rest for a few days, as he deemed himself perfectly safe from pursuers.

At the end of a week the Princess had so far recovered that the traveller determined to lose no more time in commencing his journey upward.

Princess Yobmot uttered no complaint, but it was evident she looked upon the expedition with grave misgivings. The only motive she had for startling upon such a dangerous journey was her love for Flin, as she was not even supported, as was he, by any enthusiasm for scientific exploration. But she confessed herself willing to live or die with him. And so when everything was ready, and when the apparatus for breathing had been adjusted, and the electric lamps set in motion, he turned his back towards Esnesnon and set his face upward.

He and his companion were fastened together by a rope and he took the lead.

For a long time the way was comparatively easy, and good progress was made. The gallery always trended upward, and the walls were for the most part composed of basaltic and felspathic rock. At times, however, the roof was so low that considerable difficulty was experienced in passing. But the undaunted travellers crept on their hands and knees and held their way, and when at last at the end of ten days Flin made a calculation by aid of his instruments, he estimated that they had attained a height of about eight miles above the level of

Esnesnon.

Everything was perfectly satisfactory, and the dresses fully answered the purpose for which they had been designed. But now the gallery grew rougher, and the journey became more difficult. At times it was necessary to climb up steep jutting rocks, and creep through holes that scarcely admitted the body. Moreover, the way grew labyrinthian, for the galleries trended away in every conceivable direction, and the intrepid Flin was often at his wits' end as to which one to follow. But, guided by a rare instinct, and that intuitive faculty which was peculiarly his own, which enabled him to define the right way from the wrong in most things, he did not falter, but pressed boldly forward; though there were occasions when, after terrible exertion and almost Herculean efforts, he was mortified to find himself at the end of a gallery, and was compelled to retrace his steps and strike a fresh path.

He was greatly alarmed now to observe that the strength of the Princess was daily diminishing. He saw with pain that she grew gradually weaker and thinner; and, feeling that he was responsible for her safety, he suggested the advisability of returning to Esnesnon, which he would have done at all risks. But she resolutely opposed this, expressing her perfect willingness to proceed at all hazards, and, if needs be, die by his side. He was struck by this devotion. Little did he dream that his connection with her, begun so lightly, would end so seriously. It was a grave responsibility. He felt that, and his fears strengthened every hour that his brave companion would find a grave in the heart of the earth's crust, through which they were travelling. She defined something of the thoughts which agitated him, and smiling sweetly tried to reassure him, saying that he was not to trouble himself on her account, for she would yet live to astonish the upper world people. He knew, however, that this was only dictated by her great love for him, and that her own feelings told her that this was a fallacious hope. But regrets were useless, longings were unavailing; the inevitable must be met boldly. The way now became more and more intricate, tortuous and difficult, and there were days when it was impossible to accomplish more than a mile or so of distance.

The interminable galleries stretched on and on. The unbroken silence, the awful darkness were appalling. No wonder that at last even Flin, bold as he was, should have had some feeling of despair.

"How much longer would it be necessary to travel these fearful solitudes, where neither prehuman nor human foot had ever been before?"

This was a question he was repeatedly asking himself, but the answer came not.

It was certain, however, that the way could not be interminable. The gallery must have an ending. This was at least a consoling thought. After a few days' more travelling the gallery gradually opened out, and the travellers stood on the shores of a subterranean lake. The awful desolation, the fearful melancholy, and the strange silence of this place were sufficient to appal the stoutest hearts. Flin did not feel justified in devoting any time to exploring it. Every moment was now of value, for the provisions were getting short, and both his own and him companion's strength were failing. In fact, the Princess now became so ill that it was evident she could not continue the journey much farther. Flin was distracted. He felt that in a measure he was responsible for this, though all that he had done had been done with the best possible motives. Nevertheless, had he not attempted to overthrow the power of woman in Esnesnon, things might have been different. He reproached himself a little, and he told the Princess this, but she smiled sweetly and murmured,

"Do not blame yourself. It was all done for the best, and had you not failed Esnesnon would have known an era of splendid prosperity. You have at least taught me my true sphere. To submit as a woman should submit is a woman's duty. But when she attempts to rule, and to assume a position for which she was never intended, she ceases to be a woman and becomes objectionable. This is something at least to have learnt, and I have learned it thoroughly, and would that I could teach it to my countrywomen. But that is hopeless, for my end approaches."

"Say not so," Flin answered in alarm, for there was something prophetic in the words of the Princess. "You are weak and exhausted, but I am not without hope that you may yet live to reach the end of the journey, and be honoured and respected by the great American people."

"The end of the journey has come for me," she whispered, as she sank down at his feet, "I am dying."

With a cry of alarm he knelt beside her and supported her head, and it became too evident to him that her words were fearfully true, that life was ebbing away. But he was utterly powerless to give any aid. He was unprepared for such a contingency. And all he could do was to support the head of the dying woman and whisper comfort.

She held his hand as if fearful to part from him. Belonging to a totally different race, and prehuman though she might call herself, she had yet a true woman's nature, and felt the magic of love. But she was no more exempt from death than were human beings, and the fell destroyer had stricken her. Flin Flon confesses that as he bent over her prostrate form it was the most painful moment of his life, and he would have sacrificed much could he have saved her. But that was impossible. The life tide ebbed. She grew feebler. And still clasping his hand, she at length lay dead in that strange and lonely region. It was a huge grave, but a safe one. No one was likely ever again to penetrate to those silent depths to disturb the dead remains. There they would lie in an eternal sleep until the mountains should dissolve and the secrets of sea and earth be disclosed. Flin wept. And at the moment almost wished that he too could lie beside her and sleep the dreamless sleep. He felt that he had lost a true and faithful companion, who for his sake had sacrificed much, even her life. But he must pursue his solitary journey now without her. And so, composing the dead limbs, and casting one fond and lingering look at the calm face, he went on his way.

After travelling for some distance along the shores of the lake, he was fortunate enough to hit the entrance to the gallery again. With the exception that the way was very much more difficult, the features were the same as the first half of the journey. The same gloomy, silent galleries. The same dark, hard rocks, that bore on their face evidence of burnings and scaldings, and spoke of the time when these caverns had been filled with liquid fire, that had no doubt mounted upward and upward, finally discharging itself in the upper world.

These signs gave Flin courage, because he felt convinced that the burning lava must have left an outlet, and that if his strength held out he would be enabled to gain that outlet and finally reach his beloved home.

But hope sank very low at times as he travelled upward and upward and there appeared no signs of the end. Hunger, too, was beginning to make itself felt, for his provisions were nearly

finished and the utmost care was necessary. Moreover, the greatest physical labour had to be endured, for at times he had literally to climb up walls of rock, and where a false step or the failure of nerve would have precipitated him to instant destruction, but "perseverance" was his motto, and so he struggled on. The gloom and the silence were beginning to tell upon him. He grew melancholy, he felt as if he should go out of his mind if the journey did not end, and there were one or two occasions when the very apathy of despair was reached and he felt that he could not continue another step. But these fits of depression were not lasting. He aroused himself from them with desperate energy and struggled forward, and when sight, and strength, and hope were all but gone he was at length rewarded by seeing glimmering light, the blessed light of day, and with a cry of joy he sank down and remained unconscious for some time.

But he soon recovered, and following the light, he emerged from narrow opening. Then he saw far, far above the blue sky. Yes, the sky that he had been shut out from so long was above him, and he almost went frantic with a great sense of inexpressible joy.

He was at the bottom of a huge crater, that was most perfect in its formation. The sides were nearly perpendicular, and covered with luxuriant herbage. The summit was about two thousand feet above, and to gain it appeared to be about the most difficult part of the journey. But when Flin had refreshed himself and rested for some hours he set to work to try and find a way out of the hollow, where in a great depression was a lake. After walking about for some hours he came upon a narrow track that had been beaten by sheep and goats. Up this he climbed, but it was so steep that it was a work of danger and difficulty. At length he reached the summit of the mountain, and then he found that it was one of a tremendous range. No human being was in sight. The region was solitude unbroken, save by the eagles which wheeled their dizzy flight around the brows of the mountains.

Flin's joy knew no bounds as he thus found himself once more on the exterior of the earth. And yet it almost seemed as if the most difficult part of his journey was yet to come; for unless he could meet someone to guide him, he might wander about these eternal mountains until he dies of starvation.

As the sun was setting he determined to rest for the night, and he took up his quarters in the hollow of a large rock. On the following day he commenced the descent. After many hours of hard travelling he came into a valley, and going through this for some miles his ears were at length gladdened by the sound of voices speaking his own beloved language, and rounding a point he came in sight of a party of gold diggers. As he approached the men they all stopped working and stared at him in stupid astonishment.

"Will you kindly inform me what locality I am in?" Flin asked politely, whereat all the men burst into a loud laugh, which caused him great annoyance, for he did not like to be a laughingstock.

"Well, I guess, old man, you've been in some strange region by the look of you," bawled one fellow.

"You are right, friend," answered Flin; "I have been residing for some time in the interior of the earth with a strange race of people, about whom I am going to read a paper before the New York Society for the Exploration of Unknown Regions."

This was the signal for a roar of laughter, and several of the men tapped their foreheads significantly with their fingers, thereby intimating that they thought Flin was cracked.

"Look here, old hoss," exclaimed a big burly fellow, not unkindly, "I guess you had better get away home to your friends; it ain't fit that you should be wandering about without somebody to look after you."

This was a cruel cut to poor Flin. But he felt that he could expect nothing better from these rough, uncultivated fellows; though it was rather hard to be greeted in such a manner on first returning to the upper world, and having suffered so much in the cause of science. He sighed wearily, and remarked,

"Possibly what you say, my man, is correct, but you have not answered my question. What place is this?"

"Wal, I guess you ain't twenty miles off 'Frisco. "

"San Francisco, eh?" muttered Flin. "That is fortunate; I am obliged to you for the information. Which was do I go?"

"Straight ahead down the valley."

"Thank you; good day."

As Flin moved off he heard the men laughing heartily, and one of them exclaimed ,

"He's clean gone off his mind anyhow, I guess."

Of course he took no notice of this cruel remark, but hurried on his way, and towards nightfall found himself in the busy city of San Francisco, where his uncouth appearance and strange dress caused him to be seized by the police and detained, pending an inquiry as to the state of mind. This was a cruel and bitter experience, but he consoled himself with the thought that he was suffering in the great cause of science. There was a clergyman attached to the place, and to this gentleman he told his strange story.

"But, my dear fellow," said the clergyman, "Flintabbatey Flonatin was drowned long ago in Lake Avernus through his own mad folly."

Flin persisted that he had never been drowned, but as this was considered to be a certain sign of madness, he was carefully guarded though kindly treated. Finding that no one would believe his statements he became silent, and for a whole year suffered martyrdom, until one day a visitor displayed interest in him, and Flin persuaded this person to telegraph to Barnum, who lost no time in despatching an agent to San Francisco to conduct the intrepid traveller back to New York, to Flin's intense delight. He felt now that his reward had come at last. In due course he communicated with his Society, but no one recognised him.

Of course the news of his return soon spread and for a whole fortnight he gave receptions to the general public at Barnum's Museum, whither thousands upon thousands of persons flocked to see him. But when he began to relate his adventures people shook their heads and whispered one to another that he had become very mad indeed.

Even the members of the Society for the Exploration of Unknown Regions laughed at him, and said that it was wrong of him to attempt to impose upon people's credulity in such a manner, and pose as the distinguished and celebrated scientist to whom a magnificent monument had been erected by public subscription.

"No, no," they said, "you may be harmless, but you are a wicked impostor."

It was a poor return, indeed, for all he had endured and the manifold dangers he had passed through. Such ingratitude was more than he could bear. It broke his heart, but Barnum paid him handsomely to remain at the museum, where he was a tremendous draw for a time. The novelty, of course, wore off at last, and he retired into seclusion, spending the rest of his days in making notes for the narrative of his wonderful journey and in cultivating cabbages and musing upon the base ingratitude of humanity. He consoled himself, however, with one thought, that the time might yet come when his truthfulness would be proved, and that his memory would ever be respected. And so when the poor old man had reached a century of life he passed quietly away. The world lost a genius it could ill spare. The public now know how true his story was; his wish has been realised, for Barnum himself handed me the notes from which this narrative has been written. And the wonderful nation of the screaming eagle will never allow his memory to die.

THE END

Printed in Great Britain
by Amazon

15423524R00169